THE POWER OF CONVICTION

THE LIGHT OF DARKNESS, BOOK ONE

CATRIN RUSSELL

BOOKS BY CATRIN RUSSELL

The Light of Darkness

The Power of Conviction
The Path of Salvation
The Resurgence of Light
Nefarious Echoes - July 2021
Book 5 - September 2021
Book 6 - November 2021

* * *

Prequel
Prequel

Thank you to my husband Danny, for your support and unending inspiration.
Big thanks also to my family and friends for test reading and supplying me
with plenty of advice on how to move forward ♥

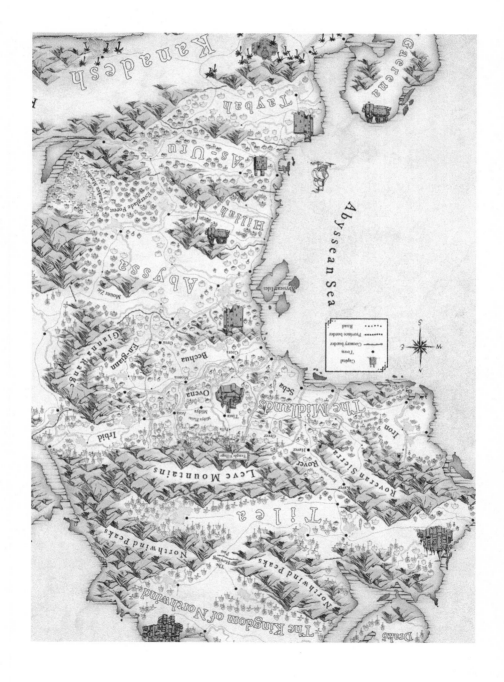

PROLOGUE

The day had been seared into her memory. It had transpired as mostly uneventful, filled with the daily chores of a priestess. She had been meditating, preparing food and offerings for the Goddess and reading books by the nearby stream. The last and seemingly trivial activity was what had led to that fateful meeting.

Standing alone by the edge of the water, she had just arrived, cradling a tome under her arm.

The stream was situated like something out of a fairy tale, connected to a small pond below the mountainside. It had a waterfall above it, trees and shrubberies spread along the edges. Willow branches hung down over the water, their leaves gently touching the surface.

Gazing across the waterways, she saw him; a tall and lean man, powerfully built and muscular, yet moving smoothly under the wild streams. His skin was pale as snow, and his hair black as the darkest of nights. The raven mane trailed down his back, reaching below the hips. Wearing only a pair of ebony trousers, he carefully scrubbed away at his hands and arms, the water staining red with blood.

He suddenly turned, his eyes piercing as he stared at her.

In no way could he have heard her, with the gushing of the waterfall drowning out any sounds. No, something else had drawn his attention.

In a single move, he sidestepped out of the flowing water and disappeared into the forest beyond.

At first, the priestess was unsure of what she had seen. Was it a human? No, a mere human would never possess such unusual features. Surely, it was a demon. But why so close to the Temple village? Had his presence been connected to the Priesthood? It was unlikely, in the manner of which he had been spotted. Indeed, it must have been by chance; a fluke. It was the only rational explanation.

1

HAVE FAITH

Awhisper sounded outside the window shutters. "Anaya! You need to wake up. Otherwise, you will be late for morning prayers."

The priestess stirred, but merely turned over and drifted off once more. The hunt the previous night had concluded only hours before dawn, and she had still to recover from the strenuous practice.

"Anaya!" called the same voice, this time louder.

Slowly opening her eyes, she blinked to focus her vision, staring blankly into the ceiling above. "Yes, yes... I'm getting up," she said, seating herself on the edge of the bed. Stretching, she yawned tiredly.

Looking over at a chair across the room, she noticed her robes hanging heavily over the backrest. They were covered in stains of dark blood, a silent witness to the treatment the demons had been given the night before. Eventually, they had all been killed, and the family living at the farm could now return to their home and continue to make use of their land.

Knowing she would have to use a different garment, she stood and walked over to her wardrobe.

Her accommodations were simple; a few pieces of furniture fashioned from pine spread about the room. They included a bed, table and chairs, and the closet she now dug through. Pulling out the first gown she could find, she quickly dressed. It was plain but well made, the linen dyed a dark green.

Traversing the room, she opened the door to her timbered cottage, peering outside. The sun stung her eyes, prompting her to shade her face with her hand. On her front step sat a young girl, no more than in her mid-teens.

It was Lenda, the one who had awoken her. "It is not like you to oversleep, sister," she said.

She was right. Anaya never overslept, often being called the most disciplined priestess to have ever walked the sacred Temple grounds. This would even be repeated by the High Priest himself.

"I know, and I'm sorry. I am causing you to be late as well," she said, sighing. She had always had a close relationship with Lenda, ever since childhood. Both being orphans, the two girls had bonded at an early age, even though Anaya was five years her senior.

"Do not concern yourself, sister. Although, I would have re-braided my hair if I were you." The young disciple referred to Anaya's tangled mess that only slightly resembled the plait she had created the evening prior.

"Oh, Goddess. Not today," Anaya complained. She removed the leather strap holding the strands together, releasing her hair completely. It was chestnut brown, slightly wavy, and reached down below her shoulder blades. Raking her fingers through to untangle the locks, she then gathered them into a ponytail, and fastened the strap once more. "This will have to do," she said.

Turning towards the Temple, they could hear bells chiming in the distance.

Filling her lungs with the morning air, Anaya slowly exhaled. She squared her shoulders, then locked eyes with Lenda. "Let's go."

As Anaya and Lenda arrived at the Temple, the rest of the priests and disciples inhabiting the village had already gathered. The girls barely made it inside before the High Priest appeared, Anaya hurrying forward to sit down in the front row.

"Good morning, my children", his booming voice sounded in the Temple. "Let this day be as blessed as yesterday, and the Light bring us blessings in the morrow. Last night's hunt here in western Ovena was a great success. Everyone, please; be seated."

Those present in the building settled down along rows of benches as the High Priest prepared the morning prayers. He lit candles and incense on top of a table below the image of the Goddess; a towering statue made from ivory, the deity tall and muscular. Dressed in flowing robes, she reached for the heavens.

The High Priest faced the crowd as he began the sermon, speaking of their work of Light and righteousness against all that was dark and grim. An hour later, the preaching concluded, and everyone was dismissed in order to resume their chores.

✶✶

Anaya's stomach rumbled as she left the Temple. Her hands quivered, her body craving nutrition. She had not eaten since preparing for the demon hunt the night before, and now found herself ravenous. Walking across the large central square of the village, she headed for the pantry building.

The area had recently been renovated, with large stone slabs creating an elegant but durable surface to walk upon. In the centre stood an ancient tree, a soaring oak with wide, twisting branches. Its canopying leaves rustled in the breeze, rays of sunlight flickering through the greenery.

Lenda ran up to Anaya, lightly touching her arm. "Should we break fast together?" she asked.

Anaya merely nodded, the two of them entering the small structure. With shelves lining the walls, it was stocked full of bread, dried meats, and plenty of fish. It also held different oats and cheeses, as well as fresh milk and seasonal fruit and vegetables. The girls settled on sharing a small loaf of bread and some cheese, then filled up a pot of water at the village well on the way back to their cottages.

"I'll make the tea," Lenda said, grabbing logs from a stack of firewood. She placed them into a simple campfire situated between the small dwellings.

The girls were long time neighbours, the younger woman still only a disciple.

Members of the Priesthood would most often live in pairs of two, but Anaya had earned the right to her own cottage due to being one of the highest-ranked priestesses. Lenda, on the other hand, was only temporarily alone in hers, her previous roommate no longer part of the Priesthood

The housing was simple but served its purpose. It consisted of two modest bedrooms, both of which were connected to a small hallway centred in the building. Each bedroom had windows facing the front and rear side, covered with wooden shutters. They also shared a chimney, with a fireplace on either side.

Anaya used her spare bedroom as a preparations and repair workshop for her gear and weaponry. One of the walls also had shelves from top to bottom, filled with books and various trinkets. For Lenda, the spare bedroom housed an empty bed and wardrobe.

"Very well, sister," Anaya said. "You do that, while I just sit down for a minute." Smiling wearily, she sunk down onto the front steps of her home. She yawned, stretching, then leaned back against the door.

Before Lenda managed to build a fire, the priestess had already fallen asleep. The young girl quietly prepared the breakfast, toasting the bread and melting some cheese over it. By then, Anaya had slept for almost half an hour. She stirred just as Lenda was about to rouse her.

"Perfect timing," Lenda said. "Here is your food, sister." She handed over the bread, and Anaya ate greedily, licking her fingers as she finished.

"Oh, my Goddess. It is the best bit of food I have ever had", she exclaimed.

"You always say that", Lenda laughed.

"And it's always true."

✶✶

It was noon by the time Anaya took the narrow path to the stream, ready to clean her bloodstained robes.

Demon blood was hard to remove. It was darker than that of humans and did not respond well to any of the soaps you could purchase at the local market. Your only choice was to keep scrubbing away at it, which was the reason why Anaya only wore black or grey while hunting. A light fabric would never get clean enough to wear again.

"Anaya!"

The sound of her name being called made her instinctively take a defensive stance, standing up with her legs wide and hands forward. She let her arms drop as she once again saw Lenda approaching.

This time, the girl held some robes of her own. "Sister, I need some help," she said. "Edric asked me to clean his clothes from the hunt yesterday, but I am not sure what is best to do. I brought all my soaps with me."

Anaya sighed, the young girl's naivety painfully obvious. She knew Lenda had asked if there was anything she could do for Edric, and the man, not having any shame, always found something.

"Do not worry, I will show you," Anaya answered kindly. "Just follow my lead. I have only just started."

Enjoying each other's company, the two women spent most of their afternoon alongside the water, chatting and laughing.

✶✶

The sun had almost set as Anaya and Lenda arrived back at the Temple village. They hung the robes up to dry outside of their cottages, then sat down by the campfire.

Lenda added some kindling, flames soon rising into the cool air. "I will go fetch some food for us," she decided.

Before Anaya could answer, the girl whisked away in the direction of the pantry house. Finding herself abandoned, Anaya noticed a young man approaching.

It was Edric, a twenty-five-year-old man with blond hair and bright blue eyes. Tall and lean, he wore a simple linen shirt and a pair of brown leather trousers. He had a handsome face, which he always kept clean-shaven. "Greetings, Anaya", he said, flashing her a smile. "How are you faring after last night?"

"Fine, thank you," she replied courteously. "However, I saw you visited the infirmary this morning, so how are you managing yourself?"

He snorted. "That was nothing. I merely wanted to be checked over."

Anaya gave him a flat look, the conceit in his behaviour glaringly obvious. He had most likely wished to avoid scarring.

Himself being an officer within the Priesthood, he should have been much more skilled at healing. However, he never honestly had the will to master anything but the arts of destruction.

Anaya maintained the presumption that there was a balance needed between the two. The power of the Goddess had the ability to consume and kill, but also to ease and restore. To become a true proficient in one, she believed that you had to master the other. The High Priest agreed, which was one of the reasons why Anaya had received a higher rank than Edric, despite being his junior.

"I see my robes have been cleaned," he said, breaking her out of her reverie. He approached the washed robes, the garments hanging over a rope stretched between two trees. "Lovely. Not a stain left on them. That girl Lenda sure has her uses."

"So you say," Anaya muttered, briefly shaking her head.

"Ah, it is still wet," Edric said, releasing the fabric. "Well, she will bring them in the morning. Good night to you, sister." He bowed deeply, then turned on his heel and strode away.

Anaya couldn't help but sigh, leaning forward and resting her arms on her legs. She watched the flames, the red and yellow colours flickering in front of her.

Edric came off as such an empty shell of a human being, but he was always hard to read, sometimes acting as if there was more to his words than what was actually said.

They had known each other for almost ten years, ever since he had joined the Priesthood. It was strange how their relationship had developed, with Anaya seemingly the only one able to work alongside him. The High Priest would often pair them up, whenever a mission called for it.

Footsteps sounded behind her, prompting the priestess to peer over her shoulder.

Lenda had returned, and this time she carried a basket filled with fresh fish, lemons, pre-cooked potatoes, and a variety of herbs. It was all left over from the day's dinner service, which they had missed being down at the stream.

"This will be great!" Lenda chirped, grinning.

The disciple loved cooking, which was why Anaya never pushed for doing it herself. It had somewhat hampered her own training in the profession, most often resulting in burning the goods as she attempted it. Soon, she had stopped even suggesting it.

Lenda was a breath of fresh air in the world of demon hunting. She was so innocent and pure, having little interest in the calamitous side of the Light. With her dark brown, chin-length hair and deep blue eyes, she was cute beyond imagination. However, she always said she wished she had green eyes like Anaya, but the priestess preferred Lenda's looks over her own. The girl was shorter, more petite, and her face round with dimpled cheeks. Having recently gone through puberty, her body had changed a lot, and with it, she had been receiving much more attention from male suitors. Such curves would make any woman jealous, even the priestess herself, despite the fact she wasn't interested in male companionship.

Instead, being strong and quite tall, Anaya had always felt like somewhat of a tomboy, with a muscular body and a humbler chest.

Anaya admired Lenda's positive attitude and resilience as she experienced courting, despite her shy and somewhat reserved nature. Anaya's way of dealing with men was to distance herself from relationships altogether. Ever since she was a child, she had instead devoted herself to her faith and the Priesthood. In essence, the clergy was like her husband, to which she was to be forever loyal.

The High Priest had seen this commitment early on and trained her personally. He had only ever taken on a handful of disciples throughout the years, so being one of them was indeed very honourable.

"Anaya", Lenda said softly.

"Yes?"

"When do you think you will go on your next hunt?" the young disciple asked.

"I do not know. It could be tomorrow or next week. It all depends on who and when someone is troubled by demons. Nevertheless, days off will not weaken my resolve. We must stay strong in these dark times."

Quietly nodding, Lenda stirred the pot in front of her. She had a wrinkle to her brow, despite the lovely scent of her cooking filling the air. "Is there ever going to be an end to this, though?" she continued. "The High Priest makes it sound as if the demons' numbers are limitless."

After a moment of silence, Anaya let out a breath. The Priesthood had been hunting demons for decades, but the number of attacks had not decreased. If anything, they had risen. "I believe that all the demons will soon be out of hiding," she said. "There will be an end to them, but they are not to give up voluntarily, which is why we see this increase in activity. They are getting fewer and more desperate. That is all."

"I suppose you are right", Lenda said, her chin lifting. "Dinner is ready now, so let's eat."

"Yes," Anaya agreed. "But remember to have faith, Lenda. We will get through this."

2

DISCIPLES

A few days had passed, and Anaya and Edric were called to attend a meeting with the High Priest. They sat around a table in the conference room, their surroundings dimly lit by candelabras. Situated at the rear of the Temple, the space could only be entered by a door behind the statue of the Goddess.

The High Priest leaned back in his chair. "Anaya, Edric," he said, offering both a nod of acknowledgement. "I have summoned you here today because there is yet again a disturbance in Tinta."

Being the second town south of the Temple, Tinta was built along the same stream as the one east of the Temple village. It was of decent size, holding a regular market, as well as supplying plenty of shops and skilled tradesmen for its populace.

"There have been multiple nightly attacks, fast increasing in frequency. The residents cannot fight them by themselves, and as such, the local lord has summoned us." Placing a large map on the table, The High Priest pointed to the area of interest. "The attacks seem to come from around here, mainly targeting the west part of the town."

"Why do you need both of us to go, your Holiness?" Edric asked. "Last time, it was only lowly demons."

"Because you are to bring disciples," the High Priest said. "This is an excellent time to practice with live prey. I want you two to sit back while a recruit, each of your choice, will fight in your stead. You will obviously step in, should it at any point become too dangerous for the disciples."

"I understand", Edric said, rising out of his seat. "I shall go and make my choice immediately, your Holiness." He showed reverence to his leader, then exited the room.

"Anaya", the High Priest said, scratching at his short, greying hair. "While we are alone, I would like to speak with you."

"Of course, your Holiness. What can I do for you?" She grinned, looking at him with a weightless gaze.

"Oh, you are too good for an old soul, Anaya. It pleases me to see you are so dedicated to our work. I know I have told you this before, but it should be repeated, nonetheless. You are truly like a daughter to me. I have seen you grow up into the most beautiful and strong woman. You are everything I ever wished for you to be." He gently placed his hand on her head, chanting a short prayer. "You know, I saw something special in you, already on that first day when you were brought here."

Anaya could remember nothing of her parents but knew she had spent most of her early childhood at an orphanage in Pella, a town not far from the Temple village.

"I am sure your mother and father took the best care of you, but once they were no longer of this world, the village sought a new home for you, and found one here." The High Priest paused momentarily, clasping his hands on the table. "I am seventy-three years of age now, my child, and soon, I am also to receive an audience with the Goddess."

"Oh, your Holiness, do not speak of such things!" Anaya exclaimed.

He raised his hand, gesturing for her to be quiet. "No, just listen." He expelled a breath but smiled. "I am merely speaking the truth. Soon, there will be a new High Priest, and I would like you to know what I have decided."

Anaya felt a heaviness in her chest. She had tried her hardest to push it out of her mind, but there was no denying it. She knew she would not be his first choice, as there were priests above her in rank. The four highest appointed within the Priesthood were Adena, Kaedin, Edric and herself, all of which were ranked as Senior Priests.

Adena was forty-three years old and, like Anaya, had been raised at the Temple. Her mother, also a priestess, chose to stay and raise her under the guardianship of the High Priest. Adena was twenty-six when she passed away, after which she devoted herself entirely to the cause. Kaedin was a forty-year-old man who had served the High Priest for two decades. Previously part of the King's Royal Knights, he had joined the Priesthood out of his own will. Being the eldest son, it had been to his family's detriment. The one thing the four of them had in common was their lack of relations with others, and their steadfast commitment to the cause.

Edric was the only one of them with a more questionable past, recruited by the High Priest seemingly on a whim. He had never been particularly popular, and as such, he would certainly not be a candidate.

"I can see your thoughts racing, my dear", the High Priest said, reaching out to grab her hand. "Listen carefully, for this is important. On the day of my death, my life shall trickle away as my blood flows along the ground. It will slowly pool underneath the one destined to usher the Priesthood into the brightest of futures. This is what came to me in a dream, created only by the Goddess herself."

Averting her gaze, Anaya's eyes settled on her lap.

"Anaya, please do not let this affect your resolve. I am still here. I may yet have years to come. I only wish to tell you about my final wishes, should the day come sooner rather than later." The High Priest clutched her hand tightly in his, gaining her attention.

She immediately felt at ease, the large man exuding an aura of certainty and trust. Sitting up straight, she attempted to focus on the mission at hand.

"Now, who will you bring with you on your quest to Tinta?"

Anaya considered her options. She could not possibly take Lenda, having already tried and failed several times. Fighting was clearly not for the young girl. Instead, she would have to take one of the newer disciples. "Enya", she finally settled on. "She has yet to experience a live hunt."

The disciple was a fifteen-year-old girl who had joined their cause during the previous year. She was quite skilled with throwing knives, as well as handling the Light, and very knowledgeable.

The High Priest agreed. "Good choice, my child."

"Right then, I best be going." Anaya rose, then bowed deeply. "Bless you, your Holiness."

The following day, the weather offered warm winds and clear skies as the officers prepared to leave for Tinta.

"Are you ready to depart, Edric?" Anaya walked up to the man as he was loading the last of his equipment onto his stallion.

The horse was dapple grey and very large, at least seventeen hands high, and with a nasty disposition. He would snap at anyone who neared, save for Edric, thus suiting his rider well.

"Indeed, I am," Edric replied. He was dressed in a grey woollen shirt, a pair of leather trousers, and a thick belt which held some of his most frequently used items. They included a sword and dagger, as well as a small pouch. On his back hung a large quiver of arrows, the strap to which ran across his chest. Edric preferred archery in combat, imbuing the projectiles before letting them fly. He wore protective bracers as well as a shoulder guard fashioned out of leather. "But I am uncertain of how our disciples are getting on," he continued, gesturing towards the stables.

His chosen one, a young man named Eden, struggled to mount his horse. The boy was broad-shouldered, seemed to be of average height, and sported short blond hair.

"Unsure of how we are to even depart if the man can't get up on a horse. City people for you, I suppose. It's embarrassing."

"Hush, Edric. We are here to teach, not scold them. Go over and help him lower his stirrup." Anaya locked eyes with Edric, her expression severe.

"Alright, alright. But only not to waste any more of our time." Edric grabbed the reins of his stallion and led it towards the stables. He was met by the young Enya, who had only just finished stowing her gear onto a horse of her own.

Already mounted, she was riding in the direction of the priestess. "Anaya! Thank you so much for bringing me," she said, grinning, her green eyes bright in the sunshine. "I will *not* disappoint you, ma'am." Like Anaya, she had braided her hair, for it not to get in the way while in combat. It was dark blond and reached below the shoulders.

"I am glad to hear it, disciple," Anaya said, even though she was doubtful the girl would be grateful after slaughtering living creatures.

The hunt for demons was not something to be taken lightly. The town of Tinta had previously experienced problems with a population of foxes. They were most often dark brown, medium-sized beasts with white-tipped tails. They could deal a powerful bite and were fast opponents. Even though this type of demon was considered an easier target, they would by no means surrender by their own accord.

✴ ✴

It was just past noon as the small party reached the surrounding community of Tinta.

With a hand over his brow, Edric peered into the sky. "We have more than enough time to finish the hunt today before the sun sets," he said.

Anaya nodded. "What do you disciples suggest we do now?" she asked, turning to the two youngsters riding behind them.

At first, they looked at each other, then Enya raised her hand.

"We are not in class," Edric snapped. "Speak up."

The girl's face reddened as she met his gaze. "I… I would suggest we go to where the demon was last sighted and hunt it from there."

"Star pupil." Edric lightly touched his heels to his stallion, causing it to resume its walk. "Let's get going then."

Riding across a field, they reached a steep slope. Down the bottom of the hillside was the edge of a dense forest.

"This is where the demon was last spotted, somewhere in the vicinity of the trees," Edric said, scanning the tree line. "The locals can't give a more accurate description since they were scared out of their wits as they saw it. We will have to leave our horses here and go on foot."

"Who would prefer to do the tracking?" Anaya asked.

As Eden remained quiet, Enya once again volunteered.

"I will do it," she said, dismounting. She pulled a row of prayer beads out of a small pouch attached to her belt. Clutching them tightly in her hand, she started chanting. Her words were assertive, the enchantment executed to perfection, and she left the two veteran priests thoroughly impressed. Light emanated from her hands, flashing out around her, then settled along the ground. Tracks flickered in the grass, just over ten yards away from the group.

"Well done, Enya." Anaya led the way as they descended the hill. "Now, tell us what you see."

Enya initially halted, tapping a fist against her lips. There were so many sets of prints, she struggled to read in what direction they were heading. "Is there perhaps more than one demon? From what I can tell, it looks like two... no, *three* demons."

Anaya smiled. "Indeed, it does. You are correct. It seems the farmers were unable to spot all of them. They did right in running the other way." She shot Edric a look.

"Fine," he huffed. "I'll mind my manners."

Grinning once more, Anaya nodded. "Now then. Let's find them."

The party had been tracking their prey for only three-quarters of an hour before they found fresh imprints, visible even without the guidance of the Light. The sun was still high in the sky as they approached a small opening in the ground, a narrow tunnel reaching deep into the darkness beyond.

"Right, any suggestions, disciples?" Anaya asked.

"Lure them out, perhaps?" Eden proposed. "There is no telling what we will run into if we try to follow them down there."

"The idea is compelling, but how do we lure demons?" Edric questioned. "Especially when they can smell us from a mile away." He paused to give Eden a chance to answer, but when such failed to come, he continued, "We will force them out and greet them as they exit." Edric moved forward, bow in hand, and started chanting. Pulling an arrow from his quiver, it glowed brightly. He aimed for the opening, then released it. Sparks flickered around the shaft as it flew into the cavern, Light instantly flashing out of the opening.

Shrieks came from within, then scuffling as something travelled up the path.

"Ready yourselves, disciples!" Edric shouted. "Here they come!"

Anaya chanted, then smashed her staff into the ground, creating a circle of protective Light around the group. She grabbed her prayer beads, pulling them over her head, then wrapped them around her wrist. Creating a sphere of Light, she hurled it at the demons as they exited. Two of them were hit, the searing powers of her magic burning their fur and skin.

The third beast pounced at Enya, growling ferociously as it extended its claws.

The girl's face went ashen, and she was unable to remove herself from its path.

Edric was about to come to her aid when Eden stepped in. Stabbing his spear upwards, he pierced through the demon's chest as it leapt for the disciples. Claret gushed from the wound, spraying the young man where he stood. He swung the body to one side, then pulled his weapon clear.

An arrow lanced through the head of the second demon, sending it crashing to the ground. With only one fox left, the party looked to Enya to redeem herself.

The young disciple pulled out two of her throwing knives, the blades lining the back of her belt. Chanting, she quickly lit them with her Light.

The last demon struggled to stand, its feet wide as it pushed itself up.

Enya hurled the knives at the creature, one slamming into its chest, the other slashing its skull open. It toppled over, blood pooling around it, the battle finally concluded.

Approaching the deceased fox demons, Anaya was careful not to step in the crimson puddles. "Good work, disciples. Now we only need to finish this," she said.

"Finish?" Eden scratched at his temple. "They are dead, aren't they?"

"You can never be too sure," Edric replied, pushing his foot into one of the corpses. "We have made that mistake before. Never again."

Edric spoke of an incident a few years back, Anaya having been seventeen at the time. She, Edric and Lia, a then forty-year-old Senior Priest, had gone on a routine mission south of a village called Midya.

The hunt had started as dawn broke. It had been reasonably straightforward with tracking, trapping and finally attacking the beast. As the demon lay dead on the ground, the group of priests had been talking for some time. Analysing the outcome of the skirmish, they had been discussing any changes to their tactics that might have been beneficial.

It all happened within seconds. The demon had seemingly risen from the dead, launching itself onto Lia's back. It had crunched down around her neck, tearing her head from the body, blood fountaining as she sagged to the ground. The rabid demon had somehow healed, despite being stabbed with a blessed weapon multiple times.

Edric and Anaya had managed to steel themselves and once more fight against the weakened demon. Delivering a clean cut with his sword, Edric had returned the favour and beheaded the beast.

"Never again," Edric repeated, unsheathing his blade.

Pulling out a large dagger from her belt, Anaya joined him as they made quick work of the fox demons' necks. "Next time, *you* will be doing this, so make sure not to avert your eyes."

The blood was dark and thick as it stained the officers' clothing.

Standing up, Anaya peered at the two disciples, crimson dripping from her weapon. "Now we will burn the corpses."

⁕⁕

"Anaya!" Lenda called as the priestess emerged from the Temple. With an upturned face, the girl hurried to meet her.

A conference had been held with the High Priest, where the officers had relayed the details of their mission and its success. Anaya walked with a loose posture, an unnatural stillness to her.

"Did it all go well?" Lenda asked.

"Indeed, it did, sister," Anaya replied. "And it was good practice for the new recruits." She peered up at the dark skies, now littered with stars. "Allow us to head for our cottages. I am exhausted."

Taking the short walk through the Temple village, they decided to sit and chat for a while around the campfire. Anaya enjoyed the warmth of the flames as she was handed a cup of tea.

"I was going to tell you, Anaya. I have good news," Lenda chirped, sitting down opposite. "I have been promoted to Junior Apprentice at the infirmary. I will be further trained as a healer, hopefully even surpassing yourself soon." Bouncing in her seat, she giggled at the prospect.

"I certainly hope so, as I am no true proficient," Anaya said, cradling the small mug in her hands. She slowly inhaled, smelling the sweet scent of chamomile.

"Now you are hard on yourself. You are very good with healing, only second to the Senior Healer herself!" Lenda always made sure to indulge Anaya in compliments, no matter if they were real or not. "But I was going to ask you for a favour."

"Go on," Anaya said.

"Well, to work full time within the infirmary, I will have to restock their herbs and materials, so I was to ask you if you couldn't... you know – when you are out and about anyway – if you could perhaps help me by gathering medicinal plants? Please?"

Anaya offered Lenda a kind smile. "Why, of course, dear sister. I will help you whenever I can. You will do very well in the infirmary. I am sure you will oversee it yourself one day."

"Oh, now you are only talk! But I will do my best, as this is what I am truly passionate about," Lenda said. Even though it was to be a hectic time moving forward, she struggled to sit still as she spoke of it. "And thank you very much. I could never have done this without you."

* *

Finding themselves increasingly tired, the two girls eventually split up for the night. Sitting on her bed, Anaya peered out the window, the shutters wide open. It was dark, but the surrounding nature lit up under the dim moonlight.

Anaya loved the night. Shrouded in mystery, it was beautiful and enchanting. Pushing her feet into her sandals, she decided to go for a stroll. It would relax her and help her sleep.

It was eerily quiet outside, and everyone had already gone to bed. The fires around the settlement were dying out, leaving only smouldering coals behind. Following the eastward path, Anaya headed towards the stream. She loved watching the water gushing past, seeing the reflection of the stars among the swirling pools. Standing in the same place as she had done when she first saw the demon, she gazed out over the pond.

Leaves suddenly rustled to her right, from the other side of the stream. Facing the sound, she saw him, the same man as only a couple of weeks prior.

The demon was now garbed in a grey shirt and a pair of black leather trousers, a dark pelt spread across his shoulders. Attached to it was a black cloak, also covered in fur, reaching down to the ground below him. His hair hung freely along his back as he stood there, staring into her eyes.

Anaya persisted. "Who are you?" she asked.

The demon did not move or utter a single word, his face lacking any expression.

"You are a demon, aren't you?" she continued. "Why are you here?"

Stepping back, he turned, then vanished into the forest.

Anaya ground her teeth. She would not allow him to escape.

20

Pulling off her prayer beads, the priestess flicked them around her hand and started chanting. Clutching hold of her skirt, she waded across the shallow stream. With her spell complete, the demon's tracks lit up across the grass, and she followed them into the shadowy woods beyond.

3

PRAYERS OF OLD

"Father Hampton! Father Hampton!"

The shouting originated from outside the village church, the voices rushed and frantic.

The priest, a middle-aged man with light brown hair, had stayed late this evening to prepare for the sermon the following day. He strode down the centre aisle, emerging through the main doors.

A group of men greeted him, gathered below the front steps of the building.

"What is going on?" Father Hampton asked, his brown eyes widening as he looked at them.

They were all inhabitants of Midya, some carrying pitchforks and various makeshift weapons. Others held torches, as the sun had already set.

"The village... We're under attack!" one of the men said. He had a hand to his chest, attempting to catch his breath. "Several people have already been killed. It is some sort of demon, Father. Please, you have to help us!"

The minister, who bore the name of Ekelon Hampton, felt his mouth slacking as he listened to the words. He owned a farm in the village, being the same as where he was born and raised. Having studied the ways of the Goddess and Her clergy throughout his teenage years, he had since moved back and taken over after his late parents. He shared the homestead with a wife and two children, along with a multitude of animals. Ekelon was unsure of how to react to the news, but as he gazed past the villagers, he could see blazing fires spreading around the edge of the settlement – in the direction of his farm.

In but a moment, his breathing shortened. His stomach clenched as his thoughts began racing. In his mind, he replayed moments from the previous summer; the sunshine on his face, the scent of freshly cut grass, and the sweet sound of children's laughter in the gardens.

Priests had long used their divine magics to repel demons. Spells and enchantments would be performed to ward them off, creating defensive barriers around a perimeter or forbidding them from entering buildings. But this was different. How was he to defend himself against an outright attack? What could he do? He was no warrior.

With a furrowing brow, he steeled himself. He had to hurry; his family's lives were at stake. He took off running, the group of villagers in close pursuit. Everywhere they looked, there was destruction. In all appearances, this was an organised attack, seemingly impossible for a lone demon to be responsible for such devastation. Houses and barns were lit on fire, and animals lay scattered in the fields. They were torn to shreds and left to bleed out, their cries heard across the Midya plains.

Approaching the east side of the village, Ekelon and his men happened upon countless bodies, dead people littering the streets. Some lay with throats ripped open; others decapitated completely. One victim lacked an arm and both of his legs, the man slumped in a vast pool of blood. The ground felt slippery as the crew passed by, heading towards the sound of battle.

Another group of farmers had joined up with whatever weapons they had, fighting desperately to fend off the rabid demons. The beasts stood in a pack of five, all in the shape of giant black felines. They growled, baring large fangs as they dug their claws into the soil beneath them. Furiously, they charged at the farmers.

Before Ekelon and his party could reach them, the second group of farmers were slaughtered, crimson splattering across the nearby buildings. Ekelon halted, now urgently seeking for an answer; for salvation. He chanted forcefully, praying to the Holy divinity as he faced the heavens above. "Goddess, we need Your strength! Show us Your supreme power in our efforts to thwart that which threatens our very existence. Lend us Your Light in order to stand up and oppose these demons. Hear our prayer, heed our words. Show us Your transcendent superiority against these wicked creatures of Darkness!"

In a whirlwind of light, a bright beam formed around Ekelon. Reaching from the skies, it illuminated the entire village. The beacon was like a roaring flame, flickering and bending before finally settling as it focused on the man. His eyes lit up, and he screamed, the light condensing into him, then bursting out through his limbs. It burned him from the inside, searing its way into his flesh. As it finally faded, his knees gave way.

Having watched the entire display, the demons stood motionless, peering at each other. Within moments, they snarled, taking a few tentative steps forward.

Ekelon grunted as he rose, holding his hands up in front of him.

The first demon leapt for him, its jaws wide open as it came off the ground. Bright lights shot out from the priest's hands, blasting the monster mid-air. The feline combusted in an instant but continued its path. Unable to swerve, Ekelon slammed back on the ground, the seared corpse weighing heavily on him. He managed to squirm himself free but felt something warm splatter across his face. Coming up on his feet, he wiped his sleeve over his eyes, the fabric staining red.

Around him lay the bodies of the remaining farmers, one of the demons still holding a hunk of someone's flesh in its mouth.

Standing alone, Ekelon hurtled forward. He blasted two more of the beasts, both of which instantly perished. The aggressive approach caused the rest to retreat, the demons quickly disappearing into the darkness.

Ekelon felt numb as he looked at the burning corpses. Never in his life had he expected this to be the outcome of his priestly training, not having participated in a single fight in all his life. He only ever wished for a peaceful existence, raising children and guiding people in search of the Salvation of the Goddess.

The town of Midya had recently expanded north into the forests, creating new pastures and fields to grow crops and for cattle to graze. It had been a massive undertaking, from which the villagers had only just started to reap the benefits. The logs from the trees had been used for fencing, new barns and houses, and some repairs on the village church.

Ekelon had been happy to do the work himself, being used to manual labour. It was only recently that he had taken over the ministry, the previous reverend father having passed away from old age. Ekelon had thus been a trained priest for years before he took on the profession, having run his family farm up until then.

The farmstead, too, had been receiving improvements, with the small house extended by an extra room, and a new barn erected for the growing flock of sheep.

Swallowing hard, Ekelon peered at the long flames licking the skies above his homestead. Leaving the dead behind, he sprinted off towards home, praying his family remained safe.

But he was met by a grisly sight.

Their black and white sheepdog lay on the front lawn, ripped in half. Scattered across the grounds were several sheep, most torn open with the intestines spilling out. The barn was engulfed in flames, but the house was still left unscathed.

Trying to ignore the massacre in the yard, Ekelon hurried towards the door. As he reached the wide front porch, he immediately halted. It was completely drenched in blood, and within it laid pieces of human remains.

An arm. A small, precious arm. In the far corner, his wife was slumped against the wall. Her throat had been ripped out, her vacant eyes staring into the distance, as she still cradled the remains of their son.

A scream rippled out; a gut-wrenching, inconsolable wail. It sounded distant, like a dampened noise echoing around Ekelon. His vision blurred as if thick mists had gathered in an instant. The shriek intensified as he realised from where it originated.

It came from him. In agony, he collapsed onto the blood-covered porch, sobbing desperately as grief overwhelmed him.

✷ ✷

Drenched in sweat, Ekelon sat up in his bed. Over forty years had passed since the events of that horrid dream, yet he still experienced it almost every night. He would see them lying there, his slaughtered family, unable to remove the gruesome image from his memory. It was a constant reminder of why he had formed the Priesthood, and why he sought to bring justice against the dark creatures and all of demonkind.

For nearly four decades, the High Priest had worked tirelessly for the cause. It took years to hone his new skills, battling using the Light. As the rumour had spread about the demon-slaying reverend, people flocked to seek his help. He had to find disciples, as the flood of demons seemed endless. Most of the original group of recruits were long since gone, having succumbed to either disease or been killed on the battlefield. Ekelon, however, remained strong. There was nothing that would weaken his resolve.

He had soon moved north towards the Leve mountains, along with his first few disciples. There, he had paid the nearby villagers of Pella to create a road into the forest. Most of the trees had been cut as they cleared a vast area within which a settlement was constructed. It took ten years to build a large temple in honour of the great Goddess. Within, a sculptor created a statue in her image, made from the purest of ivory.

Throughout the years, the High Priest appointed several officers, one of which was named Anaya Caelin. Originally an orphaned girl, she had been raised as his own. He could still remember the day he first saw her, and he cast his mind back to the very same event, so many years ago.

. . .

Riding alone through Pella, the closest town to the Priesthood settlement, Ekelon slowed his horse to a gentle walk. He often passed by this town on his way to and from the Capital.

By chance, Ekelon was homebound this day as a group of children ran out into the road before him. He halted his horse, regarding the small crowd.

But out of the corner of his eye, Ekelon noticed yet another child. She stood by the roadside, away from the others, gazing up at the sky. The High Priest flinched, taken aback as he saw the young girl with brown hair and green eyes. She was so similar to what his own daughter had looked like, all those years before.

The local reverend hurried forward, shouting for the children to return immediately, then grabbed the young girl by the arm. He started to escort her back towards a house next to the church, which functioned as the local orphanage. Realising she had no one to care for her, Ekelon called out to the reverend, who turned in surprise.

"That girl; is she in need of a home, Father?" he inquired.

"Indeed, she is, your Holiness. Her family is long gone. She is skinny as a rake, but she is a hard worker."

"Bring her to the Priesthood in the morning," Ekelon said.

And with that, her fate was sealed.

Now, so many years later, Ekelon rubbed the sweat from his forehead, the man still seated on the edge of his bed. He looked at a small cup on the bedside table. It held a mixture of different herbs, the combination of which would make you fall into a dreamless slumber. He tried to avoid using it, as he would feel faint the day afterwards, but today he had no choice.

His mouth felt dry, so he moistened his lips. Expelling a breath, he clutched hold of the brew. Demons wanted to generate nothing but pain and suffering, but he was determined to end their terror on humankind. This was no time for weakness. This was war.

4

HONE YOUR SKILLS

The pursuit lasted only minutes before the demon tracks suddenly disappeared. Anaya had reached a small meadow in the forest, and she carefully crept out into the open. She scrutinised her surroundings, looking for a continuation of the illuminated footprints, but there was nothing. *He must have come away from the ground*, she thought. *Perhaps leapt into the trees above.*

"Why are you following me?"

Spinning towards the voice, she brought her arms up in front of her, Light sparkling about her fingers. "I was the one asking the questions, demon. Why did you come to the Temple? Do you have a death wish?" Her eyes darted around, still unable to spot the demon, and his aura was too faint to pinpoint.

"Death wish?" he echoed, casually walking out from behind the trees. "Don't make me laugh, woman. There is nothing you can do to hurt me."

Anaya's expression hardened. "Do not tempt me, demon. The Goddess does not look kindly upon aggressors."

"I care nothing for you humans. I care nothing for your Goddess. I have no interest in any of it", he stated in a toneless voice. "I was merely passing by."

"Passing by?" she challenged. "For the second time? I have never seen you before last, yet now I have met you for the second time in but a few weeks. You lie, demon. Why have you come?"

"This conversation is over. Do not follow me, or I will have to defend myself." He turned away, and left unhurriedly, moving farther and farther away through the trees.

Not knowing what kind of demon she was dealing with, Anaya did not want to push it any further. She stood watching him in silence, then decided to heed his words and turn back home.

Dawn had broken, and a small group of disciples were gathered in the Temple, including Eden and Enya. A few days had already passed since the two of them had experienced their first live hunt, and they were still excited about it, telling everyone in the village what had transpired. The whispers amongst the recruits continued as Anaya walked into the room. She had a stack of books under her arm, which she placed on the altar table at the front, dropping them with a bang. Everyone went quiet.

"Time to focus, people. Today you will be learning more about demonkind. This is not like the first introductory course, where we merely scratched the surface of the topic. This will be the time to ask all the questions you might have, and discuss anything of your own experience since all of you have already participated in live hunts." Anaya looked at each of her students. "Any questions before we start?"

The disciples all remained silent.

"Alright then, let us begin." Anaya opened her first book. "During your introduction, we spoke of demons as a broad, general term. However, this is far from the truth, for demons are a very varied race. I will start by repeating some information, in case any of you were not present during the full introduction." She paused before continuing. "As you *should* know by now, demons have two forms. A human form, as well as a demonic form, also referred to as their *true form*. Why I am telling you this is so that you may get the terminology correct.

However, demons are seldom seen in human form, especially not in combat. Their demonic – or true – form is normally configured in accordance with a common animal species, such as the rodents and foxes you have seen on your hunts. But the most prevalent are predatory animals. Examples are wolves, bears, big cats, lizards, snakes, spiders, insects, bats, as well as some species of fish and birds." She gazed over the small crowd. "Any questions so far?"

The silence settled once again in the room.

"Very well," Anaya continued. "Depending on what true form they have, they might show different tell-tale signs in their human form also. This can be as subtle as their complexion, or as obvious as the person having gills on their neck." She flipped through her pages, showing the recruits drawings of the different creatures.

"I have a question, ma'am," Enya said from her seat near the back of the group. "The demons we fought the other day. I could feel their demonic aura, but they had none of the dark mists that you spoke about in the introduction. Why is that?"

"Excellent question." Opening another book, Anaya showed a drawing depicting a giant wolf demon. The beast was engulfed in a cloud of dark mist, which covered the ground around it. "It has to do with the strength of the demon. Lesser demons have very faint or no mist, such as those we fought. It also depends on the demon's disposition. The demonic mists seem to increase if the demon is agitated or aggressive." Grabbing the first book again, she carried on explaining the different types. "We have gathered a lot of material on demonic forms in this volume. I strongly encourage each of you to read through it. It includes information about where the demons are usually found, if they live in groups or hunt alone, if they are prone to attack humans, and if so, how they normally fight."

"Any demon who doesn't attack humans?" The question was posed by a female disciple in the front. She had been recruited a few months back, and had managed nicely as both a fighter and a healer.

"That is a tricky question, Gemma. Every year, new demons are added to the books. Perhaps it is because we become better at noticing the disguised creatures as they approach our settlements, or perhaps it is because they become more aggressive as the Light of the Goddess gains ground. It is impossible to estimate how many variations of demons are out there, but there could be as many as hundreds." She waited for a moment, allowing the words to sink in. "And therefore, it is hard to answer whether there are demons who wouldn't attack humans. I would pose the question: would it be worth the risk to find out? We only hunt demons who have caused a disturbance with humans, but that doesn't mean I would ever leave myself vulnerable if I randomly ran into one. So *always* be on your guard."

The table creaked as Anaya rearranged her books atop it. "Here is a fox demon. The same kind as what we killed only a few days ago." She held the tome up for the group to see. "They are, as I said, generally a lesser demon. They are medium-sized with long snouts lined with sharp teeth. They have white-tipped tails. They can be found alone as well as in packs. The packs are believed to be families and are usually no bigger than four to five individuals."

The disciples nodded, listening intently.

Anaya flipped another few pages. "Wolf demons," she went on. "They are large demons, with substantial fangs and claws. They come in colours of white, grey, black, and brown. They hunt in more sizable packs or tribes. They are a stronger type of demon, often emanating a thick demonic mist and have a distinct aura. They migrate throughout the seasons and thus can be found in most areas."

The group of disciples continued listening with keen interest.

Anaya always worried they would find all the information daunting, and found herself just as surprised every time she experienced the opposite. "Insect demons," she said. "They are a peculiar kind. We have come across very few, but they are usually some kind of bug or wasp, living together in larger numbers, in hives. And if there is a hive, there will be a *Prime* amongst them."

The recruits reared back at the mere word. During their introduction class, they had been taught to avoid Primes at all costs. Being much more powerful than the average demon, a Prime was usually the leader or a vital member of a demonic tribe or pack. Their abilities included – but were not limited to – increased size, strength, and speed, as well as enhanced self-healing capabilities. The surrounding demonic aura and mist would also be much more sinister, affecting the minds of those around it. The Priesthood rarely met a Prime, and the only one to ever slay such a demon was the High Priest himself.

Anaya continued to describe several types of demons, including bears, birds, and lizards.

"Bird demons, can they fly?" one disciple asked.

"Being so large and heavy, demons generally do not fly. Bats, birds, and insect demons can glide and jump over longer distances, but they cannot seem to fly like a common bird." Anaya had been speaking for almost an hour, and it was time to wrap up. "Any last questions before we finish for the day?"

Suddenly, all the disciples raised their hands, and Anaya stifled a groan. Had they all waited for the end of the session before taking the opportunity to satisfy their curiosity?

"Ma'am, why are demons attacking humans?" Gemma asked.

Cupping her chin, Anaya thought for a moment. "That is a question the Priesthood struggles with daily. Perhaps demons wish to taunt us, or maybe they find our presence a threat to their continued survival."

"Do demons speak?" This time, it was Eden raising the question, having previously remained silent.

"Indeed, they do, but mainly in human form. It can sometimes be hard to hear what demons say while in demonic form, perhaps due to their vocal cords, but we are not sure. It could be that we simply do not tend to speak to our targets; hence we've rarely had the opportunity to talk to demons, or learn to understand them."

"I see… Because my follow-up question was if you had ever spoken to one?"

"If *I* have?" Anaya became stumped at the inquiry. "Well… yes, but never any longer conversations, so nothing of importance." It was the answer she settled on, which was largely true. Speaking to a demon for a mere minute didn't really constitute a meaningful exchange.

Enya raised her hand again. "I know we've spoken previously about the creation of the Priesthood, but I have heard that the High

Priest himself fought off a demon for the village area to be cleared. What kind of demon was it?"

"Ah, yes. That is a story to be told. The mountainside above our village held the home of a panther tribe of quite a substantial size. And as you say, the High Priest managed to fight and kill one of them – the leader of said tribe – after which they are believed to have fled higher up into the mountains." Anaya was well-informed about the matter, this being one of the most common questions she would receive. Ekelon's battle with the said demon had happened quite a few years after the Priesthood had formed, but his win had finally proven the formidable force of his clergy.

"So, what about the panther demons then? What can you tell us about them?" another recruit asked.

"Panther demons are sizable, powerful demons. They are, like most demons, nocturnal and usually only come in black. Some are slightly lighter in colour, showing a faint leopard pattern, but they are more or less all the same. They have large fangs and claws. As far as we know, they live in bigger packs or tribes. Unlike wolves, they stay put in distinct areas which function as their territory and hunting grounds."

The questioning went on for a few more minutes before the class was dismissed.

With time, spring slowly turned into summer. Anaya held her class twice weekly as the disciples were rigorously trained in the arts of demon-hunting. They would also regularly practice their combat skills and healing abilities, Sundays being the only day allocated for rest. On their time off, they were supposed to supply their cottages with fire-wood, help keep the pantry stocked with food, as well as tend to the Temple's sacred grounds.

However, the sunny season did not only bring feelings of joy, for it was also the time of year with the most reported demonic disturbances. This was often related to humans starting to work the land, along with an increase in mining and logging, all of which took people through areas with denser demonic populations.

Despite the increased number of hunts, the priests at the Temple village were in high spirits. They were already preparing for the cele-bration of the Summer Solstice, which was only a few weeks away.

Lenda helped the Temple chefs cure meats and fish, as well as prepare herbs and preserve vegetables. Other members of the Priest-hood were busy creating ornaments and garlands for the festivities. It was an elaborate festival, taking place from noon of the day in ques-tion, until the early hours of the morning after. Most people found that staying awake was the biggest challenge, especially since mead and wine were plenty abounding at such celebrations.

The festival was to be held at the main square of the Temple village, and it was open to the general public. Most commoners would origi-nate from the nearby towns, such as Pella and Tinta, but some would come from as far as the Capital or beyond.

The Summer Solstice was celebrated all over the country, as it signi-fied the longest day of the year, therefore being the day bathed in most of the Goddess' divine Light. The Winter Solstice would also be cele-brated, but the focus on that day would be on coming together and standing firm against the Darkness. It all said so in the Holy Scriptures.

Having only just eaten her lunch by a table at the square, Anaya noticed Edric approaching.

"We have another mission," he stated. "We are to bring disciples again. I am inclined into inviting Eden once more, to see whether he would make more of an impression this time."

"Sounds like you have made your choice," she said indifferently.

"We best be going then."

A day had passed since Anaya arrived home from the latest hunt, which had taken place outside Pella. It had involved a mere few rodent demons, and the disciples had done most of the work. It wasn't until the beheading of the beasts that Enya had withdrawn. Anaya had been forced to assist, which led to her new robes being drenched in blood.

Wishing some time to herself, Anaya waited until the sun had set before she walked down to the stream. She was always disturbed if she did her washing during the day, other priests often lining the edge of the water. They would ask questions or want advice, which she was more than willing to give, but not during her time off. No, it was much more enjoyable at night. Being less crowded, and under the faint moonlight, she could tell herself it was almost pleasant.

After having sat there for about half an hour, scrubbing at the fabrics of her robes, Anaya felt the hair on her neck standing up. She instantly peered across the water, knowing what had caused her reaction.

There he was again. The demon.

Feigning her disinterest, Anaya continued to wash the black garment.

He slowly approached, stopping opposite her on the other side of the waterways. "Killed demons again?" he asked. "I can smell it from miles away – the demon's blood. Did it make you feel good?"

She laughed, the sound mirthless. "Feel good? When would killing ever be a joyous occasion? Or maybe you have a different opinion, being a demon and all." She dipped the robe into the depths again, refusing to meet his gaze, then carried on scrubbing.

"Being a demon doesn't make you evil. Being a killer *does*."

The statement caused a quiver in her stomach, but she ignored it. Instead of arguing with him, she remained silent. Finished with her layered robes, she pulled them out of the water and walked over to a nearby tree. "Who are you, demon?" she asked, hanging the garment over a branch.

"What are you really asking for?" he challenged.

"Start by your name," she said, turning around to face him.

"Why is that of interest if you only wish to kill us demons? Do you ask for all of our names?" It would have been expected to hear contempt in his voice, but there was nothing. The demon was calm and collected, showing no emotion.

"I will start then," Anaya decided, walking back to the edge of the water. She locked eyes with him as she stood there, unmoving. "My name is Anaya. What is yours... demon?"

"You really like calling me 'demon', don't you?"

"Not particularly, but I have nothing else to call you by, since you keep avoiding the question."

The demon smirked at her retort. "Very well," he said. "My name is Samael." With that, he retreated into the forest.

Once a month, all Senior Priests – or officers, as they were also called – would have an individual meeting with the High Priest. This was done to discuss the organisation, the hunt for demons and the development of current attacks, as well as the progress of new recruits.

For Anaya, it had started with a lengthy discussion of the current areas of interest within Ovena. She sat and pointed to various places on a map.

"There has been increased activity in both Midya and Pella," she explained. "The eastern parts, around Atua, have luckily been some-what spared so far this summer, including the mines. That might very well change, however, meaning we would be spread thin." She frowned. "I hate to think what would happen if there was an attack on the Capital in the middle of all this. Or worse still – activity elsewhere in the Midlands, out of our reach."

"Trust in the Goddess' plan, dearest Anaya," the High Priest said. "We are training disciples at a higher rate than we have ever done. Within a few months, most of them should be able to go on missions by themselves. But I understand that it is stressful for you officers when at least one of you must be present for their training. There are only four of you, after all." He looked over the map one last time before he rolled it up, tying it together with a string.

Anaya leaned back in her chair, placing her hands on her lap. "Your Holiness, may I speak freely?" she asked.

Ekelon raised an eyebrow. "Of course, my child. What is on your mind?"

She pulled at her skirt, twisting the fabric. "This hunt for demons... Where will it take us? How will it end? *Will* it end?"

"Oh, my child. Surely, you do not experience doubt, now when we have come so far?"

"Of course not, your Holiness. But who is to decide who lives and who dies? When do our actions cross over from being righteous and just... to being only needless violence?" The questions had been playing on her mind, ever since her last run-in with the elusive demon, Samael.

"You need not worry about such things," the High Priest said. "Demons are but shadows in our world of Light. In order to restore it, and bring it into an absolute and untainted brightness, the Darkness must be eradicated. It is as easy as that."

"But are they not creatures with feelings and desires, hopes and dreams, such as us?" she inquired, the question sincere.

"Anything in a demon's life that can be interpreted as such is but a lie, Anaya. They are driven not by love, but by hate and disdain. Any hopes and dreams of theirs only consist of seeking to overthrow the human race, were we to ever let our guard down." The High Priest sat silently for a moment, lost in thought. "No, demons have no feelings. They taunt us and gloat at our misery. That is why we should not treat them any differently. Taking the higher ground in something such as this is but a folly. We would only give them more ground onto which they can work their deadly schemes."

"I am sorry, your Holiness", Anaya said, grabbing his hands. "I should never have doubted the cause or the Goddess."

"Do not worry, my child. I understand your questioning. I have been there myself, many a time, only to return to why I formed the Priesthood, to begin with. Without having the demons affect you directly, it is easy to imagine that there could be demons who harbour no hateful feelings towards mankind. However, it is only a matter of time before they show their true nature. They lie, cheat and deceive. They use humans to their advantage and kill them as they see fit. They are master manipulators, narcissistic to the core. Never trust a demon, Anaya. *Never*."

"Of course not, your Holiness. I would never go near one unless I was killing it." She stood up, clenching her fists. "Thank you, High Priest. You have once again strengthened my resolve."

Several more hunts took place in the following days, including one outside Pella, and another along the Midya plains, north of the town with the same name. The mission outside Midya had been easier than expected, something that came as a welcome surprise, but the experience had still been strenuous, requiring the same amount of work both before and after the actual hunt.

It was dark, Anaya sitting along the edge of the stream. Grabbing at the fabric of her skirt, she rubbed at her aching legs. Her body called out for rest, but she needed the time alone, allowing her to meditate. Leaning back, Anaya placed her arms behind her, facing the sky. She felt an unexpected release of tension in her body as she gazed at the stars. The eternal stars, never changing. Some stronger than others, but all shining brightly, nonetheless. This was also a night of a full moon, the celestial body offering plenty of light, so she had suffered no issues finding her way in the darkness.

Releasing a breath, Anaya moved to sit upright. She relaxed her shoulders, steepling her hands on her lap. She needed to clear her mind so that she could enter a state of meditation. As every so often, she would initially struggle, her mind occupied with every question imaginable. She contemplated her past, her life before the Priesthood. What had happened to her parents? For both to perish at the same time, there must have been an accident. Or was it demons? Had they been attacked just like the High Priest's family? With it being so many years ago, she most of all wanted to move on. She needed to focus on the generous upbringing she had eventually been offered, and on her future.

Closing her eyes, she prayed for tranquillity, but it would not come. Instead, she thought about what her life would have looked like had her parents not died. Would she have become a farmer's wife, with children of her own? Being twenty years of age made her more than old enough. Soon the number of wooers around her would diminish, together with her beauty. Oh, but who was she trying to fool? Wooers? Anaya had received little interest, even as a young maid. By staying strong, she would not allow it to affect her. She would remain resolute instead, firmly convinced this was the path the Goddess had set out for her. She had to trust in Her divine plan.

Finally, silence settled around her, the noise from the waterfall fading away. Her consciousness filled with Light, Anaya smiled. It felt warm and serene within the embrace of the Goddess, the young woman surrounded by Her love.

Tiny spheres formed between Anaya's hands, swirling out around her. They sparkled, leaving a trail of glitter in the air as they whooshed about in an ever-expanding circle. Some travelled over the surface of the water, creating ripples as they flew past. In an instant, they were gone, leaving only a faint light where they had been.

Looking out over the pond, Anaya gazed at the reflection of the moon. She finally felt at ease, the meditation a success. "You can come out now, Samael," she said.

A faint thud was heard, then footsteps. They closed in on Anaya, the demon stopping mere feet away from her. He had never been this near.

"Why have you come?" she asked.

He shifted his weight, dragging his boot along the ground. "I wanted to see if you would still call me 'demon,'" he answered. "I now know."

Thinking he would quickly retreat, Anaya turned to watch his presumed departure, but he was still standing there. He towered over her, dressed in the same grey shirt and black trousers as last. His shoulders draped in a fur mantle, he gazed up at the moon.

Sitting on the ground, Anaya felt mere inches tall in the shadow of the dark-haired demon, but she simply couldn't avert her eyes. The heavy cloak was held on with a silver clasp, shining in the moonlight. It was circular and engraved with the top and bottom fangs of a predator.

"Why don't you sit down for a while?" she said, but instantly regretted it. Was she falling for the demon's lies, being manipulated just as the High Priest had said?

"I'd rather not," Samael said, facing the stream. He hunched down, then effortlessly traversed the water in a single leap. Pushing his mantle out with his arm, he disappeared into the forest.

Was this the effect of demons? She had never before been close enough to one for a conversation, unless she was fighting against it, and those moments rarely included any speech. This must indeed have been what the High Priest spoke of, with the demons' deceitful nature. Perhaps she would have to decrease her nightly walks to avoid additional exposure to Samael. She felt her curiosity rising, and that scared her. She had to stay vigilant.

5

AMBITIONS

M *any years earlier…*

Anaya had been but five years old when she was adopted by Ekelon and the Priesthood. An orphan since the age of three, she finally found her lifelong home. From the very start, she was determined not to let her tutors down. Any task she was given, she would execute to the fullest, no matter the significance.

The High Priest had let her move in with him during her first years. She had stayed in an upstairs bedroom in his mansion-like home, the building situated beside the Temple. Including a cellar, it was spread on three levels. The ground floor was divided into a large hallway with a magnificently carved staircase, as well as a dining room, two reception rooms, a drawing-room, and a substantial library. The library had its own door leading out, enabling priests and disciples to use it freely during the days. On the first floor, there were three bedrooms, as well as a study and a smaller library, with the High Priest's personal collection. It was next to this room, at the back, where Anaya housed her belongings and spent the nights.

Despite being her primary guardian, it was not Ekelon, but Adena, who took the young disciple under her wings, although the religious leader was still very much in charge of her training.

Adena was in her twenties when Anaya moved into the Temple village, and the two quickly bonded. She would bring her along on all things priestly and otherwise, often saying she had never seen such conviction within a child. If Anaya was asked to wash clothing, she would do it all by herself, not a spot left on the fabrics as she finished. When practising her healing, she would do so from the moment she woke up until she passed out from exhaustion. Adena often had to remind the young disciple to eat and drink, to prevent damage to her body.

Up until the age of seven, Anaya had been restricted to only practising the arts of healing and herbalism, as well as studying the Holy Scriptures and demonology. She had taken daily classes, often reading books well into the night. However, she would now advance her training to include weaponry skills and using the Light for both offence and defence.

"Well done, Anaya!" Adena parried the girl's wooden sword. "Have you been practising on your own again?" The woman smiled, dimples showing in her cheeks. She was a well-versed fighter with most weapons. In her encounters with demons, she would often bring both swords, daggers, bows and spears, all depending on their target. She was tall and robust, her short black hair cut in a men's style fashion. It was only a hindrance in battle, she claimed. Her brown eyes peered at the young priestess-to-be. "Again!"

They would sometimes practice for hours, which meant Adena had to look for signs of Anaya starting to tire. The young girl would not give in until she fainted from weariness.

Tasting blood in her mouth, Anaya repeatedly charged. She pushed forward, despite her fading field of vision.

Flinging her weapon aside, Adena caught the child as she sagged against her.

"I think that is enough for today, dear sister." She felt the girl nod, her chin rubbing on her chest. "Good. I will help you back to your room." Lifting the girl, she noticed how weightless she felt, just skin and bones in her arms. "Anaya, you really have to eat more, you know. With additional energy, you will increase your ability to learn and practice. Remember that." Again, the young girl quietly nodded. After taking Anaya to bed, Adena descended the stairs inside the High Priest's home.

"Adena, a word if you will," Ekelon's voice sounded from his drawing-room.

"Of course, your Holiness." She entered the room, closing the door behind her. He was seated in an armchair, so she placed herself before him, standing tall with her feet set wide.

"Fainted again, did she?" he asked.

"Indeed, she did, your Holiness. I have yet again reminded her of the importance of a nutritious meal, but she seems to ignore the fact. All else I ever tell her, she will do without a word of hesitation. She would jump off a cliff, if I so much as asked, but eating and sleeping..." Adena rubbed her chin. "Do you have any suggestions, your Holiness? I have tried all that I can think of. I have to keep a close eye on her even if it is something as simple as cutting wood, for she will do it until she passes out."

The High Priest nodded. "She is indeed dedicated to her training, but we need to pace her somehow. I will draft up new routines and schedules for her education, including her daily meals and hours of sleep. If I have to lock her in the dining room until she finishes her meals, I will do so. She has the foundations of becoming the strongest priestess we have yet to see. I will not let this opportunity slip us by, not when a war with the demons is on the horizon."

The following day, Ekelon introduced his new regime to Anaya. She did not look amused at wasting so many hours on what she saw as nonsense, but she agreed. Within days, she was eating her full meals, albeit in the fastest possible manner. As the routines settled, Adena took over and stood guard instead of the High Priest himself.

Anaya was still less inclined to sleeping, often smuggling books into her room ahead of time, so she could read while in bed. However, her guardians accepted it since she was at least lying down in bed, achieving some rest while doing so.

On her tenth birthday, Anaya was finally old enough to move into her own cottage. She was to share it with another female priestess called Lia, who was about the same age as Adena and well-versed in the ways of the Priesthood. They would stay up late during the nights, talking about the divine Goddess and her plans for their futures. Lia was often taken aback by Anaya's mature thinking, the girl truly wise beyond her years.

By this time, Anaya was already becoming fierce with a weapon. She had two chosen ones which she now preferred – a staff and a dagger. Being a lanky girl, she was taller than children her own age and, as such, she would more often practice against adults.

Adena was still her main tutor, teaching her everything she could. With the increased intake of food forced upon the girl a few years back, Adena had seen a leap in Anaya's development. She fought more vigorously and kept up her speed for more extended periods of time. She had developed immense strength and stamina, despite being so young.

"Well done, Anaya," Adena said, smiling at the young girl. "You make me very proud."

"Thank you, ma'am," Anaya replied. "But please tell me what I can improve on for next time."

Always the same question. Adena struggled to find fault in the girl, especially considering her age. "Remember to keep a cool head. You sometimes let your emotions get the best of you, if you feel the fight is not going your way. That is not to your benefit while out on the battle-field." It was a harsh reality. Adena had always limited her advice to the confines of the Temple grounds, but now she felt it was time to expand the horizon. "I believe that you will soon be able to come on your first live hunt, sister. And when you do, you will need to keep your head clear and your bladder under control. Next time we practice, we will increase our goals."

Anaya grinned wide, excitedly treading on the spot. "Yes, ma'am! I will make sure to step up to the task."

It took another two years before Anaya was brought along on her first demon hunt. It was to track and kill a couple of hound demons. Being smaller than their wolf counterpart, they were also less powerful. However, they would tend to be more aggressive, and therefore it was of utmost importance that the party would tread with care. Joining her on the mission was Adena, Lia, and Edric.

Edric was seventeen at the time, and he had already participated in plenty of hunts. "Why on earth are we bringing a *child* with us?" he demanded as they were preparing their horses. "Won't she only get in the way? This isn't babysitting."

"Good, then I won't have to watch your back," Anaya retorted, mounting her horse.

Adena and Lia laughed at the exchange.

"I am certain she will do alright, Edric. Don't you worry," Adena said, walking her horse forward. "Let us depart."

The group arrived in the town of Pella, then moved west in order to reach the area of the last sighting.

"Right, who-" Adena asked but stopped herself as she saw Anaya dismounting.

"I'll find them," the girl said, pulling her prayer beads over her head. She wrapped them around her hand, then chanted a short, but clear verse. The Light that formed around her sparked and crackled in the air.

Lia and Edric were lost for words, their movement coming to a halt. They had known her to be somewhat of a prodigy, but not to this extent.

"Hurry! Follow my lead," Anaya called, taking off running.

Seemingly tireless, she continued to traverse the landscape for some time, the others struggling to keep up. "There are three of them, not two as we had thought. And we seem to close in on them. The tracks are getting fresher!"

"Anaya, stop!" Adena shouted.

The young girl halted at the words. She looked up, seeing bright eyes peering at her from the shadows amongst the trees.

Adena joined her side. "You need to keep your eyes forward at all times," she cautioned. "But you did well, sister. Now ready yourself for combat." Adena had chosen to bring a sword and dagger for this fight, now hefting her blade in her hand as she awaited the demons' approach.

Lia raised her spear, pointing it towards the beasts.

Edric readied an arrow as he chanted. He let loose, the blessed projectile finding its target within the blink of an eye. The demon fell forward, the shaft jutting out of its head. The two remaining demons charged, aiming for what they believed to be the easiest target.

Anaya slammed her staff into the ground, and a large sphere of Light appeared around her and Adena. The demons screamed as they entered it, their skin searing within the blessed Light.

Swinging her sword down, Adena made quick work of the first one. She then backhanded the second beast, crimson spraying from its cracked head. It fell to the ground in front of Anaya, who found herself covered in its blood.

It had been a successful hunt.

Lia walked up to the bodies, her flashing spear held high. She recited a verse from the Holy Scriptures as she stabbed the sharpened tip through the hearts of the demons. "All in the name of the Goddess."

Ever since spring, long tables had been set up on the large square outside the pantry building, enabling people to sit down and eat together. It was still early as Anaya made the short walk from her cottage to eat her breakfast.

Rows of people had already taken a seat, most placing themselves in the shade of the large oak. She had become promoted to priestess last Winter Solstice, at the young age of fourteen. Today, she tried to stay inconspicuous, to avoid mentioning the particular date and its significance.

"Hey, Anaya!" Edric stood and pointed at a seat at his table. "Come sit with us, being your birthday and all."

Anaya felt like pretending she hadn't heard him, but she knew he would only repeat himself louder until she did, thus bringing further attention. "I will, thank you," she said. After gathering some bread and cheese, she sat down opposite Edric. A total of four men sat at the table, all trained priests in their upper teens.

"Birthday is it, Anaya?" one of them asked.

She quietly nodded, not wanting to add to the subject.

"Amazing. How old are you now then? Sixteen?"

"Fifteen."

The young man grinned. "Right. Well, how does it feel finally being all 'grown up?' Any difference?" He took a bite out of his sandwich.

"Not really, no. Sorry to disappoint." Anaya prayed for the conversation to end.

His eyes travelled across her, assessing her physique. "Ah, well. You don't look any more like a woman than before, I suppose. It's not as if you've got jugs the likes of Adena's. You could dive through them for days!"

Anaya reddened, watching them, the group of men bursting out in laughter.

Only Edric remained silent, and he immediately rose. He slammed his open hand on the table, staring at the instigator. "You take that back, right this second, Carl!" he demanded.

"Oh, come on, Edric. It was only for a laugh."

"No, you're disrespectful! Not only to a young girl, but also a Senior Priest, and women in general. You would be best off remembering we were all born from women and nursed by them. Would you talk to your own mother like that? You should be ashamed of yourself and I'll see you flogged for this. Now begone from this table, all of you! Before I have every single one of you punished for joining in!" Edric felt himself grinding his teeth, his expression severe. He had to restrain himself from making the argument turn physical.

The group of men sat speechless, their eyes flitting.

"*Now!*" Edric shouted, darting forward, finally scattering them.

Still silent, Anaya sat watching the piece of bread in front of her. She had lost all appetite.

"Anaya, don't listen to them. You might be more of a man than all of them combined, but you are still a woman. Never let anyone tell you differently. Being a woman is an advantage, not a weakness." Edric offered her a warm smile, lowering himself to his seat again. "Now, let's finish our breakfast."

✶ ✶

Taking Edric's words to heart, Anaya decided to dress up for the first time at the Harvest Festival that same year. She wore a form-fitted gown, the fabric tight against her slim waist. It was in her favourite shade of green, which really brought out her eyes. Leaving her hair down, she allowed the chestnut locks to rest over her shoulders. Happy with her reflection in the mirror, she exited her cottage and left for the festival grounds.

The party was in full swing as Anaya arrived, arranged as it was for both priests and commoners alike. A live band played music, and a dance area had been prepared on the far end of the centre square. There were rows of tables and plenty of food and beverages. Many visitors were already more than tipsy, clearly staggering around.

"Oh, Anaya, you look great!" It was Adena who welcomed the young priestess to the festivities.

"Thank you, sister," she replied, showing a brilliant smile. "I decided to be a girl today."

Walking around, the two of them watched as men and women

danced and enjoyed one another's company. The laughter and drink were plenty, people of all ages chatting away.

Anaya watched as a young couple discreetly sneaked away. They were holding hands as they slipped away into the nearby park, behind the infirmary. She stood quietly while Adena placed her arm around her.

"There might be men who would like to court you, and there might not be," Adena said. "All that matters at the end of the day, is what *you* want."

"I know, sister. I have no interest in men, nor have I ever… or ever will." Anaya sighed, wishing she felt it as strongly as she said it.

"Never say never, girl. Sometimes love develops over time. And when it happens, it might very well take you by surprise. Embrace love if you find it, but don't fret if you don't. That's what I try and live by."

The rest of the night, Anaya stayed at Adena's side and they danced and laughed. The sun soon set; the village being bathed in moonlight soon after. The two of them were among the few sober remaining people as Anaya sat down at a table.

Adena leaned forward and placed a kiss on her forehead. "I am going to retire to my bedchamber now, dear sister. I hope you have had a good night."

"It was lovely. Thank you so much for spending it with me." Anaya grinned, then looked up at the moon. "It sure is beautiful tonight."

"Indeed, it is. Good night, sister."

"Good night." Anaya stayed behind, sitting in silence and admiring the beautiful night sky.

"Damn it, Carl," she heard from a few tables away. Her posture perked up, and she rose before edging closer.

"What now?" the man answered, slurring his words.

His legs planted wide, Edric folded his arms over his chest. "You don't even manage to behave when sober, let alone when you're drunk!"

"Whatever," Carl snorted. "I do what I want." Noticing the young priestess, he cleared his throat. "Anaya, look at you! And here I thought you were one of us!" Clearly drunk, he wrapped his arm around her waist. He remained seated, pulling her close. "How about you let me woo you, dear sister?"

A flush crept across Anaya's cheeks. "Carl, please…" She tried to squirm her way out of his grip, but to no avail.

"Don't be stubborn now, girl. Surely you wouldn't mind someone like myself?" He grinned wide, his eyes barely open due to his intoxication.

"Carl, leave the girl alone," Edric said, giving him a cold stare. "Lest you prefer the whip again?"

"Alright, alright." Carl released her, causing her to fall onto the packed dirt. "That girl doesn't interest me anyway. I could never have a relationship with someone like her. It wouldn't be any better than courting yourself!" Carl strained a cough as he laughed, spilling his drink over the table.

Edric quickly rose, pummelling his closed fist into the man's face. "You never learn, you bastard!"

Carl fell backwards, bashing his head against the ground, the rest of his mead splashing over himself. Struggling to get up, he touched the back of his head, his hand coming up covered in blood. "What the hell, Edric?" he exclaimed.

"You men are disgusting," Anaya said, pushing herself up. Flexing her fingers, she drew steady breaths. "I will never in my life make myself dependent on a man. I will be devoted to the holy Goddess, *nothing else*. Men and love? What a joke! You are disgusting, Carl."

The young man scrambled up on his feet, then pointed his finger at her. "Disgusting? I will show you, woman!" Coming forward, he swung his arm out.

Anaya ducked below it, then pushed up, slamming her fist into his chin.

Falling back once more, Carl's eyes rolled into his head and he lay unmoving.

"You only prove my point, 'brother,'" she said. "Sleep tight."

Carl was once again punished, flogged in the main square before the inhabitants of the Temple village, then banished from the Priesthood immediately after.

Edric received a written warning for aggressive behaviour, having caused bodily harm to the man. Anaya was left out of it, as no one had spoken of her part in the fight.

For a long time afterwards, the priestess felt truly alone. As a young girl, she would always focus on her next task, never giving company a second thought. As she grew older, however, she longed for relationships, to bond with someone. She had Ekelon, Adena, and Lia, but they were much older and felt more parental than friendly. And that was what she truly desired – a friend.

During the winter of her sixteenth year, a young girl moved in. Another orphan from Pella, she was ten years old. Her name was Lenda Ainsley, the cutest girl with the sweetest disposition. She moved in next door to Anaya, and from that day onward, the two were inseparable. Despite the age difference, they would do everything together. They sat together in class and prayer, and performed chores in each other's company. They complemented one another in the most earnest of ways, Anaya finally having found the true friendship she craved. The two girls worked and lived closely together, even though they would follow different paths within the Priesthood. By the age of eighteen, Anaya was the youngest priestess to ever reach the rank of Senior Priest. A grand celebration was held in her honour, bearing undeniable proof of her dedication and complete faith in the divine Goddess of Holy Light.

6

FOR THE GREATER GOOD

P*resent-day...*

"Edric!" Anaya called but received no answer. He was too busy chatting to some new recruits further up the road, showing them his
embellished short sword. In her head, she imagined him bragging
about his conquests, killing the ghastliest of demons. "Edric Ramsey!"
she shouted.

He finally noticed her, instantly meeting her gaze. "Sorry, Anaya. I
didn't see you there," he said. Excusing himself to the group, he
sheathed his blade. Wandering over, he pushed a hand through his
blond hair, his face catching the morning sun. He had a slim, but well-
proportioned face with defined cheekbones. If only he weren't so
obnoxious, he would have been able to attract any girl he wanted. Lazy
to the core, he wouldn't even bother to try and change in order to settle
down with someone. Like Anaya, he would probably die an old
bachelor.

"The High Priest has summoned us," she said. "Adena and Kaedin
are already out on a mission with some recruits, so one of us has to go."

"Right. Better not make the old man wait." Edric rubbed his hands together, his eyes gleaming.

"You are so disrespectful; it's untrue," Anaya grumbled as they started walking.

"Anaya, you need to loosen up a bit. You are too strict." Edric laughed. "Any stiffer, and you'd be used as a floorboard in the Temple."

Pinching her lips tightly together, she offered no reply.

They entered the Temple, walking through to the conference room in silence, the High Priest already seated at the table within.

"Come, join me, my children," he said, motioning them to take a seat.

The two priests sat down before a map of Ovena, which was spread over the table.

"Are we to stand against demons once more, your Holiness?" Edric asked.

"Yes, I am afraid so," the High Priest replied, pointing to a spot east on the map. "Here, outside of Atua, several demons have been spotted. Their presence is a great threat as the village is holding a large feast for the Summer Solstice."

"Spotted?" Anaya questioned. "What crime have they committed?"

"None... yet." Ekelon rubbed his chin in thought. "We do not have the luxury to sit idle while lives may be at stake. The town will be flooded with people in but a few weeks. Their celebration of the Solstice is almost as substantial as our own."

Anaya's eyebrows slowly drew together. "I mean no disrespect, your Holiness, but are we not to reinforce the rule of no confrontation with demons who have not made themselves guilty of a crime?"

"You are absolutely right, my dear," he answered. "This is but a situation of extraordinary circumstances and, as such, we need to act accordingly." Placing several figurines on the map, which acted as markers for active missions, he continued. "Here, here and here, there are already groups deployed against demon activity. Here, close to the southern border outside the Capital, Adena and Kaedin are busy with a pack of wolf demons. They have started moving north for the end of summer." He paused, refocusing on the village of Atua. "You will both go on this mission, and bring a disciple each, as well as a number of trained priests. These are wasp demons you are facing."

Anaya knew very well what that meant. Wasps tended to travel alone, but as soon as one was under threat, it would signal more wasps to join, thus often turning any fight into large scale battles. "We will need to be at least six. Especially if we are to bring disciples."

"Indeed," Edric said. "We will also need to be heavy on ranged fighters, in case they can actually clear ground while in flight."

The High Priest nodded. "Choose wisely and I shall bless you as you leave. Time is of the essence."

With her arms close to her sides, Anaya stood, then offered a deep bow. "We best be on our way then, your Holiness."

**

As they left the Temple, Anaya's face reddened.

"What is the matter?" Edric asked, descending the stairs alongside her.

"What do you think?" she said. "Attacking on sight? What is that all about?"

Edric stopped in his tracks. "Are you questioning the High Priest's judgement?"

"No, only the path this might lead to." Not wanting to continue the conversation, she swiftly moved away, walking across the main square. A new cottage was being constructed along the edge of the paved centre. It was meant to serve as a tailor's shop, one of the latest recruits originally working as a clothier. The settlement was slowly becoming a genuine village, not just a training camp.

Anaya headed for the infirmary. "Lenda! Are you there?" she called.

"Yes!" was heard from inside. "Just a second, and I will be with you."

A few minutes passed before the girl finally emerged. "How can I help you, sister?"

Tapping her foot on the stone surface, Anaya sighed. "I am upset. I need to speak with you." Lenda was the only one she felt comfortable confiding to.

"Sure, allow me a moment." Lenda took half a step back through the door, speaking briefly, then rejoined the priestess. "Let us take a walk."

The couple conversed for some time as they strolled through the settlement. New houses were being erected along the mountainside, making room for more recruits. Draft horses pulled large wagons of timber past them, heading in the direction of the building site.

Lenda swallowed before speaking. "Surely, you are joking."

"I know, it is unbelievable. To attack on sight? Is this truly the best way to evolve warfare against demons?" Anaya gazed up into the sky, letting out an audible breath. "But please, do not tell anyone of this conversation. This has to stay between us."

"Of course, sister. Your secret is safe with me, no matter the subject." Lenda offered an encouraging smile. "Please, don't let it bother you for now. It's best to focus on the task ahead."

Anaya stretched, her movements more relaxed. "Undoubtedly so. Thank you, Lenda. Your time has been invaluable."

✶✶

The sun was rising on the following day as Edric strode towards the stables. He carried only his weapons, the rest of his gear already brought there the night before. The large front doors were left open as he arrived.

Inside, three horses were already readied, a stable hand tightening the girth on the last one.

Edric's stallion remained in his box, left untouched. He came forward as his master approached, pushing his snout into his hair. Letting off a satisfied snort, the horse caused the blond strands to flare out across the man's face.

"Lovely," Edric complained, pushing the hair back. It had grown too long, his bangs reaching down over his eyes. His haircut was usually kept relatively short, only slightly longer in the front, but he had neglected to tend to it for some time. Opening the door, he walked alongside the beast, feeling the strong neck and legs, and examining the stallion until satisfied with its condition for the journey.

"Sir..." said one of the stablehands, inching forward. He stopped far from the box, not wanting to be bitten. "Don't you think he would be less... disagreeable if you were to castrate him?"

Edric glared at the young boy. "Feel free," he said. "If you survive, come and tell me when you've finished."

Swallowing hard, the stablehand remained silent as he backed away.

Edric sighed. "Let's get going then, Grey," he said, leaving the box. The stallion followed without being led. "I suggest you take the other horses outside while I have him prepared."

Soon finished preparing Grey, Edric mounted up and motioned the beast forward, leaving the stables.

Anaya was outside, speaking with their chosen disciples. She turned as he neared. "No robes this time either, brother?" she asked.

Edric had donned a shirt and a pair of leather trousers again, much like he had always done. "No," he said. "They are too much work getting clean."

She laughed. "Too much work? You never clean them yourself anyway."

He shrugged. "And as such, I should not take advantage needlessly."

Lost for words, Anaya only shook her head. She eyed the group, noticing Eden scratching his chin as he looked at his horse. It was an older mare, but strong and with a good temperament. "Are you alright, Eden?"

He cleared his throat. "I, eh... Yes, ma'am. I am just not used to this... riding thing."

"Are you frightened?" Edric inquired.

Eden met his gaze. "No, but at home, they are meant to haul wagons, not to be used for riding." He managed to lower the stirrup on his own this time, placing his foot through it. Grabbing a tight hold of the saddle horn and the horse's mane, he vaulted himself onto its back.

Edric sighed. "Well done. Perhaps we'll get there sometime this week then." Shifting in his seat, he felt a slight touch to his leg.

It was Anaya, offering him a smile before she stepped into the saddle of her own mount.

"Where are the others?" Eden asked.

"Late," Edric muttered. "I will have them flogged for not arriving on time."

The thunder of hooves could be heard in the distance. Within minutes, several priests had arrived, halting their horses around the group. "Apologies for being late, ma'am. Sir." The male priest in the centre gave a courteous nod to both Senior Priests. "We only just arrived back from a small scuffle down the road. A young wolf demon was obviously lost, coming this close to the Temple village."

Anaya peered at her fellow officer.

"Fine. No flogging." He grabbed the reins of his horse, turning towards the road. "Better leave before anything else happens."

The party headed towards Atua. The officers and disciples had been joined by four fully trained priests, slowly making their way on horseback. It was a three-day ride, but after travelling through the first night, the troop managed to arrive during the second day.

The town consisted of mainly stone buildings, and it acquired the bulk of its income through mining facilities in the north. A large wall had been erected along its perimeter, as a defence against foes. The villagers also focused a lot on fishing, living alongside the nearby Atua river. It was a lively town, people always on the move, selling and trading. A lot of merchants from the Capital would come to restock on precious gems and minerals.

"Where is our contact?" Anaya asked.

"He will meet us outside the southern gates," Edric answered, walking his horse down one of the roads.

An older man stood waiting, leaning against an ornate cane with an inlay of various jewels. He wore a black coat and a pair of brown trousers, his bald head shining in the evening sunlight. "Greetings, *Lightwielders*. I have been awaiting your arrival." He welcomed the group, bowing his head in reverence.

"We will be heading out directly," Edric declared. "And unless you can send coin with us now, we expect payment in full within a fortnight."

"I shall see to it, priest. The demons have been spotted only about three hundred yards down this road, on the east side, towards the woods."

Tilting his head back, Edric watched the skies above. "It's a bit late, but we can do some investigating tonight, then head out in the morning for the hunt."

The party agreed, then proceeded to ride along the dirt road. They travelled in silence until Edric stopped according to the given directions. Dismounting, he left his stallion to graze.

"Volunteer tracker, step forward," he ordered.

One of the priests hauled himself down onto the ground. Chanting only a few words, he conjured a bright Light that spread around them.

The crew had to move further south before finding traces of demon activity, but it seemed to fit the description of the suspected bug type. The evidence lay in the shape of the prints, and in the sheer amount of them, bugs often possessing more than four legs. The tracks soon merged with seemingly human footprints.

"They must have transformed here," the tracker said.

As they reached the forest, the rest of the group dismounted, tethering their horses to the nearby trees.

"Tracker, move in and see what you can find," Edric said. "But do not, under any circumstances, engage a demon if you make contact." He then turned to the rest. "Eden and Enya. You two search the tree line towards the south for any additional clues."

"Yes, sir," the disciples said simultaneously.

The party split up as the tracker, Eden, and Enya moved away, and the rest stayed with the horses.

Anaya pulled out a map of the area, which she spread on the grass. "This is where we are currently searching," she said, her finger pressing down on the parchment. "If it is as we think, and the demons are based in these woods, I would wager for this mound, southeast of here, to be a possible hive."

"Indeed," Edric said. "As such, we need to tread carefully, with the risk of reinforcements."

One of the other priests gazed at the map. "How often is there a hive nearby, sir?"

"Seldom. These demons can travel far from their homes, but you can never be too sure."

Rolling the map up, Anaya stood. In the distance, she could see the two disciples returning. "As soon as the tracker rejoins us, we shall ride back to Atua," she said, replacing the map in one of the saddlebags on her horse.

A scream suddenly ripped through the forest. The group of priests quickly brandished their weapons and headed for the source, the disciples not far behind. Anaya flung her prayer beads out, demon tracks flashing brightly on the ground beneath them.

Edric and two of the other priests readied their bows, the arrowheads sparking.

As the group reached an opening, they were greeted by a gruesome sight. Body parts were strewn across the undergrowth, blood pooling under a torso and severed head. It was the tracker.

Eden swallowed hard, staring at the mutilated priest, whereas Enya averted her eyes, holding a hand up to her face.

Edric cursed. "I told him not to engage!"

"Perhaps it was an ambush?" Anaya suggested. With a wave of her hand, she spread her Light, revealing multiple tracks leading southeast.

"Incoming, ready yourselves!" Edric bellowed.

The beasts charged from the trees above, their dark exoskeletons reflecting the priests' Light. Large, cleave-like jaws snapped over a priest's neck, cutting his head clean off. Another demon launched itself at the two disciples as Eden's spear flashed, embedding itself between the creature's eyes. The antennas twitched as the wasp lay dying.

Her eyes wide with fright, Enya erected a protective sphere around the couple, then hurled several throwing knives at a third attacker.

Anaya chanted vehemently, filling the entire opening with searing Light.

Rearing in pain, the demons retreated a short way before regrouping.

Edric loosened several arrows, blasting gaping holes in their wings and hindering them from taking flight. He turned, sensing more demons encroaching. Grabbing hold of Anaya's robes, he pulled her away as one charged into her Light.

The wasp chittered and shrieked as its exoskeleton caught on fire, yet it managed to lock its jaws around Edric's leg. With the beast badly injured, it lacked the strength to sever the limb, but still cut deep into his flesh.

Edric screamed as he grabbed hold of his knife, stabbing it through the wasp's head.

Anaya kicked the corpse aside, chanting as her hands flashed. In an instant, she managed to heal Edric, then spun towards the rest of the party. "Regroup!" she commanded.

Eden wrenched his spear clear, joining the others as they stood back to back within the Light.

With the setting sun, it was fast becoming difficult to spot the demons. Some were only seen because of their faint patterns, but being mainly black in colour, they melded with the dark backdrop.

A tree suddenly crashed into the opening, causing the priests to scatter. A loud screech followed, the sound cutting like knives into their minds.

A massive wasp demon came into view. It was three times the size of the others, and had an extra set of arms with long sharp claws. Black smoke welled out around it, spreading across the ground. As the mist rolled into the opening, it covered Anaya's Light. The demon stepped forward, unaffected by the blessed undergrowth.

Anaya felt her knees weakening, the demonic aura so strong she struggled not to shiver. She held up her staff, then slammed it into the ground. "Steel yourselves!"

Edric looked towards the surrounding forest. He readied his bow, releasing arrows into the distance.

Shrieking came from behind the gargantuan wasp, the smaller demons darting out with the shafts jutting from their heads and bodies.

Edric sent another flurry of arrows as Anaya blasted them with Light.

The enormous wasp turned sideways, its abdomen moving to cover the smaller demons, but it was too late. They both perished, causing the massive beast to let out a gut-wrenching screech. It slashed across a fallen tree, shattering the stem, then swung at the priests.

Edric threw himself at Eden, the two disciples unable to move, already caught under the influence of the terror-inducing demonic aura.

Anaya could not reach Enya in time. Instead, she was forced to watch as the female disciple took to the air, then rendered unconscious as she hit the ground.

The other two priests had managed to free themselves from the terror, but the effect lingered. It severely hampered their ability to focus as they fought.

The giant wasp's jaws closed around the waist of one, cutting him in half. The priest's intestines spilt out around him as he dropped to the ground. The demon then grabbed the second priest by the head, effortlessly lifting him. In a loud crunch, his skull was crushed, the corpse then thrown aside.

"We need to get out of here!" Anaya cried.

Edric loosened several more arrows at the beast, but his attacks had little effect, only making it momentarily rear back.

Anaya chanted, staff in hand. Light shot out from her, forming long bands. They immediately weaved together, creating a net that slammed down onto the demon, pushing it to the ground. "Quickly, grab Eden! I'll take Enya. We have not a second to lose!" She grunted, lifting the young girl onto her back, then sprinted towards the west, hoping for clear ground.

Edric was close behind, lending a shoulder to Eden.

Breaking through the tree line, the group could hear rustling and snapping behind them. The horses whinnied and reared, then scattered before the priests could reach them. Dark mist billowed out, spreading through the grass.

"This is it!" Edric called. "This is where we make our stand. Here it comes!"

✴ ✴

The sun had long since set as Edric felt the quiver on his back. It was almost empty.

Anaya breathed heavily, the taste of blood strong in her mouth.

Arrows pierced the head and chest of the gargantuan demon. It had slowed its assault, but it showed no signs of surrendering to the Holy Light of the Goddess. Instead, the wasp swung once more at the priests, causing them to give ground.

Enya had stirred, now back on her feet, but she was too scared to act.

Eden protected her to the best of his abilities. He was surprisingly calm in the intense moment, danger so imminent. With an arm around her waist, he led her away from the attacks. He parried a hook with his spear, then seeing a chance, he let go of the girl. His weapon swept through the air, striking between two of the plates of the exoskeleton.

The limb severed, the demon's arm falling to the ground. It screeched and flung out in anger, its other arm crashing down on the disciple.

In a flash of inconceivable strength, Eden screamed, standing firm, his spear held sideways as he blocked the assault.

Edric let his last arrows fly, two hitting the demon in the eye, blinding it on one side. He drew his sword and charged the massive beast, the blade glowing brightly.

Joining him, Anaya conjured more Light, and together, the two officers managed to send the creature stumbling. Unable to use its burnt wings to straighten itself, the demon thundered into the ground.

"Now!" Edric called, rushing in once more.

The dark mists suddenly thickened and whirled up around the wasp, making it hard to see. The demon screeched and chittered again, then heaved itself upright. Instead of attacking, it reared back, grabbing a nearby tree. Uprooting it from the dirt, the demon hurled it at the priests.

Eden clutched hold of Enya, barely escaping being crushed under its weight.

Then, in an instant, the massive wasp vanished into the woods.

As the dust settled, the priests peered into the forest, looking for signs of the enemy returning.

Anaya grabbed Enya, who had fainted once again, feeling her wrist for a pulse. "She is fine," she said. Letting out a sigh of relief, she lowered the girl back down. Anaya chanted, Light enveloping the two and healing many of the girl's wounds.

Enya groaned as she came to. "Anaya?" she asked, blinking slowly.

"You will be alright, sister." Behind them, Anaya heard retching, then vomiting.

It was Eden, all the colour drained from his face.

Edric walked up to the young man. "You have nerves of steel, kid," he said, placing a hand on his back. "You did well."

Righting himself, Eden slammed his fist into the officer's face. "They are all dead!" he shouted. "How can you call that well done?"

Edric grabbed at his nose, claret pouring out. He took a deep breath to compose himself. "You are right, Eden, but that doesn't lessen your feat. We were caught in a trap, and we did what we could." He gazed over at the women. "We need to gather the horses and hurry back to the Priesthood." He wiped his sleeve across his mouth, the fabric staining with blood. Quietly chanting, he healed his broken nose.

With Anaya lending her a shoulder, Enya managed to stand. The two of them then watched the men returning with most of their horses.

"The others have scattered," Edric said, walking up to the priestess. He handed her the reins of her mount, then proceeded to help Enya.

Anaya grabbed the mane of her horse, vaulting into the saddle. "Edric," she said, her eyes narrowing as she watched the tree line.

"Yes?"

"Do you think... that was a *Prime*?"

All movement ceased as silence fell over the group.

7

_____

HEALER OF SOULS

"Well done, Lenda," the Senior Healer said. Named Maya, she was an older woman, having spent decades running the infirmary. "You have worked hard today; your efforts are really making a difference." She peered out the window at the commoners, a few still waiting to receive healing and medicine.

"Thank you, ma'am," Lenda replied, bowing to her tutor. "I am honoured by your praise."

"No need to be so formal, sister. You have earned it. Now, be on your way, and I shall see you in the morning."

The day shift had ended, and two other healers would take over for the evening.

"Maya," Lenda said, facing the older woman. "I will work late tonight, preparing for tomorrow. I have several baskets of herbs which must be cut and hung up to dry. If I leave them for the morning, they will go off."

Maya nodded. "Very well, but don't forget to rest."

Lenda watched her exit the building, then headed towards the stockroom at the back.

The infirmary was of decent size, the entry room housing several beds and plenty of equipment for the healers to do their work. A smaller office was connected to it, most frequently used for private sessions with patients, or housing a single bed for those in need of privacy.

All the way in the back was their stockroom, where they would keep and prepare herbs and medicine. It was quite large, the walls lined with shelves, some of which were filled with books, other with jars containing various medicinal products. There was a back door leading out, as well as a small window. A spacious table stood in the middle of the room, above which hung a wicker net where plants would be attached to dry. The table had drawers underneath, all filled with tools needed for the work.

Lenda grabbed a basket she had left there in the morning. It was filled with an array of herbs which she had foraged the previous night. Emptying the contents out on the table, the girl started making individual piles. She used knives and scissors, working meticulously as she readied the plants for the drying process.

She suddenly stopped as she heard the thunder of hooves outside the infirmary. Curious, she walked back into the main room, where the two other healers were bringing in patients.

"What is going on?" Lenda asked.

Both healers stood at the window, gazing out.

The door flung open, Edric stepping inside with Enya cradled in his arms. "We require healing," he proclaimed. Everyone moved aside as the officer walked up to a bed and placed the girl upon it.

"I'm only a bit lightheaded still, sir. I will be fine," Enya said, attempting to sit.

Edric held her down. "Stay in bed," he snapped. "They still need to check if you might have a concussion or even internal bleeding."

She quietly nodded as one of the healers joined them.

"My name is Padma," she told Enya. "I will check you over." Light emanated from her hands as she used her magic to scan the disciple's bruised body. "No internal bleeding. But a concussion is likely. Have you been nauseous?"

"She vomited several times on the way back," Edric said. "Although we did ride hard."

"And what about you? Are you injured, sir?" the healer asked.

"Not seriously."

"Then, please, leave us. It is best to focus on the patient alone."

The officer nodded, then headed for the door.

"Wait, Edric," Lenda called. "What happened? Is Anaya alright?"

"She is. Physically, at least." Expelling a breath, he left the infirmary.

Outside, Eden stood holding the reins of their mounts, all except Edric's. The beasts were drenched in sweat, foam covering their chests and mouths. "Will she make it?" the young man asked.

"She will be fine. We will all be fine," Edric muttered. "Take the horses back to the stables. Leave any gear in the tack room to be picked up later." He paused, glaring at his stallion. "You can leave him here."

Striding off, Edric clenched his fists, anger brewing inside him. Yet it was not only aimed at the demon who had claimed so many lives, but at himself. He had led his group into an ambush, the risk for which hadn't even crossed his mind. Walking past a tree, he slammed his fist into the stem, causing the skin on his knuckles to split. He swore. "Everyone is fine... Everyone except *them*." The image of his dismembered crew flashed before him as he pummelled the tree again.

"Edric... sir."

Spinning towards the sound, Edric found Lenda standing behind him. He gave her an empty stare but said nothing. Averting his gaze, he turned his body, attempting to hide his bloodied hand.

Lenda stepped closer, carefully reaching for him. He remained silent as she brought his hand forward, examining the wounds. She chanted a few words, and the skin closed. "Whatever happened, don't punish yourself."

Still looking elsewhere, he snorted. "You have no idea what happened. I deserve no less," he said. "Now go see to your friend."

✶✶

Anaya sat on her bed, her face buried in her hands. She knew they would have to call for a meeting with the High Priest, but she had no strength left in her body. With the memories of the fight still raw, she struggled to compose herself.

"Anaya, can I come in?" she heard from outside her door.

"Yes," she replied, immediately feeling her eyes watering.

Lenda carefully entered, then walked up to the priestess. Without a word, she sat down and embraced her tightly.

Her lips trembling, Anaya began to cry. It quickly transitioned into sobs, leaving her gasping for air.

Gently stroking her back, Lenda sat quietly, consoling her. A few minutes passed, before Anaya finally managed to take a full breath.

Releasing her, Lenda placed a hand on her friend's shoulder. "I will make us a nice, hot meal, then a cup of soothing tea," she said, offering her a warm smile. "We will talk all night, if need be."

Anaya wiped her tears. "You not only heal the body, dearest sister, you heal the *soul*. What would I do without you?"

✶✶

As night fell, the High Priest called for a conference with the survivors. It was held at his private residence, inside his spacious dining room. They had sat down around the table, the two officers on one side and the disciples on the other.

Paintings adorned the walls, and a large rug covered most of the floor, spread across nearly the entire space.

The group spoke for some time, relaying what had happened during their mission, the High Priest listening in silence.

Enya sat crying, staring blankly into the table.

Anaya had reached across, gently grabbing her hand to comfort her.

"We were but caught off guard, your Holiness," Edric explained. "We also believe that this larger, more powerful demon was a Prime."

Ekelon opened his mouth as if to speak, but paused, collecting his thoughts. "I fear you are right, my child," he said. "This amount of strength does not come with the average demon, no matter the type." His face filled with deep lines as he contemplated their options.

Enya sat sniffling but was finally calming down again.

"Adena and Kaedin are expected to be back by dawn, having completed their mission in the Rover province," Ekelon went on. "They are bringing some new recruits, which is welcome at a time like this." He scratched his chin. "One of you will accompany them to Atua and recover whatever remains of our fallen. I also want you to speak with the citizens, to pertain whether or not more demons have been spotted."

Anaya was about to speak as Edric placed his hand on her arm.

"I will go, your Holiness," he said. "I decided to move forward despite the late hour. It is, therefore, my responsibility to retrieve them."

"As you wish," Ekelon allowed, nodding. He then turned to look at Eden; the boy had been silent for most of the meeting. "You, Eden, showed great courage."

The disciple smiled, but his gaze dropped. "I only did my duty, your Holiness."

"Be that as it may, your duty still required vast quantities of bravery. Therefore, you shall be awarded the title of Junior Priest for your efforts. Your training shall continue, but you will no longer depend upon an officer to join you on missions."

"I am honoured, your Holiness," he said, bowing his head.

Ekelon once again focused on the officers. "Edric."

"Yes, your Holiness?"

"Make sure the horses are readied by the break of dawn. If there is anything remaining of our fellow priests, then buy a wagon in Atua to bring them home."

"Yes, your Holiness."

The High Priest rose, prompting the others to stand with him. "Now, I must ask you to excuse yourselves. All except, Anaya."

Edric and the disciples quietly left the room, leaving the priestess alone with Ekelon.

The High Priest motioned her to sit back down. "I wanted to speak with you, dear Anaya. It relates to an earlier conversation we had."

"I meant no disrespect in questioning your orders, your Holiness. I was merely concerned about what path we are choosing for the Priesthood."

"I know, which is why I highly respect your opinion. Truly devout members of this Priesthood will speak their mind, even if it means to question their leader. Trust that I have thought long and hard about this decision. I feel it is the only path we can take to attain an upper hand against demonkind." He sighed, gazing across the room at the open fireplace. "I wish we had a choice. Truly, I do. But surely you understand now why we must act? Imagine a beast such as the one you encountered to roam free? How are villagers to fend off such a creature?" He returned to look at Anaya, and she hung her head.

"You are right, as always, your Holiness. I only wish there was another way."

Ekelon acknowledged her words. "Until such a time, this is the path we must travel. Now, be on your way. Have some well-deserved rest."

Edric had slept for only a few hours. He was again preparing his grey stallion, this time alongside the two stablehands tending to the other horses.

Adena and Kaedin's party had only just arrived the previous hour, now meeting with the High Priest.

The sun was rising, causing the sky to glow brightly in yellow and red hues.

"Well done," Edric said to the helpers. "You are dismissed." As they left, the officer sunk down on the stable floor, leaning his back against the wall. His eyelids heavy, it took only moments before he drifted off into sleep.

"Edric."

The man jerked as his name was called. He looked around, noticing Adena standing in front of him. Yawning audibly, he rubbed at his eyes. "Must have dozed off for a minute," he said.

Adena nodded, gifting him a warm smile. "We have been given a report by the High Priest. Kaedin will join us shortly." She dragged her hand across her cropped hair. "We will recover them, Edric, and give them a proper burial."

He slowly nodded, then rose, taking on an unmoving stance.

Kaedin stepped through the open door, his brown eyes friendly as he looked at the young man. Around six feet tall, he was broad and solidly built. Previously serving as a Royal Knight for the King himself, he still wore heavy metal armour whenever he entered combat. Ready to depart, he had already donned it, along with a full-length cloak, but he held his helmet under his arm. He had dark blond hair and kept a neatly trimmed, full beard. "Edric," he said. "I am deeply sorry for what happened."

Again, Edric only acknowledged it, having no interest in discussing the incident. He wanted to get on with their new assignment instead.

Several more priests joined them at the stables, all dressed up and ready to depart.

"All here?" Kaedin asked.

"Aye, sir," one answered.

"Very well. We best be going then."

8

LICK YOUR WOUNDS

The sun was rising as Samael sat alone by the riverbank, overlooking the water slowly flowing past his home. The horizon was bright, alive with an array of colours. Despite the early hour, the air was warm, the gentle breeze caressing his skin.

Sensing a presence, he turned.

"Samael, sir, the Matriarch has summoned you."

Behind him stood a man from her personal guard.

"Fine," Samael said, rolling to his feet. At his full height, he towered over the sentry, his long hair gathered at the nape with a leather strap.

They walked a short way along the river, then ascended a hill upon which the Matriarch's house was situated. The building was quite large and spread across two stories. The bottom floor mainly consisted of a large entry hall, also functioning as a reception room for all things related to governing their tribe.

Entering the house, Samael took in the familiar surroundings. A daybed was placed at one end, near an open fireplace, and the walls were lined with bookshelves, all filled with tomes of various sizes. Below the daybed, the floor was covered by a large dark pelt.

As usual, the Matriarch sat perched on her daybed, dressed in a dark blue gown. She was slim, with long black hair and brown eyes, and her skin was bronzed after many hours in the sunshine.

Samael walked up to her and knelt. "I have come, mother", he said in a toneless voice.

"My son!" the Matriarch exclaimed, swinging her arms out to hug him. "Happy birthday."

"Mother, please." He sighed, not returning the embrace.

"Fine. You are as you are." She stood and walked over to a dresser, fetching a small parcel. "Here is my gift to you." She handed it to him, then sat back down on her daybed. "Open it!"

Giving her a blank stare, Samael pulled the thin wrapping away from the package, then started grabbing handfuls of straw from inside it. Eventually, he saw a small box at the bottom, which he carefully pulled out. Opening it, he recognised the silver necklace inside. "What is this meant to be?"

"It is the necklace your father gave me the day he asked me to be his," she explained. "You are now of age, according to the Spirits. If the prophecy is true, you will meet this someone to make yours during this year of your life."

"Mother, that is ridiculous. I do not believe in the Spirits, nor anything else for that matter. Keep your necklace." Samael dropped the piece of jewellery in her lap, then turned to walk away.

"You will find a wife, Samael! If not for your own sake, then for the sake of this tribe. I will not live forever, you know!" Before she could finish, her son exited the building, slamming the door as he left.

"Lilith... My lady," she heard whispered behind her.

"Do not sneak around, Arax. Speak plainly." It was her manservant, appearing from one of the back rooms.

"If he does not want to choose a wife, perhaps you will have to do it for him?" he suggested, walking around to stand in front of her. The man was short but well-built, with a bald head and bright blue eyes. He had been in the family for as long as he could remember. Having grown up in the household alongside his father, who served as the previous attendant, he had since taken over the position. No one could find a closer ally. "Surely, this would be an opportune time to make a most advantageous union between, let's say, two of the most prominent families within the tribe?"

"Perhaps," Lilith sighed. "But he is his own person. He is not easily forced." She leaned forward, resting her chin in her hand.

"Maybe it should be suggested as an agreement between you and him. He marries and sires an heir, then his wife and child can live separate from him thenceforth. I know it is a disturbing thought, going against tradition, but Samael is different. We know that. *You* know that. And we have already gone against practice once, so this will be no different."

"Indeed." The Matriarch looked down at her hands, slowly turning one of her rings. "I am fifty-three years old. I know not how much time I have left, and before I leave this world, he has to have sired an heir, or I shall not be able to rest in peace." Picking the necklace up from her lap, she looked at the engraved pendant. The intricate details, the love that had gone into crafting such jewellery, it was almost awe-inspiring. It was a reminder of the great love she had felt for his father. "Gather a list of women within the tribe eligible for marriage, with the closest relation being second cousin. I do not want to come off as desperate."

"Yes, my lady," Arax bowed, then swiftly left to begin his new task.

✶✶

Darkness had settled over the forest as Samael left the village, heading west. He had spent the day alone, as he most often did.

His demonic form allowed him to traverse the forest with ease, dark mists trailing behind him as he ran. Extending his claws, he felt the wind run through his raven fur. He was nigh on invisible at night, melding into the darkness.

He leapt over a boulder, then a stream.

Times like these would be the only ones where he felt truly unfettered. He was free from his mother's continued pursuit of an heir, and from thoughts of days past and those to come. He would live in the now, travelling high into the mountains, or deep into the forest. Sometimes he would hunt, and other days merely lay in a field of grass, listening to the breeze.

A life of solitude. That was what he had always wanted, but his loyalty to his mother, and his heritage, kept him in their village.

Samael knew he had always lacked emotions, disinterested in all things material, spiritual, and familial. He had never known anything different, even considering reactions to physical pain as nonsensical and merely useless distractions. It was not that he didn't feel, only that he wouldn't care about it. He had also never had any close confidants, nor had he ever wished for any. They, too, would only act as hindrances, having to be considered as he made decisions going forward.

His claws digging deep into the undergrowth, Samael kept up the pace as he passed through the woods. Finally reaching his destination, he began the metamorphosis into his human form. The process took only a few moments but was, for most demons, quite arduous. Snapping and crunching of bones echoed around him as they reshaped and realigned within his body, but he remained silent.

Walking through the last stretch of forest, Samael found himself overlooking the same waterfall and pond where he had previously seen the priestess. He was unsure why he felt compelled to go there, thinking it might stem from the rumoured expansion of the Priesthood. He was curious to see it first-hand, especially with them slowly encroaching on his tribe's territory.

The priestess was nowhere to be seen, but Samael was in no rush. Climbing high up into an oak tree, he leaned his back against the sturdy stem, gazing out over the trickling stream. An hour passed, with the demon still perching on the branch, letting the slight breeze touch his face. Blessed with a keen sense of smell, he suddenly noticed the wind bringing with it the stench of death.

Blood. Demon's blood.

The so-called holy Priesthood had once again been out on a slaughter.

On the small path below, the priestess came walking, robes draped over her arm.

Samael watched as she washed the garment, just like she had done so many times before. Jumping down from the branch, he landed silently on the ground, only strides away from her. "You just can't stop killing, can you?" he said.

Anaya clenched her jaw, looking up at him, but did not answer. With the memories of her last battle still painfully present in her mind, she had left her robes untouched until now. This evening, she had finally managed to make herself clean them, only to be taunted. Returning to scrubbing at the garment, she sighed.

Samael walked up to her, stopping mere feet from where she sat.

Turning around, Anaya extended her hands. Light blasted out, but the demon swerved out of its path. She gasped, her mouth left open as she stared at him.

"I've told you not to force me to defend myself," he coldly stated, after which he traversed the stream. Without so much as a glance over his shoulder, he walked back into the forest.

Anaya cursed. She should have known not to come out this late. "I just never learn," she scolded herself.

The party had arrived in the town of Atua, arranging for a villager to bring a horse and wagon.

Edric led them to the site of the attack, leaving their mounts on the nearby grasslands. It wasn't difficult to follow the tracks through the forest, fallen trees scattered from the demon's rampage only a few days prior.

As they reached the clearing of the primary battle, several of the priests had to immediately excuse themselves, retching as they walked away. The sight of the slaughtered crew and the stench of rotting flesh was too much for many of them.

Kaedin's eyes narrowed as he scrutinised the tree line. "I shall secure the perimeter. Begin gathering our fallen." He hefted his shield, then drew his sword as he left them.

Watching him depart, Edric wanted to tell him to be careful, but he could not. He only stood silently, as if frozen in place.

"Edric, help me lift Phillip." Adena's voice seemingly snapped him out of his state of apathy.

"Yes, of course. My apologies."

The body of the man in question lay in two parts as he had been cut in half during the assault. Having loaded him onto the wagon, they rejoined the other priests, who had managed to compose themselves before the officers returned.

"Eli and Rick, you carry Gar." It was the priest who had his head crushed. He was only recognised due to a tattoo on his right shoulder. "We will gather what we can find of Alvin." It was the man who had acted as the tracker.

Edric found himself speechless at Adena's ability to remember all their names. He felt ashamed, barely able to recall the names of those he met daily, let alone priests he seldom worked alongside with.

Being hard at work for almost an hour, the crew eventually managed to gather their fallen comrades. As they headed back out of the forest, Kaedin came walking through the trees, dragging a net of Light behind him.

"What is going on, Kaedin?" Edric asked him.

"I found this bugger not far from the clearing. I had to chase him down but managed to capture him." With a grunt, Kaedin hauled the net forward, within it a demon, but in human form. "One of the attackers, I'm assuming, as he is wearing one of your arrows on his back."

Edric came forward to have a look. "Yes, that is one of mine," he said. "But why not kill him?"

"The High Priest's orders. He instructed to capture any demon survivors in order to extract information of the Prime's whereabouts. It went smoother than expected, I must admit. The arrow is probably deep, still searing him."

The demon was sweating profusely, the skin pale as he shuddered inside the net.

"We will have to remove it if we wish for him to survive," Adena said.

"Aye. But he will have to manage on the way back. Until we have him properly confined, it will stay put. The amount of power he mustered trying to flee only strengthens my belief. We will take no unnecessary risks." Kaedin dragged the demon over to the wagon, then heaved him up over the edge. Grabbing the reins of his horse, he stepped into the saddle. "I will travel with the cargo, together with Rick and Eli. Anyone else is free to ride ahead and give the word of our success. Have them start preparing for the funeral."

Heat flushed inside Anaya's body. She felt herself grinding her teeth, striding through the village.

Clutching her robes tighter, she cursed inwardly. Not only had the demon showed up yet again, only to taunt her, but she had ruined her robes in anger because of his insolence. Several panels of the fabric would have to be replaced, so she headed for the tailor shop. Inhaling slowly, she knocked on the door, still furious. As it opened, she forced a smile.

"Oh, hi there, ma'am," the young man said as he stood in the doorway. "How can I help you?" He was short and slim, with neatly trimmed, dark brown hair and blue eyes.

"My robes," she answered, presenting them to the clothier. "They need repairing."

"I see." He accepted the garment and disappeared into the cottage. "You are welcome to come in, ma'am."

Anaya stepped inside. The shop was allocated to his main room, fabrics neatly folded on shelves and inside wardrobes lacking doors. Threads were arranged according to their colour, and a black cushion held what looked like a limitless supply of various-sized needles. The smell of dye was strong as she moved further into the building. The tailor had a wide array of tools at his disposal, many sharp knives and scissors.

"I shall try and find a matching fabric. If I can't, I will instead dye it appropriately. When would you like to have it done by, ma'am?"

"I have spares, but don't let it take too long," she answered. "I would prefer to have it back by next week."

"That is no problem, ma'am." The man placed the folded robes on a pile of several other items of clothing. "If I have it done earlier, I shall send for you."

"Thank you… pardon, what was your name again?"

"Benjamin Elton, ma'am."

"Benjamin," she repeated, committing the name to memory. "Thank you. I shall try to remember it." With that, Anaya left the cottage. She was going to find Lenda, who had asked her to join them in the preparations for the funeral. Most were already busy arranging the festivities for the Summer Solstice, so everyone had to lend a hand.

She entered the Temple, looking about the vast space.

"Anaya!"

"Lenda, I have come."

"Thank, Goddess!" Lenda exclaimed. "We are stretched thin, to say the least." She came walking with a basket, handing it to Anaya. "We need to replace every candle, in every candelabra and chandelier, as well as around the Goddess and along all the walls. Then there are the ceremonial rugs and fabrics, all of which must be rolled out, the creases removed. I am sweating at the mere thought!"

Anaya grinned at the young girl's genuine concern. "I will do my best to help, sister."

"You have no idea how much I appreciate it. The carpenters were forced to halt construction on the new accommodations, despite the fact the new recruits have already arrived, only to build caskets instead. It is all so unfortunate." She paused, staring down at her hands for a moment. "But we will make it beautiful, won't we?" Lifting her gaze, she looked up at the priestess with glossy eyes.

"It will be the most beautiful of ceremonies, sister."

Adena and Edric were the only ones to arrive back early at the Temple village. All the rest had chosen to stay behind, guarding the precious cargo. Their news had prompted the preparations of the funeral, as well as the arrangement of an interrogation room inside a mountain cave behind the Temple. Inside, the Priesthood had set up a holding facility for demons, as well as supplied a vast array of tools and weapons, all in order to retrieve sensitive information.

The High Priest inspected the grotto, walking through the entrance tunnel down into a large open space. Cages of various sizes stood along one side, and several shackles were mounted on the walls. "Well done," he said to a man standing behind him. He was the one responsible for the design.

"Thank you, your Holiness," he replied, bowing deeply.

"I believe it will come to play an important role in our work," Ekelon said, walking alongside one of the tables. On it laid several prodding irons, whips, and clubs. There were also plenty of daggers, pliers, and scalpels. "You will receive your payment by tonight." Excusing himself, he strode off, heading for the Temple. Walking through the front doors, he chanced upon Lenda and Anaya, who were standing by the entrance, together with Adena.

"Your Holiness," Anaya said as they all bowed.

"My children," he said, touching each of their heads. "Blessings upon you and your work. I am but here to prepare myself, so do not mind me." He left them, striding down the centre aisle. Coming up behind the statue of the Goddess, he entered one of the back rooms.

"Where is Edric?" Lenda asked as the door closed behind the High Priest.

"Licking his wounds," Adena answered. "He blames himself. He will need time to heal."

The young girl nodded. "Maybe the Summer Solstice will cheer him up."

"Most likely," Anaya agreed, chuckling. "Mead and girls abound... and men to fight with."

9

WHISKED AWAY

The sun rose behind thin clouds on the morning the day before the Summer Solstice. The entire village had already gathered inside the Temple, ready to attend the funeral. In the front rows sat the four Senior Priests, as well as the two surviving disciples.

The entire building was lit with candles, chandeliers hanging from the ceiling, and sconces lining the walls. White fabrics with gold stitching had been spread across the floors and tables. The caskets sat below the statue of the Goddess, also draped in fine cloth. The High Priest lit incense and put a small ivory figurine on each one.

"All rise," he called through the crowded hall.

In silence, everyone stood.

"*In the Name of the Goddess, our Mother and Holy Light,*" the High Priest prayed. "*Goddess, You are our Light, our source of life. In You, we live and move and have our being. Keep us in life and death in Your love, and, by Your grace, lead us to Your kingdom.*" He paused momentarily. "*In the name of the Goddess, we commit the bodies of our comrades to the peace of the grave.*" Walking from one side of the room to the other, he let a few handfuls of dirt fall onto each casket. "*From dust you came, to dust you shall return. The Goddess shall raise us and have mercy on our souls. At the moment of death, and on the last day, She will save us, our merciful and gracious Goddess of Holy Light."*

Ekelon faced the congregation and held his hands up high. *"Our Mother in heaven, we thank Thee for the gift of eternal life. Keep us firm in the faith, that nothing can separate us from Your love. When we lose someone dear to us, help us receive Your comfort and share it with one another. We now entrust ourselves to You, just as we are, with our sense of loss and of guilt. When the time has come, let us depart in peace, and see You face to face, for You are the Goddess of our Salvation."*

The crowds were quietly sobbing by the time the High Priest finished the prayers.

"Receive the Goddess' blessing. The Goddess bless you and watch over you. May the Goddess shine Her face upon you, and be gracious to you. May the Goddess look kindly on you and give you peace." He lowered his hands once more. "Please, be seated." Closing a book of Holy Scriptures, he gazed out over the rows of priests before him. "Our work is an important one. We stand at the front lines against the Darkness, fighting to win the war against demonkind. The Goddess' Light shall prevail, even if it means initial suffering. We need to come together during these grim times to defeat our foes and bring peace to the world. Pray for the souls of the lost. Celebrate the lives of those of us who are still bound to our vessels of flesh. The Summer Solstice is upon us. The height of power of the Holy Light. Go forth in peace. Let the Light burn brightly."

The caskets were carried up a narrow flight of stairs carved into the mountainside. Above the Temple village, another statue of the Goddess had been erected, her towering form soaring above a stone pedestal. It was the *Altar of Remembrance,* a sacred platform carved from the bedrock.

Funeral pyres had been prepared, on which the caskets were placed. The officers joined the High Priest as they lit the fires with their Light. The roaring flames burned high, lapping towards the skies. The crowds below were gathered in the Temple gardens, long into the night. Each holding a candle, they created a sea of stars as they chanted verses from the Holy Scriptures.

Ekelon gathered the ashes, then placed them upon the altar. A breeze built up, and the dead were whisked away with the wind.

The village was alive with laughter and cheering, the weather bright and warm. Despite it only being the day after the funeral, the inhabitants of the sacred grounds had come together, intent on celebrating those who were lost, instead of mourning their passing. The official ceremony of the Summer Solstice had already taken place during morning prayers. A longer sermon had been held, followed by each priest individually lighting a candle in the Goddess' honour, and placing it on her altar. Offerings were also prepared, consisting of a multitude of different foods and beverages. They were later to be consumed during the festival the same evening, believed to have been blessed by the Goddess herself.

Anaya was walking through the village with a group of new recruits, telling them about the Priesthood.

"The building with the tall windows is our Temple, where we all gather for morning prayers at six every morning, only exceptions being the day after celebrating either the Summer or Winter Solstice, as well as the Harvest Festival. Those mornings the prayers are postponed until eight. Do *not*, under any circumstances, be late for those, or you will receive a warning. Three warnings merit exclusion from the Priesthood."

Reaching the main square, Anaya halted. "The infirmary is over there. The pantry is next to it. Tables are set out over the square for breakfast every morning. More cottages are being built as we speak, as we need more skilled craftsmen. We already have an established tailor, but we should see a bowman and leatherworker set up shop soon. A blacksmith is located at the outer edge of the village, to the west. There you can have any weaponry or armour made and repaired."

Moving on, the group walked along the streets until they reached the newly built lodgings, which the recruits were meant to share. "These are going to be your homes for the time being. It is a bit cramped until we can finish additional housing, but it has all the amenities you might need."

"Excuse me, miss."

Anaya spun to find a woman, about her own age, regarding her with an inquisitive expression.

She was blond, with natural highlights running through the hair, and she had icy blue eyes. She was shorter than Anaya but well-built. Despite wearing a full set of leather armour, it was clear she had quite a voluptuous body.

"Yes?"

"I am sorry to interrupt, but as a Commander in the Rover Army, am I to cram myself in between bunk beds and sweaty men?" The woman's eyes were piercing as she watched Anaya.

"We do not mix men and women," Anaya replied. "You, being the only female recruit, shall be given your own accommodation."

"Excellent, then do-"

"Let me be clear, however," Anaya continued, her voice stern. "Whatever your position was before joining us has no meaning. Here you are a disciple, and I am a Senior Priest. Therefore, you should watch your tongue and show respect."

The woman seemed taken aback, as if not expecting a genuine show of authority. "I am impressed, ma'am. You most certainly have my utmost respect, indeed." She extended her hand. "My name is Anna Leighton, Commander of the third Legion in the Rover Army. But feel free to call me Vixen."

They shook hands. "Vixen it is then." Anaya turned, resuming her walk along the streets. "Let us continue."

A small area of the woods had been retained, serving as a communal park. A statue of the Goddess adorned its centre, the deity's hands raised towards the sky as She stood in the middle of a small pond. Benches were placed along cobbled paths through the greenery, some occupied by priests reading or meditating. A low fence had been constructed around the perimeter, fashioned out of cedar. Every board had a sacred rune carved into it.

"The Park of Serenity is open to all, at all hours. But no eating or drinking is allowed. It is not meant for picnics," Anaya explained. "You can eat either in the square, at your homes or outside the village grounds."

Further down the road, the group reached another building. A forge was visible through open doors along the far wall, and a small stream ran behind it.

"Here is the blacksmith I spoke of earlier."

Turning right, they entered a cleared area for planned construction, meant for creating streets with housing on either side.

"Further down, you will find the Proving Grounds. There, you can practice your fighting skill, either in the arena or at the archery range." The arena was a vast amphitheatre cut into the bedrock below, able to accommodate sizable audiences for entertainment or educational purposes. "We also have target dummies for Light combat, as we do not often allow that to be practised against one another."

The tour went on, walking past the High Priest's mansion before arriving back at the square, having come full circle.

"As you can see, the preparations for the Summer Solstice are ongoing. Feel free to make yourself available to help as soon as you have settled in your new accommodations. We look forward to seeing you all tonight during the festivities."

✷✷

With the funeral concluded, Adena had resumed her role as head organiser of the Summer Solstice. Garlands and pennants run above the square, stretched from the surrounding houses to the ancient oak in the middle. The tables were covered in cloths with intricate patterns, and a designated area was roped off for dancing. The live band had arrived and set up their individual instruments, including drums, cymbals, flutes and violins. The woman singing also played the lyre.

The Temple's cooks had prepared a massive feast of different meats and vegetables, as well as a variety of drinks. Caskets of mead were stacked alongside the pantry building, ready to be rolled out whenever they had to be exchanged.

It was all coming together, and Adena took a stance in the centre of the square. Looking up at the branches of the oak, she started chanting. Tiny spheres of Light formed from her hands, spreading out around her. They filled the tree, then dispersed across the village, creating a network of shimmering orbs, all leading back to the square.

"There, that should do it," she said, hands on her hips. She could see crowds of people walking along the road, heading her way. It was about to start.

10

SUMMER SOLSTICE

A naya grumbled under her breath. Her favourite dress was ripped at one of the seams. Letting it fall to the floor, she walked back to her wardrobe. She had another dress, also green, but it was much less elaborate. The gown did not hug her body as nicely either, so it wasn't quite as flattering. She halted at the thought. Flattering? Why would it even matter?

Anaya donned the gown, righted her skirt, then let her hair down. She gathered some of the locks, which she pulled back and fastened with a hairband, allowing the rest to hang freely. Leaving her cottage, she found Lenda waiting outside.

"Anaya, you look fantastic!" the girl said, as always with a smile.

Anaya hugged her. "As do you, sister."

The two took the short walk to the square, now congested with people. The night was young, but the food and drink were already running low. More bottles of wine and barrels of mead were brought forward, people having their fill. The cooks scrambled to supply more food, serving sweet and savoury dishes of every kind.

Anaya settled on a glass of red wine, then sat down on an empty chair.

Edric took the seat across to her, next to Enya and Eden.

"Hello there, Anaya," he said, offering her a full grin.

"Feeling better now, brother?" she asked sincerely.

The smile faded from his expression, Edric avoiding her gaze, and her question. Instead, he watched as the group of new recruits joined the celebrations – all men, except one.

"Vixen!" Anaya called out, waving her down.

The woman broke free from her company as she approached. She wore a bright blue full-length dress, form-fitting but simple. "Anaya, ma'am. Thank you again for the tour earlier. I believe I will like it here," she said. "And what a fantastic party you have thrown! I would never have expected this from a band of priests. No disrespect, though."

"None taken," Anaya said, then turned to Lenda, who had joined them.

Lenda held a small cup of cider, which was the only alcoholic beverage she was allowed. The wine and mead were stronger, and thus exclusive to those sixteen years of age or older.

Seeing the young girl, one of the new recruits advanced on her. "Oh, look at this pretty thing," he exclaimed, gently touching her hair.

Lenda visibly shuddered, pressing her arms tight to her sides.

Rising, Edric sighed. "Always the same," he muttered. "Keep your hands clear of the girl, recruit."

"What's that, sir?" he said. "Is it *your* girl, perhaps?" He wrapped his arm around Lenda's waist, the girl scowling as she angled away from him.

A mere instant later, the man sprawled onto the paved ground.

Lenda stumbled, but Anaya stepped in to support her, allowing the girl to remain upright.

Edric flinched, unsure how to react as he had watched Vixen down the man with a single punch.

"Disgusting filth. Get away from here!" Vixen thundered, the young man crawling backwards along the stone surface. He scrambled, then bolted off, the former Commander spitting where he had been. "He best not come back, or I won't leave his face as pretty as I did this time around."

Anaya laughed. "Thank you, Vixen. You saved Edric the trouble. And the written warning."

Vixen turned, facing the male officer. "So, you're Edric, sir?" She walked up to him, extending her hand.

Shaking it, he found himself lost for words, merely nodding as a response.

"Nice meeting you," she said.

Anaya nudged the man with her foot.

"Eh… you too," he managed to stumble.

"Alright, then. See you around." They all watched Vixen leave, the woman sauntering away towards the food and beverage area.

"What is wrong, Edric?" Anaya asked.

"Nothing is wrong. Leave me alone already." He pushed his chair against the table, then strode off.

Anaya had a sip of her wine, then turned to Lenda. "How about a dance, sister?" she asked.

"Yes! Let's dance."

✶✶

Anaya and Lenda enjoyed each other's company for almost an hour before they detached themselves from the celebrations. They took the short walk past the stables and out of the village, then followed the footpath leading to the nearby waterfall. Sitting down by the pond, they watched the sky with all its colours as the sun was setting.

"Fantastic evening," Lenda said. She took a deep breath, then slowly released it. "But very nice to come away for a bit, to get some fresh air."

"I agree," Anaya said. "It does tend to get a bit crowded." She gazed across the pond, where she had seen the demon. The spot stood empty, only the water gushing onto the rock. She watched the tree line for a moment, wondering if he was there.

Lenda noticed her stern expression. "Are you alright, sister?" she asked.

"Yes," Anaya laughed. "Only mind games. I will not let it affect me anymore."

"Is it about your last mission?"

"No, but don't let it worry you. It is nothing I cannot handle."

The girls sat in silence for a while, enjoying the nature around them; the sound of the waterfall, birds chirping, and the smell of summer flowers. They sipped at their drinks, both having brought a second glass of their individual beverages. The wine was rich and coarse, carrying hints of berries. The cider was made with apples picked during the previous harvest. It was sweet and fruity, suiting Lenda's taste well. Even if she wasn't allowed, she had tasted the wine, but not come to enjoy it.

"I was going to ask you something," Lenda said.

Anaya faced her, waiting for her to continue.

"With everything that has happened lately..." She looked down, fiddling with her thumbs. "With the funeral and the preparations, as well as the festival now... I am behind on my work at the infirmary. Could you perhaps come with me in the morning to collect some herbs?"

Anaya smiled. "Of course."

Meeting the priestess' gaze, Lenda's eyes gleamed. "Thank you! You are a life-saver."

The couple sat for some time, chatting about the small things in life, as they often did. It was everything between heaven and earth, such as new recipes of food, perhaps added books in the library, or a new discovery about demonkind.

"You know, I have been thinking," Lenda said, hugging her knees.

"Do tell."

"My hair," she went on.

"What about it?"

"Should I grow it out?" Lenda pushed a hand through it, feeling the ends. They had grown slightly, but still only reached an inch below her chin. "I was thinking a longer hairstyle, now when I'm... older."

"You are asking me for fashion advice?" Anaya chuckled. "I am the last one to give such recommendations."

"That is not true, Anaya." Lenda gave her an intense stare. "No matter how much you tell yourself that, I know it is false. You know very well what looks good and what doesn't. So, tell me, should I grow it out?"

Anaya gave her a nod. "Fine. I suppose... To an extent, you are right. I think you would look lovely with long hair. But you also look nice just as you are. As such, my answer is still not of much use."

"I appreciate the honesty. At least I know it is a possibility." She pulled her hair forward, rolling it between her fingers. "I think I will give it a try. I mean, I can always cut it if I don't like it."

"Sounds like a good plan." Putting her hand over her mouth, Anaya yawned loudly.

Lenda stood, then stretched. "Shall we go back? Perhaps before you fall asleep?"

"I think you are right," Anaya agreed. As they turned back towards the village, she halted. A rustle sounded behind them, so she spun around, but again there was nothing. Nothing to be seen or heard. And no demonic aura.

"Are you sure you are alright, sister?" Lenda asked, grabbing her arm.

"Yes. Trust me, it is only my imagination. Perhaps I am only a bit on edge... since our last mission."

As the girls rejoined the party, they found Edric seated at the same table as before, opposite Adena. He finally seemed to be in a better mood, most likely due to drinking.

Anaya and Lenda sat down, joining in on the current conversation.

"There is no way that is true," Edric huffed.

"But it is!" Adena maintained. "Bumblebees cannot truly fly; they are just too dumb to figure it out." Clearly tipsy, she giggled at the thought.

"Can you not hear how stupid that sounds?" he countered. "If even some huge *demons* can take flight, then why would bumblebees-?" He stopped himself, regretting even getting into the discussion.

"I hear you are arguing, as always," Anaya said, cradling her glass in front of her.

"Well, I suppose there is a reason why we seldom go on missions together." Adena folded her arms across her chest.

They were interrupted as a scuffle broke out at the mead caskets. Edric was quickly on-site, finding two men wrestling on the ground. One of them had managed to wrap an arm around the other's neck, depriving him of air. Edric hurtled his fist into the aggressor's face, then grabbed the semi-conscious man by his shirt, hauling him to his feet. And then instantly punched him, knocking him back down. "You two, get out of here now, or I will have you flogged!" he shouted.

The two men staggered off, both clearly drunk.

Edric shook his hand and stretched his fingers. He had pummelled them hard this time, hurting himself in the process. Ignoring the pain, he returned to the others. Adena had left, attempting to help the drunkards find their way home.

"Has there ever been a party at which you have not thrown punches?" Anaya asked as he sat down.

"No."

She laughed at the honesty of his answer, then gave him a warm smile. "Perhaps next year then."

"Perhaps," he said.

"Lenda…" The mere whisper came from behind them. They all turned to find Eden standing there. He scratched his head, looking down on the ground. "Would you…"

She grinned, her dimpled cheeks reddening. "Yes, Eden?"

He cleared his throat. "May I have the next dance, miss?" he asked.

"You may," she said, reaching for him.

The couple joined hands, walking across the square, Anaya smiling as she watched them.

"How about you dance with me then, Anaya?" Edric inquired, nudging her side.

Without so much as looking at him, she laughed. "Not even if you were the last man left in this world, brother."

He chuckled, then leaned back in his seat. "Harsh, but I can accept it. Do tell me about this new female recruit, though."

"Vixen?" Anaya asked, surprised at his change of subject.

"Yes."

Anaya finished her glass of wine, then spoke. "She is supposedly a Commander in the Rover army, having joined in order to increase their ability to fight off encroaching demons. Therefore, her aim is not to stay, only to be trained and then start her own affiliation within their province. Some kind of specialised group of warriors, anyway. However, while she is here, she will have the same rank as the other recruits."

"I see." Edric rubbed his chin. "Might be an interesting one to tutor, being someone who isn't just a farmer or tradesman. I'll certainly keep an eye on her." In truth, he already was. He watched her standing next to the centre oak, laughing and smiling as she conversed with the other priests.

"You forget yourself, Edric," Anaya said as their eyes met. "Your *own* origin."

He immediately averted his gaze.

Anaya knew it was a sensitive matter, and Edric rarely spoke of it. As far as she knew, he had joined the Priesthood at the age of sixteen, fast becoming a force to be reckoned with. He reached the rank of Senior Priest shortly after Anaya, then aged twenty-three. But his past was somewhat of a mystery. Herself being a child at the time, she was never told of it directly. As such, she had only heard it through rumours years later. There were several versions of the same story being whispered around the Temple village, all more or less grim.

One such story told of a young boy travelling with a band of thieves, nicknamed *the Haunted Shadows*. Growing up within the group, he was trained as a pickpocket and later aided in several heists and robberies. Over ten years, the band evolved, turning into murderers for hire, either as mercenaries or assassins. However, working for the wrong client, they were caught in a trap as they went to eliminate a nobleman in his home outside of Tinta. Many members of the band were killed on sight, but the rest were captured, Edric being one of them. They were all tried and sentenced to death by hanging.

As Edric and his fellow band members stood at the gallows, the High Priest had walked up onto the wooden scaffold. He asked for – and was instantly granted – a stay of execution by the local Lord. He claimed the assassin as part of a divine vision, given to him by the Goddess' herself. In it, he was portrayed as a great warrior against demonkind, a man whose *redemption* would be pivotal to their cause.

Having the noose removed from Edric's neck, the High Priest had led him down the stairs, then turned him to watch his comrades hang. Some of them had instantly sagged with a broken neck; others squirmed as they slowly suffocated. Edric had narrowly escaped death, forever grateful to the High Priest, but he remained scarred.

Some versions of the story told of much darker relations within the Haunted Shadows, where young Edric had been poorly treated and even abused, in every way imaginable. The sins against him had been mainly carried out by their leader, but Edric had also been passed around amongst the members, and raped on a regular basis. Anaya was unsure of the truthfulness to this detail, however, as Edric would never speak of it.

Adena had always told Anaya she believed it to be made up stories, only meant to induce sympathy and divert focus from the man's criminal past, but as time wore on, the priestess wasn't so sure.

Anaya watched Edric for a while, his expression now softened once more.

"Another drink, Anaya?" he asked, flashing her a smile.

"Sure, brother." She couldn't help but wonder if his often harsh exterior and unapproachable attitude indeed bottomed in some sinister events, locked away deep inside. She tried to shake the feeling, returning her focus to the celebrations of the evening.

The party continued well into the night.

Anaya and Lenda traversed the Eastern forest, each holding a basket. It was the day after the Summer Solstice, close to noon.

"Tell me then, Lenda," Anaya prompted. "How did it go last night with Eden?"

The girl instantly blushed, looking away. "Fine…"

"Oh, come on, sister. You had fun then?"

"Very much so," Lenda said. "He was sweet and nice, not at all like… every other man."

"Or like Edric," Anaya added, causing the young healer to laugh.

"You are right, as always."

"It gladdens me to hear it. But do tell me what you were up to. I thoroughly enjoyed bantering with Edric, my lifelong dream."

They both cackled at the words.

"Oh, poor Edric," Lenda said, wiping away some tears. "Let's not be too harsh on him. I am sure he has redeeming qualities."

"If I find any, I will be sure to tell you," Anaya said.

Reaching what looked like a good spot to pick herbs, the girls stopped and unsheathed a small knife each. Placing the baskets in front of some bushes, they carefully started to harvest their flowers and leaves.

"So, tell me more, Lenda."

"Not much to say. We danced for some time, and we sat down for a drink together. He didn't try to grope me or act up in any way. It was really refreshing," she said, cutting off a few more blossoms. "He would ask about my past, what I like to do during my free time, and other things of that nature. He also wondered if we could eat lunch one day this week, so perhaps we will."

"Sounds lovely," Anaya said, looking at her young friend. If Lenda didn't find a partner, she would be mighty surprised, men already circling her like moths to a flame. But perhaps this Vixen girl would draw some attention away from her. Unless she was to pummel every man she encountered.

They moved on to a slightly larger bush.

"To think it is already past the Summer Solstice now," Anaya said. "We are coming into July soon."

"Indeed," Lenda replied. "Time really flies, especially the summer months. Is it because summer is so much more enjoyable?"

"Anaya!" came a call in the distance. It was a man's voice, the source closing in behind the trees before Edric finally emerged into view. He looked tired, dark rings under his eyes. He had probably not enjoyed much sleep since the night before. "The High Priest has called a meeting, so we can discuss what to do with the imprisoned demon. He has summoned all the Senior Priests to attend."

Anaya nodded, then turned to Lenda. "I will drop my basket off at the infirmary. Will you be alright by yourself, or should I send someone for you?"

"I will be fine. Thank you for your help."

✷✷

Anaya and Edric were the last to arrive at the Temple, the High Priest already waiting with Adena and Kaedin. They all sat down along the table in the conference room, with the door firmly shut behind them. It was of great importance that no one could eavesdrop on the gathering.

"Welcome, my children," Ekelon greeted them, leaning forward. He clasped his hands, his elbows resting on the table. "I have summoned you here in order to discuss what to do with the imprisoned demon."

"Kill him," Edric said. "It cannot possibly be safe to house a demon in our midst."

"That may be, but we still need the information on the whereabouts of their Prime. Unless any of you already know where the hive might be?"

Anaya shook her head. "I'm afraid not, your Holiness. And considering the vast areas in which wasp demons travel, it is almost impossible to even guess. However, considering the Prime was present, I would suspect it's not far from the eastern province border. We did speculate about a nearby mound, but... I don't think it's the one, considering the imprisoned demon was left behind by their Prime."

"Aye, but it's likely still relatively close," Kaedin said. "A wasp

Prime, unless she is out to create a *new* hive, would not leave it unprotected for long."

Adena sat quietly, her expression severe. She merely nodded at the statement.

"So, what do you suggest, your Holiness?" Anaya asked.

Ekelon moistened his lips, considering his words with care. "I have already spoken to the demon quite extensively, but to no avail. Therefore, I suggest we add pressure to entice him into telling us what we need to know."

Anaya swallowed hard. "But surely-"

"There is no other way," the High Priest interjected. "I will see to it myself. As soon as the information has been gathered, he will be granted a swift death." He stood, looking at each of the officers. "If any of you have further objections, speak now."

The four of them sat in silence, uncertain of how to proceed. The word had not been spoken, but they all felt it on their tongues. Anaya licked her lips, wanting to call out for halting the plans, but she could not. She was unable to muster the strength, only thinking of what would now transpire. She had not yet visited the cave that had been set up, but she could imagine. In the name of the Goddess and the Holy Light... would they now resort to torture?

11

CONTRIBUTION

Vixen sat on the stone steps of the amphitheatre. A group of recruits had gathered for a lesson with Adena, the officer teaching them how to use the powers of the Light in combat.

"It is of utmost importance that you all focus your inner strength when executing these abilities," she said, pacing in front of the row of disciples. "Just as with healing, any emotional turmoil can distort the enchantment and thus yield unwanted results."

A man reached his hand up.

"Yes?" Adena enquired.

"With healing, we understood it as the flesh not fusing as it should, but what happens with this type of magic?"

"There is a multitude of consequences, all of which we would prefer to avoid. Either it will not imbue your weapon at all, greatly reducing your chances against a demon, or it might flash irregularly, also dampening the effect depending on when you strike your target. In a worst-case scenario, your powers will end up building too quickly, resulting in a blast where the Light disperses. The chances are, you will get hit and burn yourself in the process." Adena stopped before Vixen. "You will most likely find that *producing* the Light is the hardest, as you already house great skill with fighting."

She looked at the others. "The rest of you might need training with Edric before you master this part, but we shall begin today with the actual spells, so you know the words to use as you imbue your weapons."

Another man held his hand forward.

"Yes?"

"Have the officers also been blessed by the Goddess, ma'am? Like the High Priest?"

"No," she replied. "The High Priest stands supreme since no one else, thus far, has received the direct blessing of the Goddess. Therefore, we need to learn to harness our inner Light by ourselves. Our High Priest claims he was merely blessed with knowledge, not power, which is what we make use of as we become priests and fight against the Darkness."

"So anyone can learn then?" he continued.

"Again, no. Which is why your group is already smaller now than when you were initially recruited. It seems as if some are more naturally apt at bringing forth their inner Light, and those are the ones to stay. The life of a priest is also a matter of decency and moral code, but that is something judged by your actions, not your abilities with the Light." She paused, regarding the line of disciples. "I might also add that the majority of those who ask to become priests never make it past the front gates. We are very strict with whom we choose to allow participation at our preachings, and, as such, we expect the quality to be withheld. Anyone who wishes to learn needs to come here, no matter if they plan on working with the Light elsewhere in the world." She threw a glance at Vixen. "One needs to be very proficient, should they wish to teach the arts of the Light. And it should be done in a safe environment."

A third man raised a hand. "What about fighting with Light alone, ma'am? When are we to learn that?"

"Creating pure Light, such as spheres or beams, will take much more practice. The best way to start is, therefore, to use weapons as a base to project your Light upon." Adena walked over to a barrel full of blunt swords, frequently used for practice. As the recruits got more comfortable with handling the weapons, they would progress into using deadlier versions. "All of you – grab a sword, and we will start."

Vixen stood, but remained still, placing her hand on the hilt of her blade. "I will use my own one," she said, unsheathing it. The weapon was of decent length, its pommel and cross-guard made from brass, both intricately engraved.

Adena nodded. "Very well, just don't spar against any of the others," she said, smiling.

Returning the grin, Vixen stepped forward into the arena. She turned around, instantly halting.

On the top step of the amphitheatre, she saw the male officer from the Summer Solstice. He was standing silently as he watched them, holding a bow in his hand.

"Speak of the devil," Adena said. "For those of you who have not already met him, this is Senior Priest Edric Ramsey." She pointed to the man.

He lingered for a moment, then walked away, out of sight.

Adena sighed. "You will have to excuse him. He is… as he is." She turned back to the disciples. "Right, let us begin."

✶✶

It took a lot of effort and repeating the words, but Vixen finally managed the spell, her blade momentarily shimmering, before the Light faded once more. "Adena!" she called. "Something happened!"

Adena joined her. "Again."

Vixen chanted, the blade instantly flickering, then dimming again.

"You need to focus, Vixen," Adena said. "Do not let your concentration slip once the enchantment starts to take hold. That is when you have to increase your efforts for it to solidify."

Vixen nodded, clutching the hilt firmly in her hand. Starting over, she chanted the words louder this time. An orb of Light travelled along the edge of her blade, then settled at the tip. In a flash, it spread across the weapon, causing it to glow brightly.

"There you go!" Adena praised. "You have a talent, sister."

Swinging the sword through the air, Vixen could hear the sparks as they flickered off the scintillated blade. "This is amazing!" she exclaimed.

"Try managing it while in combat," a voice sounded.

The two women spun, finding Edric standing at the top of the steps once again. His quiver housed fewer arrows, the man most likely having practised his archery further down the Proving Grounds.

"I am sure I shall manage... sir," Vixen said, peering at him.

"Practice your speed," he cautioned, pulling an arrow from his quiver. It shone before it even reached his bow, the man instantly nocking it. The projectile hissed past the women, slamming into the ground further down the arena. In a burst of glaring Light, it exploded against the stone surface, the force creating a blast wave as the air whooshed past the disciples.

Adena cursed. "You always have to show off, Edric," she snarled. "Go spend time with someone who likes you. Your *horse* perhaps!"

The man strode off, without another word.

"Don't mind him, Vixen. He has never learned to mind his manners despite being a Senior Priest."

"I don't mind at all," she said. "Trust me, being in the army, you are used to... much worse."

The sun had set as the High Priest headed down into the cave behind the Temple. The captured wasp demon was now shackled to the wall, the bindings imbued with Light. As the grotto had been blessed with various incantations, the surrounding stone lined with holy runes, the demon couldn't transform. He was young, seemingly into his late teens, with short blond hair and brown eyes. Since removing the arrow, he had healed enough to stand on his own, despite the restraints burning around his wrists.

Ekelon stood in front of him, holding the demon's gaze. "You *will* tell me what I want to know."

"There is no way I will tell you where to find my brethren," the demon hissed. "You might as well kill me now."

The High Priest smiled. "So you say, demon." He went to pick up a slim blade, feeling the weight of it in his hand, then gently caressed the sharpened edge. "If so, I might as well start harvesting what I need from you. Perhaps you will change your mind along the way."

The demon winced as the old man slowly cut along his arm.

Bringing up a glass vial, Ekelon let the blood trickle into it. It was a slow process, repeated several times. Standing the flasks upright in a large wooden container, the High Priest moved on to the next item on his list. He grabbed a mace leaning up against the wall, then swung at the demon.

The boy attempted to remove himself from its path, but the shackles held firm. Crimson and teeth sprayed, the demon groaning in pain.

Coming down on one knee, the High Priest methodically gathered the teeth in a small pouch, then placed it on the table. "Fine specimens, indeed," he stated, grabbing his knife once more. "Now for some skin."

Wails echoed through the cavern, the guards outside shivering at the sound. The demon sobbed in agony as long strips of flesh were carved from his arms, legs and body.

"I beg of you... stop," he whimpered. "I will tell you what you need; just please stop."

Ekelon halted, bringing the knife up to his face. "Do tell, demon. Where is the hive?"

"East! East of Atua, in an underground cave... a mile into the forest. The Queen only left me because she thought I was dead with the rest!"

Changing the knife with a nearby sword, the High Priest placed himself before the prisoner, standing in a pool of his blood. "So not far from where your *Prime* emerged?" he questioned.

The demon swallowed, then shook his head. "It is nearby, but please. Don't hurt the Queen, she only wished to-"

"The Goddess thanks you for your contribution." The High Priest swung the weapon, cutting deep into the demon's neck.

The head lolled, claret flowing from the exposed vessels.

As the body sagged, Ekelon took a deep breath, seemingly taking in the scent of death. He clutched the demon's hair, then proceeded to scalp him, grabbing a large piece of skin. Placing the patch of hair on the table, he wiped the blade clean with a bit of cloth. "She is grateful, indeed."

The very same evening, the High Priest welcomed his officers into the conference room at the Temple.

"Thank you for once again attending, my children," he said. He motioned them to sit, then spread out a map over the table. "According to the demon, their hive is in this vicinity." He pointed at the forest east of Atua. "He claimed it was not far from where you were attacked. I suggest starting in the same area and moving onward from there, further east."

"Any chance he can tell us what we might be running into heading there, your Holiness?" Kaedin asked.

"He will not be telling us anything more, I'm afraid," the High Priest answered. "I gave him a… swift death."

Anaya felt her stomach turn. A demon would not have betrayed its Prime on a whim. She could only imagine what had transpired, the hair on her neck standing up at the mere thought.

Kaedin nodded. "Are we to depart instantly, your Holiness?"

"Preparations are to be started from daybreak tomorrow. You will all be dispatched for this, alongside ten experienced priests, as to ensure the survival of the entire party." Ekelon sat down, leaning back in his chair.

Adena looked surprised. "All of us? But what about the Temple village? Are we to leave it unprotected?"

"I will see to the village defence. I am not dead yet, dear Adena." The High Priest's expression was stern as he pulled out a prepared list of names. "These are the priests you are to take with you on this mission. I have divided you all into four individual groups." He handed it to Kaedin.

The officer had a quick look at the listed names. "Anna Leighton? But she is only a disciple."

"She is an experienced demon slayer, having fought many during her time in the army," the High Priest explained. "She might very well know more than some others mentioned on that list. Take her along. Her background as a Commander will make her invaluable in a large-scale fight as this." He once again stood. "Now, go and inform your individual groups, so they are ready in the morning."

12

RAID

To ready themselves for such a raid, the Priesthood had to plan meticulously. Everything had to be taken into account; the number of horses and wagons, what kind of equipment was necessary, and the amount of food required. They would also draft up the journey, deciding how often and where to stop and make camp. Another matter of importance was dividing up the responsibilities amongst the members of the crew, such as healing, tracking, and ranged or melee combat. It mainly depended on what qualities they had as priests, but also the constellation of the group.

Anaya would act as the primary healer, alongside Joseph and Rheas. She would also track the demons.

Responsible for ranged support, Edric had taken on Leo and Perry, both excellent archers.

Adena's and Kaedin's groups consisted of highly competent fighters, Vixen and Eden among them. The Priesthood had gone all-in with this incursion.

A couple of days had passed as they finally loaded the last of their equipment on the wagons. Kaedin stood at the main square, directing the others as he pointed to various items and where they would go. He had donned his armour, his helmet placed under his arm.

"Eli, you will scout ahead," Kaedin told the young man. "We will need an area large enough to camp outside of Tinta, so I would like for you to give them a heads up of our arrival."

Eli was a priest in his mid-twenties, relatively short but heavily muscled. He was mainly trained in close combat, both with and without weapons. He saluted the Senior Priest. "Yes, sir," he said. "I will leave immediately." Already wearing his leather armour, he mounted his horse. Touching heels to the beast, he took off down the road.

✳✳

Anaya remained in her home, standing silently in her spare room. Surrounded by her books and weapons, she tightened the grip on her staff. She had dressed in her black combat robes, now lined with a golden hem after they had been repaired.

An emptiness dropped into her belly, the priestess feeling utterly lost. It was as if her fortitude had left her.

After the morning prayers, the High Priest had attempted to strengthen everyone's morale with a long speech.

But it had not offered the desired effect on her. She felt as if Ekelon was unapproachable, something she had never experienced before. He was rarely seen in the last few days, ever since they had delivered the demon prisoner into his hands.

Anaya needed his comfort, but how would she attain it? She grabbed her prayer beads from her workbench. The rest of her equipment had already been brought to the square, ready to be loaded onto the wagons.

Leaving the cottage, she began walking up the road as she heard her name called.

It was Lenda, emerging from her home. "Wait!" she said.

Stopping, Anaya allowed the young girl to catch up.

"I wanted to see you off, dear sister," Lenda told her. "I know in my heart you will all be fine, but I still need to give you my best wishes as you go on this mission."

"Thank you, Lenda," Anaya said. "I am to see the High Priest before we depart, however, so I must make haste."

"I see. I won't keep you then. But let us walk together, for I am to start my shift at the infirmary."

✶✶

"Anaya, please, sit," the High Priest urged as she entered his drawing-room. They sat down in an armchair each, the morning fire burning beside them. "You wished to speak with me, my child?"

The room featured a desk and some bookshelves, and an array of oil paintings adorned the walls.

"Yes, your Holiness," she said, looking at him hesitantly.

His complexion seemed rejuvenated, the man appearing almost younger than previously, with bright eyes and a friendly smile.

"I feel as if you have made yourself unavailable lately, as we've prepared for our mission," she continued.

Ekelon slowly nodded. "I suppose I have, due to all the arrangements needed. It has also been necessary to continue my work."

Anaya tilted her head. "Your work?"

"Ah, yes. I have only spoken to Adena about this," he admitted. "To further increase our chances against the Darkness, I have taken on studying demons... closer."

Her eyebrows furrowed. "What do you mean?"

"Do not concern yourself, dear Anaya. Only trust that the end will justify the means. We need all the tools we can get in these hard times." The High Priest leaned back in his chair, his hands resting on his lap. "I will keep you informed on the progress of my studies, but, as of now, there is no news to tell. However, I will ask of you the same as of Adena. I want the head of the wasp Prime to be returned to me. It is of great importance to examine the remains, to improve our knowledge of them. As we increase our hunts on the demons, we will run into more settlements, and as such, most likely more Primes."

Anaya felt cold as she imagined it. Fighting against Primes on a regular basis? How would they ever manage?

"I can sense your uneasiness, my child. But do not worry. This time you will be prepared, the next even more so. We will overcome this hurdle, only becoming stronger in the process." He paused, then offered a warm grin. "Now, why did you want to see me, Anaya? What is on your mind?"

"I suppose part of it is my newfound doubt in the development of the Priesthood," she said, sighing. "I mean no disrespect; I only wish to understand it. I have always felt firm in my beliefs, but now I find myself shuddering as you speak of expanding our hunts to settlements."

"I completely understand, and I do feel the same in many ways. However, I will repeat that we must believe it is all for the greater good. We cannot, under any circumstances, falter now."

Anaya quietly nodded but remained in her seat.

"Anything else, my dear?"

"No, your Holiness. I should get back to the square."

They both rose.

"Trust in the Goddess," he said. "She will show us a way."

She bowed to him, then left. The question he had posed was seared into her mind, continuously repeating. Does the end really justify the means? She couldn't push the thought out of her head. What if they were wrong? Would it all be in vain, all the pain caused for nothing? Anaya felt as if there were more things to contemplate now than before she had walked in. She needed to meditate, but there was no time.

A knock sounded on the door to the infirmary. Alone at the time, Lenda went to answer it. As the door swung open, Eden stood outside.

"Oh, Eden! How can I help you?" she asked.

He scratched behind his head, standing silently for a moment. "I, eh… I just wanted to bid your farewell… as we are about to depart."

"I see," she said, her cheeks rosy. "Just make sure you come back in one piece, so we can have that lunch together." Her grip tightened on the door handle, but she gave him a refreshing smile.

He returned it. "I will do my utmost, miss." He bowed, then walked back to where the rest of the crew stood gathered.

Anaya had joined them, holding the reins of her horse.

As they all mounted, Kaedin and Adena took the lead. They were to ride in the front, keeping a decent pace for the caravan. Anaya and Edric would remain furthest back, making sure no one lagged behind. If the weather held, it would be a three-day ride.

During their travel, the party of priests made use of as much daylight as possible. They rode nearly ceaselessly, barely resting before moving on. They stopped in two places on their way to Atua. First outside Tinta, then at Midya, before setting up their final camp alongside the Atua river, just south of the same town.

So far, Anaya had spent most of the nights in her tent, unable to sleep.

This evening, only the day before the planned raid, she sat on her bedroll, resting her hands on her knees. She attempted to slip into a state of meditation, hoping for a sign from the divine Goddess. She suddenly jerked, a head popping through the opening of her shelter.

"Anaya! Ma'am, I mean. My apologies. This whole 'not being Commander'-thing is hard getting used to." Vixen laughed. "But come join us around the fire. We are going to discuss this Prime we are to be up against."

Anaya followed her outside to a roaring fire at the centre of their encampment. The rest of the crew was already there, most seated on sheepskins spread along the ground.

Kaedin sat down on a log, one of his legs stretched forward. He met Anaya's gaze. "I would suggest you or Edric present the challenges we are currently facing, considering you have already fought this demon."

Anaya joined them, sitting down on one of the pelts. She relayed what had happened, and how they had barely managed to fend off the massive creature. She told them of the mists and the fear, as well as the loud and distinctive screech.

"Did it ever use its stinger?" Vixen asked. "I mean... If it had one? Since ordinary wasps do."

"The smaller demons have stingers, yes, but not large enough to function as any serious weapon. I believe they might be hard to use for attacking, considering the placement. The Prime did indeed have a more substantial one but seemed unwilling to use it." Anaya gazed into the flames. "Regular wasps can sting several times, so I am unsure of why it did not. Perhaps it is cumbersome. Or maybe it felt as if it wouldn't need it, underestimating our power. Either way, with the weapon available, I would suggest staying away from both the front and the rear of this demon. Attacking the sides and making it unable to use its wings is probably our best option."

The healer Rheas seemed tense as he listened to the conversation. "Any idea of how many demons we might encounter inside a hive?" he asked.

Adena leaned forward. "We have, unfortunately, very little intelligence on the subject. However, as far as we can tell, they normally muster anywhere upwards of thirty strong, including their Prime. Nevertheless, six were killed in the last encounter, despite it being an ambush. This time we will have the upper hand, leading the charge."

Locking his arms across his chest, Edric met her gaze. "If we manage to infiltrate them, we will be able to kill most of them without alerting the Prime. It would greatly increase our chances for a clean kill."

"Aye," Kaedin agreed. "With a bit of luck, we might just be able to go home within a few days and rest for once." He shook his head, chuckling. "This summer has been nothing short of extraordinary with these hunts."

"Indeed," Anaya said. "The activity has risen lately. Hopefully, the rest of the summer shall bring us some peace."

Slapping his hands down on his legs, Kaedin stood. "Alright, you are all free to do as you please for the evening, but make sure you have enough sleep. I am to retire myself." He strode away, the priests soon scattering.

Anaya remained at the flames, watching them swirl in the light breeze.

Vixen moved in next to her, sitting down on the pelt. "Is it normally this calm?" she inquired.

"Calm?"

"Yes. In the camp, I mean. You can near enough hear a pin drop."

"It depends on the size of our crew, but it is not out of the ordinary," Anaya replied.

Leaning back, Vixen sat with her legs stretched out in front of her. "It is nice, especially the lack of vomit and piss around every corner."

Anaya laughed. "Happy you like it."

Tilting her head, Vixen smiled. "I do. I hope the current state of peace remains, so I can stay for some time." She peered towards the river, noticing a man sitting by the edge of the water.

It was Edric, his horse grazing next to him.

"Where is he from?" she asked.

"Edric?"

"Yes. He comes off as slightly different to the rest of you."

Anaya looked at the man as he leaned back, then flicked a stone out over the waterways, the pebble bouncing along the surface. "I have known him for some time, and he mainly keeps to himself. But his story is not mine to tell, so ask him if you are interested. You never know; he might surprise you."

Letting out a breath, Vixen thought for a moment. "Perhaps I will, if given the opportunity."

It was morning outside of Atua as Anaya emerged from her tent. The sun had risen just above the horizon, the sky shifting in colour.

Vixen approached her, stretching and yawning tiredly. "I can't believe I am so exhausted despite sleeping for several hours. This is indeed the calmest group of warriors I have ever encountered."

"We are no warriors – we are priests," Anaya corrected her.

"I am not so sure there is much of a difference, ma'am. I fight, you fight. It varies very little if you ask me." She paused, looking around. "Refreshing with the lack of prostitutes, though," she added.

"Being part of a Priesthood, we are rarely approached by prostitutes," Anaya explained. "If any of our priests are caught with one, they are to be instantly banished. We live by a strict moral code."

"I see. Not really a surprise, to be honest. And refreshing nonetheless."

The two joined up, heading towards the hitched mounts.

"Isn't it boring, though?" Vixen inquired.

"Boring?"

"That moral code of you-... I mean, ours. Do none of you ever find companionship?"

"Of course, we do, if we so choose." Anaya narrowed her eyes. "But it must be done through courting, with no... illicitness."

"I understand. So, none of you have...?" Vixen looked intently at the priestess, who instantly flushed red.

"No! Unless married, no such thing. Please, Vixen. Let's focus now." Anaya grabbed the mane of her horse and pulled herself up into the saddle. "And besides, you are way out of line now... recruit."

Vixen laughed, then mounted her mare. "You are right, ma'am. It won't happen again."

"Everyone ready to depart?" Kaedin called across the camp.

A resounding yes was heard from the small crowd, after which they took off south along the road. They soon reached the field where Anaya and the others had fought against the Prime.

"We will go by foot from here," Kaedin declared. "Tether the horses to the trees. Anaya will attempt to track the Prime." Donning his helmet, he dismounted.

Except for Anaya, the healers and ranged stayed in the back with Eden, who acted as a rear guard. The rest were in front, ready to defend themselves against any demons they might come across.

The woods were unnaturally silent as the group moved along, following the faint footprints of the Prime. It was as if the wildlife could sense the imminent battle, and long since left. All that could be heard was the snapping of dried undergrowth as the priests trailed a meandering path through the forest.

Soon, Anaya could sense a distant demonic aura. She held up her hand, halting.

Edric stepped forward, placing a shaft upon his finger as he kept a tight grip on the bow. He aimed at a nearby tree, in which sat a demon. It was in human form, leaning against the stem. His voice low, the officer chanted as the arrow lit up, then released it. The shaft lanced into the head of the demon, sending him falling to the ground below.

All stayed perfectly still, waiting to see if they had disturbed the nest. As silence once again fell over the forest, Anaya motioned the group to edge forward. Just ahead, they reached a clearing, beyond which was a cave mouth, large enough for the Prime to fit through. The tracks led all the way across, and down through the opening.

Leaning against the mountainside, another demon stood guard.

Kaedin addressed his group of men, giving commands using hand signals.

Rick moved away, circling the area, and re-emerging behind the sentry with his knife already drawn. In a flow of claret, he slit the demon's throat. Grabbing the body, he managed to dampen its fall.

The priests traversed the clearing in front of the cave mouth, then descended into the subterranean hollow. Coming across another two demons, the priests silently eliminated them, then dragged them aside.

Anaya felt a knot in her stomach, looking at the youths they had just killed. They could be no more than teenagers, both male. It was different, attacking the creatures in their human form. It was easier to end someone's life when they didn't appear so similar to oneself.

Walking down some narrower passages, the priests eventually emerged in a vast cavern, a faint light streaking in through cracks in the ceiling. Stalactites and stalagmites littered the rocky surfaces like imposing fangs, almost as if they had been sharpened on purpose.

Within a second, a screech echoed through the grotto, causing the priests to take formation. They had been spotted.

Several wasp demons appeared from above, chittering as they charged the priests. An array of arrows flashed through the air, piercing into their exoskeletons. With the enchanted arrows burning them from the inside, the beasts writhed in pain.

Kaedin bashed his shield into one, slashing another with his sword. He righted himself in time for a second wave to hit. He swerved left to avoid an oncoming attack; the demon's jaws spread wide. Blocking the creature with his blade, he then sent a reverse cut deep into its neck.

More arrows were released, crimson spraying as the demon corpses piled up in front of them.

Anaya chanted, her voice clear and divine. As the enchantment finished, Light formed around the crew. She had conjured a protective sphere which the wasps could not enter, forcing them to momentarily retreat. The priestess seized the opportunity to instead focus on healing those who had been wounded.

A distinctly ominous screech suddenly reverberated within the cave. The ground rumbled as the imposing wasp Prime came into view, emerging from an adjacent tunnel. Its dark mist exploded out, billowing into the room. "**I WILL NOT LET YOU SLAUGHTER MY CHILDREN!**" it roared. The distorted scream tore like claws into the minds of the priests.

Undaunted by the demonic aura, Vixen shouted at her cowering comrades. "Right yourselves, men! Get a grip over your fear. Do not let it consume you. Now charge!" The woman sprinted forward, vaulting onto the Prime's back. Stabbing her sword between the plates of the exoskeleton, the beast instantly reared. She held on, driving her blade deeper, but it swung, forcing her to disengage to avoid being hit.

The elongated body flared out into the priests' path, sending several of them slamming against the nearby cavern wall. One of the archers impaled himself on a narrow stalagmite, another crashing into Adena and her comrades.

Edric barely dodged the attack, staggering as he leapt backwards. Righting himself, he noticed the Prime's focus shifting.

Swinging its abdomen back, the towering wasp readied its stinger, aiming for Edric.

The officer saw the oncoming attack but was unable to altogether remove himself from its path. He felt the sharp, sword-like weapon travel through his flesh, piercing his thigh. He screamed as the Prime pushed upwards, propelling him into the air. The demon then hurled Edric against the wall, claret splattering the rough stone.

The group of priests immediately split up to save the archers. Kaedin amassed all his strength to lift the impaled man off the rock, dragging him away from danger.

Heading the opposite direction, Joseph sprang forward, focusing his Light on the severely wounded officer.

The Prime anticipated the move, swinging its arm out and bashing the healer across the chest, sending him flying.

"Eden!" Anaya shouted. "Save Edric!" She threw her arms out, Light pouring over the youth, enveloping him as he took off running.

Raising its front, the monster came bearing down on him. Despite the Light searing its flesh, the Prime refused to let up. Eden cried out as he blocked the attack with his spear, then swung the weapon around. Stabbing it through one of the demon's hands, he wrenched it clear, splitting the limb in half.

Vixen had once again charged the Prime, grabbing her sword as she moved across the creature, then twisted the blade. Pulling out a knife, she climbed up high onto its back, jabbing the weapon deep into the demon's neck.

Rheas managed to heal the archers, allowing for their arrows to lance into the enormous creature.

The priests regrouped for a final assault. The Prime's injuries caused an ever-growing pool of blood to spread along the floor, mixing with the dark demonic mists.

Anaya ran to Edric's side, grabbing the unconscious man in her arms. Seeing the extent of his injuries, she whimpered, swallowing a breath. Tears welled, and she wailed as she chanted, unable to remain composed. The healing distorted, but she managed to stem the bleeding. Eden stood firm in front of the couple, slashing at the Prime as it still tried to attack them.

More wasps charged, but the priests came to meet them, Kaedin and Adena at the front. Vixen slammed the pommel of her sword into one, then thrust the blade into another. Arrows flashed past, digging into their skulls.

"Anaya!" Adena shouted. "Calm yourself!" She had noticed the priestess' struggles, rushing across the room for her.

Anaya rose with her hands towards the ceiling, once again chanting resolutely. The cavern filled with a blinding Light, the demons writhing and screaming. They perished in seconds, Anaya's magic allowing for her comrades to return their attention to the Prime. Anaya focused on Edric, the man regaining consciousness as the wounds sealed.

Eden lent him a shoulder, moving him away towards the outlet, while Adena protected the priestess.

Her eyes shining, Anaya had become one with the Light. She called for the power of the Goddess, her robes flowing as searing Light shimmered underneath her. The bright rays spread, pushing the dark mists away.

The Prime shrieked as the spell enclosed around it, the exoskeleton catching alight.

Vixen dared the flames as she hurled herself onto the beast, this time hacking her sword at its neck, reaching deeper with every blow. Finally, the Prime crashed into the ground, its head rolling clear, and silence fell over the cave. They had done it, and all had survived.

As the Prime lay dead, they set fire to the hive, the screams of the surviving demons echoing in the encroaching darkness.

13

BELIEFS

S hortly after withdrawing from the hive, the priests halted. They
had to heal the wounded in order to manage the trek back through
the forest. The wind had picked up, disturbing the canopied branches
above them. The sun was setting, but there was still enough light to
examine everyone. Most had cuts and scrapes, but the archers and
Joseph had suffered more severe injuries. With little time to waste, they
were healed enough to travel unaided.

Edric limped as they traversed the forest, gritting his teeth with
every step.

As they broke through the tree line, Kaedin sent Rick to bring a
horse and wagon. They needed it to transport the wounded, as well as
the head of the Prime, which Kaedin and Eden had dragged along with
them.

Refusing additional help, Edric strenuously vaulted into the saddle
of his mount.

Anaya walked up to him, his stallion sidestepping as she
approached. "Please, let me scan you once more. You are in great pain,
brother."

Finally accepting her aid, he quietly nodded, halting his horse by
pulling on the reins.

Anaya's hands lit up as she moved them across his leg. The thigh muscle had been torn and still bled internally. Able to fuse the fibres and flesh, she could hear him exhale in relief. "There," she said. "That should do it."

"Thank you, sister," he said, then urged the beast forward.

Atua was alive with cheering as the priests returned, the massive wasp demon's head in tow. Having received word of their victory, the town had expeditiously prepared a feast in their honour. It was held at the main square, just outside the town hall.

The crowds parted as the priests traversed the streets, flower petals thrown into the air. They were welcomed as heroes.

The priests who remained uninjured stayed at the square, instantly receiving the commoners' praise. The wounded were taken to their camp, where they were healed and left to rest.

Despite being a proficient healer, Anaya still needed to recover after such feats. She had to pace herself, first healing those in most urgent need of care.

As the party commenced, the four officers gathered alongside the town hall entrance.

"I have healed those I can," Anaya said. "The injured now only need rest." She looked at Edric, who stood rubbing his leg. "Are you alright, though?"

"Yes, only sore," he replied, then straightened himself. "I will be fine."

With her arms above her head, Adena stretched. "I think I will retire for the evening. I am too old for this. And besides, I might as well keep an eye on the wounded." They said their goodbyes before she walked off in the direction of their encampment.

"Sir Kaedin Reed!" someone called.

Men from his main crew approached; Rick and Eli moved amongst them. "Come and celebrate with us, sir," they said.

"Aye, I think I will."

The burly man sauntered off, and with that, Anaya and Edric stood alone.

"Let us grab some refreshments, brother," she said to him.

He nodded, and the couple walked across to some caskets of mead. Pouring himself a drink, Edric leaned for the priestess. "So... what about that dance?"

"What about it?" she countered, smirking as she glanced at him.

"Not today either?"

"As I cry over your passing, I shall dance on your grave, dear brother."

He chuckled. "You are precious, that is for sure."

Overhearing the conversation, Vixen approached them. She flipped her blond hair back over her shoulders, gaining their attention. "I'll have that dance then," she said.

Shuffling a step back, Edric paused before speaking. "What?"

"I've heard about you asking Anaya every time, but you know she will turn you down. I will not. So, let's go then... *sir*." She extended her hand.

"No." Crossing his arms, he averted his eyes. "Besides, my leg won't allow it."

"Oh, now you are just milking that injury of yours. Don't spoil the mood now, boy!" Vixen grabbed his arm and attempted to pull him towards the dance area.

Edric instantly broke away. "Don't touch me!" he snapped, dropping his drink. It spilt across the ground, the jug slowly rolling along the cobbled surface. His eyes were wild as he stared at the former Commander.

Both women were taken aback by the sudden outburst, not expecting such a reaction. Perhaps a snarly comment, but not this.

All movement ceased amongst the group until Vixen finally removed herself from him. "Fine," she said. "*Brother.*"

Anaya stood in silence, watching Edric with wide eyes.

Planting a hand above his brow, he shook his head as if trying to clear it, then strode away.

"Apologies on his behalf, dear sister," Anaya directed at Vixen. "I will see to him." She pursued the man, but as he passed through the southern gates, he turned left, disappearing out of sight. Slowing down, she stopped at the edge of the wall, taking a glimpse around the corner. She saw how he whipped his head back against the wall, then sank down to the ground. Watching the starry sky, he let out an agonising groan, then slammed his closed fists on his legs.

"Edric?" she said, carefully revealing herself.

Edric quickly brought his hands to his face, rubbing at his eyes, then looked away. "Leave me, please, Anaya," he said, his voice strained.

Walking up to him, she ignored his request. She pushed her skirt behind her knees and sat down. "Whatever is going on, it is alright."

"No, it is not," he sighed, still covering himself with his hand.

"Edric, look at me," Anaya softly urged.

"It'll be ten years ago this autumn, Anaya. Ten!" He cursed. "How can it still be this raw?" He met her gaze, his eyes glossy and red.

"I have known you for as many years, but we have not once spoken of this subject. Would you perhaps wish to tell me now?" She carefully placed her hand on his.

Edric flinched, wanting to withdraw, but forced himself to accept it. He slowly exhaled, letting his gaze settle elsewhere. "There is nothing to tell. It matters not what I have been through, only how I let it affect my living. Or so the High Priest says." He laughed as more tears rolled down his cheeks. "Am I to punish myself forever, Anaya?"

The priestess clutched his hand in her own, then moved in to sit next to him.

He felt the urge to remove himself but halted at the soft touch of her head against his shoulder. The two of them sat quietly for a moment, looking out over the moonlit fields.

"Edric," she said. "Lately, I have had to take a good, hard look at my own beliefs. I feel as if I have been too firm and unforgiving. Amongst other things, I have been judging you harshly." She paused as she squeezed his hand. "I do not call you brother due to the Priesthood, but because I truly feel as if you are my brother. You are as close to a brother as I could ever have. You may act a jerk at times, but I know you are not. Tell me if you wish. If not, then let us sit in silence, and I'll try and give as much comfort as you'll allow."

Edric leaned back, dragging his hand over his hair. "Whatever you have heard about me… It is all true. Probably worse, if anything. Then the way Vixen…" He winced at the thought. "Those were the exact words *they* would use as I… tried to get away."

Anaya watched as tiny droplets stained his shirt, but she did not lift her head from his shoulder.

"I still felt bad, watching them hang. I thought I would have experienced some sense of justice, knowing what they had all done to me, but I did not. I only felt emptiness, as if I were but a husk; completely hollowed out and soulless."

"You are no such thing, Edric. You may have been cracked and dented in your early life, but now you are tall and strong. Don't reduce yourself to what you endured in the past." She then chuckled, considering her own life. "I am not really one to say but allow yourself to experience life. What have you got to lose? If nothing else, you can die as a bachelor alongside me, the scrawny old maid."

He laughed, clasping her hand. "I might just do that… sister. But for tonight, I think this will do."

The next morning, nearly all the priests' tents were disassembled as the group readied themselves for their return home. As people began gathering, Anaya searched the crowd. "Where is Edric?" she asked.

They all looked at each other, no one able to answer the question.

"Has anyone seen him this morning?" Adena asked from behind her.

"He wasn't present for breakfast, ma'am," Eden replied. "His tent is still to be taken down, so perhaps he is there."

It wasn't like Edric not to have joined the others for their morning meal. His love of food would not allow it.

Anaya felt her stomach tightening as she strode off in the direction of his tent. With Adena accompanying her, the priestess pulled the front section of the shelter aside. As the two of them entered, they could see Edric's silhouette under a set of covers, lying unmoving on his bedroll.

Rushing forward, Anaya turned him over. His face was pale, sweat pearling on his forehead. His skin felt as if it was on fire as she shook him, desperately trying to rouse him. "Adena, ready a wagon! He must have been poisoned by the Prime... We have not a moment to lose!"

As Adena left, Anaya started chanting, Light filling the tent. Working her way across him, she scanned his body, looking for the cause of his current state. She gasped as she realised the severity. The internal organs were failing, dissolving due to the venom flowing through his body. She focused her Light, healing him to the best of her abilities.

Edric stirred, groaning painfully. He opened his eyes, his vision lacking focus. "Anaya?"

"Stay still, brother. You have been badly injured." Finishing her spell, the Light dispersed.

In an instant, Edric arched his back, belting out a scream.

Anaya desperately tried to hold him down, scanning him again. And what she found had her stumped. As soon as her healing subsided, the organs reverted back to their state of decay, but this time the process was much more rapid.

Adena and Kaedin ran inside, grabbing the man's arms to pin him down. In the scuffle, his cover slid away, revealing his wounded leg. The cut had reopened, and the skin around it was dark blue, his veins black. It was unlike anything they had ever seen, the blood oozing out like tar.

Healed yet again, Edric settled but was left unconscious. His thigh and the surrounding tissues were discoloured and bruised.

"I need to continuously heal him, else his organs will fail," Anaya said. "We can only pray the healers at the Temple can save him, else he is lost to us."

"Adena, grab his legs," Kaedin said as he locked his arms around Edric's chest. "Heave!" They lifted him off the ground, with Anaya still healing him, then carried him outside the tent.

Eden had prepared a horse and wagon. "Place him here. I will drive you, ma'am," the youth said.

Anaya nodded, climbing aboard, with Edric then placed next to her.

"I shall have Eli ride ahead and prepare a fresh horse in the next town," Kaedin said. He smacked the mare's rump, causing her to take off running. "Hurry!"

★ ★

The journey back to the Priesthood was made in great haste, changing horses several times, with the last one still drenched in foam and sweat as they reached the Temple village. Anaya shouted for anyone to help, calling for Maya and Lenda. She was on the verge of exhaustion after her extensive healing.

Lenda emerged from the infirmary. "What in the world is going on, sister?" she asked, hurrying for the wagon. Noticing Edric, she gasped. The taint had spread, now covering large parts of his body, a spiderweb of black vessels under his skin.

Eden threw himself off the front seat and grabbed at the officer's upper body. Eli, who had joined them for the last stretch of the road, grabbed Edric's legs, and the two men managed to carry him into the infirmary.

Lenda held the door as they entered, and instructed them to place Edric on one of the empty beds.

The infirmary had been left mainly vacant the last couple of days, not allowing for the public to request healing. This was done since they were expecting the group from Atua to soon return.

Maya appeared from the office at the back. "Goddess! He is in a right state," she exclaimed, joining them. She instantly started chanting, Light shimmering around them.

Edric's breathing slowed, but he did not wake.

"Will he make it?" Eden asked.

"I cannot say," she answered. "Tell me what has happened, and I shall help him as best I can."

With the group discussing how best to proceed, Lenda went back outside to check on Anaya. Finding the priestess slumped over the edge of the wagon, she sprang forward, checking for a pulse. It was steady, and the breathing slow; Anaya had passed out. Lenda climbed up to lay her down, after which she grabbed the reins of the horse. She whipped them gently, the wagon lurching into motion, then steered towards their cottages.

Inside the infirmary, Maya swore. "It is no good. The venom only keeps coming back, eating him from within. You need to fetch the High Priest, Eden. If nothing else, then to give this man his last rights." She stood, wringing her hands. "I have never seen anything like this."

Bird song, sweet and soft. A rustling of the leaves, tranquil and soothing. Anaya slowly opened her eyes. She was lying in her own bed, the sun high in the sky as the light shone through the open window. For a moment, she wondered if it had all been a dream? Had they really fought those demons? Even killed youngsters merely for standing in their path? And what about Edric; had he really been injured? She jerked upright as she remembered. Flinging her covers aside, she rose out of bed. The world spun, forcing her to grab hold of the bed frame to stay upright. Stumbling across the room, she refused to let her body hold her back.

In front of her cottage, the horse and wagon were still present. Clutching around the seat irons, she pulled herself up, grabbing the reins. She needed to see Edric.

Arriving back at the square, the door to the infirmary stood open. Anaya's mind had cleared somewhat as she climbed down from the carriage. Sucking in a breath, she had to steel herself, not only because of her weakened state but because of what might be waiting inside. Was he already dead? Had the officer lived a cursed life, only to have it cut short in the most gruesome of ways? She took another breath, stepping inside.

The High Priest turned as she entered. "Welcome, Anaya," he said, then moved out of her path.

In the bed before them, Edric sat with his hands on the cover, a smile on his face. "Thank you, Anaya. You have saved my life, as well as Maya… and of course, your Holiness. I'm forever grateful."

Anaya hurtled forward, throwing herself into his arms, eliciting a grunt from the man. "Edric!" she cried, tears welling. "But how?"

"My work, Anaya," the High Priest said. "Surely, you must now see why the need for these experiments exists. As soon as the head of the Prime has been brought back, I shall cure him permanently. Until then, my current concoction will keep him alive and healthy."

Lost for words, Anaya felt her mouth opening, but she couldn't manage a single sound.

"The end will justify the means, dear child. Believe in me when I say this, Anaya. We will conquer the Darkness."

14

A DIFFERENT KIND OF HUNT

As the large group of priests returned to the Temple village, everyone quickly settled back into normalcy. Edric and a few other priests were kept at the infirmary, but most things were as they always had been.

Kaedin and Adena delivered the head of the Prime, with the High Priest instantly resuming his work and extracting what he could from the skull.

He stood at one of the tables inside the interrogation cave, carefully carving at the head. In the last week, while his officers were away, he had continued sending other priests on missions involving lesser demons. They were asked to bring back at least one corpse from each outing, which he then had brought to the cavern.

Additional shelving covered the walls, on which he had placed several jars containing various body parts and organs from the creatures. Next to them hung his new collection of scalps, expanding rapidly.

The High Priest managed to harvest just enough blood from the Prime to create an antidote for Edric. It would take several hours to brew, but at least the officer would be cured.

There was a tap at the door, prompting Edric to sit up in his bed. He had been placed in the private room inside the infirmary, now being the only one left out of those injured during their last assignment. He was bedridden due to the risk of the venom spreading faster, should he be physically active.

"Come in," he said flatly.

Vixen entered, flashing a smile. "How are you doing, sir?" she asked, traversing the room.

"Surviving."

"I see. Well, I thought I'd come to see you... since you are stuck in this bed anyway."

His eyes narrowed. "What about?"

She tilted her head, her expression relaxed. "I am merely jesting. I heard you are not allowed to leave, so I thought I would threaten to stay and make your life even more miserable." She offered another friendly grin, but Edric looked away. "Ah, well. I wish you a speedy reco-"

"I am sorry, Anna," he suddenly said, but would still not meet her gaze. "I overreacted in Atua."

"It is fine, sir," she said softly. "But I have a feeling I was right, about why you ask Anaya."

"Yes."

They remained silent for a moment, then Vixen put a hand on the bed frame. She slowly leaned sideways across the bed, to the point of nearly falling over, her leg stretched out as a counterweight.

Edric peered at her, an eyebrow raised. "What are you doing?"

"Getting your attention. Quite successfully, I might add." Her bright smile was infectious, causing the officer to smirk. Straightening herself, she continued. "Well, I suppose next time, I shall dress extra nice to entice you into dancing. Trust me, I shall not fail you in this mission, sir."

"What mission?"

"Teach you how to dance, sir. I understand that it isn't the real reason why you won't, but it shall be our excuse." She bowed deeply. "See you around soon, sir."

He gave her a courteous nod as she left, then leaned back against the wall. He rolled his shoulder, the joint cracking. With sleep as his only pastime, he considered lying back down to rest.

The door had barely shut behind Vixen as it opened once more. Edric sighed, not really in the mood for any additional visitors. It was the High Priest, accompanied by Anaya and Lenda. Maya joined them from the stockroom, all of them now ready for the young man to finally be given an antidote for his ailment.

With Ekelon handing him a glass vial, Edric wasted no time in bringing it to his lips. He gagged as he drank the potion, the liquid thick with a strong taste of iron. He could barely remember ingesting the last one, having been at the brink of death. And it was probably for the best, as it was hard enough to drink as it was, let alone anticipating the aroma.

"Do not spit it out, son," the High Priest warned. "You will need to drink every last drop."

Edric quietly nodded, then continued to swallow the concoction, struggling more for each gulp. The bitterness made him retch, but he stopped himself from being sick. Soon the entire antidote had been downed, and he placed the vial on the bedside table. "I've had some bad drinks in my life, but that is the most wretched thing so far. No offence, your Holiness."

Ekelon chuckled. "None taken, my son. It is not made for its taste, after all. But how do you feel?"

Edric pulled the cover aside, revealing his naked legs. They watched as the colour on his thigh changed and, within moments, the dark hues were gone. He rubbed the skin, tracing the muscles. Stunned at the speedy effect, he carefully lifted his legs over the edge of the bed.

Anaya stepped forward to lend him a shoulder as he stood.

"Thank you," he said. "I feel... alright."

She let go of him as he righted himself.

"You might still be sore for some time," the High Priest said. "Even if the skin has healed, the body has to recover." He turned towards the door, pushing it open. "Fetch me if I am needed. I will be in the cavern."

The following week, Lenda continued her training as a healer. She had been told she was nearing a promotion, her work impressing both Maya and the High Priest himself. With the rest of the village entering a peaceful state, Lenda's days were even more stressful. She would treat patients during the day, then forage for herbs and create potions and elixirs throughout the evening, often well into the night.

Finishing another shift, she rubbed the sweat off her forehead, then left through the back door of the infirmary. The view from the building was breathtaking, overlooking the Park of Serenity. She stood for a moment, wishing she could take a walk along the winding paths and gnarled oaks, but she could not. Grabbing her empty basket, she hurried around the outside of the building. As she rounded the corner, she slammed into a man's chest. Stunned, she took a step back, then looked up. Arms curled around her, offering her support.

It was Eden, his steel-grey eyes meeting her gaze. "Careful, miss," he said. "Why the rush?"

Lenda smiled politely, fumbling with the basket. "I-I am sorry, Eden. I wasn't paying attention. I was on my way to pick herbs as we are running low."

With his fingers wrapping around the edge of her hamper, it slowly came to a halt as he lowered it. "Do you want company?"

"Oh, um… I wouldn't want to keep you. You probably have much more important things to attend."

"You are one of them, Lenda, as I came to see you. Give me a moment, and I will meet you outside the stables. Wait for me there."

She stood silently as he disappeared from view. Walking down to the stables, she had only waited a few minutes before he reunited with her. He held a basket of his own, its goods covered with a piece of cloth.

"I am taking it you have not eaten since breakfast as you weren't present for lunch," Eden said. "So, I've brought some food." He held the fabric up for her to see. Inside, there were a few pieces of bread, several fruits and vegetables, and a bottle of freshly pressed juice.

"Heavens! Thank you very much." The apprentice healer felt herself blushing at the gesture, the young man showing such consideration for her wellbeing. Despite being busy with his own work, he looked out for her.

The two of them followed the path east, towards the pond. A new bridge had been built across the stream, finished only days earlier. It was small, no wider than for one to cross at a time, and it was fashioned out of natural stone, suiting the environment well.

Walking along the tree line, the couple eventually came across a large patch of raspberry bushes.

"I need lots of leaves from these. We have started receiving more women as they are about to give birth, and the plant can help reduce pains and shorten labour." Lenda brought out a knife and started cutting individual leaves from the tall shrubs.

Eden nodded, joining her. "I have noticed an increase in pregnant women. I am sure you make a great midwife."

Cheeks burning, Lenda stared at the bush as they continued harvesting leaves, soon filling the entire basket.

Heading back, the couple sat down alongside the trail, looking out over the grasslands. Lenda felt the warmth of the sun on her face, taking in a deep breath. They spoke for a while as they had their meal, both in a cheerful mood.

"It is nice to be just the two of us for once," Eden said.

They had previously only managed to eat together in the square, amongst the other priests. It was fine for talking and getting to know each other, but it was indeed refreshing to feel a bit of freedom as they conversed.

"Mm, I very much agree," Lenda said. "I like spending time with you. You make me feel relaxed, not at all as uneasy as most men do. I often worry about their intentions, but not with you." She placed her hand down on the grass, accidentally grazing his. Feeling the warmth of his skin, the two of them allowed their fingers to intertwine.

Their eyes met, and her cheeks instantly flushed. Eden leaned in, the young girl tilting her head as she closed her eyes in anticipation of his touch. Their lips met, the two joining up in a slow, soft kiss.

Edric slowly recovered. Over two weeks had passed since he received the antidote, and he felt his strength returning. Stealthily moving through the forest, he held his readied bow in his hands. The soft undergrowth brushed against his legs, his high boots carefully touching down on the ground as he traversed the terrain.

The deer was close.

The man was used to hunting, having spent many hours of his life perfecting the art. Ever since he was very young, he had performed the assignment alone, often bringing game home for the Haunted Shadows. As he joined the Priesthood, he had continued, supplying the pantry with plenty of meat.

Reaching for a nearby bush, Edric touched one of the leaves. The edge was ragged, still wet from the creature's bite. Silently crossing a mound, he knew the encounter was imminent. He moved up to stand behind a tree, surveying a small opening in the forest.

The horns were majestic, and the coat shimmered in the sunlight breaking through the trees. The stag was grazing, slowly moving along a thick set of brambles.

Edric pulled back the string. Taking a deep breath, he exhaled, the arrow hissing through the air.

One shot. One kill.

Walking up to the beast, Edric bent down. He grabbed hold of its back legs, hauling the dead animal over his shoulder. It was heavy, but good practice. The officer was about to resume his role as a trainer in both ranged and melee combat, and he needed the exercise to assess his own physical condition.

Hiking back through the woods, Edric soon reached the road he had travelled earlier in the day. His grey horse stood beside the same birch as where he had left him, whinnying as it saw the man approach.

Stowing his cargo on the back of the stallion, Edric quickly mounted, then rode off towards the Temple village.

★ ★

With his sleeves rolled up, Edric bit down on the blade end of his knife. He pushed the stag further up the table, then returned the tool to his hand. He proceeded to gut the animal, removing the intestines and the individual organs. Carefully slicing through the layers of fat underneath the skin, he began removing the hide.

"Been hunting… sir?"

Looking over his shoulder, he saw Vixen standing behind him. "Yes," he said.

Her head tipped to one side. "And you are now butchering the thing?" she asked.

"No. I'm preparing the stag for tenderising."

Stepping forward, she examined his work, her hands held behind her back. "Why do you bother with such things, being an officer?"

Folding the skin up, Edric took a fresh grip on his knife. "We all have to pull our weight, high-ranking or not."

"I suppose you are right. There are many differences between the army and the Priesthood."

The man remained silent as he ran his arm across his forehead, removing sweat. His shirt was already stained with blood, but he continued to flay the animal. Bending down, he pushed the blade deeper before standing back up. Throwing a glance at the woman, he noticed her observing him. He clenched the handle of his knife, meeting her gaze. "What?" he hissed.

"Have you cut your hair?"

His eyes narrowed. "Why do you care?"

"Oh, nothing. I just noticed." She walked around the table, scrutinising the animal. "I was only going to remind you of our dance. I believe the Harvest Festival would be a good time for it, so I've ordered a new dress for the occasion. I visited with the tailor's today."

Grabbing the legs of the stag, Edric turned it over. "I was hoping you would have forgotten about that," he muttered.

"Forgotten?" Vixen echoed. "Are you crazy? I can barely wait!" Her grin spread. "Anyway, I will leave you to it then. Your... tenderising." She strolled down the road, heading west.

Watching her leave, Edric merely shook his head.

15
INTENTIONS

The height of summer had passed. It was late July, and demon activity had been ever low since the attack on the wasp hive.

Anaya had refrained from taking her solitary walks for some time, especially at night. However, feeling increasingly restrained, she decided to go for a wander. It was just past noon as she entered the Eastern forest, the sun high in the sky. With a small basket, she was going out to pick berries.

It was early in the season, so finding ripe ones would be difficult at best. But eventually, Anaya happened upon a patch of wild strawberries, which looked promising. She sat down, her robes fanning out around her. Taking in her surroundings, she listened to the birds chirping, and the light breeze rustling the leaves. The outdoors was where she belonged, not cooped up in some cottage.

In her mind, Anaya would often imagine leaving the Temple village behind. She would dream of a day where she could live high up the trees, alongside the squirrels and birds; to live off the land, making her own way through life. Yet it was a utopia, never to be realised. She knew the Goddess had more significant plans for her, and she had pledged her life to whatever that may turn out to be. Living out her days in a peaceful meadow in the woods didn't seem to be part of it.

134

The wild strawberries were sweet and plump, the priestess eating a couple before she started filling her basket. They looked perfect and would make for a delicious jam. Or perhaps pie? Whatever Lenda preferred making, Anaya would eat it. The wind picked up, the branches creaking in the trees, but it also caused a different sound, like cloth whipping above her. She looked up, seeing a black cloak moving in the breeze. Knocking her basket over, she scrambled back along the ground.

Watching him jump, she could observe his nimble movements. How he, despite his size, dampened the fall to the point of nearly not making a sound. The demon bent down, righted the basket again, then scooped some of her berries back into it. "Where have you been?" he asked.

Anaya frowned. "What do you mean, 'where I've been?'"

"Your late walks. You stopped taking them."

"Who... well, who wouldn't, with a stalker such as yourself!" she exclaimed, still sitting on the ground. "There is no way this is a coincidence. What's this, the... the *fifth* time you return now?" She tried to regain her composure as she stood. Brushing grass and leaves off her robes, she took a deep breath, then stared at him. "Are you here to punish me?"

"Keeping count, are we? And punish you? That's funny." Samael gave a sly smile. "If you mean that Light you tried to burn me with, then forget about it. Is that why you stopped going out at night? Fear of me?"

Anaya's face reddened. "I'm not afraid of you!" She crossed her arms, looking away. "But I am concerned about your intentions, whatever they may be."

"Is that not a distinction without a difference?"

Anaya slammed her foot on the ground. "You be quiet! Stop your taunts, demon!"

"Back to 'demon' are we? Ah well, it was fun while it lasted." Samael turned and walked away.

Anaya couldn't bear to watch him, emotions churning inside her. *How dare he?*

Taunting, stalking, bullying. All entertainment, nothing else. Not even daytime was safe any longer. But how was she to stop it? She couldn't possibly tell the High Priest, or even Lenda. They would only question why it took her so long to ask for help. She would have to find the answer herself instead, whatever trials the Goddess might be planning.

Edric's group of disciples had once more gathered for practice. Amongst them were Enya and Vixen, as well as most of the newer male recruits. They would meet inside the amphitheatre at the Proving Grounds.

Enya should have already been past this part of her training, but after her encounter with the wasp Prime, she found herself freezing in battle. However, since the girl was a hard worker and very knowledgeable within Demonology, she would not be given up on just yet.

Vixen only had to attend due to tradition, despite having both fought and killed a Prime. With her skills as a warrior, she would regularly join in when Edric meant to demonstrate a new move, the two of them sparring in front of the other students.

As the class was dismissed, Vixen often lagged. This day was no exception, and she sat down, watching Edric clean his sword. She sat perched on the stone seating carved around the amphitheatre, the officer standing below her.

"You have great talent, Edric. Sir," she said, then cursed. "This whole formality thing is hard, I'm sorry."

"No need to call me sir, Vixen," he replied, but did not lift his gaze from the blade.

"That's a relief." She leaned back, her elbows resting on the step above her. "I only ever have to be formal with the generals and the King himself, which is quite seldom."

"I see," he said, sheathing his sword.

"Tell me something, though, if you will."

His expression hardened as he looked at her. "Depends on what you want to know."

"Well, I try not to listen to rumours," she began, but noticed how he flinched, then taking a step back. "No, listen, Edric-"

"I'm leaving," he said, grabbing the last of his gear before he strode off across the arena.

Vixen raced after him, placing herself in his path. "Please, listen," she repeated. "I have only heard you come from a less conventional background compared to most of those trained here."

"So?" he challenged.

"I'm sure it won't come as a surprise when I say that I am not here due to my devotion to the holy Goddess. I believe in Her powers, but I am not wholly convinced She is the sole cause of how my life is paved before me. I only wish to know why you fight alongside the Goddess?"

"I am not here to discuss my beliefs," he said, but remained unmoving.

Vixen stood firm, her eyes peering into his.

"Fine." He paused as he momentarily glanced away. "No, I am not a perfectly gracious and devout believer in the Goddess. However, I know She saved my life, twice now, through the High Priest's actions. It doesn't matter what I believe, for I shall be forever grateful and, as such, I intend to give my life to the cause."

"Would you ever consider leaving the Temple village behind?" she asked.

Unsure what to say, Edric blinked, his mouth falling open. "I... As I said, I intend to give my life to the cause."

"And if the cause, the path which is given, would lead elsewhere, would you take it?"

He hesitated for a moment, then spoke. "Yes," he said.

Satisfied with the questioning, Vixen smiled. "That's all I wanted to know." She stood facing him as he left, then sat back down, gazing up at the sky. Clouds were gathering, a rainier season fast approaching.

Anaya stalked through the Temple village, her lips curled as she seethed with anger. She firmly clutched the basket with both hands, to make sure she wouldn't fling it at an innocent victim. Heading towards the Temple, about to hold a class in Demonology, she stopped by the infirmary. She found Lenda inside, the girl carefully bandaging an old man.

"I have healed what I can," Lenda said in a loud voice. "However, the long-term damage to your knee might still cause you pain. And any numbing spell I place upon you now will only last for so long. I shall send some herbal remedies with you, which I suggest you take twice daily for at least a fortnight." The man was clearly half-deaf but nodded as he listened to her instructions. Satisfied he had understood, Lenda turned, noticing her friend. "Oh, hello, Anaya!"

The priestess gave her a warm smile, then presented her hamper. "I have a gift for you. Well, for *us*."

Lenda looked into the basket and squealed with delight. "Strawberries!" Grabbing a handful, she began feasting on them. "I haven't eaten lunch yet, so I am starving."

Anaya laughed. "I was hoping you could make a dessert to have after dinner tonight. If you have time, that is."

"Oh, I will make time. Especially now, when they have finished building the stone oven outside the pantry. I shall bake a pie, no exception!" Lenda ate a few more, then placed the basket in the stockroom. Coming back out, she stood close to her friend, keeping her voice low. "Is it fine if I invite someone?" she asked.

"Of course, dear sister. But who is this someone?"

Lenda moistened her lips. "Eden," she said, blushing.

"I see." Anaya nudged at her side. "Any more kisses lately?" she teased her.

"Stop it, sister." Lenda's entire face was now bright red. "We can speak more in the evening. I have to get back to work."

Anaya chuckled. "And I must get to class if the recruits are to learn anything today. I will see you later." She leaned forward and kissed the young girl on the forehead, then departed for the Temple.

✶✶

Pulling the fresh pie out of the oven, Lenda took a deep breath, her lungs filling with the sweet scent. She padded it with layers of fabric to not burn herself as she carried it. Moving for the exit, she grabbed a bowl of whipped cream, already prepared, then hurried across the square. She instantly cowered at the sound of her voice being called, believing it was the cook catching her take the last fat-rich milk.

"Lenda!" she heard again. This time closer, she recognised the voice. It was Edric, the man joining her. "That smells delightful, whatever that is." Pulling back the top layer of fabric, he revealed the fruit-covered dessert. He helped himself to one of the strawberries, quickly devouring it. "Oh, my Goddess. That is divine. Are you having it now?"

Lenda sighed but smiled. "Yes. Anaya, Eden and I have only just finished our dinner. Would you care to join us?"

"Don't mind if I do," he said, shrugging, but left her to carry the food.

"What is this smell?" came from behind them.

Gritting her teeth, Lenda exhaled, thinking there would be no pie left by the time she reached the cottages. Turning around, she saw Vixen.

"Would you look at that! Amazing pastry you have there, Lenda. Any chance I could snatch a bite?" she asked.

Lenda lightly poked the inside of her cheek with her tongue. "Sure thing, just come along," she said.

The three of them arrived at the cottages, where Anaya and Eden sat by the fire.

"Oh, hello everyone," Anaya said, standing to greet them. "I will fetch a few more bowls."

Lenda placed the pie and cream on a wooden plank along the ground, then faced the group.

"Do not, under any circumstance, tell the cook about this. I stole the last cream."

Their joint laughter pealed out, Edric seating himself beside Eden. "Your secret is safe with us," he said. "And besides, the cows will need milking tomorrow also."

As Anaya emerged from her home, she handed everyone a bowl and spoon. Soon they had all had their fill of pie, the sweet and fresh taste a welcome change to the otherwise strict and mainly savoury foods. They spoke for hours as the evening transferred into nighttime.

"Thank you for inviting me," Vixen said. "It is nice to mingle with people during our spare time. If I am to stay here for any lengthy such period, I feel the need for socialising."

"You are always welcome to join us, Vixen," Anaya said.

"I think I will, sister," she replied. "But now, I will retire for the night."

"As will I," Edric said, stretching.

"Well, good night then," Lenda said. "See you all at prayer tomorrow."

"Do you want to join me to the square?" Edric asked Vixen.

"That's alright," she said. "I will take a shortcut through the woods... But thank you for tonight, Edric."

"And you." He gave a slight bow, then turned on his heel and strode away.

Vixen watched him, his body language tense. He had seemed unsure of how to detach himself. During the evening, she had been pleasantly surprised, the man allowing her to sit beside him at the fire. Perhaps, some progress had been made. She waved goodbye to the rest, then headed off.

Anaya yawned audibly. "You will have to excuse me now, dear sister and brother. I am up well past my bedtime." She stood and gave the couple a warm smile, especially looking at Lenda, who instantly blushed.

It was close to midnight as Anaya retired, now only Eden and Lenda left around the dying flames. He grabbed her hand and rose, motioning her to stand with him. He pulled her into a warm embrace, which she returned. Joining hands, they walked over to her front door, the young girl traversing the steps.

"I will see you soon, miss," Eden said, kissing her hand.

Lenda's cheeks flushed once more as she found herself lost for words. He was so sweet and sincere. Before she knew it, his arm had encircled her waist, pulling her in. Warmth spread throughout her body as he kissed her.

Their lips parting, the young man lowered her back onto the cottage steps. "Breakfast tomorrow?" he asked.

Still struggling to speak, she quietly nodded, then watched him depart for the night.

A few days later, Lenda had again asked for help in foraging herbs. Anaya had accumulated her own personal collection of books on the subject, which lined the walls of her spare room. Due to the extensive reading, she was excellent at distinguishing plants from one another. Healing could only do so much, and therefore the medicinal herbs were of great benefit to treating various ailments, anything from a severe illness to the common cold. Anaya wondered if these problems were caused by something the Light could not touch. Was it so small perhaps that without knowing the target, a priest could not aim for it? Pushing the thoughts aside, she focused on her current chore. Today she was out to look for evening primrose. The yellow flower, having several positive effects on the human body, was quickly being used up by the infirmary.

Carrying a wicker basket on her back, Anaya crossed the new bridge over the stream, then followed the path along the forest, overlooking the nearby fields. Preferring full-sun, evening primrose often grew along the trail. After an hour-long walk, Anaya located the plant. Soon, her basket was full to the brim, and she sat down on the grass. She brought out a small bread roll, which she had prepared before leaving the Temple village. The snack was well received, and she drank her fill with water before slumping down amongst the soft greenery. The sun was hot on her face, but a cool breeze made it comfortable. Always hard at work, Anaya comfortably dozed off where she lay.

"Priestess."

There was a soft push to her side, followed by the same voice. It was as if it was all so far away, cushioned in the world of dreams. Up until the touch became uncomfortable, causing her to open her eyes. It was the demon.

"What are you doing kicking me?" Anaya shouted, scurrying backwards to get away from him. She felt the retreating manoeuvre was fast becoming a habit.

Samael folded his arms across his chest. "How sensitive are you anyway?" he asked. "Are you not supposed to be some tough demon-hunter? Surely, a nudge like that won't affect you."

Anaya's expression hardened. "That's beside the point. What do you want?"

"What I want? Yes, I suppose that is a valid question." Samael gazed up at the sky, now filled with ominous dark clouds. "How about waking you before lightning strikes the area?"

Rising, Anaya glanced upwards, then let her eyes settle on the demon once more. "Fine. But why would you care?"

"I don't." Samael turned and walked across the nearby path, heading for the forest.

"Wait!" Gathering her things, Anaya hurried after him. "Tell me why then. Why would you bother? If you demons are incapable of feelings, how come-"

He instantly halted, then spun on his heel. "Incapable of feelings? What do you think you are, you humans? Some divine creature above all else? How absurd a statement."

"Oh? And you are just as emotional as any one of us, are you? You are the only proof I need. As you said, you don't care." Anaya turned, facing down the road.

"And the way you are representing the entire human race? Devoting your life to your cause, avoiding relationships whenever possible? I can't see humans surviving for long if that is the aim of your lives."

Anaya immediately glared at him, her face flushed red. "Don't talk as if you know me! You know nothing about me."

Showing a faint smile, he leaned forward. "Your response to what I just said tells a different story."

"Damn you!" Anaya charged him, her hands flashing with Light.

Remaining still, Samael simply grabbed her arms and pulled her close. Lifting her off the ground, he held her tightly as to not allow her to discharge her powers. "I have said this before; do not make me defend myself. You are no match for me."

"Let me go!" Looking up at him, Anaya snarled and aimed to spit in his face, but he angled away.

"Charming."

Being released, Anaya quickly retreated as she dropped to the ground. Stumbling backwards, she fell, landing on her behind. "You are such scum, Samael! You are only proof of what we already know, that you demons only feel hate and wish for destruction. You gloat in others misery. You are lowly creatures of Darkness, only wanting to extinguish the Light of the Goddess and us humans!"

Watching her stand and dust off her robes, a full grin bloomed on his face. "Are you trying to convince me, or yourself? Because if you ask me, then you suddenly do not sound as sure as you usually do."

"I said, stop talking as if you know me!"

Thunder rolled in the distance. The skies opened up, and rain started pouring down.

"I *hate* you!" She turned and hurried down the path.

16

A NEW ACQUAINTANCE

It was evening as Samael entered the Matriarch's home, thunder roaring outside. Water dripped along the floor as he traversed the entrance hall in long strides. His hair was soaking wet, as well as his cloak. Without so much as looking at his mother, he unclipped the mantle and pulled it over his shoulder, revealing his dry clothing underneath. He sat down next to the open fireplace, removing the leather strap from his hair.

Lilith watched as he ran his fingers through the raven strands, attempting to speed up the drying. "You really should leave it out more often, my son," she said. "Most would kill for a mane like your own."

"So you've said," he replied coldly.

Sitting up on the daybed, Lilith frowned. "Tell me something," she said. "Why do you smell of human?"

Samael's eyes narrowed. "No reason."

"Have you been in contact with a human?"

"It has nothing to do with you, mother. Leave it."

"I demand to know, Samael!" The Matriarch rose, striding across to him. "You know not to interact with humans! Especially now, after what happened to the wasps. What if they hurt you? If they *kill* you?"

With her arms close to her sides, she clenched her fists, but her eyes sparkled with unshed tears.

"Mother, please." Samael stood, reaching for her hand. "Nothing has happened. I have been in no danger. Trust that I will not place myself in harm's way."

Pulling away, she snorted. "If you had children of your own; if you had experienced what I have… then you would not take this so lightly." She turned and walked back to her daybed, sitting down once more. "Do not dare approach this human again – whoever it is."

Samael remained silent, grabbing his cloak. He threw it over his shoulders and walked back out into the rain.

As the door closed, Arax entered from one of the back rooms. "My lady," he said, walking up to the daybed.

"Yes?"

"Have you had time to look over the list of names for me to send out invitations?"

"I have," she said, expelling a breath. "But there are not many of them who would seem a good match for Samael." She brought out a rolled-up parchment from under the daybed and gave it to her manservant.

"Mm, I see," he said, poring over the Matriarch's notes alongside the names. "I would have thought at least Elena Grey, or Brook Knox would have stood out."

"Indeed, but Elena is only fifteen, and Brook has a bit of a reputation amongst the men within their part of the tribe. Nonetheless, they shall be invited, along with the others I have marked on the list. At present, we have little to lose." She brought out another parchment, which she also handed him. "These are the arrangements for the gathering. Send out the invitations and place the orders for all which is needed. We will hold the gathering here, at my house. By leaving the doors open, the courtyard will be included as a reception area, should the weather allow."

"As you wish, my lady."

With only two weeks left until the Harvest Festival, Edric finally felt as if he had adequately recovered, almost a month after his injury. He rubbed at the leg; the muscles only slightly tense.

The moon was high in the sky, the white crescent bathing the Proving Grounds in dim light. Using his sleeve, Edric wiped the sweat from his temple, then replaced his grip on the practice sword. He swung at the target dummy, hacking away at its battered armour. He appreciated being alone, the lack of distractions enabling him to focus. He had been cleared by the infirmary to resume his personal training.

Fighting seemed to be the only thing that would quiet the voices in his head, the rush of combat drowning out his inner demons. Never truly proficient in the Goddess' Light, he kept up appearances with his archery and sword skills. In a way, nothing had changed. He was part of a group which had taken him on out of pity, then forced to survive through pure willpower, one day after the next. He was also unable to ever make a single human bond. Anaya was the closest he had experienced, but the relations she offered was not what he longed for.

The sudden sound of a sword hissing from its scabbard caused him to spin on his heel.

Vixen stood there, weapon in hand, and her feet planted wide. "Want to spar? For *real* this time," she said, grinning.

Edric let out a breath, chuckling. "Sure," he said, then charged at the woman.

Lancing his sword forward, he struck at nothing as she sidestepped, then her sword crashed down from above. He swerved, deflecting the blow, then sent a reverse cut up behind her. She rolled under his swing, lunging upwards. The sword stung his upper arm, and she retracted it in a spray of crimson.

Pulling back, the officer groaned. He swung his sword down, burying it into the ground. Chanting, he healed his wound, then once again armed himself.

Clashing rang out as the blades continuously collided, again and again.

Edric's sword suddenly shattered under the pressure, the shimmering pieces flying in all directions, spreading around his feet.

Flinging the hilt aside, he drew his knife, then hurled himself at the woman.

Taken by surprise, Vixen only just managed to block the oncoming attack, then attempted a counter. Her sword sliced air to his left as he sidestepped, the man's shoulder bashing into her. She struggled to retain her grip on the blade, slamming into the paved surface, then felt the edge of his knife graze her neck.

"I give," she said, laying her hands above her head.

Edric held perfectly still as he sat over her, panting from the exhaustive exercise. When his breathing eventually slowed, he discarded the knife. His expression softened, all while holding her gaze.

Keeping her hands upwards along the ground, Vixen smiled. "Would you... like to kiss me?" she asked softly.

Edric was silent for a moment, then averted his eyes. "Yes," he replied. "But I can't." Pushing himself off, he rose.

Vixen remained on the ground, but seated herself. "That is fine," she said. "We can watch the stars instead."

There was a wrinkle to his nose, the man uncertain of what she meant. "What?"

"Come sit with me, Edric. We shall only do what we both want to." She peered up into the night sky. "And I suggest looking at the stars for a while."

With the current lack of demon hunts, Anaya had taken on all the more pursuits for herbs. She was increasingly concerned with encountering Samael, but she had no choice but to go out, unless she wanted to tell someone about her previous run-ins with him.

Sitting underneath an old oak, the crown broad and dense, she was once more collecting plant material.

"Picking herbs again, are you?" The voice was all too familiar, dark and brooding.

"Yes," she replied.

"What this time?"

Taking a glimpse at the demon, she found him perched in a maple tree. He had a foot planted along the branch, the other leg hanging over the edge. "What's it to you?"

"Ouch, it stings when you do that, dear priestess," he said, gracefully descending the tree. "Surely, I do not need a reason to speak with you? Getting to know you?" He smirked as he approached.

"Yes, I can really see you being genuinely interested." Turning her attention back to the leaves, she felt a sudden chill. Gooseflesh covered her arms as he leaned over her, his cloak draping her gown.

"Peppermint, I see," he said.

"Mm, you are indeed of high intellect," she muttered.

Coming to his full height, he sidestepped. "I sense some sarcasm here."

"Proof of my previous statement, clearly." Pushing herself up, she spun to look at him. With the closeness, his sheer size was daunting, the demon likely to be seven feet tall. Her mouth dry, she gulped down a breath. "Look, I don't know what it is that you want, or why you keep appearing. I followed you once to question you about it, but you got defensive and threatened me. The least you can do is explain yourself if you want any further conversation."

"Explain myself, huh." He slowly nodded, his slender eyebrows furrowing for a moment. "I suppose our last conversation intrigued me. I want to know more."

"Know more? What about? The Priesthood? Or perhaps why I'm not interested in the male sex?"

He instantly grinned. "Aha! Now you came clean. See, I knew it."

Anaya's face reddened, even more so than when they last spoke of the subject. "Fine! I'll admit it – you were right. Happy now?"

Throwing his arms out, he shrugged. "I can die a happy man."

"Not a man. *Demon*."

Samael's features lost all signs of his previous smile. He was back to what the priestess now knew as normal. "I suppose I shouldn't be surprised," he said, turning around and walking back towards the maple tree.

"Finally, you're leaving," she said, resuming her work on the peppermint plant.

"Leaving?" she heard from behind her. "Who said anything about leaving? No, I'm just taking a seat." Samael sat down, leaning against the stem, but retained his focus on the woman. "I will just do it from here, considering you are such a killer of moods. Amongst other things."

"Other things? Like what? What have I ever done to you?" Throwing her tools aside, she rose, then headed for him.

He remained unmoving, only his gaze lifting as she gained on him.

With her index finger pointed at him, Anaya felt her cheeks burn. "As far as I know, you are the one who always follows me around. You don't see me visiting you, wherever you're from! I have never asked for your company, nor will I ever do so. All you do is taunt me, for your own entertainment. Had it not been for our Priesthood's strict rules against engaging demons who have not shown aggression, then I would have done so a long time ago." Standing directly in front of him, Anaya saw his arm whip out. He grabbed hold of her dress, pulling her down. She desperately clawed at the tree behind him, as to stop herself from crashing into him.

"Listen, girl. I have told you, over and over again; do not *dare* attack me. I will not, under any circumstances, hesitate to defend myself. And trust me, you do not want to go there." As he sounded out the words, Anaya could clearly see fangs in the demon's mouth. Was he getting agitated? Was this a show of emotion coming from this cold-blooded being? Albeit aggression, it was the first she had ever seen from him.

"Fine! Now let go of me!" She still clung to the stem, her muscles beginning to cramp. Finding her dress released, she bounced back and toppled over, landing on her behind.

Samael didn't even flinch as she fell to the ground, his face flat and emotionless.

"Always these threats of yours, that's all you ever do. You have not a caring part in your soul, Samael."

Drawing a knee up, he rested his arm upon it. "Well, at least you didn't refer to it as being part of my demon nature. Perhaps it is all personal nowadays?"

Anaya did not reply. She merely got back on her feet, patting her dress to remove dirt and grass from it. "If you really want to get to know me, don't be such an asshole about it." Her arms tight against her sides, she stared at him, waiting for him to reply or make a move. A silent minute passed, but it felt like a lifetime as she held his gaze, determined to receive an answer.

"Get to know you?" he finally asked.

"Why, yes. If you are to 'know more,' surely, it would be to your benefit to make my acquaintance."

He contemplated the idea for a moment, rubbing the stubble on his chin. "I am intrigued by your suggestion. How would I go about... making this acquaintance of yours then?"

"Stop threatening me, for one."

Samael nodded. "Duly noted. Does that mean you will stop trying to burn me with your magic?"

"Yes," she replied, then her eyes tightened. "Even if it doesn't make a difference to you."

"It does not. However, I believe it is the thought that counts," he said, offering another one of his deceitful smiles.

"You are very convincing," she listlessly stated, then walked back to the patch of peppermint. "Perhaps you wish for me to introduce myself properly then?" Receiving no answer, she looked across her shoulder, only to find the demon gone.

By the end of August, Lenda had done it. She had received the official title of Healer through her work at the infirmary. She was indeed a true proficient within the trade, able to now perform most healing spells single-handedly. She was only second to Maya when it came to herbalism and the arts of creating medicine and potions, thus exceeding even her own expectations.

Telling her friends, they held a small gathering where they ate lunch together. The weather was poor, so the little party, including Anaya, Eden, Edric, and Lenda, had gathered in Edric's spare room since it was only used for a minor amount of storage.

Like a bloodhound, Vixen had again managed to join them, clearly able to smell Lenda's cooking from miles away.

"She followed me from the kitchen," the young girl had said as she emerged with the last of the food. She had whipped out a feast, and they all ate until they could not muster another bite. They laughed and chatted, all the while listening to the rain hammering down on the roof of the cottage.

"Are you helping with the preparations for the Harvest Festival?" Vixen asked the newly promoted healer.

"I am, yes. Mostly with the edibles and decorations."

Vixen's face brightened with a smile. "If this is the kind of food we can expect, then count me in!"

"It gladdens me to hear it," Lenda said. "I only hope we get hold of all the ingredients we need."

"What are you missing?" Vixen asked.

"Mainly fresh produce, like fruits and vegetables. We have nearly bought all the stock from the nearby towns, but we will check the markets tomorrow as well. We also lack some herbs and, of course, truffles."

"I will go and hunt for some truffles, Lenda," Anaya said. "Hopefully, there will be a spare hog available."

The healer drew a cleansing breath. "I appreciate your help, dear sister. I am sure we will manage." Redness unexpectedly crept across her face as she felt a nudge under the table. It was Eden, sitting opposite. He flashed her a smile, then silence fell over the room. As they looked across at the others, they were now the centre of attention.

Vixen huffed. "Oh, come now. We all know what is going on. Why try and hide it?" She waved her hand in the air. "Kiss the woman already, Eden. She is entitled, receiving her promotion and all!"

Now it was the young man who blushed, smiling bashfully. He stood, walking around the table, then extended his hand. Lenda accepted it, rising to meet him. The two embraced, their lips meeting in a slow and affectionate kiss.

"Just make sure to invite me to the wedding," Vixen added, grinning as their faces further reddened. "I wouldn't miss that kind of food for the world."

The sun shone as the priestess carried her basket through the forest, the rays dappling the undergrowth. Birds sang and piped all around her, so she closed her eyes for a moment, enjoying the sounds to the fullest. As promised, she was out to collect truffles, but she was the only one from the village to enter the Eastern forest. She had so far obtained three of the subterranean fungi, two of which were of decent size. They had a few hogs trained for the chore, but unable to snatch one up, she had to make do on her own. Either way, she enjoyed the stroll.

Looking around, Anaya saw a promising area underneath a grey birch. Sitting down, her robes fanned out around her. Her already dirty fingers started clawing at the undergrowth, trying to feel around for any truffles. She spent a few minutes removing soil, but, as in so many other places, she found no fungi. Sighing, she started scooping the dirt back into the hole.

"No luck?"

Without looking, she knew who it was. "No, unfortunately not. Especially not when *you* show up in the midst of things."

"Ouch. You almost hurt my non-existent feelings." Samael stopped beside her. "Now, what is it that you are looking for today?" Before she answered, he peeked into her basket. "Truffles, is it?"

"Yes. We need them for our Harvest Festival." Anaya stood and cleaned her hands using the hem of her robes. "But none of our trained pigs were available for me today, so here I am, searching by hand."

He raised an eyebrow. "Pigs?"

"Why, yes. A pig has a keen sense of smell, so we train them to find the fungi."

"I see. I might have heard of that." Samael grabbed the hamper from her and retrieved one of the truffles.

"Hey! Give me that," Anaya cried, attempting to snatch it back, but he held it out of reach.

Bringing the fungi to his face, he carefully inhaled the scent. "Mm, I can see why that works. They do smell an awful lot."

Cursing under her breath, she tightened her fists. "Why do you always have to be such a jerk?"

He smirked, handing her the basket. "Well, you said it yourself. It's in my nature. You can't fight what's in your blood, right?" He turned, edging away from her.

With a hand across her mouth, Anaya strangled a laugh. "If this is one of your 'vanishing moves,' then I have to say it isn't particularly impressive." She held her head high, awaiting his retort, but it never came. Stepping forward, she decided to follow him. They walked some ways, past a large oak, then stopping below a lesser one. It grew low to the ground, the stem split along the middle.

Samael halted and dropped to his hands and knees, his gathered hair spilling over his shoulder. He seemed to sniff the area, then looked up at her. "This is it. Dig here," he said. Pushing his hair back, he moved aside and sat down.

Pursing her lips, she locked eyes with him. "Are you serious?"

He returned her glare. "Do I seem like the joking kind?" he replied coldly.

Coming down next to him, she was hesitant at first, removing only a little dirt. Glancing at him, she felt his callous stare, immediately returning to digging through the soil. Within minutes, she had uncovered three sizable truffles.

Her eyes wide, she faced him. "How did you do that?"

"I can smell them. My sense of smell is somewhat greater than yours, priestess." He remained on the ground, watching her clean them.

Placing the truffles in her basket, she rose. "Fine, but why? Why help me?"

"Ah, yes," he said, tracing his jaw with his thumb. "This why-question again. To be honest, I am not quite sure. I'm easily bored, and you offer entertainment, so I suppose that is the answer to 'why.' Anything else you would like to know while we're at it?"

His dark eyes were piercing, freezing her movements. "I, eh... I have nothing else to ask." Attempting to shake the feeling, she focused on her basket, arranging the truffles within, then pulling a piece of cloth over them. "I... think this will do."

Samael assumed an upright position, sneering at her. "Pleasure to be of help, priestess."

Her eyes narrowed. "I didn't thank you."

"Oh, I know. But you would have. I just saved you the trouble. Until we meet again." With that, he silently moved away amongst the trees.

17

THE HARVEST FESTIVAL

O nce every few years, Lilith would gather all the leaders within the tribe. This function would sometimes be combined with a great feast, where the families of the most prominent houses would be allowed to socialise, including the Matriarch herself, and her son, Samael.

The conference held had been lengthy, mainly due to the ongoing discussions on the development of the Priesthood. Several members of the Wasp tribe had encroached on the Matriarch's land while trying to escape nearby human settlements.

Lilith had not experienced the issue first-hand, but it needed to be dealt with, as the tribe was already low on acreage.

As the day slipped into night, the banquet commenced. Luckily, the weather held up, so the Matriarch's entrance hall was not too crowded. Samael sat on a chair beside her daybed, a foot pulled back underneath the seat. Looking about the room, the demon noticed the abundance of women this year, and he had a feeling he knew why. Having dressed for the occasion, he wore clothing much more elaborate than usual, shirt and trousers matching. His long hair draped his back and shoulders, and his cloak hung unused on the wall beside the fireplace.

"You look lovely tonight, son," his mother told him, but there was no answer. Crossing her legs, she leaned towards him. "I have invited a few women to be introduced to you."

Angling away, his eyes narrowed as he looked at her, but his silence persisted.

"You will be introduced, after which we will speak in one of the back rooms." She waved at Arax, who started gathering the girls from the crowd.

Samael slowly sunk into his seat as the first was brought forward. His legs wide, he stared blankly at the young woman. She was short but pretty, her face round and sweet. Her black hair reached the small of her back, and she looked to be about twenty years of age.

"P-pleased..." she started, but her voice failed her. "Pleased t-to meet... you, your Highness." She curtsied, her knuckles white as she clutched at her skirt. She had not once looked him in the eye.

"And you," he answered, his mere voice making her noticeably tremble.

Arax presented the second girl. She was the one called Elena Grey, a young girl of fifteen. She was taller, but very slim and with childlike features.

"Your Highness," she said, also curtsying before she righted herself in front of the heir. Despite being calmer than the first, she, too, could not hold his gaze.

And so, it continued, twelve girls presented, all eligible for marriage. Most were the eldest daughters of their family. As it finished, Samael rose without so much as a word. He gathered his cloak from the wall, readying himself to leave.

The legs of Lilith's daybed dragged along the floor as she came to her feet, grabbing his arm before he could walk past. "You come with me this second, Samael," she demanded.

His mouth opened as he released a breath, but he followed. The two of them scurried off into a back room, the door firmly shut behind them. "Mother, this is ridiculous," he said. "There is no way any of these women would willingly give themselves to me."

"Do not concern yourself. Arax and I have discussed the matter. Even my brother has joined in on the subject. There is no need to exert yourself with traditions any longer. We will only arrange a marriage in which you stand to sire an heir, no more. You will have no obligation to stay with them after the fact."

Samael flinched, his brow slowly lowering. "To marry and have a child, then I would go free?"

"Yes, I believe it might work… with you. And it is the only way for the lineage to survive," she replied. "I shall personally see to the education of your choice of mate, to assume the role as Matriarch and rule as I have."

His stance stiff, Samael flattened his lips. "No matter the relations, if I am to ever choose a wife, it shall be someone who can at least look me in the eye."

"They will learn, dear. It just takes time… getting used to." The Matriarch paused as she creaked the door open, taking another glimpse at the girls. "I believe Elena Grey will be a mighty handsome woman in but a few years. Perhaps she is a match?"

"Mother, she is half my age."

"I was only sixteen when I married your father," she protested.

"Yes, but he was twenty at the time. I am *thirty*." His muscles tensed as he bared his fangs. "I am not to force myself on a woman, let alone a child!" he snarled.

Refusing to back down, Lilith stood firm. "Elena has gone through her *Evolution*; she is of age," she maintained, her voice steady and low-pitched. "You will choose a wife, Samael, even if it is the last thing I shall see to as I walk this earth."

"And I will, whenever there is a woman who can stand my company." He whipped the cloak over his shoulders, clasping it shut. "Which is clearly not today." Unwilling to walk past the prospective wives, he headed for the rear door. Forcedly closing it behind him, he left for the forest.

The very same evening, the Priesthood hosted their Harvest Festival. It was held together with the public, to celebrate the oncoming harvest season for all fruits and vegetables, as well as honouring the last days of summer. As the night encroached, the food had been consumed, and the drinking had begun.

Anaya and the rest were seated around a table, still trying to recover after the great feast.

"Amazing, Lenda," Vixen said, releasing a satisfied groan. "The Goddess smiles upon you and your... fantastic cooking skills."

Edric chuckled. "Spoken like a true devout."

Seated next to him, she playfully pushed her elbow into his side. "I'm making an effort here!" she hissed.

Leaning back, he stretched his feet out underneath the table. "Fine, alright. You are an exemplary recruit," he allowed, his head tilting as he examined her. The former Commander was dressed in a form-fitting gown, her luscious body apparent under the crimson silk. Her hair was worn up in a high ponytail, the sides braided into it.

"Thank you, even if you don't mean it," she said, grinning wide. "Now, I'm going for refreshments. Who wants any?"

"I'll have some," Edric replied.

Anaya also showed interest in the offer, but Lenda and Eden still sipped at their previous round of drinks.

Vixen soon returned with a glass of wine for Anaya and two jugs of mead for Edric and herself. She sat down, her fingers wrapping around the metal pitcher. "So, is this the last celebration of the year?" she asked.

Sampling her wine, Anaya lowered her glass onto the table. "We celebrate the Winter Solstice as well," she said. "It is a bit more formal, however, as it is most often held inside the Temple."

"I see."

"Unless we have other occasions," Edric added. "Such as promotions or weddings, but they are usually much smaller."

Twirling a lock of hair between her fingers, Vixen quietly nodded.

Some minor conversation ensued, and the group listened to the music for a while, until Vixen unexpectedly faced Edric. She slammed her hands on the table, the man jolting in his seat as she pushed herself up. "That dance," she said.

Everyone halted, an uncomfortable silence settling over the group. Their eyes darted between Edric and Vixen, in anticipation of the officer's refusal.

Dragging a hand over his head, Edric rubbed at his neck. He struggled to maintain eye contact with her, forcing a smile. "Sure," he said, leveraging himself to his feet. He accepted her hand, the young woman leading him away towards the dancing area.

Anaya rubbed at her eyes. "Did that really happen?" she asked the others.

Lenda laughed. "I really think it did. Amazing!" she exclaimed. "Can we also dance, Eden?"

"Of course, miss." He stood, offering her his hand.

"If it is fine with you, dear sister?" Lenda directed at Anaya.

"Certainly. Enjoy yourselves. The night is young."

The current song allowed for dancing with little to no touching between the partners, which suited Edric well. He had learned the dance as a youngster but had since never practised.

Vixen made sure to give him space while instructing him, the man soon following her lead nearly perfectly. Her bright smile was contagious as they moved and clapped to the cheerful tunes. As the song ended, everyone stopped to show each other respect with a bow.

Within a moment, a new song began. Slow and soft, the dance would require close interaction. Edric shuffled a step back as Vixen approached. His shoulders curling forward, he averted his eyes.

She halted, her face bright as she looked at him. "Edric, think of this as sparring," she suggested.

He frowned. "Sparring?"

"Yes. Focus on *moving* me, not our contact. Kind of as if we're wrestling, but all the while holding my gaze."

He remained hesitant, but obliged, his breathing quickening as they joined hands. Vixen guided his other hand onto her hip, then gently placed hers on his shoulder. "Now lead."

Edric took a deep breath, his heart racing with his first step. Their movements were initially rough and rigid, but as he got comfortable with her closeness, the two slowed, settling into the pace of the song. Not once did she laugh at him or give him a demeaning look. Instead, her grin was genuine, and her touch soft. They danced for some time, before heading back across the square.

**

Finding Anaya alone, Adena joined her, their table lit by shimmering orbs. They conversed long into the night, and plenty of drink was poured between them. Anaya soon lost track of the amount she had ingested, her head spinning as she rose. She swayed, feeling unsteady on her feet. "Oh, my Goddess," she yelped, placing a hand over her flushed cheeks. "I think I have had too much."

Adena's laughter rolled out. "Indeed, you look it. Perhaps some fresh air would do you good?" she suggested.

"Do you need an escort back to your cottage?" Edric offered.

"No, it is fine. I think Adena is right. I will take a short stroll." Heading down the road, Anaya carefully placed one foot in front of the other, focusing on not falling over. She turned left, taking the path towards the stream, hoping to find the area empty. Noticing Eden and Lenda sitting along the edge of the water, she halted.

They embraced, kissing in the moonlight. The young, sweet love they felt for each other. It was nothing Anaya had ever experienced, nor would she ever do so. She felt a sense of relief, knowing her friend would be fine. Eden was an honourable young man who would never mistreat her. She was sure he would soon ask her to marry him.

Warmth radiated throughout her body, the priestess elated as she thought of Edric. He had taken a giant step in the right direction in his acceptance of Vixen. She was sure it would all work out in the end.

Walking across the stone bridge, Anaya headed out into the forest.

**

Feeling as if he had drunk enough, Edric excused himself from the table, leaving the others behind. But as he walked through the village, he noticed someone following him. Turning around, he found Vixen standing behind him.

His hands briefly clenched as he watched her. "What do you want now?" he asked.

Reaching for him, she ran a finger down his arm. "Walk together," she said, moving past him.

Rubbing at his brow, he merely shrugged, the two joining up as they strolled along the winding roads. There was a bounce to her step, Vixen humming as they traversed the street leading to the northeastern cottages.

Soon stopping outside his home, Edric spun, his back turned towards the wall. "Why do you interest yourself in me?" he questioned.

Carrying a building smile, she took a step forward. "Because I am attracted to you," she answered candidly.

"Me? Of all the men you have come across in your life, commanding your own legion, you find yourself attracted to someone such as me?"

"I have indeed met my fair share of men, currently being responsible for over a thousand strong in the Rover army, but I did not achieve my rank by warming their beds. Sure, I have accompanied some men into their bedchamber, but it has never been to affect my position in or outside of my career. But here, within the Priesthood, things are different. For the first time, I can feel like a real woman, not like one pretending to be a man." She paused, coming closer. "And as a *woman*, I find myself drawn to you."

Having taken a wide stance, he stood firm despite her approach, their bodies nearly touching. He clenched his jaw as her hand landed on his chest.

"Tell me if you want me to stop," she said softly, but he remained silent. Her heels coming away from the ground, she pushed herself up, her half-open mouth verging upon his.

His heart pounding, Edric saw her eyes closing. He trembled, a shiver shooting through him as their lips met. Her skin felt soft, her breath sweet and warm. At first, the movement was slow and temperate, but the kiss soon developed, Edric allowing his arms to encircle her. His knees felt weak, the young woman seemingly reaching his essence with her touch. Hesitant to further advance on her, his hands remained still, but they ached with the desire to feel her.

Reaching back, Vixen gently moved his hand to her hip. Slowly guiding it upwards, she allowed him to gently cup around her breast. The kissing instantly intensified, the young woman opening her mouth to invite him in. Their tongues met, swirling as her fingers spread out behind his neck. In the excitement, her hand travelled down Edric's back, causing him to instantly retreat, bashing into the wall of his cottage.

"Damn this!" he cursed, slamming his fist against the wood.

"I'm sorry. I got a little ahead of myself," Vixen said, her hands falling to her sides. "The alcohol clouds my judgement. I should have been more sympathetic to the situation."

His eyes wild, Edric stared at her. "Don't you *dare* pity me!" he shouted, a haunted look on his face.

Silence fell over the two, seemingly disarming the infected scene.

Vixen stood perfectly still, holding the officer's gaze as his breathing slowed with each passing moment. "I pity no man," she said. "But I sense a void which I can fill."

"Blasted woman!" he snarled. "Why..." He stopped himself as she cocked her head to one side, her hands held behind her back. The innocent and almost childlike body language completely disarmed him.

"Do you want me to stop?" she asked.

Dragging a hand across his face, he sighed. "No," he whispered, but found himself unable to act.

Vixen lifted her arms and slowly let them encircle his neck, granting him enough time to stop her. She gently pulled him in, their lips locking.

Embracing her once again, he returned the kiss, melting against her.

As they finally parted, Vixen offered him a radiant smile. "Let's do that again sometime," she said. "Goodnight, Edric."

He returned her smile. "Goodnight."

The Harvest Festival had almost come to an end. During the early morning hours, Anaya traversed the forest. Strolling along, she touched the trees and plants, almost as if trying to reach the spirit of the woods. She took a deep breath, inhaling the scent of leaves and needles, flowers and undergrowth. Looking up at the vacant skies, she saw the dawn light in all its glory. It shone in red, orange, pink and purple. The air was still warm, even though nighttime had only just passed. She felt at ease.

At the edge of the forest, Anaya sat down next to a great oak. It was hollow inside and had made for a perfect hiding spot back when she was a child. She smiled at the memories growing up within the Priesthood, so free of worries, despite relentless education. Peering out over the nearby fields, she leaned back, enjoying the breathtaking views.

"Samael, come sit with me," she said. Just like previous times, she heard a light thump behind her, then footfalls. "See, I knew you were there."

Closing her eyes for a moment, she lifted her chin, flipping her hair over her shoulders. Opening her eyes again, she blanched, finding the demon looking down on her. "Heavens! I said *sit*, not stand over me."

Without a word, he did as she asked. Reaching for the silver clasp on his cloak, he unclipped it. With one smooth pull, he removed it from his shoulders and laid it on the ground beside him.

It was the first time he had taken it off. Anaya couldn't help but wonder if he was becoming more comfortable around her. Taking a closer look at him, she noticed he wasn't wearing his usual clothing. Instead, the garments were much more elaborate. Silver stitching made patterns along the hem of his sleeves as well as the bottom of his shirt. His trousers matched, still fashioned out of black leather but with several rows of silver threads and buttons. He was clean-shaven, lacking his previous stubble, and his hair hung freely.

Leaning in, she looked at him. "Do you always watch me?" she asked softly.

He leered at her, as if making sure the question was genuine. "Do you honestly think I'm stalking you?" he countered.

"No," she replied. "But you do tend to show up more often, especially when I leave and travel east. Do you live in the east? Somewhere in the forest?"

His boot scuffed along the ground, but Samael did not reply. He merely gazed out over the expanses of grass, the vegetation slowly moving in the breeze. There was little use pushing the question.

"You are nicely dressed tonight," Anaya chirped. "And you've shaved!" She lightly clapped at the heel of her hand, her smile growing. "Was it all for me? Or are you perhaps coming from a party yourself?"

There was a slight movement to his jaw, yet he would still not answer.

Anaya sat forward, her eyes narrowing. "Tell me something…" She moistened her lips. "What kind of demon are you?"

Samael gave her a cold look. "What questions are these?" he said, his voice flat. "Why does it matter? And what do you mean by 'what kind?'"

"Well…" Her mind racing, she contemplated how to ask. Every way that surfaced inside her mind only made her sound like a prejudiced demon-hunter. "I… come across a lot of demons. And… well, demonic forms seem based on various animal species." She paused again, scratching at the back of her head. "So, what are you?"

"Why does it matter? Do you wish to see that which you call our 'true form?'" He smirked, his canines coming into view.

"No, nothing like that. But you wear fur, which makes me think you are a mammal. You have fangs, pointing towards a predator of some kind. Probably black, looking at your hair. So, again, what are you?" Still tipsy, Anaya giggled as she envisioned her own suggestion. "Perhaps the big bad wolf?"

Samael smiled at the thought. "That would have been something, wouldn't it? You are sharp, however, and closer than you think. But a wolf? No." He sat back, his posture relaxed. With no intentions of answering her question, he instead posed one of his own. "Why do you avoid men?"

Anaya felt taken aback by the inquiry, seemingly sobering up with the abrupt change of subject. "How did you-"

"You have already said you are disinterested in males. It's also obvious in the way you act, and whom you spend time with; I have watched you enough to know such, so why is it? Have you been violated?"

Her face immediately reddening, Anaya crossed her arms. "No such thing! I am but a pure woman, living detached from the opposite sex."

"The word 'pure.' How laughable. Is it only because you have not laid with a man that you call yourself *pure*?" Samael peered at her, but she averted her eyes.

"Yes, but no." Anaya pulled her knees up, wrapping her arms around them. With her chin resting over them, she released a breath. "Truth be told, I have devoted myself wholly to the Goddess and Her divine plan. I have thought that if I were meant to be with a man, I would have received the proper foundations for such a relationship, both spiritual and... physical. I have neither." She looked dispirited, hugging herself, almost as if she attempted to hide her body within the fabrics of her dress.

Samael rubbed at his chin. "You find yourself less of a woman than other females?" he questioned, a hint of surprise to his voice. "You, who are amongst the strongest of your kind?"

"I suppose I do. But that doesn't affect my strength as a priestess. No, quite the opposite. I have nothing to distract me in my line of work. My focus lies elsewhere than in human desires, living above those worldly things. Besides, I am soon too old for such." She paused momentarily. "What about yourself? Do you have a family?"

"Perhaps we are not so different, you and I," he answered, ignoring her questions. "I have no interest in any of that. I prefer to spend my time honing my skills, living a life of solitude." He paused for a moment, flicking a leaf off his trousers before continuing. "And too old?"

"Why, yes. I am over twenty years of age now. To still have no companion or prospects concerning a steady partnership, I would, unfortunately, be deemed as somewhat old now." Exhaling, she shook her head. "But as I said, it is of little importance."

As their conversation stalled, the couple looked out over the grasslands once more.

"Anything else you wanted to know?" he asked, finally breaking the silence.

"Yes," she replied, perhaps too quickly. Her hands suddenly damp, she swiftly ran them over her skirt. "Something… I have been wondering about for a while now."

"Continue."

"Well…" Anaya was unsure how to pose the question, but it had played on her mind for some time. "Why is your aura so faint? I can usually sense demons long before I can see them, but not with you."

Samael acknowledged her words with a slight nod. "Valid question. It is true, but not because I have a weak aura. It is because I can manipulate it." Turning to look at her, he extended his hand.

Initially hesitant, she decided to grasp it, the demon embracing her hand in a firm grip. The skin was rough, but warm, exuding strength. Samael's demonic aura was stronger with the touch, but it was still faint. In an instant, it flared, causing dark mists to seep out between their fingers. Fast becoming ever more powerful, Anaya pulled away, placing distance between them as she shifted along the grass.

Clutching his wrist, the joints cracked as he stretched it. "So, you see, my aura is there, only repressed when I have no use for it."

The potency of the demon was unlike anything she had ever felt, his aura having instantaneously sent emotions of despair through her. Unwilling to tempt him into using it again, she did not question him further. It was best left for another day.

Grabbing his cloak, Samael silently rose, facing the path that abutted the edge of the forest. "People are coming."

"Wait," Anaya said, pushing herself up. She held her arms wide, waiting for her surroundings to stop reeling. Hearing voices, she spun towards the path. It was Rick and Eli, both drunk and blabbering as they staggered along. And they still drank, each holding a jug of mead.

Anaya's eyes widened. She couldn't risk being seen with a demon. "Quick, come with me," she said, grabbing Samael by the hand.

Pulled towards a nearby oak, he became intrigued. He followed her lead, the woman pushing him into an opening in the stem.

The entrance faced away from the road, so Anaya was positive they would not be spotted. Backing up against Samael, she pressed herself tightly against him, the two of them barely able to squeeze in together. "Now, keep your demonic aura in check," she hissed. Still somewhat inebriated, she suddenly lost her footing, struggling to straighten herself. She heard his mantle flutter as it gathered around their feet, then she instantly covered her mouth, hindering herself from crying out.

Samael's arms flanked her, his hands clutching over her hips.

A flush crept across Anaya's cheeks, his body warm and substantial, offering a sense of strength and reliability she had never experienced. But it didn't strike her as sexual, the way he held her. On the contrary, it felt most natural, as he made sure she would not come crashing out of the tree. She could feel his chest move as he breathed, giving off a sense of calm.

The minutes inside the tree transpired like hours as they waited for the voices to fade.

Finally emerging from the oak, Anaya stepped away, her face still red as she struggled to look at the demon. "Alright, Samael. I'm... I, eh..."

Samael smiled. "Yes, that is probably for the best. I beg your leave, priestess." He offered her a modest bow, then disappeared into the forest.

18

A RUSE

The four officers had once again assembled for a meeting with the High Priest. Autumn was on the horizon, and darkness was fast encroaching. They could hear the rain outside, the glass panes in the windows shuddering from the downpour.

Ekelon sat in his chair at the end of the table, the Senior Priests lining the sides. His hair looked darker, even more so than before, and his eyes gleamed. His skin seemed revitalised, the wrinkles in his forehead shallower.

"I am afraid our recently blissful everyday life has been nothing but the calm before the storm," he said, rolling out two separate maps on the table. One was of Ovena, the other depicting the neighbouring province of Rover. "The most urgent is in Rover, outside the city of Greer, where there has been an unusually large amount of reports on bear demons. Some villagers claim to have been attacked and even suffered casualties. I received word about this as late as this morning, and intend for a party of priests to be leaving by daybreak tomorrow." He paused, regarding his Senior Priests. "Kaedin and Adena. You two will be responsible for this mission."

Kaedin nodded, then grabbed the map. "It will be a four-day ride, your Holiness. You should expect us back within a fortnight, should all go smoothly. I shall send a messenger to bring the news of our arrival."

"Splendid," Ekelon said. "Don't forget to bring back remains. I have yet to study a bear."

"Aye, we shall."

The High Priest then turned his attention to Anaya. "There is another matter to attend, up at the Stricker mines. As they breached a wall inside the mountain, a cavern was exposed, in which lived a small group of lizard demons. From the description given, I believe they might be iguanas, but I cannot be certain. If so, they would be unusual for this area."

"Do they not normally live in warmer climates, your Holiness?" Edric inquired.

"Indeed, hence the surprise. But if they are iguanas, then I welcome remains here also." He clasped his hands, leaning forward. "However, this mission will be for Anaya, as you will remain off duty, Edric."

His breath caught. "Off duty?" he echoed. "But I have been cleared by Maya."

"For your personal training, yes, but there is no way of knowing the long-term effects of the Prime's venom, especially if your body is to be put through the strain of combat. I have already discussed this with Maya."

With his lips pressed tight, Edric paused before speaking. "But, your Holiness, I'm sure I am the best judge of my own abilities."

"Be that as it may, this is a decision already made. You will be stationed here at the Temple until six months have passed since your injury."

"But that's in the new year!" Edric exclaimed, rising from his seat. "I implore you to reconsider!"

"No, my son. I will not risk your life needlessly. Please, accept it."

Edric slammed his closed fist on the table, then stormed out of the room.

Anaya stood, about to follow him as the High Priest held his hand up.

"Leave him," Ekelon said. "He will have to learn to take orders, no matter if they suit him or not."

She sat back down but remained silent.

"You will be dispatched to the mines within a few days," he continued. "We are still to receive word from the scouts, to confirm what type of demon we are dealing with. I suggest you savour the last days of peace before we are yet again neck-deep in blood."

"Yes, your Holiness."

★★

Vixen and a group of disciples had come back early from a class in herbalism, with the tutor none other than Lenda. The increased rain had forced them to return to the Temple village prematurely. Walking along the road leading up from the stables, Vixen saw a man further up a side street. She recognised him as Edric, his body language stiff as he strode away at a high pace.

"Lenda, ma'am," she said.

"Yes, sister?"

"Can I please excuse myself?"

"Of course. If the weather is better in the morning, we shall all meet at the stables again. It is fine for everyone to leave for today."

Vixen hurried after the officer, soon coming to a jog. She caught up with him just as he opened the door to his cottage. "Edric!" she called.

He turned, still holding the door handle. "Vixen? What is it now?" He was clearly flustered, his face stern.

Lightning flashed above them, followed by a roar of thunder. The rain increased, drenching her where she stood. She said something, but the loud noise from the hammering rain on his roof made it impossible to hear.

"Just come inside!" he shouted, waving her in. As they entered, he threw a few logs into the fire, renewing the flames. Putting his hands to his hair, he shook it, removing as much water as he could.

Vixen still stood in the doorway to his bedroom, droplets from her clothes creating a small pool of water below her.

"Well, don't just stand there," he snarled. He pulled out a chair and placed it before the fire. "Have a seat. Dry yourself off."

Kicking her boots off at the door, she silently moved across to the fireplace, which now supplied a comfortable heat. She sat down, swinging her hair over her shoulder to help dry it.

Grabbing another chair, Edric placed it beside her, then proceeded to change into dry clothing. He pulled his shirt over his head, dropping it over the backrest, then went to fetch a new one.

Vixen watched him intently, his muscle-bound upper body making her smile.

"What?" he said, noticing her gaze.

"Oh, nothing," she replied, still grinning. "I just like what I see."

He couldn't help but smirk, his mood improving. "Thanks, I guess."

"Indeed, it is a compliment." She pulled at the thongs on her leather vest, then removed the garment. Underneath, she wore a shirt made from bone white linen. It was damp, but still dry enough to wear.

Edric had moved himself to the bed, still holding his new shirt. Sitting on the edge, he watched her stand and unravel the strings of her leggings. "What are you doing?"

"Getting undressed. I am soaking. Else you want me to suffer from a low temperature?" Sitting back down, she pulled the trousers off, then hung them over the chair with the other clothing. She held her hands up to the fire, rubbing them together. "There. That's nice."

Blushing, Edric couldn't even make himself look at her.

She glanced at him over her shoulder. "It's alright. I'm wearing undergarments. I'm not naked if that is what you think." Rounding her seat, she rose. She traversed the room, dragging the chair, then spun it around in front of him. Sitting down, she forced him to widen his legs to accommodate her closeness. He could no longer ignore her. "What had caused you grief, Edric?" she asked.

He huffed, blowing hair from his face. "Nothing of importance."

Leaning onto her elbows, she offered him another one of her inviting smiles. "The way you looked walking back here tells a different story. Do tell."

He rolled his neck, his eyes settling elsewhere. "I was in a meeting with the High Priest. I am to be off duty until the new year."

"I see. I know the feeling, having once torn my shoulder out of socket quite badly." She gently prodded above her right collar bone, recalling the event. "Is it due to the injury you suffered?"

"Yes. He has discussed it with the Senior Healer, and because they cannot say for sure that I am cured, then I am not to put myself under unnecessary stress. Ridiculous if you ask me since I feel fine." He cursed but decided to meet her gaze. "Is that why you came? To check on me?"

"Yes," she said, her blue eyes piercing. "It is one of the by-products of caring for someone."

He chuckled. "So I hear."

Vixen unexpectedly came to her feet, forcing Edric to straighten himself. The skin on her naked legs shone in the dancing lights of the fire. The damp shirt hugged her body tightly, raised nipples showing through the fabric. Her wet hair trickled over her shoulders as she refused to break their eye contact. "Do you want to touch me?" she asked.

Licking his lips, Edric felt his throat go dry, his heart thumping wildly. "Yes," he exhaled.

"I want it also... So, please do," she whispered, reaching for him. "I'll help you."

Edric took her hand, swallowing hard. His mouth opened as he found himself guided underneath her shirt, stopping at her chest. He circled one of her breasts, running a soft thumb over the nipple.

Closing her eyes, Vixen nibbled at her lip, revelling in the sensation.

Her skin was like velvet under his touch, her scent sweet like apple blossoms. Trailing downward, past her belly button, Edric reached the undergarments, aching to advance on her. Sliding them down, his hand settled between her legs. He felt her soft hair, then the warm, luscious centre. Pushing a finger inside, he shivered, hearing her moan with delight. He pulled her in, his lips brushing against her belly as he continued to pleasure her.

With an overwhelming desire to become one, Vixen shuddered from her building arousal, fighting not to grab at the man. Another finger entered her, a lustful sigh slipping from her lips. The excitement urged her to caress him, to explore his body, but she could not. She knew her touch could impede their union, and she would never risk it.

Reluctantly releasing her, Edric came to his feet. He freed her from her top, revealing her naked body. For a moment, they stood watching each other, the young man looking down at her with hungry eyes.

Vixen motioned for them to turn, allowing her to position herself upon the bed. Lying down, she placed her arms above her head, her hair spread out over the mattress. "I'm ready," she whispered.

Expelling a breath, Edric braced himself for how he would react. He had not once laid with a woman, for fear of the lingering effects of his traumatic experiences. But now, he could not help himself, gazing across her flawless body. She was divine, her skin soft, the breasts perfectly formed. He stepped out of his trousers, then climbed over her onto the bed.

Giving him a welcoming smile, Vixen remained still, her eyes bright and cheeks flushed.

Edric faithfully traced her body, rounding the breasts once more. He pressed kisses to her neck, then her lips, their tongues instantly swirling around each other. No matter the passion in their connection, the woman below him allowed him to explore freely. Edric needed time to build up the courage to breach her. He felt her again, the inner lips wet and silky. She was indeed ready. Holding his breath, he settled over her body, bearing down on her. A groan escaped him as he delved into her, the feeling surprisingly different from what he had anticipated. It was sensual and gratifying, the warmth inside him spreading like wildfire.

Rich sighs left Vixen as he moved above her, the sensuous sound punctuating his every thrust, again and again. Yet, despite the thrill of having him, she resisted the urge to claw at his body. Ever since she had first laid eyes on him, she had felt the attraction. Edric's tall but lean frame was pure perfection, his blond hair roughly cut, and his blue eyes full of expression. He was a man close to his feelings but unwilling to show them.

The bed creaked with the movement, the fire crackling in the back-ground, and the rain spitting on the roof.

Edric had never known sexual urges, the mere thought of the act only bringing painful memories to the surface. Yet at this moment, as he felt her sheath him, it was as if all that was gone. He yanked at her hips, increasing the intensity as he dived into her, deeper and deeper with every hungering plunge. He watched as she grabbed at the bed frame behind her, whipping her head sideways in enjoyment.

She suddenly began to tremble, her body hot and flushed as a sharp moan burst from her lips. She bit down, fighting against her oncoming climax, yet there was no escaping it.

Edric felt feverish seeing her elation, a throbbing sensation spreading from his centre. With a final roll of his hips, a rasping groan left him, and their entwined bodies shuddered as their pleasure culminated.

Resting over her, Edric cradled her head with his arm, kissing her again.

"I enjoyed that… very much," Vixen said, moistening her lips. "That too, I wouldn't mind… doing again."

He gave out a breathless chuckle. "I… I think we can come to an agreement."

Moving aside, Vixen allowed him to slump down beside her. Her finger slowly traced the side of his face, stopping at his lips. "When you are ready for me to touch you, do tell."

He planted a kiss on her fingertip. "I will," he replied. Rolling onto his back, he stared at the ceiling above. They remained silent for a moment before he brought a hand to his head, sighing. "I wish to never speak about it after this, but I will tell you."

"Don't do it for my sake," she quickly said.

"No, I will tell you so that we can… make this work." He paused, unsure how to continue. "You heard of my background… as a criminal. It all happened while I was in a thieves band, where I spent most of my childhood. When we travelled the lands for robberies and murders, the supply of women was sometimes… lacking. I would then be used to make up for it. My memories are muddled from the time, but I think…

174

it went on for about nine years... until they said I became too manly for them to pleasure themselves on."

Vixen quietly nodded. "I assumed something had happened, for you to react as you do. But it is of no concern to me. I am happy to work around it... like we just did." She blushed as he looked at her.

"It gladdens me to hear it. Perhaps... it will get better with time."

"I believe it will."

It rained for several days, lightning forking across the skies from dark clouds. As it finally let up, the inhabitants of the Temple village hurried outside to bask in the unaccustomed sunshine, Anaya no exception. She decided she would spend the day doing something she loved – fishing. It would be a much-needed break from the severity of demon hunting, which she knew was soon to be on the horizon.

The day was unusually warm, allowing her to wear only a modest, single-layered dress and a pair of open-toe sandals. She had walked some way through the forest, soon reaching a small but deep lake. She knew it well, the water containing plenty of fish, as well as supplying a diverse bird population. Closing her eyes, Anaya faced the sun, feeling the warmth of its rays caress her skin. It was only past noon, and she had managed to leave the Temple grounds undetected, with a fishing rod and lure. She was going to attempt catching some perch for the evening meal. Lenda loved to smoke perch, and it would make a delightful supper.

A light breeze whirred past, whipping Anaya's hair up in the air. She had it untied, allowing for the locks to move freely. It had grown long and worn in the last months, but she would soon have Lenda tend to it.

There was a tug on her rod, prompting her to look down. A small school of fish had gathered, swirling around the glittering lure. As Anaya slowly moved it past them, they followed, darting back and forth as if undecided on what to do. She would let them continue, as one would soon become greedy. They always did; she only needed to be patient. The rod bent, the surface disturbed by the flitting line. Anaya quickly retracted the tackle, catching a large perch.

Stretching her legs out, she whistled a happy tune. She had always liked fishing, the pastime being relaxing but exciting at the same time. Ever since a child, she would go out to fish on her own, leaving all the priestly duties behind. Breaking the fish's neck, she unhooked it and placed it in a basket together with another four perch, all of a decent size. Lenda would be happy.

Returning her attention to the school of fish, Anaya clutched the lure. Bringing it to her lips, she kissed it good luck, then flicked it out across the water. The line suddenly snapped, the embellished hook sinking to the bottom of the pond. "Oh, no!" she exclaimed, hurrying forward. Unable to spot the lure through the surface, she retreated to her basket, placing the rod on the ground. Pulling her knees up, she let out a profound sigh.

"Favourite lure?"

"Yes," she huffed. "Just my luck, I suppose. The same with you always showing up to gloat at my misery."

Samael did not reply as he approached. For a moment, he stood observing her, the priestess wincing before she looked away. She wiped at her nose, further slumping where she sat. He walked up to the edge of the water, peering into the depths.

"An old keepsake," she continued, her voice on the edge of break-ing. "I should have known better than to use it still, but it works so well fishing perch. It spins in the flow of water and gives off a shine that attracts them."

Kneeling, Samael leaned forward to identify the location of the lure. He felt a sudden push to his back, causing him to come off balance. In a cascade of water, he fell face-first into the lake.

Throwing herself back on the grass, Anaya could not contain her laughter, the enchanting sound pealing out. The priestess had finally hunted her demon, although in a less deadly manner than usual. Rolling onto her side, she rested her head on her arm, still giggling wildly. She expected to find him climbing to safety, but instead, he merely stared at her.

He was motionless, standing tall on the bottom of the lake with only half his face above the water. His hair had loosened and fanned out over the surface.

Unable to see his expression, Anaya slipped into silence, the colour washing away from her face.

In an effortless move, Samael placed his hand on a rock, then swung himself out of the water. Leaping across the priestess, he landed behind her, his drenched cloak slamming down on her. With the cold water seeping through her dress, she shrieked, scrambling to get out from under the wet fabric.

"Damn it, Samael!" she cried. "*I* was the one who meant to play a prank on *you*, not the other way around!" Her cheeks red, she stomped at the ground, but as the demon looked back at her, she quickly calmed.

His face displayed a brilliant smile, his fangs gleaming in the sunlight. "I think I like you, priestess!" he said, laughing. "You really did take me by surprise just then. Was it all a ruse? Did you do all that to trick me?"

Blushing, she found herself unable to hold his gaze. "Yes," she quietly replied. "I... suppose I did." She smiled bashfully. "But then you went on to spoil it and completely drenched me. Look at this mess!" Her dress was soaked, the wet cloth adhering to her body like a second layer of skin. Having turned almost translucent, her breasts, a narrow waist, and wide hips were showing through.

His head tilting to one side, his smile slowly began to change.

"No, not like *that*!" she shouted. "Turn around this second!"

Spinning on his heel, Samael did as she asked. He unclasped his cloak, letting it fall to the ground. Pulling his shirt over his head, he dropped it over the mantle, then settled down alongside the water. The wind created ripples across the surface, lily pods swaying with the motion.

Secluded within some dense bushes, Anaya changed into her robes. She had brought them with her, ready to be used, should her linen dress adopt the scent of fish. Reemerging, she halted, the demon now half-naked as he sat by the edge of the lake. His hair had begun to dry, the ends flowing in the wind. Fiddling with a blade of grass, he discarded it as he noticed her presence.

"May I look at you now?" he asked.

"Yes, you may." She pulled her shoulders back, standing tall with her arms close to her sides. She was awaiting his characteristic sly smirk or rude and cold comment, but instead, she saw warmth in his face.

"You have nothing to fear, dear priestess. It was all for fun, I know that. I can appreciate a good joke, even if I do not seem like the kind." He let out a breath, facing the pond once more. "And if there were ever any doubts of you being female, they have all been but eradicated. You truly are something to behold, fierce in more ways than one."

Hearing the words, a flutter rose inside Anaya's belly. Attempting to shake the feeling, she clenched her fists. "You don't mean that," she said.

"Don't make me tell you twice. You heard me. Do with it what you will."

Her face reddening again, she glared at him. "Did you just admit you saw me, through that wet dress? You pervert!"

"You did ask me to look at you. I won't hide the fact that, yes, I did perhaps see more of you than you would have liked. Why does it bother you? I am a demon, nothing more."

"Fine, but as a gentleman-"

"I am no such thing, especially not to you." Pulling a foot up underneath him, he locked eyes with her. "As I said, I am merely a demon, so why would it matter to you?" He rose, gathering his belongings.

Seeing his muscular physique in such close vicinity, she found the similarities striking. Demon? Human? For a moment, it was hard to distinguish between the two. Were it not for his unworldly pale skin, she would not have been able to tell. But what was he?

"Why are you not like other demons?" she asked.

Samael stood unmoving, his expression hardening. "What do you mean?"

"You know I cannot sense you as much as other demons; that you can manipulate your aura. Why is that? Why do you appear different? I can track you all the same, but your spirit is unlike any other. Tell me why."

Taking a step forward, his eyes darkened. "And what if I do? Are you to try and use it against me?"

Despondent with his reaction, she shook her head. "Is that what you think? After I just pushed you into a lake, you suddenly believe I'm conducting an investigation?"

With his brow relaxing, he fell silent. He dragged a hand through his hair, contemplating how to proceed. "I am different, but not in the way you might think."

"Do tell," she said. "I'm all ears."

"It has to do with my origin. I am no less demon than those you have previously fought. Quite the opposite, which is why I have told you to be careful." His emotionless tone shifted, sounding more menacing with each word. "I doubt you have ever battled against one such as I."

The hair rose at the nape of her neck, the priestess regretting the question.

"Your Priesthood preys on the weak and desperate. I'm none of that. **I AM A PRIME.**" With his last words, his voice deepened. It turned into an ominous, anamorphic growl, clawing at the priestess' mind.

Within an instant, all fell silent. It was as if time froze as they stood there, listening to the leaves swishing in the trees. The previously cheerful mood vanished.

In all her years within the Priesthood, she had only once experienced a Prime first-hand. She thought back to the fight with the wasp demons, how they had suffered so many casualties, and then required over a dozen priests to kill their Prime. If Samael was indeed something similar, then she would not want to fight him alone.

She took a deep breath, determined not to let his demonic aura affect her. "Is this it then?" she questioned, breaking the silence.

He blinked, his features instantly softening. "What do you mean?"

"You and I; we are vastly different. Let us speak plainly – we are each other's opposites. This was my attempt to somehow normalise whatever... *this* is." She pointed between them as she spoke. "You only want amusement. I gave you that, but it still ended in this, only because of my curiosity. There is nothing more I can say or do. It is like you said, I need to tread carefully around you as to not risk my own life. I cannot trust you, so what am I to gain from our relations?"

His demeanour still, he peered at her. "Trust is it? Is that what you want?"

"If I am to spend time with someone, then yes, I would prefer that person to be trustworthy. I put myself enough at risk to not do so in my spare time. There are enough dangers for women as it is, let alone being in the company of a demon."

"Ah, this demon thing again. Demons are no different from humans. You seem to think there is some inherent evil amongst my kind, but this so-called evil is just as prevalent within your own race as it is mine. I have no interest in harming you, nor have I ever entertained the thought. I am curious about your Priesthood, but no more than that. And yes, I find entertainment in you, priestess or not. That is all. I have no ulterior motives." With a tight grip on his clothing, he turned towards the forest. "I must beg your leave, priestess."

Anaya did not answer. Instead, she watched him as he walked away with soundless steps.

19

PRIMAL

M *any years earlier...*

Dust billowed around the children, two of the youngsters wrestling on the ground. "Let the boy go, Samael," Arax said, approaching them. All of similar age, most of them were boys.

Releasing his grip, Samael withdrew, allowing for the other boy to get up on his feet. He sighed, lowering his head as he dragged his foot along the dry soil. "I am sorry," he said.

"Pah! I do not care, Sam. It is *always* the same." His arms folded across his chest, the boy motioned to the other children. "Let's go."

As they left, Arax placed a hand on Samael's shoulder. "You need to remember your strength, boy. You are not like the other cubs. You must always hold back if you are to join them in play fights. It is not like practice with me."

"I know, sir. I just never *learn*." Looking down at his hands, the boy flexed his fingers. "It is as if I can't control these," he said. "Whatever is inside me comes boiling to the surface, no matter how reposed I am, to begin with."

Arax knelt before him. "I may not be a Prime myself, but I promised your father that if anything would ever happen to him, then I would take care of you as if you were my own son. We will get through this together, no matter how many years it takes us. Your inner power *will* be contained, used only when you wish it. That is our goal and my sole purpose in life." Arax stood, then patted the youth on the head. "Now then, we might as well begin today's lesson."

Pulling away, Samael glared at his tutor. "Fine, but do not belittle me."

The man grinned at his show of integrity. "Very well. You are eight years old now, so I suppose that time has passed." Heading for the sparring area, the two walked in silence. Arax could still not fathom how it was already three years since the boy's father had been so cruelly murdered. Of all members of the tribe, of all Primes, why him? And why would he have placed himself in such a high-risk scenario? He shook his head in disbelief, just as he had done on the day the news had reached him.

Arax had been out on a hunt at the time, receiving the news from a messenger. There was initial uncertainty about the Patriarch's ability to heal his injury, but as Arax had arrived back at the Patriarch's home, it was already too late.

The manservant's heart still ached as he recalled Lilith's reaction, how she had sobbed and desperately held on to her husband on the day of his death. She had rocked back and forth on the floor of their entrance hall, seated in a pool of blood. Arax was the one who had lowered the Patriarch to the floor, and brushed across his brow to close his vacant eyes. No matter her wails, as she had pleaded for him to return to her, he had been long gone.

Now walking alongside Samael, three years afterwards, he led the boy a short distance through the village. The training grounds were already prepared. Arax placed himself in the middle of the small arena, motioning young Samael to step forward. "Until such age as when you learn to transform, you will always have to be able to protect yourself in human form. Even as an adult, combat as a human is sometimes necessary, depending on the circumstance. It is especially important to keep in mind now, as we live an even more secluded life, further away from humans."

With a curt nod, the boy joined him.

Taking a wide stance, Arax raised his arms. "We will focus on hand-to-hand combat today."

Arax practised with Samael almost daily, varying what weapons they would use. They often avoided weaponry altogether since members of the tribe rarely used them as adults, their demonic form more than powerful enough to defend themselves with. His only issue was the boy's strength. Despite his young age, he was extremely robust and much larger than other children his own age. Arax already found the practice fights exhausting.

Studies of the world were much more gratifying and tranquil for the tutor. Samael was a great student, taking in everything he presented to him. Arax would hold daily classes for the young Prime, on all subjects, such as mankind, economy, agriculture, history, astronomy, and architecture. His mother was responsible for teaching him demonology, law, and traditions.

Samael would often read between classes, bringing books on the subjects with him as he sat perched in the highest trees, away from everyone. His outings would increase, both in frequency and length, but he would always return to resume his education.

The Matriarch often called on her manservant, indeed her closest advisor, to discuss their progress with young Samael. As he neared his teenage years, the youngster was already taller than her. With his father having been close to seven feet tall, she was not surprised. However,

Samael's appearance didn't help when trying to make him warm up to new acquaintances.

As Arax approached, she looked deep in thought. "What is the matter, my lady?" he asked.

Seated low on her daybed, she brought her fingers to her mouth. "It will soon happen," she said, her voice low.

"It can still be years away, my lady."

She bit at her lip, then let her hands fall to her lap. "I know... but he is twelve, to be thirteen in only a couple of months. We need to prepare him further if he is to function as the Prime of this village. But who are we to ask? My brother has his own family and village to deal with."

"True, but I think we can manage," Arax said, offering her a comforting smile.

Lilith met his gaze. "Yes?"

"If you can spare the two of us, I propose travelling to Sia, staying there for Master Prime Leviathan to teach Samael." He paused, anticipating a reply, but there was none. "I will continue his tutoring in all other areas, of course."

Gripping at her dress, she smiled, but the expression would not reach her eyes. "I know it is the only way. You will leave in the morning. Start the preparations."

"As you wish, my lady." Arax bowed deeply, then left the room.

✶ ✶

Departing the next day, Samael and Arax journeyed together with a small group of Lilith's personal guard, heading for the Sia village. The Matriarch had grown up in the settlement, and it was where her brother Leviathan now ruled as a Master Prime. He was a tall, burly man with wild black hair and green eyes. As the party arrived, Leviathan met them in his courtyard. He wore a bronze shirt and a pair of brown trousers, a black mantle spread over his shoulders.

"Samael!" his uncle called as he saw him. Coming forward to meet him, he embraced the boy. "Goodness, you grow faster than weeds."

His face flat, Samael left his arms hanging.

"As talkative as always, I see," Leviathan said, grinning. "Ah well, one need not speak in order to prove he listens." He patted the boy on the shoulder. "Let us begin your training then."

The room was dimly lit by candelabras, a low fire flickering in the background. Lilith, Leviathan, and Arax had gathered for a meeting in the Matriarch's dining room. The young Samael was to turn fifteen this summer, often being the year of the *Evolution*. He had already shown signs of the initial transformation, with oncoming nausea and fever at the last full moon.

Lilith rubbed at her brow. Circles had formed under her eyes from lack of sleep. "How are we to deal with this, brother?" she asked.

"Obviously, his father would have-"

"I know!" she snarled. "But we all realise that is not possible."

Leaning forward, Leviathan placed a hand on hers. "I will undoubtedly be the one to help him, but it will require that you send for me at the earliest possible sign of his change. Considering his reactions already, and the power he holds, I would expect him to show plenty of symptoms in the week prior."

Clenching her fists, Lilith dug her nails into the palms of her hands. "Will he survive this?"

Leviathan had hoped for the question not to arise, as he sat pursing his lips.

For any demon, the *Evolution* was gruesome, but for Primes, it was outright dangerous. The pure strength of their demonic form risked overtaking them, both physically and mentally. Some would die from the change alone; others would go insane, becoming one with the feral. They would have to be hunted down and killed, else they would risk running amok, slaughtering anything on sight. This was the main reason for another Prime to be present, as regular demons would never be able to thwart a Prime on their own.

"I cannot say, dear sister, and you know why. Samael was a risk ever since conception, or even as early as when the marriage was arranged between Forcas and yourself. Our predecessors knew it could very well result in a serious backlash, but they were willing to take the risk... so here we stand. I have done what I can to prepare him; the rest is up to Samael. I will come as soon as I receive word."

She merely nodded, looking down at her hands as blood trickled onto the table.

Leviathan rose, placing a hand on the backrest of his chair. "I will beg your leave, your Highness. Pray for the Spirits' blessing."

✶ ✶

Soon alone, the Matriarch sat in silence, her heart heavy. Seeking anything to use as reassurance, she thought back to an event long ago. In the coming autumn, it would be ten years since she travelled north, to meet with the great Oracle. Grief-stricken after her husband's passing, she had been desperate for answers.

Her dress in tatters, Lilith finally reached the top of the mountain, standing in front of an old hut. Veiled by the branches of a dead tree, it was small and dilapidated, the wood grey after years of weathering. She approached the building, seeing light dancing through the gaps in the walls, but no smoke rising from the chimney.

"Welcome, child of Darkness," sounded an old crackling voice.

Lilith could not tell from where it came, almost as if it originated from inside her own head.

Following a narrow path sunken into the rock, the Matriarch arrived at the entrance. Ascending a few creaking steps, she reached for the door handle. As her hand neared, the door swung open, revealing the modest main room of the hut. Bones and feathers hung from the ceiling, the walls covered in pelts and various crystal trinkets. In the centre, a white fire burned, leaving no smoke and providing little heat. On the other side sat the Oracle, perched on a wooden stool. She had long, grey hair, her face lined with deep wrinkles. "You have come for me to tell you the fortune of your child," she said, without looking up from the gleaming blaze.

Seating herself in front of the magical flames, Lilith watched her intently. "Yes, I wish to know-"

"Whether or not he shall sire an heir", the Oracle supplied. "Yes, I know, my child. You worry about the continued survival of his lineage, as well as that of your tribe." The old hag picked up a worn leather pouch from the floor, pulling on the strings to open it. Digging into the small bag, she retrieved a handful of powder which she spread over the fire. The flames instantly changed, turning bright blue and only reaching inches off the floor. A minute passed in complete silence, the Oracle still not lifting her gaze. "This is what the Spirits tell us," she continued. *"The man with hair the colour of ravens, within his thirtieth year in this world, shall have a Prime form in his shadow. It is like no other, wanted by no one, but revered by all those touched by it. And thus, the world shall never be the same."* The flames flickered back to white, reaching high into the air. "The Spirits have spoken. You have your answer. Now leave."

Knowing the Oracle would only ever answer one question, Lilith exited the hut. She had her answer, but still not. Did this mean the lineage would survive? Was Samael to sire an heir? Or would he perhaps choose one? And why would this child be unwanted, yet revered?

Almost ten years had passed, and the questions were still unanswered. Lilith walked into her entrance hall, slumping down onto the daybed. She tried to find comfort in the words *within his thirtieth year*. If the Oracle was right, it would mean he would survive the *Evolution*. Lilith needed to believe in the Spirits, to trust in their wisdom, else she would lose herself to the anguish of uncertainty.

It was a night of the full moon, wispy clouds slowly drifting across the ebony skies.

"It is almost midnight, my lady," Arax said, entering her grand house. "We need to go outside."

Lilith sat on her daybed, her knuckles pale as she clasped at her son's hand.

Samael sweated profusely, his long hair clinging to his face and neck. It was the seventh day of his transformation, and he had experienced severe symptoms throughout. His skin was sickly grey, and his eyes bloodshot and raw.

The Matriarch's gaze flitted around the room. "Where is my brother?" she demanded, her speech rushed. "Has he still not arrived?"

"I'm afraid not, my lady. The villagers have been told to stay clear, and the bonfire is lit."

"Not without my brother!" she cried. "I am *not* to lose my son also!" She felt tears welling as she turned towards the young demon. "Samael, you need to focus. Do not let this engulf you. You will make it through this!" She grasped his shoulders, attempting to steady him, but he sagged.

Sliding off the daybed, Samael fell to his hands and knees. "Mother-" He hurled, emptying the last of his stomach contents on the floor. Unable to finish a single meal in the previous five days, he shuddered, his muscles cramping.

A beastly roar sounded from the courtyard.

"Finally!" Lilith sprang out of her seat, heading for the door. Once outside, she saw a massive silhouette standing within a cloud of black mist, the bonfire flaring in the background. "Brother! I beseech you – help my son, *please!*" Her voice breaking, she felt a tightness to her chest, as if she was being smothered. With shaking hands, she wiped tears away from her face.

Cracking noises filled the air as the black creature started to change. Within moments, Leviathan emerged from the mist, his cloak whipping behind his feet as he headed for Lilith. "Bring him quickly!" he urged her.

Samael was immediately dragged out into the courtyard. His uncle snatched him up by the shirt and pulled him to his feet. "Listen carefully, or you will not survive this. You will experience the worst pain imaginable. You will feel as if your mind is shredded and your heart is breaking. Your whole existence will be challenged as you go through this first transformation. As such, you need to *focus*. You need to make sure you, yourself, are grounded. Do *not* lose yourself to the feral!"

Gritting his teeth, Samael nodded. "For the sake... of my father, I will survive this."

"Good. Now ready yourself. The time is upon us."

As the moon reached its peak position in the heavens, Samael belted out a scream, the first bone in his body snapping. The crunching noises quickly increased, sending the boy into a state of agony. Lacking any strength left to stand, he slumped against his uncle, who instantly righted him.

"Focus, Samael! Your mind must be burning as bright as the fire before you!"

Samael's skin ripped, bleeding wounds spreading like lightning across his body. His every muscle spasmed and swelled, showing through the expanding lacerations. His raven hair floated up into the air, then slammed back down. He growled painfully, the dark mass advancing along the cracks in his skin and creating a thick pelt. The damage to his body fuelled a state of rage, helping him remain upright, but his mind dulled. His inner self drifted as he desperately sought relief. The sight of the bonfire began to fade as the demon's field of vision slowly diminished.

"Samael!" his mother wailed. She lunged for him, but she was held back, Arax folding his arms around her.

"No, my lady!" he urged. "You may not disturb him. You might do more harm than good. Your brother will deal with this."

With swollen eyes, she merely whimpered. She wanted to avert her gaze, but she could not allow herself to ignore her son's hardship. "Forcas... send us your strength, my love," she prayed.

Leviathan grabbed at the youngster and shook him, the pain stirring Samael back to consciousness. "You cannot let the mind phase this out. You need to experience it in order to conquer it. Now, step forward!"

His legs leaden, Samael initially found himself unable to move. In the fire, he could see lights flicker and change, his father's face coming into view. He seemed to nod, motioning him to keep going. Letting out a gut-wrenching scream, Samael lifted his foot off the ground. By willpower alone, he slowly started to walk, focusing on one step at a time. The movement lessened the great torment of the metamorphosis, making him believe it might finally be over. The cracking of bones suddenly resumed, and the demon shrieked, falling to his knees.

Once again, his uncle pulled him up. "This is it, Samael. You will turn. Do not forget who you are!" With his last words, he stepped back from the youth.

Thick, black smoke burst out from the wounds on Samael's body, enveloping him in seconds. Unsure of what happened next, he found himself staring at the long flames of the bonfire, reaching high against the dark skies. Turning around, three strangers stared at him. They were speaking, but he could not make out what was said. He bared his teeth, ready to defend himself. Growling, he sidestepped, his tail flicking along the ground.

A word was repeated. *S. S-what? Sam. Sam?* It sounded familiar, but he knew they could be dangerous. He refused to let his guard down. Seconds felt like minutes; minutes felt like hours. *Sam. Sama... el? Samael! Who is that?* His eyes widened. *It is I!* "**I AM SAMAEL!**" he roared, his raging voice distorted. Dense, black mists once again whooshed around him. In an instant, the young man slipped into darkness.

Leviathan threw himself forward, catching him as he passed out. "You can relax now, sister," he told Lilith. "Samael will make it."

Years passed as Samael honed his skills as a Prime. He would often visit with his uncle, going on lengthy hunts, or duelling for practice. Prime against Prime, the spectacle would often gather a large audience.

The fearsome roars reverberated as the black beasts used their fangs and claws, slashing at each other. Despite being an exhibition, crimson would spray as they lunged, dark mist exploding out and causing the crowds to cower in fear.

On Samael's eighteenth birthday, he was summoned to his mother's home. As he walked inside, Arax came to meet him, the manservant leading him through to her dining room.

Seated at the table with Lilith, another man was present.

"Leviathan?" Samael questioned.

"Greetings, nephew. And congratulations." The imposing man pulled out the chair beside him. "Have a seat."

Arax followed behind Samael, placing himself opposite the Master Prime.

Samael's eyes narrowed as he regarded the three of them. "What is going on?"

Tapping her finger on the table, Lilith stared at him. "Just sit down, son."

He followed her orders, leaning back in his seat, and folding his arms across his chest.

The group sat in silence before Leviathan came forward. "We have been discussing the Patriarchy," he said.

Looking elsewhere, Samael offered a half-hearted shrug. "I am not interested."

"We are already aware of the fact, nephew." The man clasped his hands on the table. "We suggest a different solution, albeit somewhat untraditional."

Samael gave them a look of suspicion. "I'm all ears."

Clearing her throat, Lilith gained his attention. "I am to continue serving as ruling Matriarch, with you acting as our Protector Prime."

"But that is only meant for families with more than one Prime offspring."

"Indeed, it is," she granted. "But we are in a situation which will have to be solved using unconventional methods. This will allow us to retain power, despite you not taking your place as the rightful heir."

He nodded, his gaze low as he avoided eye contact. "I can accept it."

"However," Leviathan intervened. "If you are unable to sire an heir, the Patriarchy shall be passed down to my eldest, being next in line for the throne."

"Fine," Samael said. "Whatever you think is best. I only wish to remain undisturbed."

20

THE MINES

P *resent-day…*

Anaya had gathered a small group of priests, about to leave for the Stricker mines and fight off the reported lizard demons. The scouts confirmed they looked to be iguanas, a medium-sized beast with equal power. Anaya had decided to bring three trained priests, all of whom had joined the raid on the wasp Prime. Battle-hardened and ready, they set off.

The road to the mines was long but easily travelled due to its regular use by the industry. There was a known shortcut through the forest, connected to a narrow mountain pass. It led up to the rear side of the iron-rich caverns, but it was perilous. Riding on horseback made it hard enough, but travelling with a wagon rendered it unusable for the crew. Instead, they journeyed along the conventional road via Atua. It took four days for them to reach the mines, which had laid abandoned since the lizard demons appeared.

The priests tethered their horses some ways down the road, then made the rest of the stretch by foot. Anaya took the lead, using her magic to check for tracks. There were none present among the dirt, indicating the demons had separate access to the mines.

"Ready your arms," she said, her voice low. As they neared the mountainside, the four of them slowly edged forward. "Michael, you're up."

The young man had brought his bow, as well as his sword. He looked at the others, Scott armed with a sword and dagger, whereas Joseph held a mace. Clutching her staff, Anaya had already wrapped her prayer beads around her wrist.

As they moved past the ridge, they saw a group of men sitting around a campfire. Their demonic auras were clearly present, but no mists emanated from them. They were busy cooking something, the smoke bringing with it the scent of charred fish.

Readying his bow, Michael chanted under his breath, then released the glowing arrow. It lanced through the skull of one of the demons, the man toppling over into the flames, pieces of coal sent scattering. The other demons instantly retreated, scrambling away from the fire, all while trying to spot the source of the single projectile.

Michael let off a second shaft, but the moving target made for poor aim. He hit the demon in the leg, watching him stagger off behind the others into the nearby woods.

"Quick, before they transform!" Anaya shouted, the four of them charging the demons.

A lizard appeared through the trees, large spikes spread across its head and back. It was covered in green and black scales, with the tail longer than its body. The claws were long and sharp, teeth showing between its lips as it hissed. Another one appeared, then a third, the last one with an arrow still protruding from its leg.

Anaya cursed. "Focus on the injured one! Do not get hit by their tails!"

Hurtling forward, Scott raised his sword. Making room along the hilt, he grabbed it with both hands before slashing down on the demon. The beast swerved to avoid the blow, only to find its skin burning. A sphere of Light seared against its scales, Anaya standing behind it with her hands and staff raised. Momentarily stunned, it stumbled to one side, allowing Scott another way in. He stabbed with his sword, piercing the lizard just below the eye. He pushed his weapon deep into the demon's head, to the sounds of crunching bones and ripping flesh. Blood flowed along the blade as the beast sagged.

Michael loosened more arrows as Scott charged another target, Anaya supporting him with her Light.

Preserving his spiritual power, Joseph was standing back, ready to heal if need be. The third demon, with arrows now littering its body, noticed his inactivity. It spun, its tail whipping towards the priest. Swinging his mace, he blocked the oncoming attack. He let the weapon crash down onto the beast's flank, the blessed head burning through the scales. It wailed, rearing back with its front legs flailing in the air. A sword slashed past, and the demon's eyes rolled back in its skull.

Retracting the blade, Scott lunged again, the man driving it deep into the lizard's head.

The three demons lay dead, and the priests surveyed their surroundings. All they could hear was their own shortness of breath, and the gurgling water from the nearby river. Unable to sense any additional demonic aura, they were satisfied they had killed all demons present. They proceeded to behead the beasts, including the one at the fire, still in human form. It was gruesome work, the dead eyes staring back at the priests.

Fetching the horses and wagon, Joseph halted alongside the corpses, all lined up at the dying fire. They loaded the demons onto the wagon, covering them with a thick woollen blanket and strapping everything down with cotton cords.

As they stood in silence, Anaya watched the cave mouth. Something felt amiss, but she could not pinpoint the source. Attempting to shrug it off, she turned to her fellow priests. "Well done," she said. "Let's head back."

Within a few days, the party managed to return safely to the Temple village. The journey had been uneventful, but their cargo was starting to give off an unwelcome smell.

It was morning as they halted outside the Temple, about to unload the demon corpses.

Joseph and Michael carried one, then Scott meant to grab a second with Anaya. He stood on the wagon, hauling the lizard over the edge.

About to grab her end of the creature, Anaya lost her footing, slipping on blood left from the previous cadaver. Toppling over, she found the dead demon falling with her. Then, as if the tumble had made its heart spring back into life, claret poured from the severed neck. The scales became slick with blood, the priestess squirming as she struggled to remove the beast. "Get this thing off me!" she squealed.

Scott leapt down, clutching hold of the demon's legs. He managed to pull it clear, dragging it away from Anaya. "I'm sorry, ma'am, I should have kept a tighter grip on it."

Pushing herself up, Anaya held her arms away from her body, blood dripping from her fingers. "It is alright, but I need to wash myself, obviously. You deliver the body, brother."

His legs wide, he saluted her. "Yes, ma'am," he said.

Looking down at herself, Anaya cringed. She would have to fetch a change of clothing, then head for the stream.

That stench again. Demon's blood. No matter how many times Samael approached the village of the Priesthood, he could never get used to the smell. And today, it was worse than usual, reeking well before he reached the pond. He stood amongst the trees, finding the area empty of people. Coming up to the edge, the source seemed to be the water itself.

It had to come from higher up.

Ascending the cliff face, Samael continued up into a tree, placing himself on the branch of a dense oak. Above the waterfall was yet another pond, albeit smaller than the one below. This, too, was sustained by a waterfall, but it was much broader, yielding a thinner cascade. Makeshift wooden planks had been erected towards a nearby path, leaving people at the pond out of sight from onlookers. From what the demon could tell, it seemed to be used for washing *oneself*, more than one's clothing.

On the other side of the pond, she stood. Unsure how she had managed it, she looked to be drenched in blood, this time from head to toe. Only her hands had so far been cleaned.

With her hair tangled, Anaya removed the strap holding it together, then gently pulled her fingers through the strands. Standing at the edge of the water, she gazed at her reflection as she tried to unravel the locks. Seemingly satisfied with her progress, she started to untie her bodice.

An eyebrow raised, Samael leaned back against the stem. Things were getting interesting, so he decided to make himself comfortable. This trip could very well have been worth it. He was curious to see what she was hiding under there, claiming to be plain. From what he had already gathered, she couldn't possibly be as repulsive as she made herself out to be.

Anaya dropped the bodice onto the ground, pieces of coagulated blood splattering the stone surface. Reaching in under her skirt, she pulled out her undergarments, then moved to untie her dress. She let it slide down her arms, leaving it to gather around her ankles. Now naked, she again peered at her reflection in the pond, turning around, and lifting her arms up. Perhaps looking for bloodstains on her skin.

Her skin.

Her sun-kissed skin shone in the sunlight. Samael found himself stunned at the sight. She was a strong woman, long and muscular, but with plenty of female features. Wide hips, firm thighs, a slim waist, and a pair of round, defined breasts graced her luscious forms. He watched as she walked over to the waterfall, reaching her hand out into the cascades. She yelped, pulling it back while she visibly shivered.

Samael instantly bent over, choking out a laugh, not wishing to be heard.

It must have been cold, he mused.

Clenching her fists, she dared the freezing waters, and stepped in. Allowing the water to soak into her hair, she held her arms up, washing out the blood. Her hands trailed down as she cleaned her neck, shoulders, and arms, rubbing them carefully. She moved on, brushing her hands across her breasts and stomach, then her back and buttocks. Last, her legs and feet, after which she sat down. Facing upwards, she seemed to enjoy the water surrounding her, droplets forming on her flawless skin.

Feeling like he had seen enough, Samael descended the tree.

She was a fierce thing to behold, indeed.

It was the last day of September, and Lenda had been given temporary leave. It was her birthday, a day she would always spend resting and enjoying the outdoors. After morning prayers, she had whisked away, retreating to her bed. Allowing herself a sleep-in, she huddled up within the soft bed linen, soon drifting off into the world of dreams.

After only an hour, the sun shone through the open window, slowly waking her from her slumber. She stretched, touching either side of her bed as she inhaled the morning air.

There was a faint knock at the door, the girl pulling the covers over her shoulders. "Come in!" she called.

The door slid open, Eden stepping inside. He was carrying a basket and some flowers, and a warm smile split his cheeks. "Good morning, beautiful," he said.

"Oh, Eden!" Lenda exclaimed, seating herself on the bed. She threw her arms out, inviting him into a loving embrace.

Placing the flowers on her table, he left the basket at the end of her bed. Sitting down, he moved in to kiss her, then offered her the contents. He had prepared breakfast; rolls and cheese, as well as freshly pressed apple juice.

Lenda blushed, her eyes sparkling as she gazed over the gifted edibles. "Is all of this for me?" she asked.

"Yes. Happy birthday, miss."

Clutching his hand, she pulled him in, pressing her lips against his. "Thank you so much!"

"I am glad you like it, miss." He paused, placing a hand on her leg, gently caressing her through the covers. "I was going to invite you to a dinner party tonight, hosted by myself and a few of your friends."

Her mouth opening, the girl peeped with delight. "Amazing!" She clapped her hands but suddenly stopped. Changing her position, she angled for him. "Um... Anaya isn't cooking, is she?"

Eden rubbed a knuckle at his temple. "I am not sure. Why?"

"Well, if she is... you will find out tonight," she laughed.

21

THE ORCHARD

With the arrival of autumn, the trees bore plenty of fruit. Anaya left early in the morning together with a group of disciples, heading southeast. They had brought baskets, gathering apples in a nearby orchard. The priestess needed hers for an apple pie Adena planned to make for Lenda's birthday party that evening.

Anaya found herself picking slowly, not wanting to fill up her basket just yet. She was soon alone, the disciples having left with their woven containers full to the brim. However, their plentiful harvest posed a new problem for her; most of the remaining apples hung too high up, out of her reach.

Strolling through the orchard with light steps, she spotted the apples she wanted. The most giant tree seemed to hold the ripest fruit; big, red orbs shining in the sunlight. Stretching as far as she could, she would still not reach them. She tried poking about with a stick, shaking the branches, but to no avail. With her hands on her hips, she stared at them, as if attempting to will them down.

"I'll help you if you wish it."

Anaya swung around to find the demon standing only yards away. She hadn't noticed his presence, being too busy with the apples. Still upset with the fruit ignoring her request to fall on their own, she glared at him. "Alright," she said. "What do you propose? Can you fly, perhaps? Because as far as I can tell, they will be too far up for you as well." She turned back, looking up at the produce in question, then studied the tree. "And the branches seem way too fragile to support your-"

She squealed as her feet lifted off the ground, a great fluttering erupting inside her.

With his hands pushing her skirt over her thighs, he had grabbed her sides, then gently placed her on his fur-covered shoulders.

Her face red, she wrapped her arms around him. "My Goddess, have you no shame?" she exclaimed. "Putting your hands up a lady's skirt like that!" Her heart hammering inside her chest, she looked down at him, their eyes meeting. It was strange, how his demonic aura only heightened her already jubilant state, adding a slight tingle as she sat perched on him.

His eye contact was intense, and he offered her a smile before motioning for her to resume her chores.

It didn't take long for her to fill her basket, the priestess soon ready to come down. With a tight grip on the hamper, she braced herself. "Right, I'm finished. Lift me down, please."

Samael stood for a moment, letting his hands continue to rest on her exposed legs. The skin felt smooth, just as he expected. Her feet were dressed in light sandals, securely tied around the ankles. Even they were nicely kept with clean, trimmed nails. Everything about her was neat and precise. Her scent much stronger with the closeness, it was sweet and fresh, when not tainted with blood.

Anaya leaned forward. "Samael?"

He blinked, clearing his throat. "Yes, sorry. My apologies." Grasping at her hips, he lifted her over his head once more.

Back on the ground, she brushed at her dress, righting it. "Thank you, Samael. That was... *fun.*" She rubbed at her face, her cheekbones beginning to hurt from her persistent grin.

"Fun?" he retorted. "Nice to see that you are easily pleased with *something*, at least."

With her back against him, Anaya pushed a playful elbow into his side, causing him to step back. "You're the one being funny now, aren't you?" she said, spinning around. "Telling jokes! Oh, how the mighty have fallen!" Her bright smile was genuine and pure, a cheerful aura exuding from her. Holding her basket close, she began reversing away from him, releasing an infectious laugh.

Samael couldn't help but smirk, watching her.

"Oh, not so heartless anymore, are you?" she teased him. She bounced, then broke into a run, her delighted giggles echoing across the orchard as she increased the distance between them.

Pushing his boot into the ground, Samael instantly raced after her. His cloak flared out behind him, the heavy cloth horizontal with his speed.

The flutter returned, stronger this time, as the imposing demon gained on her. She fought not to cry out, the exhilaration bordering on terror. Hefting one of her apples, she hurled it at him.

Ducking under the red projectile with ease, he sidestepped a second, then caught a third.

Anaya hurried behind a wide maple tree, her hands sweeping across the stem. She darted left and right, avoiding capture as she made sure to stay on the opposite side to Samael. Feigning going left, she swerved right, bolting towards the next tree.

Disposing of his apple, Samael dashed after her, grabbing her from behind. With one hand over her grip on the basket, his other snaked around her chest, up to her neck. Coming to his full height, he lifted her off the ground, inhibiting her from running any further. "Fleeing, are you?" he hissed. "Attacking me with apples? I don't suppose this is the newest tactic against demonkind?" He pushed his face against her head, sniffing above her ear, then lowered his voice. "I can smell your *fear*, priestess."

Ceasing all movement, Anaya tensed, the increased aggression in his behaviour unexpected. She suddenly heard a low rumble as he growled, the sound reminding her of the purr of a cat. Her face flushed as she burst out with laughter once more. "Let me down, Samael!"

"Oh, fine," he huffed, carefully lowering her to the ground. Bending down, he replaced a few apples in her basket that had fallen out in the scuffle.

"And I was sure the apple tactic would work," she continued, barely able to speak through her fit of giggles. "I need to meet with the High Priest at once!"

Samael showed a dubious smile. "If these are the new types of fighting styles you are bringing out, then I have no issue being the test subject."

"Fantastic, I'll note that down, for sure," she said, lightly touching her chest. She rubbed at her neck, a faint red mark showing on her skin. "Although, you do play a bit rough."

His hand lifted, but he stopped himself. "I am sorry about that," he said. "I wasn't thinking. Please, forgive me, priestess."

Taken aback by his sudden concern, she blinked, then her smile grew. "It is fine. Don't give it another thought." Placing the basket on the ground, she sat down next to it. "It's nice to be surprised by you, Samael."

The demon slumped down beside her, one of his legs extended forward. "I suppose there is a lot you do not know about me."

Anaya forced a laugh. "That can't be much of a revelation though, surely? You never answer a question straight, ever. Obtaining information from you is like getting blood out of a stone."

"Alright, fine. That might very well be true." He rubbed his chin, his thumb chafing at the stubble. "What do you want to know?"

"Really?" she asked. Her fingers brushed against his shoulder, the demon meeting her gaze. "Would you answer honestly?"

"Yes," he said, offering a curt nod. "Try me."

She grinned, her eyes instantly gleaming. "Oh, this is so hard! I barely know where to start." She paused for a moment, a finger tapping at her lip. "Well, let's start easy. Your age. What is it?"

"Thirty."

"Really?"

"Yes," he said, frowning. "Why would I even lie about that?" Peering at her, he angled towards her. "Do I look old?" he added.

She brought her hands up between them. "No, no. Nothing like that. I am only making sure I am receiving the correct information now. So, when was your birthday?"

He sat back again. "Fifteenth of June."

Anaya was quiet, counting briefly on her fingers. "Didn't we meet around that time?"

"Yes."

"And you didn't mention it?"

"Why on earth would I have mentioned it? As far as I can remember, you tried to blast me at that time." Scratching at his head, Samael let his eyes wander, attempting not to get agitated. He somewhat regretted agreeing to the interrogation.

"My apologies. I shouldn't have said anything." Placing her hands on her lap, she looked down, fiddling with her thumbs.

Joining the silence, he watched her. The woman seemed upset by his reaction. "Next question," he said calmly.

Her shoulders pulling back, she perked up where she sat, but remained undecided on what to ask. "Um... Do you have any siblings?"

"No."

"Perhaps a mother and father?"

"Mother. My father passed when I was five."

"I'm sorry to hear it. My condolences." Again, she felt awkward, not expecting the answers to come so quickly and be so genuine. "Any favourite colour?" she eventually asked.

Samael looked down at his outfit, then back at the priestess. "What does it look like?"

"Right, I suppose I should have deducted that myself." She pulled a few blades of grass out of the ground. "What is your full name?"

"My full name?"

"Yes. Title, name, surname. You know, full name."

"Yes, I know what it means. It is just that the question was unexpected." He paused but decided to oblige. "Prime Samael Fahd of the Panther Tribe."

"Aha!" she said, her hands coming up into the air in celebration. "I *knew* you were a panther. That purr gave you away earlier."

Samael chuckled, unable to mask her spirited influence on himself. "True. I didn't think of that. What is yours then?"

"Senior Priest Anaya Caelin," she answered, the demon nodding as a response, but then fell an unnatural silence. There were so many things she would want to know, but most pertained to his demonic background, and she didn't wish for the mood to sour. "What about your favourite food?" she blurted out, but instantly regretted the silly question.

He thought for a moment, then grabbed hold of Anaya's arm, pulling her close. He licked his lips. "Small, succulent *babies*."

All the colour drained from her face, her mouth falling open. She gulped down a breath, unable to utter a word.

His laughter rumbled out. "Honestly, you should see your face. I cannot believe you still fall for this. Am I not any less frightening to you?"

She released a whimper of relief at his return to normalcy. "I do not know why, but it kind of catches me off guard."

"I understand. I seem to have that effect on people, demons and humans alike. I am clearly socially inept." Samael released a breath. "What about you, then? You like *babies*?" He sneered at her, making a last attempt at the joke.

Choking on her own saliva, Anaya expelled a strained cough. "I-if I would like to have a baby?"

Samael's face reddened, his eyes widening.

Covering her mouth, Anaya gasped. "My Goddess, are you blushing?"

"Oh, stop it, will you?" He looked away, praying it would fade rapidly.

"You surprise me yet again, Samael. This meet is truly something else." She gave him a warm smile, the demon locking eyes with her again. "Can I perhaps ask you a more serious question?"

"I said I was going to answer honestly. I have no intentions of going back on that now."

"Right, well... this has been on my mind since you told me that... you are a *Prime*."

His eyes narrowed, but he said nothing.

"Just listen. I am merely curious." Anaya steeled herself. "As far as I know, Primes are the strongest amongst their kind, and as such, they usually have some sort of leadership role within their faction. Is that true for you also?"

"That is true, but my situation is... complicated. I am unsure of how to answer that lest you spend the rest of the evening in my company." With no intentions to tell her as much, he decided to assume the role of the interrogator. "Let me ask the questions now."

She felt a knot form in her stomach, worried that the Priesthood would be part of his chosen subjects.

"Since you are so keen to know about my family situation, what is your own? Do you have a family? Or friends?"

"No family," she answered. "No one blood related anyway. The Priesthood has been my family ever since I was five. However, I have a close friendship with Lenda."

"Ah, is that the young healer who is sometimes with you?"

"Yes, mister Stalker."

He smirked. "You got me there. No wonder your complete devotion to the Priesthood then."

"Truth be told, it is all I have ever known. I was orphaned at the age of three, so I have no recollection of my real family."

"I see," he said. "Well, I already know your age. When casually dressed, you often wear green, which makes me believe it is your favourite colour. In the mornings, you often carry the scent of mild cheese, and as such, you most likely have that as a favourite food. Then, by your own accounts – as well as what I have gathered – you are well respected and highly ranked within your Priesthood. You are popular amongst your kind, often spoken to and asked for advice. You also clearly enjoy the outdoors, taking long walks in the forests, prefer-ably at night, to watch the moon and stars."

Placing a hand to either side of her face, she felt the increased heat on her skin. "My Goddess, Samael. If it weren't for the lack of affection in our relations, it would almost sound as if you shoulder great fond-ness to me."

"I am merely observant," he answered. "It is true then?"

Anaya nodded. "You are, indeed, right. Regretfully, however, I need to get back to the Priesthood, else they should start looking for me." She grabbed her basket and stood, then straightened her dress. "Thank you for today, Samael. It was a true pleasure."

The demon silently rose as their eyes met. "The pleasure was all mine, priestess." He bowed, then left the orchard in the direction of the Eastern forest.

Braziers and torches lined the outside of the square, their flames flickering in the slight breeze. Adena had created a network of small glowing orbs which she spread over the ancient oak at the centre. The weather was mild despite the time of year, with a clear sky and warm air.

Lenda had dressed in a comfortable but pretty linen gown, dyed in two different shades of blue. It had been gifted to her by Anaya the same morning. With her hair left to grow throughout the summer and autumn, the young girl had managed to gather it into a short ponytail. Her eyes were bright as she entered the square, regarding the people seated around a long table.

Anaya and Eden were present, but also Edric and Enya. On the other side of the table sat her tutor Maya, and her colleague Padma. Furthest down on the left, Vixen cheerfully waved as the young girl approached.

"She always shows up anyway, so I thought we might as well invite her," Anaya supplied.

Lenda smiled, tearing up. "Th-thank you all so very much," she said, her voice choked. "You have no idea how happy I am to see you all."

Standing up, Anaya embraced her. "It is a big day for you, being sixteen years old. You are officially a woman now." She kissed her on the forehead, then turned to the others. "I propose a round of cheers for her."

Everyone seated brought their glasses up into view, all cheering before taking a sip out of their drinks.

"Please, sit, Lenda. We will bring the food." Anaya motioned for Adena and Edric to join her, the three of them heading for the pantry building. As they re-emerged, she noticed a hesitant look on the birthday girl's face. "Oh, don't worry, dear sister. Adena did the cooking. I only helped pick the ingredients."

As Lenda let out a sigh of relief, laughter rolled out amongst the party-goers.

The group ate slowly throughout the evening, enjoying several courses. They spoke of various subjects, all the louder as additional drinks were poured. Discussions eventually centred on the unusually warm weather, Edric leaning back in his seat. Sitting across from Vixen, he peered at her. He was silent, with his arms folded over his chest and his legs stretched out underneath the table.

Coming forward, she opened her mouth but said nothing. Holding his gaze, she placed a hand to her face, nibbling at her thumb. A smile developed, the woman moving her foot along the paved ground. She gently grazed his leg, but he immediately retracted it.

He sat up, averting his gaze.

Lenda moved towards Anaya, the priestess seemingly smiling at nothing. "You look mighty cheerful today, sister. Has something happened I should be aware of?" She gave her a suggestive look.

Her glowing cheeks flushed, Anaya's complexion became distinctly red despite the dim lighting. "Oh, no. I'm... only happy to be able to spend the evening in such great company... before I head off for a scouting assignment tomorrow."

Lenda shrugged, but continued to stare at her. "If you say so," she said. "I did hear about this from Eden, though. Was it something with the orchard?"

"Yes. Someone had spotted one or more demons in the area. I spent the day there today harvesting apples, but I, eh... I saw none." She tugged at her ear, then brushed some hair behind it. Lying was clearly not part of her skillset. "Anyway, I will be leaving early, so I won't be attending morning prayers."

"I see."

"How did your last mission go?" Anaya inquired, looking at Adena. "With the bear demons." Before she could receive a reply, several of the guests booed at the table, all directed at her.

"Shameful! Speaking about work at a time like this," Edric admonished, holding his drink up. "Cheers, everyone!"

As the celebrations resumed, Eden rose from his seat. The chattering instantly died down, eyes focusing on the young man. He extended his hand to Lenda, the girl immediately blushing. "Will you speak with me a moment?" he asked.

"Of course," she said, accepting his hand. The two left the square, heading down the road.

✶ ✶

The stars littered the sky. Eden stopped as the two of them stood on the stone bridge across the stream. He faced Lenda, clasping her hand.

With rosy cheeks, the young girl looked up at him, her smile spreading.

"From the moment I met you, I was taken by your beauty and your devotion to your profession. I love your patience and kindness to others; your innocent and sweet character. I have come to realise that you are everything I could ever want in a woman. We might be young, but I would like to spend the rest of my life with you." He dropped down on one knee, holding her gaze.

Lenda's eyes glittered as she watched him, knowing what he was about to say.

His grip on her hand tightened. "I love you, miss Ainsley. Will you do me the honours of marrying me?"

Throwing herself into his arms, she grabbed at him, pressing her lips against his.

Rising, he returned her affections, kissing her softly. "I take that as a yes?" he said, his grey eyes fixed on hers.

"Yes, yes, yes!" she shrieked, leaping onto him again, her arms wrapping around his neck.

Eden had to grasp at her legs as she jumped up, the young girl planting kisses all over his face. Lowering her back down, he blushed. "Goodness," he said. "That went above and beyond my expectations."

"Oh, how can I not wish to be your wife, Eden?" she said, her eyes glossy yet again. "I love you too!"

The couple soon rejoined the party, telling them about their engagement, to the great cheers of their comrades.

It was late by the time Samael returned to the village, his cloak fluttering as he kept up the pace. He walked along the road leading to his mother's house, noticing her presence on the front porch. The bonfire was lit in the courtyard, and the perimeter lined with flickering torches.

Lilith sat in a neatly carved chair with a high backrest, her feet resting on a small stool. She had been enjoying the sun this day, reading books, but now she merely watched the flames of the roaring fire.

"Samael," she said as he passed her, halting him.

"Yes?" he asked, without looking at her.

"I can smell human on you again. Stronger this time. *Female*." She met his gaze, the demon glaring at her over his shoulder. "Tell me why. *Now*," she demanded.

He clenched his jaw. "Mother, just leave it."

She rose, coming down the front steps. "The scent is unmistakable. Have you… *embraced* a human?"

"I'm leaving." Taking a step, he felt a grip around his arm.

"You tell me *now*, Samael. Who is this woman?"

He turned, tightening his fists. He was met by a pair of wet, dull eyes, glistening in the firelight. He exhaled, his features softening. "A priestess."

The Matriarch reeled back. "What did you just say?"

"She means nothing. We touched, nothing else."

Her eyes wide, Lilith let her arms drop to her sides. "But a *priestess*?"

"I know what you're thinking. You are right. I should know better."

He paused, avoiding her gaze. "But she intrigues me, mother. I feel the need to know more."

"Intrigues you?" She laughed in disbelief. "A human, female priestess? Of all women in the world, it has to be a *human priestess*?"

"Mother, please. It is no more than entertainment. I am in no relation with her."

"You better not be!" she exclaimed. "To fall in love-"

Samael recoiled at the word. "Don't be ridiculous," he snarled. "I am incapable of such feelings!"

"No one is immune," she hissed. "Not even you. Do not go near this woman ever again."

He grunted. "I do as I please," he said, turning on his heel. He swiftly left, heading elsewhere than his home.

22

WEDLOCK

The evening of Lenda's birthday had indeed been cheerful, and the alcohol plentiful. Edric swayed, rising from the table. He left a hand resting on his chair, waiting for the world to stop spinning. "Right, I think that's it for tonight," he decided. "Since the birthday girl has gone to bed and all."

Vixen rounded the table to join him. "I'll help you home, sir," she offered, squeezing herself in underneath his arm.

"I'm not *that* drunk," he snarled, attempting to pull away. His sudden movement caused him to stumble further, but the woman righted him again.

"Sure, because you are as steady as can be," she stated, shooting him a flat look.

"Fine," he muttered.

She grinned. "Goodnight, everybody. I will also go to bed, as soon as I take this drunkard home."

Adena chuckled, waving at them. "You do that. We shall see you at prayers tomorrow."

They all said their goodbyes, most retiring to their beds. Staggering the majority of the way, Edric eventually straightened himself as they reached his cottage. "I'm fine," he said. "Now, let me go."

Releasing him, Vixen stepped back. "Certainly," she said, but lingered at the bottom of his front steps.

"What do you want?" he asked, his hand planted on the door handle.

"To be invited in, of course," she replied, holding his gaze. "Will you have me?"

Edric felt as his breaths shortened, his grip tightening around the metal handle. He knew she was blunt with her words, always to speak her mind, but her openness about their sexual relations caught him off guard.

Several weeks had passed following their last intimacy, but she had occupied his thoughts ever since. Every time he saw her, he felt the warmth flair inside him, his heart throbbing in his chest.

This time was no exception.

The whole evening, he had fought not to reach out and touch her. For her to now offer herself freely, the temptation was too great. "Yes," he finally said.

"Fantastic," she replied, traversing the steps to meet him. She placed her hand on his, opening the door.

Walking across his bedroom, she released the threading of her dress, leaving it to fall to the floor. She proceeded to remove her undergarments, after which she placed herself on the bed.

Stumped, Edric ground to a halt. He had barely entered the room, and there she lay, naked amongst his dishevelled bed linen.

She pushed herself up on her elbows. "Edric?"

He shuffled a step forward, but stopped again, as if he couldn't make himself come to her.

Swinging her legs off the bed, Vixen rejoined him by the door. "Can I touch you?" she inquired softly.

Edric swallowed hard, then exhaled. "Yes."

In silence, she reached up and embraced him, motioning for him to meet her. Her lips travelled along his neck and cheek, then claimed his mouth. They locked together, their sultry movements gradually building.

Returning the enchanting kiss, Edric could smell cider on her breath. Infused with alcohol and apples, the essence mixed with the perfume in her hair, like sweet summer blossoms. His heart raced as he placed his hands on her hips, but then stopped. Despite his burning desire for the woman, he found himself unable to advance on her.

Vixen set to unbuttoning his shirt. "Tell me if you want me to stop," she whispered. As the garment spread open, she pushed it off his shoulders. She pulled at the thongs on the front of his black trousers, then released them to fall to the floor. She clenched her jaw, desperately wanting to explore his masculine physique, but she had to pace herself. Her hands carefully traced his collarbones and chest, then across his defined abdominal muscles. She brought them back up, caressing his back. As they travelled down, she noticed how he flinched.

His eyes tightly shut, Edric felt his whole body surging with the need to remove itself. "S-stop," he pushed out.

In an instant, her hands lifted. She placed them on either side of the man's face, pulling him in for another kiss. Her lips parting, she brushed her tongue against his mouth, allowing for them to deepen the connection. Almost instantaneously, he relaxed into her hold, his posture loosening. Satisfied he had snapped out of his state of discomfort, Vixen took a step back. "Waist up, no problem," she chirped, nudging him with her arm.

Edric offered a strained smile. "Yes… I suppose that is right."

Grabbing him by the hand, she led him across the room, her thumb gently caressing him. In silence, she placed herself upon the bed, her arms resting above her head. Releasing a slow breath, she locked eyes with him. "I am all yours," she said. "Trust me when I say, I have longed for this."

Sitting down on the edge of the bed, he rubbed at his brow. "I, eh…" His words trailed off, and he cursed, struggling to speak. "I still… want to touch you."

Blushing, she let out a light-hearted laugh. "Then go ahead."

Moving closer, Edric leaned in, allowing his hands to explore her body. He trailed every inch of her sensuous curves, enjoying the soft-ness of her skin, and the roundness of her breasts. He caressed her hips, then swept down over her centre. Pushing his fingers inside her, he shivered with anticipation, her sheath smooth and hot. The memories of their last tryst came to life, adding to his already building arousal. He watched as she closed her eyes, her mouth falling open before she released a low-pitched moan. Kneading and rubbing her inner lips, he felt a tantalising satisfaction, resisting the urge to breach her.

Her breaths quickening, more for each time his fingers entered her, Vixen suddenly grabbed his wrist. She looked at him intently. "I want you. *Now.*"

Edric disengaged from her, clenching his jaw. Even though it was their second time together, he still struggled for courage. Releasing a breath, he moved up to settle between her legs, his hands running along her thighs. He grasped at her, pushing them apart. Trailing down to her buttocks, he lifted her slightly, then leaned in. His jaw slacked as he sunk into her, a wild groan escaping his lips. He trembled, overcome with desire, as he began plunging into her.

Vixen moaned softly, shuddering as she watched him, her fingers curling around the bedsheets. But she longed for more, if only just a simple touch. Carefully wrapping her arms around him, she pulled him in, nibbling at his lip. A trickle of sweat ran down his face as he moved over her, the two of them joining in a hungry kiss. Edric had started out slow, as if savouring the moment, but now, his rocking motions gradually intensified. He entered her, again and again, their kiss soon broken by another pleasurable groan.

Caressing his chest, Vixen brushed her fingers down his front, then lifted them back up. Her soft sighs echoed about the room every time he filled her, a fiery heat burning in her belly. She raked her fingers into his hair, clutching hold of the blond strands. She wanted to urge him on, to wrap her legs around him, but she could not. Instead, she claimed his mouth once more, their tongues dancing to the rhythm of their passion.

Parting from her lips, Edric gasped for air, then lowered his head beside hers. Grabbing below her hips, he lifted her away from the bed, delving deeper, riding on the rush of having her. Edric feverishly groaned, feeling Vixen's breath beat against his ear, the naked woman crying out with elation.

Overcome by euphoria, the two of them moved as one, their pleasures soon soaring into a climax.

The sun had not yet risen as the priests gathered in the Temple for their morning prayers. Adena had placed herself at the front, as all officers should, but found herself short of fellow comrades. Only Kaedin was present, sitting on her left. Anaya had been excused, leaving early for her scout, but she wondered where Edric might be.

The sound of chiming bells interrupted her thoughts, the prayers commencing.

Adena peered over her shoulder, scrutinising the massive hall behind her. Ekelon's voice boomed out as he began his sermon, but Adena continued to search the gathered priests. She could see Lenda and Eden at the back, together with Enya. The rest of the healers were present only a row away.

Adena's eyes narrowed. Vixen was missing. She had noticed her spending more time together with Edric, last night being no exception. Edric was often late to prayer, but this was too much of a coincidence. Facing forward once more, her lips tightened. She hoped she was wrong, for Vixen had so far been a promising recruit, but her intuition told her otherwise.

As the morning prayers concluded, Adena approached the High Priest, who was stacking the tomes of Holy Scriptures on the table before him.

"Your Holiness, may I speak with you?" she asked.

"Certainly, my child. What about?"

Adena looked around, waiting until the Temple was cleared. They stood alone, except for the High Priest's guards. "Edric and Anna Leighton," she said. "They left late last night for his home, and none of them showed up this morning."

Ekelon's expression tightened. "And you fear something might have happened?"

"Indeed, your Holiness."

"I see," he said. "Go and investigate. Bring two of my guard." He paused, lifting the pile of books. "And should you find something... unlawful, then bring them to me. I shall be present in the conference room for now."

Adena nodded, then waved for the guards to approach. "Come with me," she ordered, then exited the building.

Edric had been outside to relieve himself. Entering his bedroom, he yawned, rubbing his eyes. Only dressed in a pair of black drawstring trousers, he neared the bed. Vixen lay there, quietly watching him, the man dragging a hand across his head.

"I think we have missed morning prayers," he said.

Sitting up, she smiled. "I'm sure the Goddess will let it slip. She is forgiving, after all."

He smirked, stopping at the edge of the bed. "Indeed, She is, so let's hope you are right."

Vixen brought her hands forward, pinching hold of the thongs on his trousers.

"Again?" he asked.

"Always," she replied, moistening her lips as she looked up at him. With the thongs loosened, the trousers dropped to the floor. She reached for his hands, their fingers entwining as she pulled him over herself. They kissed feverishly; all signs of tiredness gone in an instant. Her centre throbbed as he trailed down and played with her, fuelling their simmering moment.

Clutching her legs, Edric spread them apart, his mouth falling open as he entered her. He exhaled, relieved at his ability to transition their union this swiftly. As he continued to push into her, he felt the excitement building faster than ever before. A passionate groan burst from his chest, the man unable to hinder himself.

Already shuddering with ecstasy, Vixen moaned eagerly, caressing Edric's chest as he moved over her.

The door unexpectedly flung open, Adena stepping into the bedroom.

The couple reared out of bed, Edric scrambling for his trousers as Vixen covered herself with a blanket.

"What the hell, Adena!" he exclaimed. "Have you ever heard of knocking?"

Adena raised her chin, glaring at him. "Have you ever heard of morale and living by the *law*? I suppose old habits die hard, after all."

Vixen watched as Edric's expression changed, his brow twitching, eyes flickering. His state of rage shifted to grief, but he clearly fought to hide it. He remained silent, clenching his fists.

"I suggest you both get dressed," Adena continued. "The High Priest will want to speak with you." Retrieving Vixen's dress from the floor, she flung it at the woman, who quickly donned it.

Edric pulled a shirt over his head, then stood unmoving.

"Guards," Adena called, two of them entering the room. "Arrest them."

The wardens stepped forward. Using tightly woven cords, they bound the couple's hands behind their backs, then led them past Adena out into the open.

"Take them to the High Priest," she instructed.

★ ★

The square stood empty as the guards led Edric and Vixen to the Temple. Being October, the tables had been removed outside the pantry, as people were now meant to eat indoors due to the changing weather.

Adena ordered them to wait at the entrance, so she could speak with the High Priest alone. As she re-emerged, she called for Vixen's guard. He guided her up the stairs, leaving Edric outside with the other sentry. They walked through the main hall of the Temple, reaching the conference room. Another two guards stood at the door as she entered, Adena remaining outside.

The High Priest pointed to a chair opposite himself. "Miss Leighton, have a seat."

She sat down, meeting his gaze.

"You have been accused of fornication with Senior Priest Edric Ramsey. How do you plead?"

Vixen's mind raced for anything she could say to soften the blow, but in the end, there was no way she could talk herself out of the situation. Her posture slumped, and she clutched her wrist. "Guilty, your Holiness."

"I see." He leaned forward, resting his elbows on the table. "You are therefore found guilty of this crime. Your punishment will be house arrest for seven consecutive days."

Her eyebrows raised, she gave him an incredulous look. "Only house arrest?" she questioned. "I am relieved to hear it, your Holiness, but is this not usually cause for harsher punishment?"

"For the man, yes. Not for the woman. You can be excused."

The guards moved to grab her, but she interjected. "Please, your Holiness, listen."

The High Priest raised a hand, halting the guards. "Anything you wanted to add, my child?"

"Edric," she said. "What punishment does he face?"

"Flagellation and banishment," Ekelon answered, his eyes narrowing. "Extramarital sex is strictly forbidden."

"We intend to marry," she exclaimed. "At earliest possible opportunity."

"You should have done so beforehand, miss Leighton. It is a bit late now." He once again motioned to the guards. "Take her away."

"No, please, your Holiness, show leniency!" Vixen was dragged out of the room, the door closing behind her. There was nothing she could do. The guards took her through a side exit, following the path past the High Priest's mansion. As she was led down the road, she could see Edric being pushed up the front steps of the Temple. It would be his turn to speak with Ekelon and receive his penalty.

· · ·

"Master Ramsey," the High Priest said as the officer had entered the room. "You have been accused of fornication with Disciple Anna Leighton. How do you plead?"

Eyes on the floor, Edric sighed. "Guilty, your Holiness."

"Mm, unfortunate, to say the least. The evidence is not to be rejected, as you were caught in the act." Ekelon paused momentarily. "Miss Leighton claims you are to be wed at the earliest given opportunity. Is this true?" he asked.

Edric instantly met his gaze. "Yes," he said.

"I see. Your response rings true. I have to say, I am surprised to find you in this situation, my son, considering your... background. However, I am happy to see you developing relationships finally. I only wish it had been a lawful one. Be that as it may, you are found guilty of fornication."

Edric stood silently, awaiting his sentence. He knew banishment would be part of it.

"You are to be sentenced to flagellation, three hundred lashes with the cat."

The cat, also called a cat o'nine tails, was a whip only used for severe punishments. It was a multi-tailed whip, sporting nine knotted thongs of cotton cord.

"After which, you will lay to self-heal for seven days under house arrest. Guards will be stationed to make sure no outsider, or yourself, attempt with the Light to heal your wounds. On the eighth day, you will be taken to the infirmary for treatment, then here to the Temple, where I shall wed you with Anna Leighton."

A brief silence passed as Edric waited for the High Priest to continue, but he merely looked back at him. "No banishment, your Holiness?" he questioned.

"No. You will not be banished, but only on the condition of you two entering wedlock."

"I agree."

"Good. Miss Leighton has been put on house arrest for the time being. You shall see her eight days from now."

Edric nodded. "Thank you, your Holiness."

"Thank the Goddess. She is the reason why you stand here today, Edric. As the *Redeemed*, you are part of my vision, so I shall not let you go lightly. But punishment you shall receive, nonetheless. It will be carried out tonight when darkness falls."

23

DARK HOLE

Anaya had always handled her missions with severity and dedication, the same as with all the education and training she had received during her years with the Priesthood. Despite this, scouting missions were still quite mundane. She had never grown to appreciate the day out, speaking with the populace and gathering information. The vast amounts of interviewing bore the priestess to no end. The point of the conversations was to try and discern what type of demon had been spotted. Without such knowledge, hunting the beast could be right out deadly. To know one's enemy was key in becoming a successful demon-hunter within the Priesthood.

Sighing heavily, Anaya peered out the window. It was noon, and she had still not left Tinta. More than thirty people had been waiting for her as she arrived, all wanting to tell her what they had seen in the orchard as they went to collect apples.

A Senior Priest would typically never be sent on investigative missions, but all the regular scouts were already dispatched, and most others were out on unrelated hunts.

Anaya, now barely able to stay awake, leaned forward on the table. She rested her head in her hand, quietly nodding in response to the man sitting opposite. She wasn't listening anymore, only watching the movement of his mouth, how he would spit every time he said the letter S. It annoyed her, but she had no interest in telling him.

Despite the several hours spent with various people, she had still not managed to narrow down what demon it was. They were all giving contradicting statements, some of the descriptions making absolutely no sense. The demon would have two heads in one witness account, six legs in another. Then it would be black before it was turned into green. Or a shade of deep red. It had once been seven-foot-tall, then only about three. It was also hairy but had scales. Clearly unable to piece the picture together, Anaya knew she would have to manually scout to attain the correct information. The only valuable piece of intelligence was that the demon had been spotted again, that very same morning.

Finished speaking with everyone involved, Anaya consumed a light snack before heading for the orchard, staff in hand. Entering the fruit garden, she couldn't help but reminisce about the previous day, a warmth spreading inside her. She slowly walked the grounds, stopping at the tree where Samael had lifted her over his shoulders. She smiled, recalling the event.

Anaya shook her head. She needed to concentrate. Bringing out her prayer beads, she wrapped them around her hand, then started chanting. Light flashed around her, then spread out, settling along the ground. Tracks instantly glowed in the grass, but they were not the ones she was looking for. They were Samael's, large and spaced out with long strides. Again, she had to shake the pleasurable feelings bubbling up inside her. She was there for work, not leisure.

Surveying the area, she found another set of tracks, but much smaller. Some in the shape of paw prints, and others human, but they were both emanating the same demonic aura. It looked to be a lesser demon of mammal type. Perhaps a smaller feline, canine or vulpine, such as a lynx or a fox. She followed the tracks across the orchard. The demon was probably there for the apples, more than anything else. *Such a pitiful hunt,* she thought, *wanting to punish a demon for filching fruit.*

The tracks seemed to speed off towards the woods. This was probably where the demon was last spotted, sprinting off when it realised it had been seen.

Anaya followed the prints, now distinctly animal. *The demon must have transformed as it fled.* Walking into the woods, the tracks crossed the larger ones from earlier. Samael's footprints. She stopped, her mind drifting again. What if she was to follow him? Would she find him? Unable to fight the temptation, she trailed his impressions in the undergrowth. Reaching a small clearing, she came to a halt, noticing how they abruptly changed. Her eyes widened as she stared at the gargantuan paw prints. She could only imagine the size of his demonic form. Perhaps following him was unwise.

Deciding to turn back, Anaya resumed her mission. She cursed, finding it unfathomable that she had even drifted away from it, to begin with. A knot formed in her stomach. What if the High Priest was right? Was Samael using some kind of manipulation on her, trying to get close to the Priesthood? Pushing the thoughts out of her head once more, she focused. It was time to figure out what demon she currently searched for.

The smaller tracks led north, closer to the Temple village. Considering her options, Anaya looked up into the sky. It was bright with the various colours of dusk. She had spent too much time in the orchard and… drifting off, so she had to hurry.

Picking up her pace, she ran through the trees, Light flashing from her hands as she clutched a firm hold on her staff. The tracks became tighter together. The demon must have slowed with the uneven ground.

Coming around some thick bushes, Anaya suddenly found herself face to face with the demon she was hunting.

Startled, the beast reared back, then flashed its teeth at her. It was a fox demon, just as she had thought.

She slammed her staff into the ground, a circle of Light appearing around her. Despite it being a scouting mission, she was forced to defend herself.

The beast charged, but pulled back as the Light seared its skin. It shrieked, then took off running.

Against her better judgement, Anaya decided to pursue it. It was fast becoming hard to see in the dim light, so she created a sphere above her head to guide her way. Running along a dark crevice, she glanced down into the depths. She had to be wary of her steps not to fall in.

There was a rumble underneath her, the soil unexpectedly collapsing. Dropping her staff, Anaya desperately clawed at the ground, trying to locate a place of anchoring, but all came loose as she gripped it. She plunged into the cleft, screaming as she fell.

✶ ✶

Placing a hand to her forehead, Anaya forced her eyes open. She felt dazed, lying at the bottom of the cleft. On her way down, she had managed to dampen her fall by grabbing some roots, but her back ached, and her right ankle throbbed. Slowly sitting up, she touched the back of her head. It was sore, but not bleeding. Chanting a few words, she healed herself as best she could, then rose to inspect her surroundings.

The soil was too soft to grip, and there was no vegetation available to climb on. With the setting sun, she could barely see in the fading light. And unable to make out the edge of the pit, she wasn't even sure how far she had fallen.

She muttered under her breath. It was long since she found herself unable to hunt down a demon. It was even longer since she had failed at safely returning to the Temple village. Calling out for help was not an option; the demon still out there in the forest. Perhaps it would come back and take the opportunity to kill off the huntress, making her the prey. For the same reason, she could not create a Light sphere, in fear of the wrong creature finding her. She would have to stay put and hope that, within a few days, someone would come for her.

Sitting back down, Anaya hugged her knees. She wished days such as these were behind her, that her training had made her nigh on impossible to break, let alone kill. And now, stuck in a dark hole in the middle of a forest, it became all too clear she was only as human as she had ever been.

Rubble trickled down the far side of the pit, Anaya hearing a single pair of footsteps above. She stood and quickly retreated, her back pressed against the soft soil. A rope appeared, curling up in front of her, the other end extending up and out of reach. Anaya cautiously stepped forward, grabbing it. As she tugged at the rope, it felt firm. "Who is there?" she called.

"Just grab it already."

She recognised the voice. "Samael? Is that you?"

"Damn it, woman, just grab the bloody rope."

Anaya could hear the impatience in his voice. She gathered the rope, then wrapped it around her waist. Holding it tightly, she once more looked up towards the dark skies. "I'm ready."

As she was elevated along the side of the crevice, she noticed how far she had fallen. When she eventually cleared the edge, she hurried forward to get away from the hole, should more of the side collapse. Settling in front of Samael, she looked down at herself. Her robes were coated in dirt and mud, so she bent down to brush it off. Unsteady on her feet, she slipped and stumbled forward, finding herself face first in the demon's shirt.

Saving her from falling, he had stepped forward and embraced her, his cloak fluttering around them.

Her cheek pressed flat against him, Anaya could hear his heart pounding and feel the warmth of his broad chest.

Releasing her, Samael stood firm, allowing her to find her footing.

She looked up at him, her cheeks flushed.

For a moment, they stood perfectly still, Samael gazing down at her. The only reason why they did not touch was the demon's sheer size. His expression softened as he watched her. There was something about her that he just could not distinguish. He found himself utterly lost in her emerald eyes, like glistening jewels reaching into his soul. The moonlight created a glittering surface on her flawless skin, and an ethereal shine to her hair. Then there was her scent. The same as before, sweet and fresh, almost... *divine.*

He reeled back, removing himself from her as he averted his eyes. "Try to not... get yourself into a hole you can't get out of," he said, then quickly made his way into the forest and out of sight.

Anaya stood in silence, not quite sure what had just happened. Trying to shake the feeling of a sudden closeness, she looked around for her staff. She created a small sphere of Light to guide her way, the orb floating above her.

The demon hunt would have to wait. Now she only wanted to return home.

✷ ✷

Anaya kept to a westward direction, hoping to reach the edge of the forest, and with it the path leading up to the Temple village. She was in luck, as it only took about an hour to reach it. In the end, she had travelled so far during her hunt that she had almost made a full circle. She could soon traverse the stone bridge across the stream, heading towards her cottage. Walking along the road, she decided she would go past the pantry for a late snack.

Nearing the square, Anaya noticed it was full of people. Many were holding torches, a large bonfire lit outside the Temple. Below the front steps, the whipping pillar had been brought out. Pushing herself through the crowds, she reached the oak at the centre, managing to pull herself up along the stem. To her dismay, she saw how Edric was pushed through the open doors of the Temple, his upper body bare, and hands bound behind his back.

She hurried through the crowds, but before she could reach the front, someone grabbed her arm. Turning around, she found Adena holding onto her.

"Anaya, do not interfere," she cautioned. "He was caught rutting with Anna Leighton. There is nothing you can do."

Her eyes wide, Anaya watched as the guards strapped Edric to the pole. "Th-that's not possible!" she exclaimed, attempting to pull free.

"I walked in on them myself, sister. He shall suffer three hundred lashes."

227

Anaya stared at her in disbelief.

Silence fell as the crowds waited for the punishment to begin. With each passing moment, Anaya noticed the hum of whispers building around her.

Isn't he a criminal? It was only a matter of time before he would act.

I knew taking on a thief would end badly. How can the High Priest even contemplate letting him stay?

He should be banished this instant.

Such a rotten man! No respect for women. Copulating outside of wedlock? He should have known better.

This was certainly not his first time. Arrogant, and egotistical, that's what he is.

He deserves what he gets.

The first lashing. Edric groaned, leaning against the whipping pole. The second lash. The third and fourth. It was one of the newer guards who delivered the punishment. He had been taught well, as he stopped between each lashing, allowing the skin to regain tactual sensation.

The cat o'nine tails had previously been used for self-inflicted flagellation, the priests chastising themselves for wrongdoing or lack of faith in the Goddess. However, the High Priest had since forbidden its use, except for severe punishments. The whip in itself was small, requiring the guard to stand close as he delivered the strokes, thus yielding a weaker blow. But it also meant for longer abuse, and all the more suffering with the added multitude of onlookers.

The guard had been trained not to hit the same place in close succession, covering the entirety of the back instead. The skin would go red and raw but not easily tear. It was merely the large number of strokes that would eventually break through, slowly ripping the flesh and leaving bleeding gashes in its wake.

Had a longer whip been used, Edric would have been lucky to survive even a portion of his penalty.

Even thus, blood started to trickle down his back. He sagged but righted himself again.

More lashings. Then more.

Ceaselessly falling.

More and more blood was drawn, as the whip rippled across the man's already raw skin. Edric let out a scream, the pain unbearable.

Anaya felt empty as she stood watching, tears flowing down her cheeks.

For almost three-quarters of an hour, the beatings continued. Edric desperately clawed at the pillar to remain on his feet, but several times he would fall to his knees. The blood pooled beneath him, crimson flicking each time the guard pulled the cat back into position.

As the lashings neared their conclusion, Anaya could no longer see. Her eyes were swollen as she shrieked, Adena still holding her firmly. When the crowds parted, Adena led her back to her cottage, so that she would not interfere with the aftermath.

24

CONFINED

Anaya walked the short distance to the Temple. Unable to sleep, she arrived early for the morning prayers. Kaedin and Adena were already present, but Edric's seat was empty. She winced, thinking back to the previous night. She could only imagine what agony he must still be in, left to self-heal in his bed. Adena had told her of his given punishment and that he would not be banished, which offered some comfort. Anaya would personally make sure Maya and Lenda performed his healing when the seven days were up.

Kaedin greeted the priestess as she sat down. "You look downcast, lass," he remarked. "Are you alright?"

She gave him a courteous smile. "Yes, dear brother. I am merely tired."

"Aye, you only just came home yesterday. A day early at that. Did everything go well with your investigation?"

"It did. I am to relay it to the High Priest after the sermon." She sighed, looking up at the statue of the Goddess towering above them. "But the demon is no threat," she added.

"I see." He pinched hold of his bearded chin. "Feels strange with Edric missing."

Anaya met his gaze.

"The boy should have known better," he continued, his brow drawing together. "I certainly hope that this so-called arranged marriage between them will be to his benefit."

"Arranged marriage?" This was something Adena had failed to mention.

"Ah yes, I apologise, dear sister," she said. "The reason he was spared banishment was because they were already engaged to be married. He had apparently answered yes, to the question of whether this was true, within an instant. The High Priest took this as proof of his honesty, but I am not so sure."

Anaya sat quietly, merely nodding. She knew now what had happened, and Adena was right in her suspicions. There was no way Edric and Vixen would have made such an arrangement beforehand. This was their only way to lessen his sentence.

The Temple slowly filled up with people. It was almost time for the prayers to begin, and the High Priest emerged from a back room. He placed the books of Holy Scriptures on the prayer altar, then proceeded to preach. It was shorter than usual but contained a strong message: All those of the Darkness were to be eradicated.

Ekelon had hinted to it before, especially with the hunt on the wasp demons, that they were to start raiding their homes and settlements. It would be in an effort to stem the renewal of demons, by slaughtering every man, woman, and child.

Anaya felt herself shiver. He did not say the exact words, but that was what he meant. She felt sick as the sermon ended, the crowds of priests slowly leaving the Temple.

"It is about time we do something," Adena said, as the officers stood alone.

Kaedin shrugged. "I'm not so sure. I stand undecided. Purely from a military perspective, this tactic has never been a very successful one. Ignoring the moral aspect."

"Moral aspect?" she asked. "They are demons."

"That may be so, but would you cull a litter of puppies only because the mother bit you?" he challenged. "As I said, I stand undecided."

Anaya couldn't even speak, worried she might give away more

than she would like. Instead, she mumbled some words of goodbye before leaving to see the High Priest. Entering the conference room, she found him sitting at the table as usual, but with the opened scriptures in front of him.

"Ah, Anaya," he said. "Nice to see you back so soon. Please, sit down and give a report on your mission."

"Yes, your Holiness." Sitting down, she placed her hands on her lap. She proceeded to describe how she had interviewed a multitude of people, after which she tracked and located the demon. However, she avoided telling him how she lost sight of the creature, only saying she attacked it, and it fled.

"Very well," the High Priest allowed. "We shall wait and see if we receive word on any further sightings. You might have scared the demon off if it was only a case of stealing apples, as you say."

"I believe so, your Holiness."

"Good." He paused, clasping his hands. "Unfortunately, I must tell you that you will have to return to the Stricker mines."

Anaya raised her eyebrows. "Really, your Holiness?"

"Yes. More demons have been spotted, so the mining operations have halted once more. I have already sent out scouts to confirm the sightings. When they are back, you will lead a new party to clear the strays."

"Certainly," Anaya said. "I will bring the same group as last since they know what we are up against."

"Indeed. But considering the demons are of a lesser kind, I would also like you to bring a disciple. One of the newer ones."

She nodded. "I will do so, your Holiness." She stood to leave but halted.

"Did you want something else, my child?" Ekelon asked.

"I do… I would like to know about Edric, your Holiness."

"Ah. Undoubtedly so, I should imagine. I heard you arrived in time for his sentence to be carried out."

Anaya's mouth felt dry as he mentioned it. "Yes," she said.

"And regretfully so, I might add. I am sorry you had to see your brother in such a position, but he was tried and found guilty of fornication. There was nothing else to be done."

"I understand… But why so harsh, father?" She leaned forward over the table, her eyes already welled up with tears.

"Shed no tears over such a thing, dearest Anaya. Edric was caught in the act and admitted to the crime. There was no way to show leniency in something as serious as this, thus the three hundred lashes, being the norm. However, he was relieved of banishment in exchange for their wedlock. You must understand that I cannot be lenient against the Senior Priests, no matter their background. I had to set an example."

Anaya knew it was true. Had he been soft on Edric, he ran the risk of the crime spreading amongst the Priesthood, knowing the punishment was not upheld. The same was with respect for officers. Had he not been found guilty, all of them would have lost face with the subordinates. Anaya nodded, straightening herself. "I shall go and choose a disciple for the hunt. I beg your leave, your Holiness."

Ekelon chanted a short prayer, then held up his hand towards her. "You may go, my child."

✶ ✶

Leaving the Temple, Anaya immediately headed for Vixen's cottage. As a Senior Priest, she could visit with those serving sentences, no matter the crime. Other than the officers, it was only the High Priest and whatever guards present who were allowed near a prisoner.

Reaching the residence, she motioned for the guards to allow her passage. They stepped aside, the priestess entering the building.

Vixen sat on her bed, hugging her knees. Her eyes were red and swollen, her breakfast left uneaten on the table. She briefly looked at Anaya, then back down on the bed. "I am so sorry," she whimpered. "It is all my fault. I only wish I was the one serving a sentence, not him." She covered her mouth, fresh tears trickling down her cheeks.

Sitting down on the bed, Anaya placed a hand on the woman's

knee. "Edric will be fine," she assured her. "Heaven knows, he has been through worse."

"But not because of me," she whined, her hands shaking as she attempted to dry the tears. "And to add insult to injury, I have now *forced* his hand, and made him marry me."

Anaya gave her a warm smile. "That is true, but it saved him from banishment."

Vixen's lips parted, a shine of hope in her eyes. "The High Priest lessened his sentence then?" she asked.

"Yes, but only on the condition you just mentioned."

"But what if… he doesn't want it?" Grabbing a piece of cloth, Vixen wiped her face again.

Anaya chuckled at the thought. "If you managed to bed him, Vixen, he will have you in a heartbeat."

More tears spilt down her face, but the former Commander still managed to smile. "You think so?"

"Rest assured, dear sister. He accepted your proposal and did so without hesitation."

Throwing her arms around the priestess, Vixen squealed with delight. "Thank you! Thank you for everything."

"It will all work out in the end, sister. I shall go see to him now. I will tell him that you look forward to your married life."

**

Anaya hurried along the streets. It was a lengthy walk, spanning the entire village as she strode across from Vixen to Edric. Standing outside the officer's cottage, Adena emerged from the front door.

"Hi there, sister," she greeted. "What brings you here?"

"I am here to visit with Edric," Anaya answered. "What about you?"

"I only questioned him further," Adena said. "I'm not entirely convinced of their cover story."

Anaya's eyes narrowed. "The High Priest has already passed his verdict."

"True," Adena granted. "But I am the curious kind." She offered a modest bow. "I shall see you later, sister."

Anaya returned the gesture, then stood in silence, watching her leave. Walking inside, she found a guard present in the room.

Edric lay on his stomach on the bed, his arms bound above his head, tethered to the headboard. His back had been dressed in cloth, the fabric laced with medicinal herbs to stop infection. Only wearing simple breeches, he was awake, taking short, shallow breaths. His face was pale, and the skin drenched in sweat.

Anaya sat down on a chair beside the bed, then placed a hand on him. He felt cold, his body shivering. "You have to lay a blanket over him," she told the guard.

"We have received instructions not to, ma'am," he said. "He is only allowed one at night."

"I-it is… fine," Edric stuttered. "A-at least… they didn't… b-bind my… legs." He had to physically push every word out as he spoke, the pain overwhelming.

"Guard," Anaya said, her voice authoritarian. "What time is it? I am to be preparing a disciple for a hunt." As the sentry turned, she carefully placed a hand on Edric's head.

Looking out the window, the guard used the positioning of the sun to estimate.

With a flash, a dim light travelled across Edric's body.

"I'd say about nine, ma'am," the sentry declared. "Yeah, midmorning."

Anaya leaned forward, pressing a kiss to Edric's forehead. "Anna is fine," she whispered. "She is thrilled to be yours."

He forced a smile. "Thank you, Anaya," he said, relief in his expression.

She had not healed his wounds but numbed the pain. The spell would rarely be used, as it required much greater power than fusing flesh. Yet, at this moment, it was Anaya's only option.

"It should last for tonight," she told him. "Try and get some rest. I shall see you soon, brother."

In the days ahead, Anaya prepared for their new mission. Luckily, the men present on her last mission to the mines were available. She found it repetitive, speaking to the priests and going over the same tactics as before, the only difference being a disciple accompanying them. Anaya had chosen Bran Elliot, a young man of fifteen. He was an excellent student, well-versed with ranged weapons and daggers. He was not yet much of a proficient with healing, but that was nonessential for the current assignment. He was a good fighter, and that was all the skill he needed.

The party had decided to journey along the conventional roads again, like they did for their previous mission to the mines. They would also join up with Rick and Eli, who were to scout for a different undertaking only a mile away from the mines.

It was the seventh day of Edric and Vixen's sentences, and the next day, they would be released and wed. Anaya was scheduled to leave after the union, first serving as a witness together with Adena.

The scouts had returned and reported that the lizard demons were indeed back. They had seen tracks from three individuals, all of lesser strength. The party had their equipment prepared inside the stables, ready to be loaded up while they would wait for the priestess to join them the next morning.

Having briefly met with her crew members at the square, Anaya excused herself. "I have an errand to run, but make sure you are all ready by tomorrow at dawn." She hurried across the square, running into Lenda and Eden. They had gathered some food from the pantry, on their way to the girl's cottage.

"Hello there, sister," Lenda chirped, offering a friendly smile. "Busy?"

"Unfortunately, yes, dear sister. I have preparations to make for the mission tomorrow."

"What a shame. I would have invited you over for food otherwise. Perhaps you would like me to save you some?"

"That would be lovely. I shall see you later." Anaya waved at them, then left for the blacksmith.

"They are going back to the mines, right, Eden?" Lenda asked him.

"Aye," he said. "I would have liked to go myself, only to see the type of demon. I am yet to fight against lizards, but I have a different assignment only two days from now."

"Oh? What is that then?"

"Routine mission, nothing exciting. A pack of wolves, but they have been spotted dangerously close to the Capital. It might take as long as two weeks before I am back. Kaedin will lead the charge and bring Rheas, Leo and Perry. Adena will be busy in Rover at the time, with Ken and Robert, as well as Enya." He clasped her hand, motioning for them to begin their walk back to her cottage.

She took a hesitant step, following him. "But… are we to be left without officers then? And most of our experienced priests will be dispatched."

"Aye, considering Edric will be in no shape. But the High Priest reckons it is no cause for alarm, as it is highly unlikely a demon would come to our base of operations. It would be suicide."

"I suppose you are right," she said. "I shall miss you while you are gone."

"And I, you, miss," he replied, then halted, prompting her to stop. "I would like to marry you soon, Lenda." Placing a hand on her cheek, he leaned in, kissing her softly.

"We will arrange it when you come back," she said, her face flushed. "Now, let us eat."

The High Priest descended the cavern. Light spheres lined the walls, brightening the space as he walked down the narrow path. Reaching the grotto below, he surveyed the room. He was always suspicious of someone uninvited paying a visit while he was away, despite two sentries consistently guarding the entrance.

Ekelon had started to feel immune to the reek of dead corpses. He barely noticed it anymore, whenever he resumed his work. Removing his robe, he hung it on the wall. He looked down at himself, seeing the body of an old man. His potions had an effect, his muscles flexing and swelling under the wrinkled skin, but he would have to tweak it, as the results did not appear to be permanent.

The antidote produced for Edric seemed to work long term, but that was perhaps because it was created for a specific ailment. What he was doing here was much more experimental, the effect meant to enhance the priests' powers, hopefully supplying the Priesthood with the upper hand even against Primes.

However, most of the parts from the wasp Prime had already been consumed, leaving very little to work with. He would soon need another Prime. Attacking settlements would be the only way to lure them out since most would have a Prime present as a leader and protector.

Ekelon ran his hand over his collection of jars, looking at their contents. Eyeballs, teeth, blood from different demon types, hair, fur, nails, claws, and scales. Many were organs. Hearts, brains, kidneys, livers, even testicles and a uterus. So many things to experiment on, to extract contents and use against disease and famine. The regenerative powers of demons could revolutionise their infirmary, able to cure people of such things not previously possible. But for now, he had to focus on their cause – to eliminate the imminent threat of demons.

The brew from the previous evening was ready, the bottle standing on the alchemy table. The High Priest held it in his hand for a moment, feeling the weight of the contents. It was a large batch, but perhaps precisely what would be needed. Grabbing it with both hands, he chanted, Light enveloping him and the potion, infusing the brew with his magic. He carefully popped the lid open, then held it to his face. The stench was overpowering, but he knew it had to be done.

As the liquid reached his mouth, it seared his tongue, burning as it travelled along his throat. Gulping it down, the High Priest watched as dark shades of blue swirled underneath his skin. They spread, seemingly alive as they crawled inside his flesh. After a few minutes, it all settled, and the colour faded.

Ekelon flexed his muscles again. It felt good, his joints no longer aching, and his mind sharper. Now it was only a matter of calculating the duration of the effect, taking into consideration the amount of material. He returned to his books, scribbling notes. He would need more specimens.

25

DRAGON

As morning came the following day, the door opened to Vixen's bedroom.

Adena stepped inside. "Disciple Anna Leighton," she said. "You are hereby to be released after serving your sentence for fornication with Senior Priest Edric Ramsey. You are free to go."

Vixen instantly sprang from her bed, scrambling for clothing.

"However, you are not to see him," Adena went on.

Halting, Vixen glared at her. "Why not, ma'am?"

"He is preoccupied at present, being healed at the infirmary. At noon, you are to be located in the Temple for your legal joining. I suggest you not be late."

Vixen's features grew austere. "Trust that I won't be... ma'am."

Adena turned and left the cottage, leaving her to get dressed.

It wasn't long until Vixen traversed the streets. She could feel eyes upon her and hear the whispers. Everyone could mind their own damned business, as far as she was concerned. Coming up to the square, she saw two guards stationed outside the infirmary. Unable to spy what went on within, she spat a curse. She would indeed have to wait to see him.

Vixen decided to go to his cottage instead. As she arrived at the door, she momentarily stopped, her hand planted on the door handle. She looked at it, thinking of how she had instigated their sexual relations, only because she had lusted for the man. Walking inside, she reeled back, a horrendous smell assaulting her nose. It was like death had been present, blood and decay creating a musky and rich scent, overwhelming her senses. As she stepped forward, she saw where the man had been lying; dried blood covered the bed, and the shackles were still left attached to the headboard.

Steeling herself, Vixen clenched her fists. "Whether you like it or not, Edric, I will take care of this... take care of *you*."

⋆⋆

Ascending the front steps of the Temple, Vixen suddenly felt a warmth spreading inside her. She was finally to be with Edric again, and now stand as his wife. It was unfathomable that her stay at the Priesthood had resulted in this, but here she was, ready to pledge herself to a man.

Taking a deep breath, she entered the building. At the altar, she could see Anaya and Adena already present. Looking around the room for Edric, she found him sitting on a chair along the wall. He leaned back, his head slumped against the stone behind him.

"Come forward, Vixen!" Anaya called out to her. "If we are all present, we might as well begin." She went to fetch the High Priest, who emerged from the conference room.

"Ah, we shall begin then." He motioned to Adena. "Bring Edric."

Adena grunted but followed orders. She nudged the man, attempting to stir him.

Edric's eyes slowly opened, but he remained still.

Adena reached out and grabbed him, pulling him out of the chair. "Get up already," she snapped.

He stumbled, but righted himself, then noticed Vixen in front of him. Having been passed out in his seat, he had not seen or heard her come in.

Her mouth ajar, she stared at him, distressed at how his punishment had affected him. His skin was pale, his face grey. His usually fair hair was crimson with dried blood, and his eyes were red. He winced, staggering forward to place himself beside her, the two of them standing before the High Priest.

"Are we ready to begin?" Ekelon asked.

Edric's knees buckled, but he felt a supporting arm around his waist. It was Vixen, catching him as he was about to fall. She draped his arm over her shoulders, then stood firm, eyes fixed on the High Priest.

"We are, your Holiness," she declared.

Ekelon nodded, then cleared his throat.

"*Dear Mother, we humbly invite Your presence and Your blessings to be upon these two as they enter into the ceremony that will unite them in the bonds of holy matrimony. Impress upon them the solemnness and the impact of their actions today that will influence their lives for eternity.*" He paused, observing the couple. "I ask you now, in the presence of the Goddess and these people, to declare your intention to enter into union with one another through the grace of the Holy Light. Anna Leighton, will you have Edric Ramsey to be your husband, to live together in holy marriage? Will you love him, comfort him, honour and keep him, in sickness and in health, and be forsaking all others, be faithful to him as long as you both shall live?"

Grasping at Edric's hand, Vixen held her head high. "I will."

"Edric Ramsey, will you have Anna Leighton to be your wife, to live together in holy marriage? Will you love her, comfort her, honour and keep her, in sickness and in health, and be forsaking all others, be faithful to her as long as you both shall live?"

"I... will," he forced out, his voice coarse.

The High Priest looked at the small gathering. "Are there any rings to be given as tokens of this union?"

Vixen was about to speak when Anaya darted forward.

"Yes!" the priestess exclaimed. "I almost forgot." She brought out a small box. Opening it, she revealed two simple gold rings, which she handed to Edric and Vixen.

"Very well," the High Priest said, then continued the ceremony. "The wedding ring is the outward and visible symbol of inward and spiritual bond, which unites two loyal hearts in endless love. Edric, will you take Anna's ring and put it on her finger, then repeat after me."

Edric's foot dragged along the stone floor as he pulled back from Vixen. Taking a deep breath, he fought to remain upright. He clasped her left hand, placing the ring on her finger, then repeated the words as the High Priest spoke. "I give this ring... to you, Anna... as a constant reminder of my devotion of love. I dedicate myself in... righteousness, to the pursuit of our mutual good and happiness, and I will...willingly and gladly share with you all that I possess... till death do us part."

Vixen remained silent, droplets gently rolling down her cheeks.

The High Priest faced her. "Anna, will you take Edric's ring and put it on his finger, then repeat after me."

She nodded, wiping her sleeve over her eyes, then followed his lead. "I give this ring to you, Edric, as a constant reminder of my devotion of love. I dedicate myself in righteousness, to the pursuit of our mutual good and happiness, and I willingly and gladly share with you all that I possess, till death do us part."

Ekelon dipped his head. "For as much as Edric and Anna have consented together and pledged their faith to each other in holy wedlock, and have witnessed their vows before the Goddess and Her company of friends and loved ones, and have sealed the same by giving and receiving rings, I therefore, by the authority vested in me as High Priest of the Goddess of Holy Light, pronounce that they are husband and wife. Thus, what the Goddess has joined together, let no man put asunder."

✶ ✶

Kaedin waited outside the Temple, making sure no one would disturb the ceremony. He helped bring Edric back to his cottage, then excused himself as they arrived.

"Your marital home now," he said. "I shall not enter."

"I will... be fine," Edric replied, Vixen helping him up the steps. "Thank you, brother."

243

"Recover now, lad. I shall see you soon." Kaedin turned on his heel and left them.

"Let us go inside," Vixen said, opening the door.

Edric merely nodded. He was truly exhausted, with no strength left to even warn her of the conditions inside. Stepping through the door to his bedroom, he halted. The room was bright, the window shutters open, and the fire was roaring, keeping it warm despite the chill of the outdoors.

"I had to leave the windows open for the air to clear," she explained, moving over to shut them. Darkness fell inside the cottage, but she brought out a piece of burning cinders from the open fireplace and proceeded to light candles spread about the room. In front of the fire, a bathtub had been brought in, as well as several buckets of water.

Edric's eyes flitted around. "What is going on?"

Vixen blushed. "I, um… I have prepared a hot bath for you," she said, leading him to the bed where he sat down. The bed linen was fresh, and she had wiped down the bed frame, not a speck of blood left on it.

"Did you do all this?" he asked.

"Yes. I was released early this morning and came here." She looked around. "Truth be told, I was shocked. I can only imagine the suffering you have gone through… and still are." Her eyes settled on his, glossy in the dim light.

"Anna," he said, grabbing her hand. "Please, don't blame yourself for this. I knew the consequences of my actions."

"Yes, but I was the instigator. But for me, none of this would have happened. And to then force you to marry me…" Tears welled, the woman looking up into the ceiling. "Damn this crying!" she snarled. "I have never cried like this in my life."

He pulled at her hand, the two of them locking eyes. "No matter the way you would have asked me, I would have accepted. Unless… you didn't really want me?"

Vixen laughed through the tears. "Of course I want you! Silly man." She caressed his face, rubbing some dirt off his cheek.

"Good, because now you are stuck with me."

"That is what I wanted all along," she said. "I meant what I said in the Temple. I will cherish and comfort you, *love* you, until death parts us."

Edric blushed, but his smile brightened. "I... I love you too."

The two joined together in a warm and affectionate embrace, kissing thoroughly before they parted.

Looking down at her hand, Vixen examined the gold band. "I can't believe she did this for us," she said.

"Anaya is one of a kind," he chuckled. "It wouldn't surprise me if she went and measured our sizes as we slept."

Vixen laughed. "That is probably true." She wiped her tears away, then motioned Edric to stand.

He groaned, coming to his feet, but he said nothing.

Carefully opening his shirt, she removed it, then undid the thongs on his trousers. As they fell to the floor, he stood naked before her. "Come," she said softly, then led him to the half-filled bath, supporting him as he climbed in. She allowed him to get comfortable while she gathered some bars of soap from the nearby table. Returning, she lifted the first bucket over his head. Slowly emptying it, she allowed it to soak into his hair and run down his face and body. Rubbing one of the soaps between her hands, she used its froth, massaging his head. Water and blood trailed down him, creating a network of small red streams.

"I take it you are fine with being Mistress Ramsey now then?" he asked, leaning back.

Sitting down on a chair behind him, Vixen came forward, gently pulling his head back. Their lips met, the kiss slow and smooth. "I never liked Leighton anyway," she said, releasing him.

Edric laughed. "Happy to hear it."

"I do have to stress the fact that I am truly sorry for what they did to you." Her fingers hovered over the red marks on his back. Even though he had received healing, the days the wounds were left open had resulted in scarring.

"They will fade. I will not deny the fact that flogging is gruelling, but you should not concern yourself with it. What is done is done, and we were equally to blame. Trust that I do not, nor ever will, hold this against you." Edric turned to face her. "As we said; love and cherish, until death does us part."

Vixen blushed, then reached for another bucket. "You are right. Now, let us enjoy the evening. Close your eyes."

Having prepared a light meal, the couple ate after the bath was done with. Then they lay in bed and spent their first night together as husband and wife, sleeping in each other's arms.

It took several days for the priests to reach the mines. They camped not far from the site, together with Rick and Eli, after which they split up at daybreak. They planned to rejoin at noon, not expecting either mission to be particularly lengthy. Like the previous time, they had a wagon available to bring any demon corpses back for the High Priest.

Taking the lead, Anaya had her party follow the dirt road towards the mines. This time, both Michael and the disciple Bran used a bow and arrow. She motioned for them to ready themselves as they neared the cave mouth.

Around the corner, there were indeed demons present. However, they stood guard at the opening to the mines, not leisurely sitting around a campfire. Anaya's brow drew together, a knot forming in her stomach. Something was wrong.

The arrows lanced through the air, hitting their marks, and the demons slumped to the ground.

As the priests remained still for a moment, all was quiet.

Michael flinched. "Was that it?" he questioned, looking back at the others.

"I am not so sure," Anaya said, her voice level. "Keep your guard up." An eerie silence enveloped the crew as she led them out into the open, stopping in front of the mine entrance.

Dark mists suddenly exploded from the mines, immediately covering the surrounding area. The priests couldn't discern anything through the blackness, but their bodies shook violently, an immense fear rippling through them. The demonic aura was strong, much more so than that of the wasp Prime.

Chanting, Anaya created a defensive sphere around herself and the others. "Ready yourselves!" she bellowed. "Focus your Light!"

An enormous black and green, heavily scaled tail came swinging through the mists. Cutting through the Light around them, it tore through Scott. The appendage smashed into his body, ripping it apart, his intestines hurtling towards the other priests. In a whoosh of towering mist, a leg came crashing down, crushing Joseph under its weight.

As the remaining priests scrambled to get away, the Prime charged, massive jaws and fangs flashing in the air. The mouth closed over the disciple, crunching down on his flesh and bones in a sickening squelch.

With the mists finally settling along the ground, the priests could see what they were up against. Like a dragon from the fairy tales, the demon's body was covered in scales, long spikes running along its back. It stared at them, eyes agleam, and a forked tongue darted from its mouth as it hissed. Then, the Prime spun, its tail once more whipping towards them.

"Run!" Anaya shouted, but it was too late. The tail shredded through Michael, then slammed into her. She flew through the air, coming to a stop against a tree. Having cracked her head against the stem, she slumped to the ground, struggling to regain her bearings. She rolled to her stomach, then pushed herself up to her hands and knees. Desperate to escape, she clawed at the undergrowth, but lost her footing, tumbling down a short slope along the Atua river. Unable to stop herself, she bounded over the edge, fully submerging into the water.

For a moment, all was quiet, almost... serene, the gushing water seemingly washing away her pain. A large gash in her head left a red trail of blood along the surface, the claret swirling downstream with the current. Realising she needed to breathe, Anaya managed to breach the water, then desperately gasped for air.

The nearby vegetation shook, trees creaking and breaking as the demon hissed. It was looking for her.

Anaya struggled to crawl along the ground, her elbows digging into the dirt beneath her. Whispering an enchantment, she managed to heal herself enough to get back on her feet.

Now running, she headed down the riverbank, trying to escape. A tree suddenly crashed to the ground behind her, the Prime emerging within moments. It had found her. The black mists burst out around them, then Anaya was batted aside and sent flying yet again.

Landing uphill, she found herself back in the clearing outside the mine entrance. She lay still for a moment, her thoughts the only thing keeping her strong. *Stay awake. Stay conscious. Live. I must live.*

Anaya dragged herself along the ground, dazed and unable to focus, darkness edging her vision. She tried to locate the other priests, grasping at anything to traverse the terrain.

Bodies. She could see bodies scattered around her. A severed arm laid as a deserted island in a pool of blood, only feet away from her. Her eyes welled up with tears. *Is this the end?* Feeling her body lifting from the ground, she found herself flung again into the stem of a tree. But this time, she felt no pain – only numbness. The world around her dimmed with every passing moment, and she readied herself for the final strike.

A roar. Like a beastly, raving, gut-wrenching scream. Anaya could barely see anything anymore. Teeth. Claws. Fur. Blood. *Am I dead now?* All went dark.

26

SPAWN OF DARKNESS

L enda sat alone as she finished her dinner. Most priests were still away on their individual missions, and Edric and Vixen mainly kept to themselves. The day was warm, so Lenda had spread a blanket out on the ground outside the stables. It had been a long day, but she was to enjoy the evening with a new book on herbalism.

Finished with her soup, she unexpectedly froze, the skin on her arms turning to gooseflesh. Her bowl slid from her grasp, the young girl unable to keep her hands from trembling. Her mouth fell open as she watched a demon carelessly walking through the entrance to the Temple village. His pale skin and dark hair stood out like snow in summer, and his immense demonic aura whirled around him, creating a thick black mist. It billowed out, covering the ground like an unholy tidal wave.

Despite the distance, Lenda felt herself shaking, paralysed in fear. Even as she spotted her dearest friend thrown over his shoulder, she couldn't utter a single word.

The demon stopped, peering at her. "You! Where is the infirmary?" he shouted.

Still frozen in terror, Lenda could not mouth a reply.

"ANSWER ME, GIRL!"

His overwhelmingly powerful voice snapped her out of her state of immobility, the girl instantly dashing into a sprint. "Come this way!" she called, grasping at her skirt as to not stumble on it. She felt chills running down her back, hearing his footfalls behind her, knowing he was undoubtedly gaining on her. But strangely enough, all the fear was gone, now replaced with the urgency to give Anaya the care she so desperately needed.

Lenda gulped down a breath, unable to spot a single priest in the village. Of all the days for the streets to be deserted, this had to be the day.

Entering the infirmary, Lenda found it empty as well, all the healers having left for the day. She pointed to the nearest bed. "Place her there!" Without watching him, she immediately started preparing her prayer beads, wrapping them around her wrist. "What has happened to her?" Joining the couple, she chanted a few words, Light forming around her hands and arms. Allowing the magic to envelop Anaya's body, Lenda worked diligently, cuts, wounds, and bruises gradually disappearing.

The demon shifted from one foot to the other, dragging a hand through his hair. "She has been tail swiped by an iguana Prime, hit straight into a tree and was knocked unconscious. I have not had time to stop and look; I just came straight here." He stood close to the bed, his expression tight as he gazed down at Anaya's battered body.

"I can sense no inner bleeding," Lenda told him, then paused over Anaya's head. "No trauma to her brain, only concussion. With enough healing and rest, she should pull through."

Expelling a breath, the demon let his arms drop, the intensity of his aura slowly lessening. "I'm glad to-"

"Demon! Come out this instant, you foul spawn of Darkness!" boomed from outside the infirmary. The voice was clear as day, strong and righteous. It was the High Priest himself. "I will not let you leave this place if you take the women hostage!"

The demon had a last look at Anaya, his eyebrows tightly drawn together. "Take care of her." He turned, then exited through the front door of the cottage, forced to duck through the low opening. "Hostage? Who do you take me for?"

The High Priest stood underneath the great oak. He had gathered quite a large crowd of priests around him. "Why a filthy demon, of course!" he spat. "You are capable of *anything*, no matter how despicable."

With the aura dampened, the priests no longer felt the fear as when the demon had entered the village.

"If you come with us of free will, we shall grant you a swift death," the High Priest continued.

The demon forced a laugh. "Really? Is that how it is now? No 'hunt only if the demon has wronged?' You really think I would have brought your dear priestess back if I were indeed the one who caused her harm?"

A hum of whispers spread amongst the priests.

"Silence!" Ekelon demanded. "You have wronged by merely walking onto our sacred grounds, not to mention what wounds you most likely inflicted on poor Anaya."

The demon's eyes narrowed. "Perhaps you are but jealous of the fact I got to hold her?"

The High Priest's face went grey, his mouth opening.

"To touch her," the demon continued. "The soft skin. Her sweet scent." He licked his lips. "Do you wish to take her as your own?"

Ekelon's eyes bulged as he took a step forward. "You bastard!" he cried, the priests around him retreating a step, taken aback by his lost composure. He reached up, chanting for only seconds, then brought his hands back down. A massive cage of Light formed above the demon, slamming down to encase him. "You will suffer for this!"

✴ ✴

Secured to the cavern wall, the demon had been shackled with handcuffs made from Light alone. Satisfied he wouldn't be able to escape, the High Priest motioned his guards to step aside, then let the cage disperse around his new prisoner.

The demon scrutinised his surroundings. "Nice room you have here. A lot of souvenirs, I see."

Ekelon glanced at the guards. "Everyone, leave us," he demanded. "Now!"

The priests initially looked at each other, then quickly retreated.

"Now then, *demon...*" Ekelon began to slowly pace the room. "I shall enjoy this, truly. You are indeed a fine specimen."

"Wait, are you just going to torture me? No questions?" Samael's flat voice mirrored his emotionless expression, his gaze tracking the High Priest. "How very disappointing."

"Silence, demon!" His face red, Ekelon reached for a nearby whip, immediately infusing it with Light. He swung the weapon, lashing at the demon, the enchanted leather rippling across his torso. Standing back, the High Priest swallowed a breath. To his surprise, and to further anger him, he got no reaction. "You will suffer for your insolence!" he shouted, whipping the demon again, then again. But still no sounds. No groans, no words, and certainly no pleads for mercy. Veins bulging on his neck, the High Priest lashed until he was out of breath, the whip sliding out of his hand.

"Is that all you have?" the demon taunted him. "Is that all the power you can muster?"

Flexing his fingers, Ekelon unleashed his magic, Light shimmering around his hands. "You will beg for your life before I am done, demon. *Beg* for it!" He came forward, blasting the demon's chest, sending him rearing into the back wall. "See, even *you* have your limits. And I *will* find them."

"Lenda?" Anaya whispered, straining to open her eyes. In the distance, she thought she had seen the girl's silhouette.

"Anaya!" Lenda threw herself over the bed, hugging the now conscious woman. "You are finally awake! You have been sleeping for hours."

An emptiness clutched hold of Anaya's inner, her stomach churning. "The others? Where are the others?"

Lenda shook her head. "We have sent a search party out for them, but it does not look good. It will take at least a day to reach them, even if they take the mountain pass."

Tears welled in Anaya's eyes. "But how... how did I make it?"

"A demon. He just walked straight into the village, carrying you and asking for the infirmary. I was at first completely frozen in fear... due to his aura, but my mind cleared. He has since been captured. The High Priest is questioning him now as to what he did to all of you."

Anaya stared at her. "What? What he did? What did he look like?"

"Oh, he was something to behold. He must have been around seven feet tall, with long black hair, and wearing a fur cloak."

Clawing at the bed, Anaya attempted to sit, but found no purchase. "Oh no, I have to-" Grasping at Lenda's dress, she felt faint, and the room spun around her. She struggled to remain upright, praying she would not pass out. Her mind screamed for Samael, then darkness claimed her once more.

"Hush, dear sister," Lenda soothed, gently caressing Anaya's forehead. "Do not worry about a mere demon." She pulled the covers over her, then left to relay her status to the High Priest.

"Your Holiness!" a voice echoed from the cave entrance. The sound had Ekelon halt, and he held his whip back as he listened. "The scouts who travelled with Anaya's group have returned with grim news!"

Ekelon held the weapon up to his face, allowing the dark demon's blood to touch his skin, then moistened his lips. "How unfortunate to have to pause in the middle of all the fun we are having, demon."

The demon glared at him, but remained silent.

Placing the whip on the table, the High Priest rolled his shoulders back. "I will return shortly." He walked out of the cavern, then across to the Temple. They had gathered around the altar under the statue of the Goddess.

Scraping a hand over his head, Rick stepped forward. "While Eli and I were busy scouting for the assignment close to the Stricker mines, we heard screams and shouting. We hurried over there, but by the time we got there… none of the other priests had survived, and Anaya was missing. It was a horrible sight." He stared at the floor, placing a hand over his mouth. Standing silently, he despondently shook his head.

"A… a lizard demon also lay dead, an iguana, the creature much larger than anything I have ever seen. We hurried along the mountain trail to get back as soon as possible."

His eyes round, the High Priest threw his arms out. "I knew it! It was that scum of a demon who did this to them! Surely, as they fought against the iguana, he took advantage by attacking them from behind! Then to come here and continue his taunts, bringing Anaya with him… For all accounts, he looks to be a panther demon. The most *hellish* of demons!" He slammed his fist onto the table, cracks appearing in the wood.

Rick visibly swallowed. "Your Holiness," he said softly, "I must, unfortunately, disagree on this statement."

The High Priest stared at him. "Speak then!"

"Well, you see… The iguana demon looked to have been killed by claws and fangs, not by our means. So, if this is indeed a panther demon, as you say, then would it not be more plausible that he might have saved Anaya?"

"Lies!" the High Priest shouted, spit flying through the air. "These beings are incapable of such acts. It goes against every fibre of their being! I will *torture* the answer out of him. I *will* get to the bottom of this!" He turned on his heel, his face flushed in anger as he stormed out the side entrance of the Temple.

Outside the front doors, Lenda felt a coldness seep into her bones. She had initially not wanted to interrupt the conversation, waiting for her turn to enter, but then found herself shocked at what had been said. Moving around to the corner of the Temple, she watched the High Priest as he traversed the gardens, heading for the cavern.

⁎⁎

Descending into the grotto, Ekelon felt a sense of calm wash over him, laying eyes on the shackled demon. He took a deep breath, relishing the smell of fresh blood. Retrieving his whip, he resumed position before the prisoner, then suddenly blanched.

There was not a single wound left on the demon's body, only faint welts showing through the ripped shirt. A wicked grin snaked across his features. "Welcome back, *your Holiness*."

Pursing his lips, Ekelon tightened his grip on the whip handle, then held the weapon up across his shoulder. "You know, these are the things that make life worth living. I will wipe that smug look off your face, soon enough." With that, he resumed his lashings on the demon.

His fangs gleaming in the flickering torchlight, Samael smiled. He breathed heavily, having been severely beaten. His shirt was all but torn to shreds, blood pooling beneath him. "Are you done yet, old man?" He continued to taunt the High Priest with every breath.

The whip ripped across the demon's body as the High Priest spat a round of curses. "If I so have to keep you locked away for eternity, the lashings shall never seize!"

"Eternity?" Samael questioned, an eyebrow raised. "I'm afraid I cannot spare you that amount of time. I would advise releasing me, or I will have to force my way out."

"Ha! I have fought your kind before. And guess who made it out alive?"

Samael's eyes narrowed. "I am not as merciful as my father."

"Mercy has nothing to do with it. All is allowed in *war*." The High Priest hefted his whip again, lashing the demon, blood sent spraying across the nearby walls. As he made a second swing, his arm suddenly stopped midair. He felt pressure around his wrist, the demon squeezing it tight.

Samael had pulled himself free from his bonds, hauling the High Priest in. He exposed his fangs, bringing forth a thunderous growl.

"I'm not wasting any more of my time." Throwing the old man aside, he stalked away towards the exit.

Ekelon quickly rose, then chanted resolutely, Light filling the entire cavern. Gleaming bars emerged, blocking the entrance. "You will not escape, demon! Come and face me!"

"That's it! **YOU HAVE FORCED MY HAND, PRIEST.**" Samael grabbed at the bars, his black mists spewing from his hands, shattering the barrier. The aura grew increasingly stronger, sending the mists flaring out around him.

Two guards stood shaking by the exit, unable to lift their gaze as he strode past.

The High Priest cursed, running after the demon. He hurried through the Temple gardens, catching up with him as he reached the great oak in the square.

Black smoke billowed around Samael, all priests around him frozen in fear.

"I will not let you get away with this, demon!" Ekelon yelled, barrelling towards him. Light shot out from his hands, sparks flickering through the air as the magic slammed into the demon's back.

Samael grunted, then instantly turned, stepping in to clutch hold of the High Priest's throat. He lifted him away from the ground, viciously snarling. "You are like a bad smell, *your Holiness*. I would suggest you leave-" Unable to finish the sentence, Samael momentarily felt all power leave him, his blood running cold. Staggering forward, he dropped the old man, a ferocious pain erupting from his core. Looking down, his eyes fell upon an arrow protruding from his chest. He lifted his gaze back up, spying a single priest on the other side of the square, who held a bow with trembling hands.

The chilling sensation spread throughout his body, and, for the very first time, Samael felt as if his life was trickling away.

In an explosion of dark mists, the sound of cracking bones rang out. Priests around the square threw themselves onto the ground, few able to lift their gaze as an enormous black feline rose from the fear-inducing smoke. Larger than a horse, its paws were spread wide, and its long claws scraped against the paved surface on which it stood. In an instant, the beast took off, sprinting towards the Eastern forest.

Ekelon pushed himself upright, chanting as his light spread around him, dispersing the mists. He locked arms with one of the priests, helping him to stand. Reaching out to another, he halted, hearing shouts echoing from the east. As the frantic voice grew louder, a young disciple emerged, running along the road.

"Help!" he screamed. "Demons are attacking!" He stumbled forward, slamming onto the ground, a black iguana locking its jaws over his head. With the maw snapping shut, the demon crushed his skull, and more iguanas appeared in the distance, hissing and shrieking.

27

DESTINY

L ight spread around Ekelon, crackling with potency. He wasted no time meeting the demons in their charge, slaying them one by one. Within moments, three of the lizards lay dead, the man stopping a fourth as it pounced. The incinerated corpse crashed beside him.

"We demand the whereabouts of the Prime killer!" one of the beasts hissed. Its red tongue darted as it slowly gained on Ekelon.

"We already know you are colluding with the panthers. Now prepare to die!" As his foot hit the ground, the High Priest's Light whooshed out, searing the oncoming demons.

The road suddenly milled with priests, all coming to the defence of their village. Arrows hissed past, slamming into several iguanas. Edric stepped forward, readying another shaft.

Vixen bolted past the High Priest, her sword instantly licking out. She slashed through a lizard, then backhanded another. Rolling under a tail swipe, she came up beside the demon, stabbing her blade into its head.

Wiping the sweat from his forehead, Edric followed the woman's onslaught. She spared no expense, fighting ruthlessly as she left a trail of dead demons behind her.

She had heard the commotion from their house, only grabbing her sword on her way out.

Another tail swung around, and Vixen brought her blade up to block it. Yet the hit was heavy, sending her flying backwards.

Out of arrows, Edric discarded his bow. He drew his sword, lunging at the demon, driving the weapon deep into the creature's head. He spun as another jumped for him, his blade flashing up through its chest.

Another wave of Light swept across the ground, demons writhing in front of the priests. Ekelon came forward, pushing it further as he intensified the enchantment. *"We drive you from us, whoever you may be, unclean spirits and all demonic powers; all hellish invaders, all wicked legions, assemblies and tribes. Tremble before the mighty Goddess; the Light that broke the Dark prison walls asunder and led souls forth into Salvation."* The Light whirled into a tempest, driving through the throng of iguanas. "The Light shall prevail!"

Anaya slowly opened her eyes. "Lenda?" she asked.

"Anaya! Finally, you are awake again. It is almost sunset now." Lenda turned away from the window, coming to the priestess' side. "Let me help you sit."

Bringing her legs over the edge of the bed, Anaya rubbed a hand over her forehead. "I feel as if I've been smashed under a boulder," she groaned, allowing her pressured touch to travel across her temple.

"You had so many bruises... It was hard to find and heal them all, even for me," Lenda admitted. "But you will be fine; I'll make sure of it." Her eyes flitted towards the window, then back again.

Frowning, Anaya watched her intently. "What is going on?"

"The village... we're under attack."

Anaya blanched. "Under attack?"

"Yes. As soon as Edric shot that other demon and he fled, then all these lizards came out of nowhere. The High Priest seems to think they are in allegiance with each other, but he has since managed to push them back. I can no longer see them fighting."

"Edric did what? What demon?"

"The demon who brought you here," Lenda explained. "He broke free but was shot, after which he transformed and escaped. I have never felt such fear. I could hardly lift my head high enough to see what was going on, and that was from in here."

"No!" Anaya blurted out, instantly covering her mouth. "I need to see the others!" She heaved herself out of bed, staggering before she managed to right herself.

Lenda came forward, grabbing her arm. "You need to be careful. You still have to recover!"

"There is no time for that, sister. Now, let me go." Anaya twisted free from her grip, then rushed out the door, ignoring her wobbling knees. She knew time was of the essence. Even if Edric had been shaking at the time, his aim would still be true. Samael had to be found.

Running through the village, Anaya saw dead bodies littering the streets. Most were demons, but there were also priests. Ekelon stood with a large gathering further up in the north-eastern district, Edric and Vixen among them. They were piling up corpses, so the fighting must have already ended.

Pulling her prayer beads over her head, Anaya wrapped them around her lower arm. As she reached the far side of the stream, she cast her tracking spell, instantly finding Samael's prints in the under-growth. They were deep and spread far apart, so the demon had most likely travelled at high speed. Stepping forward, she felt something slick underneath her foot. With another enchantment, she created a small sphere of Light to illuminate the area.

It was blood, the thick liquid still warm to the touch. Samael was indeed injured. Anaya ran as fast as she could, in a desperate attempt to find him.

Darkness had fallen by the time Anaya noticed the imprints slowly narrowing. *He's running out of strength,* she thought, swallowing hard. She felt sick thinking about the staggering amount of blood along the trail. As the splotches of claret led up the mountainside, Anaya cautiously approached the rockface. A shiver rippled down her back, the priestess sensing a potent demonic aura nearby. Looking up, she saw dark mists rolling out from a cave mouth, the trickle of fog resembling the cascade of a waterfall.

Carefully climbing along the rough surface, Anaya began to shake as she closed in on the opening. She had to focus not to succumb to the fear, gritting her teeth. Inhaling deeply, she silently peeked above the ledge, as to not make a sound. But despite her best efforts, she gasped as she saw him.

On the stone floor in front of her, lay the badly wounded demon. His fur cloak had been left in a heap beside him, Samael having collapsed only a stride further into the cave.

His breathing strained and coarse, Samael had a hand resting on his chest. His bloodied shirt was merely held together by a few threads, and the mist dampened with every passing second. He could hear Anaya approach, but he had no strength left to look at her. A gurgling noise erupted from his throat, his rasping breaths turning into coughs. Blood spilt from his mouth, choking him.

Anaya ran forward to help lay him on his side, then gently placed his head upon her lap. Unable to speak, the demon merely looked up at her with bloodshot eyes.

He was dying.

Anaya's eyes welled with tears, a lump forming in her throat. "Samael, I am so sorry... I will do my best to help you," she whispered, her voice on the verge of breaking. "Oh, dear Goddess, guide my hands. Let Your divine ascendancy heal this child of Darkness, as it does those of Light." She started chanting, fighting against her emotions as to not distort the spell.

Light enveloped the couple, the shimmer whirling out across the demon, healing wounds and burns all over his body. His breathing slowed, and he closed his eyes. A faint smile was hinted in his expression, almost as if he was enjoying the moment. As the Light dispersed, he had fallen unconscious.

Remaining by his side, Anaya carefully removed the remnants of his shirt to inspect the wound. Only a red mark was left in its place, just below the heart. The head of a blessed arrow fell to the floor as she pulled the fabric free, likely driven out of his body when the flesh fused. Picking it up, she recognised it as one of Edric's.

It was all as Lenda had said. The arrowhead would have killed him in the end, searing him from the inside.

Using the torn garment, Anaya gently cleaned Samael's cheek, removing the blood. She brushed her fingers across his powerful chest, feeling the shapes of several old scars. Grinning to herself, she wondered how he might have acquired them, every single one telling tales of his past. Reaching his collarbone, she noticed him gazing back at her.

"They are from..." He winced, shifting his position. "When I was young... before my self-healing was strong enough to avoid scarring."

She blushed, her smile growing.

"I am in... your debt, priestess."

Brushing hair away from his face, she lightly caressed him. "No," she said. "I believe we are even now. Especially since it's the *second* time you saved me."

He chuckled, but the sound twisted into a groan as he pressed his hand against his ribs. "I suppose... you are right." He looked at ease, resting his head on her lap. With Anaya's hand still on his chest, he grabbed it with both of his, then held it tightly. "But I... still feel the need to thank you. Had anyone else from the Priesthood come after me... I would have perished by now."

She offered him another smile. "Samael, I know not why the Goddess made our paths cross, but it cannot be because we were destined to end one another." Folding his shirt, she placed it underneath his head. She moved back in order to stand, but her head violently spun. She was lightheaded; her already weakened state further drained of energy from her healing spell. She slumped down, falling over him, the demon grunting as her chest pressed against his.

Their faces were now closer than they had ever been.

Samael's expression softened as he locked eyes with her. Gazing up at her, he reached behind her neck, gently guiding her in.

Their foreheads touched for a moment, and Anaya closed her eyes, slowly exhaling. She felt a thrilling heat inside her, a throbbing sensation travelling through her body as she longed for his show of affection.

Samael pressed his lips against hers, the two of them joining up in a slow, smooth kiss. It felt like the most natural thing, their mouths eagerly uniting as they revelled in each other's energies. Wrapping his arm around her, Samael ushered them on, deepening their contact. Her mouth opened, their tongues briefly meeting, as if testing the connection. The passion intensified as they entwined, lovingly brushing against one another. It was unlike anything Anaya had ever experienced, the fluttering inside her turning into a burning flame. Unsure of where it would lead, she opened her eyes, and their lips parted.

Removing herself from him, she felt him tense, but he said nothing. She held a hand to her mouth, leaning against the cavern wall, then backed away. After only a few steps, she spun and descended the mountain, leaving Samael behind.

28

TO BLOODY ONE'S SWORD

T he High Priest had urgently ordered for increased defences. A high wooden wall was erected around the perimeter of the Temple village, enhanced with magical runes and spells to deter demons from coming in. An alarm system would also be triggered, sending a signal high into the sky, should any demon approach. The enchantments would need to be renewed regularly, but it was worth the effort. The wall was only weeks from completion.

Ekelon was determined to never again make the same mistake.

Standing inside the interrogation cave, he worked away at the recently brought in body parts of the iguana Prime. The scouts sent out to retrieve them had managed to bring the head, most of the organs, a leg, and the tip of its tail. Anything more than that, and the horses would not have been able to pull the wagon along. The demon was too large.

Primes being scarce, the High Priest was happy with what he could get his hands on. He would attempt to enhance his brew further, now using the Prime. He was confident that their strength would be the key.

Despite his collection of iguana demons, including both dead and live ones, he had dispatched Kaedin and Adena to procure more material. They had scouted out a fox den only a day away from the

Temple village and, with a bit of luck, that would also include a Prime.

Placing his knife down on the table, Ekelon stepped away from the remains of the iguana Prime. He cursed, thinking about how easily the panther demon had pulled himself free, the power of his aura genuinely unforeseen. He needed to create something which dulled the fear-inducing effects, so his priests would not feel such despair. Either as a potion to be drunk before combat, or perhaps something to disperse the mists. It was something worth pondering about, the solution not as straightforward as Ekelon would have wished. With the added need to try such a concoction on live demons, he instructed his officers to bring any and all home, should they be given the opportunity.

A dull ache developed in his back. The High Priest was no longer used to the pains of ageing, regularly ingesting the renewal elixirs he had designed. He walked over to the shelves and brought one down. Infusing it with Light, more so than before, he quickly devoured it, feeling the effects almost instantaneously. He let out a sigh of relief, as he could now get back to his work.

Lenda took a deep breath. The air felt fresh and crisp, being the end of October. Seated at the back of the Temple, she was amongst the first to step out as the morning prayers concluded. It was still dark outside, the streets lit with small orbs of Light.

Eden joined her, placing an arm around her waist. "Waiting for Anaya, miss?" he asked.

Her dimples showing, she nodded. They were meant to have breakfast together.

Anaya emerged through the doors, grinning wide as she stretched. Her eyes bright, and her cheeks rosy, she seemed to have recovered well. Spotting Lenda through the train of priests, she pushed herself past them. "Ah, there you are, sister," she beamed.

"You will have to excuse us, Eden," Lenda told him, turning around to embrace him. She felt her chin lifting from a soft push of his knuckles, then he leaned in for a kiss.

"I am off to practice. I shall see you later, miss. And good day to you, ma'am." He waved at both of them, then headed off towards the Proving Grounds.

As the two girls got comfortable inside Anaya's cottage, Lenda brought out a basket of food she had prepared earlier that morning. "How are you faring, sister?" she asked.

"I believe I am recuperating nicely," Anaya answered. "I have probably never felt so good in my life." Her face warmed, unable to release its smile.

"You do seem awfully happy lately. Has something happened I should know about?" Lenda leaned across the table, seeking eye contact with her.

Anaya blushed, her cheeks burning. "Oh, no, nothing like that!" She waved her hand, shielding her face.

"If you say so... You just remind me of myself whenever I am around Eden." Lenda laughed. "He makes me giggle about anything."

"I can imagine he does." Anaya's thoughts drifted, and she found herself thinking of Samael, a flutter emerging in her belly. She reminisced about their time in the orchard, how he had chased her, and their talk when he detailed his observations about herself. Then there was his brilliant smile, so genuine and contradictory to the rest of his personality. Emotions flared within a moment, the pulsating sensation returning as she recalled their sensuous kiss, and the desire raised by his touch. What might have happened... had she not left? And where would it lead now? He was, indeed, something else.

Lenda tilted her head. "A copper for your thoughts, sister," she asked.

Cradling her drink, Anaya watched the ripples on the surface of the water. "Maybe some other time," she said. "I want to know something about you instead. How is your new work coming along?"

"As Head of Midwifery, you mean?"

Since Samael's alleged attack on the village, Lenda had received another promotion, this time for her bravery in healing Anaya despite the demon's presence. Officially no longer of Junior position, she had taken on an area of responsibility within the infirmary.

"Yes," Anaya said.

"It is coming along, I suppose. I am young, and obviously have no children of my own, so I have a lot to learn, but no one else really wanted the position. The expectant mothers seem to like me, though, which is a relief." Lenda scratched her head in thought. "It is a bit surprising how quickly my reputation has spread. Some know me by name as they arrive now."

Anaya laughed. "I'm not surprised at all, dear sister. You have a gentle heart, which I am sure they all receive a piece of as they are under your care."

Lenda's cheeks turned scarlet. "Maybe so. I only do my best." Taking another bite of her food, she was quiet for a moment, then locked eyes with the priestess. "I have something of importance to ask you."

"Oh? What might that be, sister?"

"The demon."

The colour drained from Anaya's face. She slipped into complete silence, as if unable to move, but her mind raced as to what her friend might want to know.

"He... acted strangely."

Anaya feigned a chuckle, rubbing at her neck. "Strangely? In what way can a demon act strangely?"

"Well, first of all, it is the fact that he brought you here." Lenda paused, watching her intently for any reaction to her words. "He obviously rescued you, most likely injuring himself in the process. Then proceeded to risk his life yet again by bringing you here, only in an effort to save you." She noted Anaya's increasingly softened expression, and that her mouth slowly opened. "As he had lowered you on the bed, he would not leave your side. He showed great concern for your wellbeing, Anaya. Who is he? Do you know him?"

Biting at her lip, Anaya sat in silence, her gaze dropping. The description of his actions seemed unreal. Had he really done all those things? Followed by their shared closeness after she had healed him, it made her wonder. Did he perhaps... *love* her?

"Anaya, please. You need to tell me," Lenda pressed her.

"I..." Anaya was lost for words, her mouth unable to create the sounds. She shook her head, staring down at her hands. "I do know him," she finally admitted.

"I had the feeling, which is why I am asking you. I have told no one, however. Not even Eden. Whatever relations you have with him, your secret is safe with me."

Her face reddening once more, Anaya clutched a firm hold of her mug. "I am in no relations with him!" she exclaimed. "None whatsoever! I... I merely know him as an acquaintance. We have met on a few occasions, in the forest, speaking only briefly. I reckoned he wanted information about the Priesthood, so I played along... to do the same to him."

Lenda's eyes narrowed briefly, but she nodded, accepting the answer. "I see. And he just happened to be nearby while you were attacked by the iguana demon?"

"I don't know where he could have come from. The mines are far away from anywhere we've previously seen each other." Anaya questioned it herself, how he had possibly known of her whereabouts. "Please, Lenda. I wish not to speak about this anymore. It is still too raw." She felt her eyes watering, images from the fight appearing in her mind.

Lenda gifted her a comforting smile. "Of course, sister. I am sorry to have pushed it so far."

"It is of no concern. My spirit will heal in time."

The funeral for those lost to the iguanas had taken place only days earlier, all members of the Priesthood sobbing as the High Priest spoke of each of the fallen. He had said it was in the name of the Goddess, as part of Her divine plan. It gave comfort, but also raised even more questions.

"I have to ask, though... about the demon's behaviour," Lenda said, her fingers wrapping around her mug. "If... if demons are – as everyone says – incapable of compassion, then how come he saved you?"

Anaya found herself stumped once more. She had thought about this so many times while getting to know Samael. Even if he wasn't the most attentive of creatures, he clearly had a wider spectrum of emotions than what the priests were taught, especially judging from his ability to save and care for herself. "I do not know," she answered. "I fear there is more to demons than we think." She sighed heavily, peering out the window. "I stress the fact that this has to stay between us... but I am in more doubt now than I have ever been. I dread the path we are heading down."

Placing her hand on Anaya's, Lenda held it tightly. "No matter what happens, we have each other, sister."

Anaya nodded, then the two of them finished their meal in silence. "Perhaps a change of subject?" she suggested, wishing for a more cheerful prospect to be discussed.

"What might that be then?" Lenda inquired.

"Your wedding, of course. When is it to be held? Have you made arrangements yet?"

Lenda smiled shyly, looking away. "We have. We are to be married on the morning of the Winter Solstice."

"How lovely," Anaya said. "We shall go visit with Benjamin. He will make you the most exquisite of dresses."

Raising his shield, Kaedin blocked the oncoming attack, bashing the fox demon aside. Bringing his sword down, he cleaved through its flesh. He had already killed several of the beasts, and ensnared another within a net of Light. Rick and Eli pulled it away, out of the battlefield with the hopes of bringing it back alive.

Adena was occupied with their main target – the fox Prime.

It was more than three times the size of the others, lighter in colour and with a greatly elongated tail. The beast pounced again, crashing down over her sword, its claws curling around the blade. Unable to hold its weight, she dropped her weapon and swerved, avoiding its snapping jaws.

As Adena moved out of the way, Leo released an arrow into the Prime, the projectile digging into its neck. As he readied another one, he could hear creaking from the branches above him. Hurtling down over him was another demon, its teeth sinking into his shoulder. He screamed as it tore through his flesh, ripping a chunk away as it leapt to the ground.

Blood fountained from his severed jugular, the priest desperately clutching around his neck to stem the bleeding.

Light whirled out as Rheas hurried forward, his enchantment swirling around the injured man.

Adena charged, thrusting her sword through the demon's head, ending its life. Turning back towards the Prime, she hurled a sphere of Light, forcing the beast to retreat. She infused her weapon, the blade glistening as she advanced. Hacking away at the Prime, she seared through its flesh.

Screeching, the Prime increased its dark mists, flooding the nearby undergrowth, then bolted for its den. It staggered along the way, crashing into Kaedin's group.

Rick was knocked off his feet, but Eli skittered away, taking a defensive stance.

"This is it, demon!" Kaedin shouted, his sword pointed at the beast. "Surrender, and we will grant you a swift death!"

"THERE WILL BE NO END TO US. YOUR PRIESTHOOD IS DOOMED TO FAIL." Standing over Rick, the Prime sunk its claws into his chest, dark mists spewing out. But before it could end the priest's life, it ducked, dashing towards Eli, arrows flashing past as they missed their target.

Kaedin pushed Eli aside, receiving the brunt of the force himself. Thrown back by the blow, he slammed into the ground, losing hold of his sword. The Prime furiously roared, its mouth closing around the man's armoured head. In a shower of blood, it sagged over Kaedin, the limp creature weighing him down.

Adena pulled her sword clear from the severed head of the Prime, then helped to roll it over. "Are you losing your touch, old man?" she asked, offering Kaedin a hand.

"Aye, I believe I am," he replied, accepting it. Back on his feet, he removed his helmet, then looked at Rick. "How are your injuries?"

"Fine, sir. They were not deep enough to puncture a lung, so I managed to heal them."

"What about your group, Adena?" Kaedin asked.

"Leo has lost a lot of blood, but he should pull through," she said. Walking up to Kaedin's sword, she grabbed the weapon, then handed it to him. "We need to make sure the den is empty before we leave. The rest can stay and load up the corpse of the Prime."

Kaedin followed her into a narrow underground tunnel. They soon reached a spacious opening; a system of corridors and rooms dug out into the soil. There were furniture and belongings set along the walls, including clothing, food, and toys.

Taking the lead, Adena made sure to clear the rooms for any survivors. As they entered the last one, a small door at the end of a hallway, it creaked open. Inside, a young woman sat huddled up in the corner with two children, both only a few years of age.

Kaedin instantly halted, looking at Adena, then back at the demons. They all emanated a demonic aura, but were in human form.

The woman had long ginger hair and peered at them with green eyes. "Please, at least let the children go," she begged.

Flicking her hand, Adena motioned Kaedin forward, but he stood firm.

"I may be the killer of many things, Adena, but women and children are not amongst them," he said, spinning on his heel.

She followed him, grabbing his cloak. "This is the order we have been given, Kaedin. We are to *clear* the den."

He looked back at her, his face stern. "I'll take whatever punishment it might lead to, but I am not to bloody my sword on defenceless women and children." He snatched his mantle out of her grip, then disappeared out of the den.

✶ ✶

The party of priests soon finished loading their cargo onto the wagon, including their live fox demon, carefully bound.

Adena emerged from the den. She held her sword up, wiping the blood off the blade.

Averting his gaze, Kaedin shook his head, then hauled himself up onto his mount.

About to join the crew, Adena halted, a feeling of sickness washing over her. She walked away from the others, grabbing a tree to stop herself from falling. She hurled, vomiting on the ground, shuddering violently. The experience had shaken her to the core. "In the name... of the Goddess... of Holy Light," she whispered feebly, then spat on the ground. Wiping her mouth, she straightened herself, still leaning against the tree. Taking a deep breath, she then returned to the others.

29

AS YOU WISH

With time, the scars on Edric's back became only faintly visible. Lenda had made him a special iron-rich potion to restore his depleted blood levels. He drank it daily and was to do so for another month. He entered his cottage, the second bedroom now furnished with extra storage to accommodate Vixen's equipment.

She had made it more homely, hanging up curtains in the windows, and spreading a large rug across the floor. She was a fierce fighter, but she was just as ferocious when it came to decorating their home.

Despite his disinterest in the subject, Edric was happy with the change. And as the new bow maker made himself comfortable in the Temple village, he started offering general woodwork too, so the couple had a bigger bed ordered up.

Edric carried the last piece of it into their bedroom.

"It will be amazing, Edric!" Vixen squealed at the mere sight of the bed, as it was finally coming together. "And with the new mattress that Benjamin helped me sew together... It will be doubled up, all for extra comfort!"

Edric laughed. "I'm sure it will be the most comfortable bed in the village."

Her hands to her hips, she leaned over him, watching him nail the pieces together. "Make sure you do it properly now. We don't want it squeaking too much when we... you know."

He glared at her. "Do you want to do it?"

She giggled, kissing his forehead. "No," she replied, then headed for the door. "I will go and fetch some dinner, so we can stay in for the night." Leaving their cottage, she walked in the direction of the pantry building, meeting plenty of people on the way. She let out a sigh of relief, the whispers around her finally gone.

It had taken a couple of weeks, but things had now settled. The inhabitants of the village had bought the idea that the couple was already engaged by the time they were found out, falling for temptation only in the days ahead of marriage. After serving their sentences, they had been largely forgiven, only a handful still holding a grudge. Adena was one of them, always trying to find fault in Edric's reasoning. And how she had muttered, as the High Priest praised the man for shooting the attacking panther demon and then defending the village against the lizards. He had received a full pardon, as well as the Symbol of Bravery – a statuette of the Goddess holding a shield.

Edric had told her it had always been such with Adena, yet Vixen could not let it go. She felt the need to defend her husband, knowing how wrong other's had been about him.

Despite the hardships at the start of their relationship, their love had flourished, becoming stronger by the day. Vixen was surprised at her own ability to harbour such feelings, smiling as soon as she thought of him. Even their sexual relations had developed, albeit slowly. She was able to touch him more, explore his body. Some areas were still too connected to dark memories, but she could participate more in the act, which she much enjoyed. She shivered at the mere thought.

Edric and Vixen had another two weeks of honeymoon to enjoy, which was given to all those married within the Priesthood. It mainly functioned as a way for couples to integrate their lives, often having to move to a separate cottage. With Edric already living on his own, the choice of housing was simple. It was the renewal of the place that proved more work, but it was worth it. He was worth it.

Vixen soon returned, and the two cooked a meal over the outdoor campfire. They finished it inside, sitting on the floor in front of the warm hearth. The rug beneath them was made from spun cotton, soft and comfortable, dyed a dark grey. The young woman lay back, feeling the carpet around her. "I impress myself with this purchase," she chirped.

Edric flashed her a smile. "It is nice; I have to agree."

"Come join me," she said, tugging at his shirt.

Edric placed himself beside her, lying on his side.

She felt his hair, blond and soft, grabbing at the strands. Taking a deep breath, she inhaled his scent. It was light and fresh, like a crisp winter breeze. His blue eyes peered into hers; the emotions so close to the surface. Pulling him in, she embraced him, planting a kiss to his forehead.

Edric pushed himself up, their lips delicately connecting, the kiss gradually building. His hand trailed along her side, settling over her breast.

Unbuttoning his shirt, Vixen opened the garment, feasting on the sight of his toned body. She traced his chest and stomach, feeling the smoothness of his skin under her fingertips. Intensifying the kiss, their tongues met, slowly whirling against each other. She felt his hand as it swept down, reaching in under her dress, removing the undergarments. Her centre already throbbing, she spread her legs, allowing him to caress her. A moan broke their kiss as he pulled her close, his fingers prodding and kneading inside her, the woman shivering with desire. His touch firm but gentle, he lovingly pleasured her, building her excitement. He knew exactly what she wanted, slowing and speeding up to tease her to the point of climax.

Grabbing his hand, Vixen removed it, their fingers interlocking. Her eyes narrowed as he smirked back at her. "You are *evil*," she hissed. Biting her lip, she untied the front of his trousers. Their eyes locked again, but he was silent. "Tell me when to stop," she said, her voice now low. Reaching in, she took him in her hand, then gently caressed. She watched him take a deep breath, his mouth opening, but he said nothing. With a grin, she clasped his manhood, letting her hand move across with increasing momentum.

Moaning in pleasure, Edric leaned his head back on the rug. His eyes closed; his thoughts dispersed within the moment. His voices were silent, all doubts gone within a second. In her company, he could feel complete, concentrating solely on their lustful union. His fingers curled around the fabric of the rug as she continued to fondle him. Her touch brought a delight greater than any rush he had ever experienced. A heat spread through him, and he felt himself on the verge of his pinnacle. His hand flashed out, grabbing hold of her arm. Breathless, he pulled her in, staring at her. "I suggest you stop... should you wish for us to lay with one another."

"Fine," Vixen said, releasing him. "I was only returning the favour." She slid his trousers down, then let her lips brush against his as she straddled him. Their kiss was slow and deliberate, in anticipation of their union.

Edric pulled her dress over her head, revealing her naked body. He flung it aside, the gown expertly landing across the back of a chair. Tracing her belly, he felt her soft skin, eventually settling over her hips.

They looked at one another, Edric offering her a silent nod.

She carefully lowered herself over him, enveloping his length. Sighing softly, she bit her lip, revelling in the sensation of him filling her. Her arousal soared in an instant, forcing her to pace herself as she would lift, then slowly drop on him.

Reaffirming his grip on her, Edric added to her delicious move-ments, pulling her in. She couldn't stop her passionate swaying, her excitement further heightening. He caressed her supple breasts, running his fingers across her nipples before finally travelling down. He clutched over her legs, feeling her muscles tensing as she rocked against him, again and again. His breathing became increasingly strained, an overwhelming arousal flooding him as he watched her. She was the most beautiful woman he had ever laid eyes upon, her inner strength just as striking as her appearance.

Vixen licked her lips, throwing her hair back in euphoria as she pushed down on him. Gripping his hands, she clasped them, bringing them up above his head. She leaned forward, wantonly claiming his mouth, tongues dancing between them. Vixen moaned against him, abandoning herself to the pleasure of sensation, moving faster and faster, so very close to release.

Delighting in her pleasure, Edric could no longer hold back. The overload of emotions burst through all his control, driving him to spend himself inside her. He felt her shudder as she grabbed at his hair, crying out with her own orgasm. With his satisfaction fulfilled, he looked into his wife's eyes. They were bright, and her cheeks rosy.

She bent down, kissing him slowly. "I like the development of this," she said.

"So do I," he replied.

"I bet you couldn't see this happening when you first saw me?"

Edric chuckled. "No, I certainly could not."

Lying down beside him, she pushed her back against him.

He turned to embrace her, kissing her neck. Brushing his fingers down her side, he gently caressed her.

"Want to go again, do you?" she asked, glancing back at him.

He smirked. "Maybe later," he answered. "I was just thinking about something."

Pushing herself up on her elbows, Vixen rolled over to her back. "What about?"

"Well…" Edric trailed her body, his hand settling beneath her belly button. "What if… I were to make you with child?"

Tilting her head, she contemplated the idea for a moment. "I have not really thought about it," she admitted. "I have so far never become pregnant, so I have somewhat assumed I might not be… very fertile."

Edric held her gaze. As he considered his past, the question in his mind felt so improbable, but he needed to word it. "Would you want to have my child?"

Vixen instantly blushed at the sincerity of his inquiry. "I have never had that feeling, whenever I have been with a man… except with you," she said. "If I were to carry your child, I would gladly deliver it. However, maybe right now is not the best time if we were to choose."

A smile graced Edric's lips. He felt honoured. "I am glad to hear it. But yes, you are probably right. Perhaps we should be more careful. Is there a way to reduce the chance for conception?"

She shrugged. "I am sure there is, but I have not exactly been the most in tune with my... femininity. I might discuss the matter with Lenda. She would know what to do, being in charge of the midwifery and all."

Another day passed, and all the Senior Priests were present in the conference room. Adena and Kaedin had returned the same morning, now ready to give their report.

"The den has been cleared," Adena said after being seated. "The only survivor is the one brought to you, your Holiness."

"Excellent," the High Priest replied. "We will have great use for him." His gaze set on Kaedin. "I heard you would not execute my orders, son. Do explain."

Kaedin's expression hardened. He had expected Adena to tell, but not for him to be questioned in front of the other Senior Priests. He was quiet for a moment as he considered his answer.

Anaya struggled not to gape, astonished at the words. Not once since he joined the Priesthood, had Kaedin refused to follow orders. She did not know the details of their mission, but as it was given to them, she had been glad she was still off duty. The raid of a settlement ran the risk of encountering those the priests would not usually kill.

"I said this to Adena, so I'll say it to you, your Holiness," Kaedin began, then cleared his throat. "I am not to bloody my sword on women and children. Punish me for insubordination if you will, but I will not kill a mother cradling her young."

All the colour drained from the High Priest's face, then he slammed his hand onto the table, springing to his feet. "The demons did not show mercy when my wife desperately clutched my son and daughter! Instead, they ripped them apart as if they were rags. Never did they think twice of the moralities of such actions. I am not, under any circumstances, willing to show mercy to those unable to even fathom the concept!" His face red in anger, he gritted his teeth.

Kaedin stood. "Be that as it may, but I have morals, and my

conscience is clear. If this is to be the new norm, I will regretfully have to ask for my immediate resignation, your Holiness."

The other Senior Priests stared at each other, Anaya no longer able to contain her disbelief.

Ekelon inhaled a breath, then sat down and clasped his hands on the table. "Please, sit down again, Kaedin."

The former Knight did as he asked, but his gaze settled elsewhere.

"There is no need for your resignation, my son," the High Priest said. "I can recognise your standpoint, even if I do not agree with it. With that said, we are at a crossroads." He leaned back and regarded the faces of all those gathered. "With some luck, the material you have brought me will further advance my experiments. I have recently been working on a potion which forces a demon to go into a state of rage. I am to test it on this live one you delivered today. If all goes to plan, you will all soon be out of work, for we shall no longer need to burden ourselves as executioners."

★ ★

Anaya needed to clear her mind after the meeting. With daylight still present, she headed for the Eastern forest. Red and yellow leaves laid scattered along the undergrowth, blanketing nature for the coming of winter. As it was late in the year, the days were shortening rapidly. Walking for some time, she halted under a large willow, the long branches almost touching the ground.

Anaya stood unmoving amongst the slender sprigs, closing her eyes. Few birds were left singing, and it was a windless day, making it eerily quiet. She could practically converse with her own thoughts, being so crisp in her mind. But she needed them to disperse, not only her doubts about the Priesthood but to wash away the memories of her last battle. The blood and gore, the severed limbs. The horrific screams and sounds of crunching bones. Her eyes welled with tears. If only they had known, they would not have taken the mission so lightly. How could this have happened, for the second time this year?

Placing a hand on the stem of the tree, she let her fingers run along the bark. It was cold and rough in its rawness, but still so very beauti-ful. Its scent reached her nose, clear and distinct, like a concentrated perfume of wilderness.

"Anaya."

Stepping back, she looked up. In the very same tree, a black cloak hung down from a branch high above her.

The demon grabbed it as he swung himself down, landing silently beside her.

"Samael," she whispered, but couldn't continue. She wanted to reach out for him, to touch him, but she could not. She was unsure of what to say or do, thoughts about recent events overwhelming.

"Are you alright?" he asked.

She remained silent but nodded. With a hand to her mouth, she couldn't speak in fear of bursting into tears. The guilt of leading her group into a death trap was crushing, not to mention the fact that she was the sole survivor. Never would she forgive herself.

"Anaya, talk to me." Samael came forward, grasping her arm.

His demonic aura flashed through her, the perception of terror too much like what she had experienced with the iguana Prime. "Let me go!" she cried, instantly pulling away.

Releasing her, he averted his gaze. "Fine. I get it," he said. "Don't give it another thought, priestess. We were both out of our senses."

She held her breath, a coldness flooding her. "No, it's not-"

"Yes, it is. And you are right – you're a human; I am a demon. There is nothing between us, so consider it a mistake." Samael paused, pushing a hand through his hair. "I only came to check on you… to make sure you pulled through."

Running her hand along her arm, she gripped at the fabric of her sleeve. "I'm alive," she said. "What about you?"

"Me?" He looked at her again, his eyebrows raised. "You removed the arrowhead, so I healed. There isn't much more to it."

The couple slipped into silence, the demon shifting his weight as he stood there.

Hugging herself, Anaya clutched her sides. She swallowed, attempting to moisten her dry throat. "We… we are building increased defences for the Temple village," she finally said. "Since you just walked in there like nothing, followed by the iguanas attacking. We are raising fences with demon repelling spells and enchantments. New buildings are being erected as well, as we have more recruits. The Priesthood is becoming ever more in demand, so we... we need to expand."

Samael let out an audible breath. "How I wish that at least you, of all people, would recognise what is happening."

"What do you mean?" she asked.

"You mean you don't get it?" He held his arms out in disbelief. "Where do you think this will lead? To the well-being of the populace? Perhaps to farmers and hunters? What about us demons, are we just going to stand by while you slaughter us? Every man, woman, and child?"

"Demons must be... taught a lesson." Anaya cursed inwardly, forcing the words out as she recited the High Priest. "Not all demons know to stay clear of humans, or at least to remain neutral. If they would just stay away, there wouldn't be a need for war against them."

"Neutral?" he challenged. "Is there even such a thing? Where do you think that timber of yours comes from? How many times is my tribe to up and move only for your people to expand your territories? To build your homes? To grow your crops? You and your Priesthood are a fallacy."

"How can you say that?" she demanded, her fists tightening. "I thought you had grown to at least understand our Priesthood!"

"Understand it? The very same Priesthood which is out to hunt each and every single demon, to rid the world of them? The same Priesthood whose members tell themselves how some divine creature up in heaven gives them the right to end another's life, purely because of how they were born? The same bloody Priesthood whose High Priest cowardly murdered my father by stabbing him in the back!"

Anaya gasped. "You lie! Ekelon would never-"

"Oh, first name basis now, is it? You realise he *tortured* me as thanks for saving your life? Perhaps he didn't mention that small detail?" Samael's eyes narrowed. "You are no more 'devout' than any other, human or demon. The only difference is you believing your violence is somehow justified."

"How dare you!" she exclaimed. "After all the time we've spent together! All to have it now thrown back in my face? Was it just for entertainment, after all, only for me to be cast aside? I mean nothing to you?"

Samael looked at her for a moment, his face cold, lacking any emotion. "No," he said. "You don't."

To her own surprise, Anaya felt as if she was about to break apart, pain engulfing her soul. Grief stabbed at her, tearing through her body like daggers. She fought to keep her eyes from welling up with tears, slamming her foot into the ground. She prayed for strength, but there was nothing to dull the agony in her heart. "Then why?" she asked. "Why did you save my life?"

He stood in silence, unable to answer the question.

"If I mean nothing to you, tell me why!" Tears began streaming down Anaya's face, the young woman unable to repress her emotions any longer.

Samael flinched, taking a step back. "Why are you crying?"

"Damn you!" she screamed. "Go to hell, you unfeeling bastard! I never want to see you ever again!"

Pushing his cloak aside, Samael clenched his jaw. "As you wish, priestess." He backed away, then turned and strode off.

Barely able to see through her tears, Anaya watched as his black shadow drifted away into the forest.

30

EVIL

A rax closed the door behind him, walking through the entrance hall. "My lady," he greeted.

The Matriarch sat at the back, atop her cushioned daybed. "Yes?"

"You have visitors. They are messengers from the Iguana tribe."

She sighed. "They have come then?" Her scouts had already relayed to her the slaying of their Prime, so she had expected them to arrive. As her village was the closest settlement to the scene of the crime, it had only been a matter of time.

"Indeed."

"Very well. See them in."

"Yes, my lady." Arax returned to the doors, opening them. He motioned for the messengers to enter, who then proceeded to approach Lilith.

The two men knelt, eyes on the floor. "Greetings, your Highness. We are honoured to be allowed in your presence."

"Welcome to the Panther tribe," she said. "Rise and introduce yourselves."

Both men were relatively short, one with a shaved head, the other with cropped blond hair. Both had green eyes, now peering at the Matriarch.

"I am Kleen Arroa," said the first man. "And this is my brother, Eti Arroa. We are messengers from the Iguana tribe."

"I have gathered as much." Her voice flat, she kept her expression stern, showing no emotion. "What is your purpose for coming here?"

Kleen cleared his throat. "I don't assume you have heard of... an incident to the north, pertaining to our tribe?"

"I have," she confirmed. "What about it?"

Kleen nudged his brother, who instantly pulled a parcel from a pouch strapped to his belt.

"The one dead is no other than Protector Prime Typhos Illixa of the Iguana Tribe," Kleen went on. "Our investigation on the corpse, Spirits rest his soul, has reached some conclusions which we would like to discuss with you."

"Continue."

A pearl of sweat ran down his forehead. "Well, you see, we are led to believe that our Prime was attacked and killed by another demon, most likely a Prime also, considering his level of strength. The first arrivals at the scene reported human corpses in the area, but no signs of man-made injuries on Prime Typhos' body. The group followed a trail of demon's blood along the mountain pass westward from the mines, eventually reaching the parts of the Eastern forest closest to the Priest-hood. Typhos' guard led a charge against them, but they were all killed."

"So I heard."

His sleeve swept over his bald head. "As we continued to investi-gate the occurrence, we were forced to leave Prime Typhos' remains, and we believe the priests have salvaged body parts after his death." He paused, grabbing the box from his brother. Opening it, he brought out a tuft of raven fur.

Lilith tensed, attempting to mask her reaction. Already, she could smell from whom it came.

"Connected to the Priesthood or not, we have managed to obtain a sample of fur from whom we believe is responsible for this crime. Just by eye, we can determine that it comes from a mammal, most likely feline, canine or ursine." Kleen took a step forward and held it up towards the Matriarch. "Would you be so kind as to tell us if you can recognise the scent?"

Angling away, she snorted. "You need not come so close, messenger. It reeks from where you are standing." She held a hand to her nose. "And no, I do not recognise the scent. It is not from anyone in this village. The only one strong enough for such a feat would be my son, Protector Prime Samael Fahd. However, he was dispatched elsewhere at the time." As she spoke, she prayed he would not arrive home while the men were still present.

"My deepest, most humble apologies, your Highness," Kleen said, bowing courteously. "Never would I have meant to offend you."

"Your apologies are accepted, messenger. Was there anything else you wished to discuss?"

"Only a message from our Patriarch, Sobek Illixa of the Iguana Tribe. A warning due to the recent events with the demon settlements. He wishes for all to tread with great care, as we are unsure of the Priesthood's plans, with them collecting corpses at a large scale."

"Duly noted. You are dismissed."

The two messengers bowed deeply, then backed away before exiting the building.

Arax approached as the door shut behind them. "I was able to smell it from the back of the room, my lady. What would you have me do?"

"Send for him. Immediately."

Anaya slammed the door shut to her cottage, then grabbed her now cold morning tea and hurled it into the wall. "Damn you, Samael! *Damn you!*" Her tears had long since dried, the priestess left with feelings of hurt and anger. It had been for his entertainment – all of it. Not once had he showed her a genuine smile; an honest expression. How could it have gone so far? Had he only brought her to the village to survey it, assessing their defences? Using her as a means to get out? And how she had fallen for it! Even when his plan had backfired, she had followed him and *healed* him.

Grabbing a chair, she raised it over her head and smashed it into the floor, the legs snapping. Panting, she halted to catch her breath, then kicked the pieces aside. She cursed, walking over to her bed and slumping down. Burying her face in her hands, she released a painful cry before she once again sobbed. She had failed, both as a woman and a priestess. Not only had she forsaken the cause, but also her comrades and herself.

A sudden knock on the door had her startled, the priestess staring in its direction. Not really wishing for company, she pressed her lips together, remaining silent.

"Anaya, can I please come in?" It was Lenda. "I heard something happen, and now I can hear you crying. You needn't tell me; I shall only offer you comfort."

"Come in then, sister," Anaya whimpered, desperately trying to wipe away the tears with her sleeve, but they kept coming.

"Oh, dearest sister! Whatever has happened, I am truly sorry." Lenda hurried forward to embrace her. Sitting down on the bed, she clasped her hand. "As I said, you need not tell me if you do not want to."

Anaya merely nodded. She had no wish to speak of it now. Perhaps in the future, but not at this moment. "It is nothing of importance, only my own failure as a priestess."

"I do not believe that for a second, sister, even if you feel doubt in the cause."

"The cause," Anaya repeated, forcing a laugh. "The cause has never been so clear as it is now. Demons… they are indeed evil."

The Senior Healer had cleared Anaya for duty, only a few weeks after the encounter with iguana Prime. She was to resume both hunts and classes as soon as possible. And it was not long until the High Priest called for her to join him in the conference room at the Temple.

"Anaya, Adena. I have summoned you here because of troubles within the province. I know you have only just been cleared, Anaya, but there are two separate matters of importance, both of which need to be dealt with. Kaedin has been given stationary duty here at the Temple, training the new recruits for the time being." The High Priest motioned the two women to sit down as he spread his map out on the table. "One hunt is in the south, outside Tinta. The sightings of these demons have been close to the Capital, making this quite an urgent matter. It is believed to be bear demons, so whoever takes this on should bring at least another priest – perhaps more – for the hunt."

Everyone knew that any demon activity so close to the King had to be stopped immediately. This was due to a fear of rising mobs against the monarch, in case the general public thought the royal family no longer cared for their loyal subjects.

"The other one is outside Midya, the townsfolk requesting help against one or more panther demons... Again."

Anaya felt as if her heart stopped, already sensing where this would end.

"While the villagers have been foraging in the woods, they have seen a panther prowling. Several sheep and cattle have been taken or killed and left in the pastures. A child is also missing. However, that is unconfirmed to be the demon. Thus, you must find and slay this panther." The High Priest stood, ready to leave, but he paused momentarily. "I highly doubt this is the demon we encountered last. From the villagers' accounts, it seems too shy and weak for such, which leads me to believe it is nothing but a lesser demon. However, considering our latest casualties, we cannot spare any disciples, despite it being a good opportunity for a live hunt. As such, you may divide the two missions amongst yourselves as you wish, but they both have to be dealt with as soon as possible." Exiting the room, he left the two Senior Priests alone.

They sat there for some time, none of them uttering a word. Instead, they merely stared at the map.

Adena eventually leaned forward. "Should we take one each? It would save us time, completing both missions simultaneously. Especially if it is only a lone demon in Midya." Bringing her hand to her head, she ruffled her hair. "How about I lead the mission in Tinta, and you go search for this elusive panther? You should track it with ease. If there is more than one demon, then abort the hunt and send for us."

The choice made sense. Anaya had been away from hunting for a while, and a single lesser demon would be no trouble for a Senior Priest. And as Adena said, should she find evidence of more than one demon, they would come within a day and join her for the hunt.

"Agreed," Anaya said, leveraging herself upright. "It is the best option. I shall start preparing immediately." Before Adena could say another word, she left the room. She had to pack quickly before anyone could stop her. If there was a chance this was Samael, she needed to make haste. He would have to answer for his sins.

Samael came through into his mother's entrance hall, but found her daybed empty. She was standing at the roaring fire instead, her arms crossed over her chest.

She glared at him as he traversed the room. "You have been gone for several days," she remarked. "Tell me what you have been up to."

"Nothing of interest," he said. "Why?"

"Do not dare lie to me. I obviously already know." Her dark mists began seeping out from below her dress.

He paused before speaking. "What would you have me say?"

"Tell me the truth. Did you kill a Prime?" Lilith took deep breaths, attempting to stay composed.

Samael pressed his lips tight, averting his eyes. "Yes."

"Damn it, Samael!" she snapped, the black smoke whooshing out from her. "You killed *Typhos*! You realise that? The brother of their Patriarch!"

"I know!" he ground out through gritted teeth. "It couldn't be helped."

"Oh, I already know what happened. Do not even entertain the thought of lying to me." Her face red, she walked up to him. "It was that priestess, wasn't it? The Priesthood has already collected Typhos' body parts after the fact."

Samael met her gaze. "Yes."

Lilith did not want to believe it, but she knew it was true. She stood motionless, her eyes wide. "But why? Why would you kill one of our own, a Prime at that, for the sake of a human? A *priestess*?"

"I cannot answer that," he said, once again letting his gaze settle elsewhere.

"Do you *love* her?"

Demonic mists instantly flared around him. "She wants nothing to do with me!" he growled. Swinging his arm out, he bashed his closed fist into the wall.

Lilith's expression hardened. "That is not what I asked."

"Women! Damn the lot of you!" he snarled, his exposed fangs reflecting the nearby firelight.

The Matriarch walked across to her daybed. Sitting down, she folded her arms back over her chest. "We have to be extra careful in times such as these, my son."

"What?" He turned to look at her, his mists receding with the change of subject.

"A second raid on a settlement has taken place, the Prime's body removed. They killed everyone."

"I heard." Samael leaned himself against the wall, crossing his arms, his head tilted down.

"I assumed so. And as such, we need to be vigilant, and not put ourselves in dangerous situations." She peered at him, but he would not meet her gaze. "We have a rogue panther roaming the Midya plains. You have to deal with it."

Finally, he looked up. "A youngster, is it?"

"Indeed. He is but fourteen years of age, only gone through his *Evolution* a couple of months ago. He needs to be… taught a lesson."

Samael nodded. "I shall see to it." He motioned to leave, but the Matriarch held up her hand.

"You will do this, but only this. Afterwards, you are to rejoin me and be placed under house arrest."

Samael's aura raged once more, mist spewing out underneath his cloak. "What?" he demanded.

"The iguanas already know a Prime killed Typhos. They also know your scent very well, having tracked you as far as the Temple village. As they move to investigate this, they will swamp the forests with their scouts. I shall not have you roaming around with the risk of you running into someone recognising you." Coming forward, she stood, her voice rising. "If the Iguana tribe so much as suspects you of the crime, they will demand your *head*, Samael. This priestess makes you lose your senses. If you cannot stay away from her by your own accord, then I shall *force* it!"

No matter if her reasoning was sound, Samael felt his inner powers seething as he listened to her. He cursed, then stormed out of the building.

31

DEFILE

It was around noon when Anaya arrived in Midya. The journey had taken two days by horseback, after a stop in Tinta, where she spent the night with Adena's group. Dismounting, she walked along the main street, holding the reins to her mare. Most of the houses were set alongside the road, with only a few side streets visible. The wooden structures were slowly being replaced by stone counterparts, scaffolding plenty abound throughout the settlement. Anaya could see very few people, the atmosphere eerie considering the time of day.

A door swung open, a man stepping out from one of the more substantial buildings.

"*Lightwielder!*" he called. "Finally, we have been waiting for so long!" He presented himself as the town mayor, inviting Anaya inside. Short and stocky, the man wore a ring of hair around the sides of his head, the top completely bald.

Leading her along the corridors of the building, he would not stop talking.

"Lately, we have barely been able to approach the forest lines. Families are scared to death, hiding in their homes, and the panther prowls closer and closer. Some sheep have been taken, as well as cattle. We think it is the demon. Worse as well, is that a child is missing. Surely, it must be the demon. Who else would take a child? Horrible thought indeed, what those demons can do to poor little children." The mayor shook his head, then led her into a vast hall, over to a table prepared with a map.

"Do not worry, mayor," Anaya said, her assertive words echoing in the room. "I will hunt this demon down."

He held a hand to his forehead. "Makes me happy beyond words to hear such a thing! Oh, thank you, Goddess, for sending us the help we prayed for." He gazed up into the ceiling, seemingly conversing with the Goddess Herself.

Anaya spoke with the mayor, the man showing her a map with markings placed for each sighting.

"I will show you to your accommodations, priestess. Make yourself at home for as long as you need it." They walked back outside, then into the building next door.

The structure housed the local inn, within which a small room had been prepared for her. Simply furnished, it held a bed and a desk.

"Thank you, this will do just fine," Anaya said, then proceeded to unpack her satchel. "I will begin the hunt within the hour. Now, leave me, so I can prepare."

"Yes, of course, priestess." The mayor excused himself, bowing deeply, then left the room.

∗ ∗

Anaya did not expect the hunt to last for very long. If the sighted demon were indeed Samael, he would come out of hiding soon enough, if only to taunt her. Her enchantment finished, the Light settled over the ground, and demonic footprints emerged within moments. They were smaller than she had anticipated, clearly not Samael's. She felt hope building inside her, wishing he would not be capable of terrorising a village, let alone abducting a child.

No! Do not think such things! she scolded herself.

The emotions would need to be repressed, as they were assuredly

The Power of Conviction

only caused by his demonic influence. He did not deserve to be held in such high regard.

Riding across the plains, she faithfully followed the set of tracks. The sun was still present, offering plenty of light as she pressed her heels into the mare's flanks. Giving her horse its head, they sped off, the priestess feeling the wind across her face as they thundered across the grasslands. She was enveloped into a sense of tranquillity, becoming one with the beast as they enjoyed wondrous freedom.

Soon reaching the edge of the forest, Anaya pulled on the reins. Her mount slowed, coming to a gentle stop next to a set of birch trees. Tethering the horse, she would have to continue on foot, as the vegetation was much too thick for the beast. Walking only a few yards into the woods, she saw a second set of prints. They were fresher and much more significant, the strides long. There was an instant flutter inside her as she recognised them as Samael's, the aura unmistakable.

Her grip around her staff tightened. Could this mean he was part of the attacks after all? Colluding with the other demon? Or was this a way to lure her out? Either way, he would have to be stopped.

Tracking for some time, Anaya eventually slowed, darkness creeping in. Illuminating her surroundings with a sphere of Light, she pressed on. She did not wish to waste time and perhaps lose the demons' trail, should they move faster than her. Having travelled far north, she reached the ridge of the Leve mountains. With little to no natural light left, she thought it wise to stay hidden for the darkest hours of the night. She attempted to find shelter, soon spotting a small crevice amongst the rocks. She looked about the surrounding area, but saw no signs of demonic activity. Satisfied she was not followed, she climbed to the elevated hollow.

The cave mouth was lower than herself, so Anaya had to duck as she entered. Various sized bones and remains covered the floor, but none seemed to be of human origin, which was in her favour. To avoid unnecessary attention, she made no fire for the night. Instead, she huddled up into an extra blanket she had brought, knowing she would soon move on, even deeper into the forest.

The night wore on, Anaya enjoying very little rest. She contemplated what could have transpired in and around Midya. Was it really Samael? Or was he perhaps pretending to be on her side, already going after the same demon, most likely a member of his own tribe? Was this all part of manipulating her further, of making her trust him? She laughed at the mere thought. Trusting a demon; is there such a thing? Yet she couldn't help but feel torn. Torn between her growing attachment to Samael, and her duties and beliefs as a priestess. If the High Priest were right, then this would all end in a hard-fought battle.

In the light of the predawn, Anaya gathered her staff and satchel. Returning to the trail, she chanted once again, sparkling Light setting around her. The demon footprints instantly emerged. With steadfast conviction, she hurried through the forest, pushing leaves and branches aside as she forced herself through the vegetation. She soon observed how the larger of the two demonic imprints became fresher, noticeable even to the naked eye as they la crisp along the ground.

Samael must have been dormant for some time, but he was active now, and on the move. She would find him this day; it was only a matter of time.

Anaya chanted a short prayer, creating a faint sphere of Light around her. The shimmering surface would protect her against evil. Looking up, she watched the swaying branches of the trees. The wind blew against her. It made for a more strenuous run, but the demon would not catch her scent.

Ascending a steep hill, she grunted as she reached the top, then pushed herself through a set of brambles. Only strides away, she spied an opening, causing her to halt. It was a meadow.

The rays of the sun created a swirling pattern along the grass within, ever-changing with the light breeze. As the moving gusts reached her, the flutter inside her belly returned. At the far end, she saw him. *Samael.* As he stood in the shadows of the trees, only his black silhouette was visible, his back turned against her. The fur mantle shifted in the wind, his gathered hair lifting from his right shoulder. Samael bent down, touching the soil beneath him, then smelled the dirt on his fingers. He surveyed the area in a westward direction, brushing his hand on his trouser leg. He seemed to hunt something of his own, but what?

Anaya took a step forward, then stopped again. How could she possibly face him? She knew she would have to stop him before he could find his intended victim, but her whole body revolted at the mere thought.

Forcefully expelling a breath, she broke through the tree line, heading for Samael. Chanting resolutely, she sent Light flashing around her, creating a glittering trail as she ran.

Samael swerved at the last second, her Light whooshing past him. "Anaya?" he questioned. "What are you doing?"

Standing with her feet wide, she hefted her staff. "You shall answer to your sins!"

✷✷

Anaya conjured sphere after sphere, hurling them at Samael.

Continuously retreating, he avoided her attacks, allowing her to gain ground. "Killing livestock? Attacking humans? *Children*?" He sounded genuinely offended at her allegations. "Are you so angry with me that you would make up stories to justify attacking me? I thought we were past this!"

"Fabricating stories?" She charged him again, the demon once more dodging the oncoming Light. "Was it not enough with what you did to me? Did you have to cause others grief too, only to further enhance my suffering?" Out of breath, she let her arms drop, briefly pausing her attacks on him.

The hunt had gone on for an extensive amount of time, the demon constantly questioning her assault on him. They had travelled north during their altercation, the priestess now cornering him where the forest met the mountain. The ancient rock was shaped like a crescent moon around them, allowing no passage to escape; except past Anaya. Samael had nowhere left to run.

"What I did to you? I *saved* you!" Stepping out of her way, avoiding more of her magic, he flashed his fangs. "And I committed a grave sin in doing so!" he snarled.

"How can you be so cold? Are you truly so heartless?" she cried. "Is it only because you are satisfied with your entertainment that you would forsake me?" Coming forward, she hurled another sphere at him.

Samael swerved again, then righted himself. "I do not want to hurt you!"

Her eyes glossy, she felt the building ache of her heart, her emotions churning. Her knuckles turned white as she clutched her staff. "How can you not see? You truly do not realise it is already too late for that?" Holding her weapon up, she smashed it into the ground. The act caused the soil to become blessed, a glowing circle forming around her. Bars of Light now blocked the entrance, as she held her prayer beads and started chanting. Her hand extended, she gained on the demon, her words louder and louder. The spell shifted into an exorcism of his spirit, the Light burying deep as it seared him from within.

Clawing at his shirt, Samael twisted, writhing in pain. He bent down and charged at her, burning himself within the Light. Knocking her out of the circle, he forced her back, the two of them rolling onto the ground. "Anaya, stop this! Talk to me," he urged, standing on his knees over her.

"And say what? How you ruthlessly toyed with my emotions? You uncompassionate son of a bitch!" She brought her elbow up, smashing it into his face, then pulled her knee up.

Before she could connect with his groin, Samael threw himself off her, springing to his feet. With a hand to his face, he felt blood pour from his nose. "What the hell, woman! If you make an attempt on my life, trust that I will not go easy on you."

"Enough talking! I should never have trusted you, Samael! Everything you have ever done or told me was a lie. You couldn't be more malevolent, even if you tried. Your kind are nothing more than what the High Priest said all along!" She threw herself at him, blasting him with a gleaming Light.

Samael winced, rearing back, but remained silent. His shirt had been ripped open; scars burnt onto the skin of his chest. Hurtling at her again, he grabbed her arms, slamming her back down to the ground.

The air whooshed out of her lungs, making Anaya unable to chant. She knew she would stand little chance in hand-to-hand combat with him, so she needed to keep him at bay. She focused her Light back into her arms. With a flicker, it seared into Samael's hands, causing him to momentarily loosen his grip. Freeing herself, she grabbed his face and pushed her thumbs into his eyes, burning them.

Samael screamed, pulling away from her, his vision gone. Blinded, he staggered back, forced to rely on his other senses to make out Anaya's location.

Light on her feet, she rose, regripping her prayer beads. Clutching them tightly in her hand, she recited another hymn. An aura of Light formed around her as she marched on him.

Still unable to see, Samael retreated to a nearby tree, pulling himself up onto one of its branches.

Finished with her enchantment, Anaya glared at him. "I will not allow you to escape. Not this time!" Bashing her closed fist into the stem, her knuckles split, claret staining the bark as the entire tree lit up. The leaves blackened, swirling into the air as the branches immediately crumbled.

Landing silently beside her, Samael clutched hold of her hair, cracking her head against the now-dead willow. "How can you call your magic *holy*?" he growled. **"YOU *DEFILE* THIS FOREST WITH YOUR ABHORRENT HUMAN SPIRIT!"**

The words sliced into her mind, being that voice, like a primal, ominous roar reaching the furthest corners of her soul. Dazed, Anaya wobbled, barely able to stay on her feet. A wound had opened over her left brow, bleeding profusely, the claret running down into her eye and blurring her vision. Uttering a few words, she raised her hand over the cut. In a quick flash, it closed, just in time for her to dodge a second swing from the demon as he attempted to grab her. She ducked beneath a third, then dropped down. Swinging her leg out, she tripped him, causing him to fall back.

Throwing his arms out, Samael arched his body, pushing himself back up. His vision gradually returning, he searched the area for a way out. No matter how much she wanted to fight, he had no intentions of retaliating further.

Seeing his moment of inattentiveness, she seized the opportunity to blast him. She aimed for his chest, focusing all the strength she could muster. "I will incinerate your heart!" she yelled, her voice choking despite the aggression.

His knees buckling, he attempted to withdraw but staggered with the motion. He grunted, unable to draw breath through his Light-scorched lungs. Coughing strenuously, he spat blood on the ground, then his inner Darkness surged into life. Within an instant, his demonic aura flared out, enveloping the couple in black mists. "**ANAYA, STOP!**"

Steeling herself, she ignored his words. She reached skywards, her eyes glowing brightly. As glaring rays spread around her, they pushed his dark mists back.

With the Light reaching him, Samael retreated further. Their fight had to come to a stop; otherwise, his Darkness would force him through a transformation to hold his ground. It was now or never. Gritting his teeth, he rushed at Anaya, slamming into her. He screamed as the Light blackened and blistered his skin. Grabbing at her arms, he locked them in place as he lifted her off the ground.

Anaya squirmed feverishly to remove herself from him, but he would not release her.

Stepping forward, he pushed her up against the mountainside, the woman settling on a ledge amongst the rough surface. She struggled in his vicelike grip, but this time, he held firm. Not even as the Light burned him again would he weaken his hold on her.

For the first time in her life, Anaya felt truly powerless. Not even when she lay beaten in front of the iguana Prime had she felt so frail. Was this Samael's real strength? Had he been going easy on her the entire time? He hadn't even transformed into his demonic form, and barely spread any of his aura. Did she have a death wish, going into a fight against someone who had made the entire village of priests cower in fear?

"What are you doing?" she shouted. "If you are going to kill me, then finish me already! Damn you!" Not yet ready to leave this world, she felt despair inside her, clenching her fists. Tears welled as she continued twisting within his grasp, her eyes forcedly shut.

She suddenly felt his hands go slack, and she saw her chance, ready to release her Light upon him and break free. She opened her eyes, only to find him mere inches away from her face. But before she could make a move, he leaned in, pressing his lips against hers.

Anaya pushed at his shoulders, attempting to fend him off, but he would not part his lips from hers. Deep inside, she knew her efforts were only half-hearted, a warmth spreading through her body. She finally relaxed, leaning back onto the rock.

Samael reached behind her neck, his tongue seeking hers as their connection developed into a passionate testimony of harboured feelings within both of them.

It was nothing like the hate Anaya had assumed he felt. To her own surprise, there was an unexpected urge to return his affections, fuelling her inner fire.

Placing a hand on his forehead, Anaya spread her fingers, Light flaring out. He flinched as he withdrew, believing she would burn him yet again, only to find his vision restored. She healed him, her hand running down his face and chest, spreading the Light and closing all his wounds.

Unclasping his cloak, Samael let the black garment flutter to the ground. He quickly moved back in, his lips locking once more with Anaya's. He spared no expense, kissing her ferociously as his mouth travelled along her neck and shoulder. Extending his claws, he cut through the thongs of her bodice, leaving long tears in the garment. He lacked his accustomed composure as he attempted to remove her clothing, his body language tense, and his movements rushed.

Seeing this change in his demeanour, Anaya gently traced his cheek. She knew not what to do, only what her heart so profoundly ached for; *him*. Clutching Samael's hands, she drew him in for another kiss. Her centre throbbed as he brought forth a slow, rumbling growl, the velvety thunder caressing her senses. His brow drew together, yet an apologetic smile graced his lips.

A redness crept across Anaya's cheeks as she reached down, grabbing the bottom of his torn shirt. She wanted it gone, longing for the sight of his muscular body. With him stepping back, she pulled the garment over his head.

Retracting his claws, Samael advanced on her again. He removed the rest of her bodice, pulling it clear. Grabbing at the robes, he found that they, too, were greatly damaged. The gown tore as it slid off her shoulders, the remnants settling on her lap. Dipping his head, he kissed her, over and over, inching across her body. He yearned for her skin; the beautiful, flawless, sun-kissed skin. His lips brushed against her neck and shoulder once more, then her collarbone and breasts. His hands cupped them, his fingers curling the roundness of her perfect chest. He kissed one of the raised nipples, baring his fangs. In excitement, he nibbled at it, his canines grazing the skin. A single drop of blood trickled down her body, the demon's mouth closing over it. Licking his lips, he continued to caress her, his hands unable to stop.

Shutting her eyes, Anaya moaned softly, but not in pain. His touch was highly intensified by his demonic aura, sending shivers through her body, the tingling sensation heightening with every passing moment. She had never done nor felt anything like this before, but it was all so natural, as if it was meant to be.

Pushing her skirt up, Samael discarded her undergarments, then knelt before her. Their eyes met, the priestess instantly blushing.

A hunger churned inside Samael as he clutched her legs, spreading them apart. Running his fingers along the inside of her thighs, he focused on the centre of her natural allure; the force of his carnal desires. With his fingers sliding in between her inner lips, he felt the hot and luscious sheath. He took a deep breath, his eyes falling shut. Utterly intoxicated by her scent, he grabbed at her buttocks, pulling her in.

Anaya arched her back as he tasted her, his tongue swirling, athirst for her essence. Warmth flushed within her, her heart pounding wildly in her chest. Her hands wandered aimlessly, craving a place of anchoring. Overcome by need, her breathing quickened, the short exhales carrying the soft sound of her lustful voice. Her fingers crept over his head, entwining with his black strands as she urged him on.

Pleasures soared as Samael's tongue danced across her essence, but Anaya craved more. Grabbing at his raven hair, she motioned him to stand. A thrill washed across her body as he towered over her, the imposing demon's eyes wild as he looked at her. He leaned in, his mouth locking with hers in another raw, enchanting kiss.

Trailing down his athletic front, Anaya reached the edge of his trousers. She no longer thought as she unravelled the thongs, her mind completely void of anything but her desire for him. As she slid the leather garment open, she felt his hand encircle her wrist.

Samael pushed her to the wall, then seized hold of her hips. It was the moment of no return as he thrust forward, a deep breath rumbling from his chest as he entered her.

Anaya immediately tensed with the unexpected discomfort of their union. Her fingers whitened as she grasped at anything around her, praying it would fade. Enduring the sensation through each of his indulgent motions, the furrow of her brow slowly released. Her overwhelming lust overshadowed everything, for all she could think of was her need for his being to weave with hers. Soon, her covet sighs resurfaced, escaping through parted lips.

Clasping his hands with hers, Samael pressed them against the stone behind them, delving into her, again and again. He snarled, struggling to retain focus as his inner power seethed. He shook his head, fighting desperately not to lose control. It had been over fifteen years since he had felt his mind numb as it did now, the sensation overwhelming him.

His grip over Anaya's hands tightened as he shifted his attention to her. He listened to her cries of passion, watching her flushed cheeks and the sweat creating a perfect sheen on her marvellous skin.

Perfection. She was absolute perfection.

His vision blurred, the demon cursing under his breath. In a last attempt to not lose himself to the feral, he slid from her.

Anaya let out a plaintive cry as she felt him leave her, not yet ready for his departure. Her hands instantly closed over his, pulling him back.

Craving a continuation to their union, he lifted her off the ledge. He paced himself, knowing he needed time for the effects of his encroaching feral state to dim. He gently lowered her onto his cloak, the black fabric creating a cushioned layer across the ground. Angling over her, he gritted his teeth, hungering to enter her again. He took a deep breath, the mere scent of her spurring him on, thrilling to no end. It was a high he had never experienced, his focus drifting once again.

Sensing Samael's struggles, Anaya graced his cheek with a feathered touch. They gazed at each other, her scarlet cheeks brightening with her smile. She invited him in for a kiss, their mouths tenderly connecting, slowly opening as their tongues met. She so longed for him to continue, to settle inside her again, but she was unsure of how to achieve it. Feeling his fingers inch along her body, she quivered, his hand coming to a stop over her hip. He renewed his grip on her, pulling her in. A moan left her lips, the demon sinking into her, then lifting to do it again. He moved with a restrained rhythm, and she listened to his breathing as it deepened.

They lovingly watched one another, revelling in the sight of the other's enjoyment as they united. Rolling his hips in a seamless motion, Samael filled her, over and over again. He leaned forward, gently brushing some stray strands away from her face. Their foreheads touched, the two joining up in an increasingly affectionate kiss. Time seemed of no importance as they melted against each other, utterly lost in their lovemaking.

Embedded inside her silken sheath, he greedily grasped at her, his hands forcing her to meet him.

Anaya wanted to cry out with his rising intensity, moaning aloud as the excitement soared. Her fingers ached with the need to touch him, to feel his muscles tensing as they joined. Running her hand down his powerful chest, she watched his half-open mouth, baring the elongated canines.

Samael snapped them shut, clenching his jaw with a snarl. Burying himself inside her, again and again, he sensed an overbearing rush flaring through his body, surging into a thundering tremor. He felt a sudden gravitational pull against Anaya, weighing him down as if his body desired to become one with her. He strained to remain elevated, the raging emotion wreaking havoc upon his physical being. He could feel her tremble beneath him, her sensuous cries echoing out around them. Pleasure burned within him, the demon barely able to stay in control as the illicit twosome climaxed together. His breaths rasped as he leaned over her, his hair spread out around them, merging with his dark mantle.

Examining his features, Anaya caressed him, his eyes closed. She touched his firm brow, the strong jawline, and his short stubble. He had a mighty handsome face, a small scar visible above his left eyebrow. She brushed some hair over his ear, then reached behind his neck and drew him in, their lips touching once more.

Samael returned the kiss, then suddenly flinched. Peering at her, his eyes grew wide. "Anaya, I..." He cursed, slamming his closed fist on the ground. Pushing himself up, he immediately retreated, disappearing into the forest beyond.

Before Anaya even managed to get up on her feet, he was already gone. Her torn skirt rippled over her legs as she stood there, with her arms across her chest to cover up her bare breasts. Her mouth fell open, the young woman unsure of what had just happened. She felt cold inside, as if drenched with icy waters, a chill clawing at her gut. *Why did he leave me?*

An overwhelming pain assaulted her chest, her eyes welling up with tears. Did he not love her after all? Had he left her, never to return? Was she ever to see him again?

Her body damp with sweat, and her dress torn to shreds, she soon found herself shaking in the cold weather. Looking down, all she had was his black cloak. Retrieving the garment from the ground, she wrapped it about herself. It felt heavy, but it instantly returned her body heat, reducing her shivers. Unable to carry anything else, she headed west, hoping she would soon find a road leading home.

EPILOGUE

In the coming year, he was to turn fifteen. He ran his fingers through his dark hair, the strands tangled from days out in the woods. Sitting inside a shallow cave, his green eyes watched the fire before him. He knew the Protector Prime had been on his trail, so he had fled, but he was now running low on food. He would need to return to the village soon unless he was to starve.

Holding his hands up to the flames, he felt the comfortable heat on his skin, but all he could think of was to return and face judgement. The notion sent chills crawling down his back, spreading into his stomach where the emotion laid grinding. The sensation suddenly grew, a tremble reaching his arms and legs. Looking towards the entrance of the cavern, he noticed black mists rolling out along the stone floor.

The boy slowly rose, his hands pressed against the wall behind him.
"COME OUT THIS INSTANCE, BOY."

He gulped down a breath, but stepped forward. His legs felt heavy as if weighted down with rocks, each step slow and cumbersome. Reaching the entrance, he saw the silhouette of the Prime, the moon shining brightly behind him. His long hair was worn down, the ends flowing in the wind.

"Have mercy, your Highness," he begged, falling to his knees.

"This is no time for mercy. You risk *everything* with your foolishness!" Grabbing the boy's clothing, Samael lifted him away from the ground, then hurled him into the mountainside. "Enough demon villages have been wiped out for you stupid younglings to stay out of trouble! You know the punishment for your crimes. Now, stand and take it!"

The youngster tried to crawl away, but he felt a hand clutch around his leg before he was slid back along the ground.

Turning him around, Samael bashed his closed fist into his face. Blood sprayed as a tooth loosened and fell out of the boy's open mouth.

Flexing his fingers, Samael hit him again, then again.

The youngster desperately tried to remove himself, clawing and kicking at the ground, but it was to no avail. He flew up again, then slammed back down onto the hard surface of the rock. Another fist pummelled into his face, then another. "P-please!" he cried, tears now streaming down his badly beaten and swollen face. "H-have you no compassion?"

Samael instantly halted, Anaya's words echoing in his mind. *How can you be so cold? Are you truly so heartless? ... Uncompassionate ... Malevolent ...*

His mind suddenly flooded by regret, he stepped back from the youngster. He let out a breath, averting his eyes. "I... I am not heartless."

ABOUT THE AUTHOR

Catrin Russell is a Fantasy author from northern Sweden. Her books are all written in English and are mainly part of the Epic and High Fantasy Genre. However, she does use influences from Dark Fantasy, and a touch of Fantasy Romance.

With a background in digital design and holding a degree as a registered nurse, she writes novels in medieval settings, with plenty of action and romance. She often brings moral struggles, or issues in society, into her writing. Another subject that is often highlighted is mental health.

Catrin also creates concept art, bringing her characters to life on paper, much of which can be seen on her social media pages!

Catrin's Website: http://catrinrussell.com/

Amazon Page: https://www.amazon.com/Catrin-Russell
Catrin's Blog: https://blog.catrinrussell.com/

BOOKS BY CATRIN RUSSELL

The Light of Darkness

The Power of Conviction
The Path of Salvation
The Resurgence of Light
Nefarious Echoes - July 2021
Book 5 - September 2021
Book 6 - November 2021

* * *

Prequel
Prequel

Made in United States
Orlando, FL
09 March 2023

30875339R00189